Praise for Breaking the Cycle

"More than a war novel, this is a chilling exploration of legacy and liberation. Jak Bazino weaves together the parallel journeys of Anthony Preston and Khin Yadanar, showing that while the faces of conflict change, the struggle remains the same—until a new generation finally dares to break the cycle. Set against the harrowing frontlines of Myanmar's Spring Revolution, Bazino finds a fragile thread of hope in the quiet resilience of those determined to change the future."

Esther Htusan, former Foreign Correspondent for the Associated Press, 2016 Pulitzer Prize Winner

"*Breaking the Cycle* is a must-read for anyone interested in Myanmar's affairs. Although it is classified as a novel, it is written based on true events and historical facts. It is a book that not only provides a deep understanding of contemporary Myanmar but also fosters a profound empathy for the feelings and experiences of its people.

It goes even further than that. While reading about the Myanmar people's enduring struggle under colonialism, fascism, and military dictatorship, it prompts a reflection on the broader human condition. It is a book that vividly depicts the struggle of humanity as it remains caught in a recurring cycle of conflict."

Khin Maung Soe, News Director, Democratic Voice of Burma (DVB)

"A great read. Impeccably researched and wonderfully written, Jak Bazino's *Breaking the Cycle* elegantly weaves important chapters from Myanmar's modern history into a captivating novel."

Dr Ronan Lee, Leverhulme Trust Early Career Fellow, Rohingya Futures Research Project, Loughborough University

"*Breaking the Cycle* evoked a strong emotional response in me because it reflects the lived reality of people in Myanmar. It is deeply moving to learn how individuals in active war zones demonstrate remarkable resilience while carrying their own complex trauma. This book is a must-read for anyone who wants to understand what frontline responders in Myanmar are truly facing. Not reading this book would be a significant loss to one's intellectual and moral growth."

Jue Jue Min Thu, Mental Health Leader, Lecturer at the University of Hawaii, Founder of Jue Jue's Safe Space

BREAKING THE CYCLE

BREAKING THE CYCLE

Jak Bazino

Chinthe House.

This work was first published by Chinthe House in 2026.

Publisher: Chinthe House.

ISBN: 979-8-90243-056-8

Legal Deposit: 2026

"When you go home, tell them of us and say:

For your tomorrow, we gave our today."

John Maxwell Edmonds,

Kohima Memorial, India

"The tree of liberty must be refreshed from time to time

with the blood of patriots and tyrants. It is its natural manure."

Thomas Jefferson

This novel is dedicated to the youth of Myanmar,

who sacrifice their lives and their today

to make way for a better tomorrow.

May they never be forgotten.

To my wife, for her love and support at every stage of this journey, from the path we have walked together to the one still opening before us.

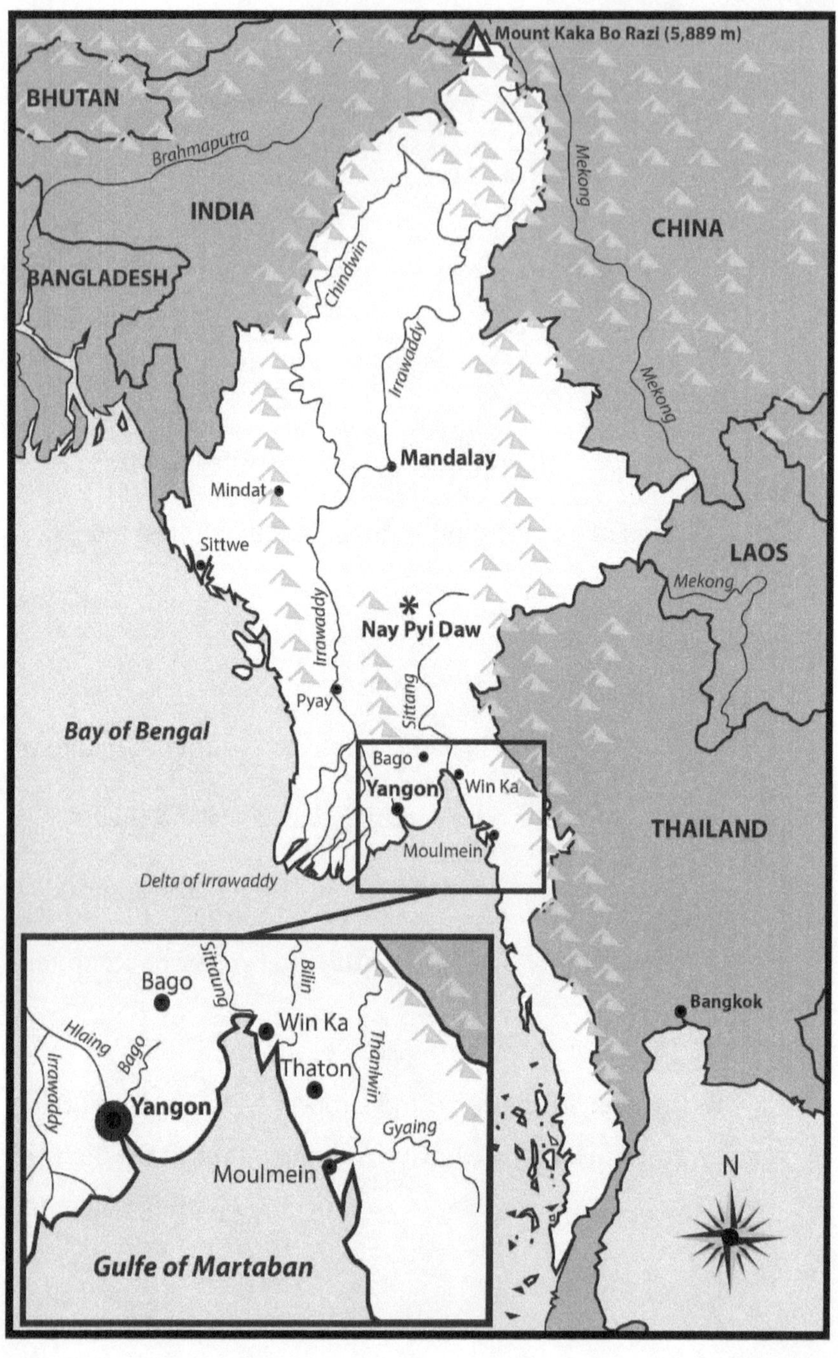

Mount Kaka Bo Razi (5,889 m)
BHUTAN
Brahmaputra
INDIA
BANGLADESH
CHINA
Chindwin
Irrawaddy
Mekong
Mekong
Mandalay
Mindat
Sittwe
LAOS
Mekong
Irrawaddy
*
Nay Pyi Daw
Sittang
Pyay
Bay of Bengal
Bago
Yangon
Win Ka
THAILAND
Moulmein
Delta of Irrawaddy
Bangkok
Bago
Sittaung
Bilin
Hlaing
Bago
Win Ka
Thanlwin
Irrawaddy
Thaton
Yangon
Gyaing
Moulmein
Gulfe of Martaban
N

Prologue

Burma, March 1942

- "The rounds pierced the tank! We've lost too much kerosene! The engines will pack up!", declared the pilot before returning his attention to the instrument panel.

Anthony Preston was going to die. At scarcely nineteen years old, he had believed, with the presumption of youth, that death was but a distant abstraction. Yet now the moment imposed itself, brutal and inexorable: he would cease to be.

The revelation seized him viscerally, awakening within him that *Dorian Gray* lurking in the shadow of every man, a beast ravished by hunger for eternity, driven into a corner and quivering, not before death itself, but at its approach. Convention would have it that life flickers before one's eyes, a reel rewound at frantic speed by an invisible hand. But this evening, no images came. Perhaps, this superstition had been born of a romantic's fever, greedy for meaning. His own existence, he sensed, had none.

His love, his hopes, those near to him, his country, all had dissolved, evaporated, leaving him only with the worn, absurd object, swaddled in the battered leather satchel clutched against him like a useless talisman, itself promised to oblivion. No, he possessed nothing exceptional, nothing unique. He was, quite simply, as billions of beings had been before him and would be after. No design had guided him through the labyrinth of his ephemeral existence. He had been the plaything of Fortune, swung from one probability to another, propelled by a series of accidents that had brought him here. Had he seen the film of his autobiography unspooled before him, he might have discerned a pattern, a *leitmotif*, if only to give it a title? Perhaps. Had only his life actually flickered before his eyes.

He would have wished to see again, if only for an instant, the walks of Rangoon University, the house on Battery Road, the Sundays at Dalhousie Park after service at the Cathedral of the Holy Trinity, the summers in Maymyo, and the faces of his parents. Memories redolent of frangipani and jasmine. But his mind, once docile, now escaped him like a dog gone wild. As the aircraft began its inexorable descent toward certain death, he was left only with the present: the glacial fuselage, the smell of machine oil mingled with something acrid, the scent of fear, that telltale trickle of urine betraying the body's collapse. None of it held 'great' meaning and that was meaning unto itself.

His breathing quickened without filling his lungs, his nostrils clogged with mucus, his eyes streaming with tears. He was suffocating, panicking, thoughts exploding in incoherent showers. The pilot seated beside him, bellowed in sharp bursts above the twin propellers of the Bristol Blenheim:

- "Haven't got a clue where we are. We're over mountains now: the Pegu Yoma or the Chin Hills, Lord knows. Not a sign of a road or clearing. Just jungle."

He had delivered his report in a toneless voice, with that particular British RAF phlegm which transforms lucidity into a form of courage. The order fell, dry and impersonal:

- "Cut those rope lines securing the bomb bay hatch," he shouted, extending a hatchet and pointing toward the middle of the fuselage where the bay lay. "I'll reduce speed at the critical moment. When I give the word, you jump. Keep your body tight. The trees will break your fall. With luck, you'll make it through."

- " What about you?" shouted Anthony, suddenly terrified by the solitude of the jump.

The pilot cast him a look heavy with meaning, then fixed his gaze once more upon the void before him. Each man travels toward his own death, but by separate roads. After all, every man is born and dies alone. Between these two moments, there are only meetings.

Anthony made his way, bent-over, toward the center of the narrow fuselage, bent nearly on his knees. His satchel hampered him, choking off his breath in that cramped space. He tore off the cursed bag with anger and threw it away. It was because of what it contained that he had lost everything. So much suffering for an old artifact, a stone forgotten by all. The bag abandoned on the metal floor seemed to mock him, to remind him of his powerlessness. Fear, anger, sorrow, and despair awakened in him like beasts battering against their cage. He seized the hatchet and brought it down with fury upon the lines holding the hatch shut, striking again and again with fierce groans, continuing even after they gave way and the door swung open onto the void. At last, exhausted, he stopped, his gaze fixed upon the abyss, an endless rectangle of darkness that stared at him in return. A gust of warm air rushed into the cabin, granting him at last the sensation of being able to breathe again. Calmed, he sat upon the edge of the precipice, his legs dangling over nothing, his eyes lost in the abyssal darkness unfolding beneath him.

He was going to die, this much was certain. Crushed within this coffin of metal, swallowed by the jungle, what did it matter? In this glacial acceptance, an intuition rose within him, sudden as lightning, an illumination: no single life has meaning. Only the connections, the points of contact between impermanent beings, possess their own existence, absolute and independent of those who engendered them. Like the threads upon a loom, only the connections matter, binding, creating coherent pattern from chaos. Emergence. Death itself changes nothing.

He saw her again in his mind, she from whom he had been separated. They had loved each other. A certainty that would persist even after his death and which, like the circular ripples of a stone skipped across water, would continue to influence the world around them. *Amor mundum fecit*[1]. Both of them had occupied a common space and moment, had undeniably been, together. Their lives had intersected, and the "I" had become "we," if only for a

------

[1] Latin saying meaning "Love created the world".

time, like two overlapping circles. Each meeting created a connection that existed for and by itself.

These connections were the memory of the universe itself. Their sum, their reverberations, shaped reality, lent meaning to the absurdity of existence taken in its individuality. He sensed them, these fortuitous junctures that had led him thus far, through the ages, through an irremediable succession of causes and effects. He stood amid a row of falling dominoes. Who had pushed the first, if ever there had been a first? Who would fall last, if indeed there were a last? He was but one of the indefinable points that form a line. The law of cause and effect, *karma*, this was the pencil stroke connecting all these infinitesimal, trivial, futile points that formed a line only when united.

In a flash, he beheld all the points that had preceded him, all that had led to this precise instant. A series of causes, a series of effects. And the same causes produce the same effects, ceaselessly and without fail. A cycle. This play that was performed and re-performed, each new act plagiarizing the last, was nothing but farce. The actors succeeded with one another, but the lines remained unchanged. And all in the audience laughed and wept, again and again, each time as though for the first. They were all prisoners of a cycle, these blind ones who applauded. And if the same causes produced the same effects, what effects would his death produce?

- "Stand by! At my signal!", bellowed the pilot without even turning.

Anthony felt the aircraft slow and dive. The loss of speed brought a surge of turbulence. The bomber began to pitch, and he had to resist with all his strength to keep from tumbling into the gaping aperture that sought to draw him down. The vibrations intensified in crescendo until they bruised his eardrums. He cast another glance at his satchel, lying several meters away. He could not leave it. However much he hated what it contained, it was all that remained to him, all that connected him to his past. If he lost it, it was as though he had never existed.

He was rising to retrieve it when an engine suddenly coughed, then ceased abruptly in a roar. The aircraft lurched violently. Anthony felt his body lifted into the air, his legs pedaling through emptiness, his arms opened by reflex. In the same moment, he saw with horror that he was falling through the gaping opening of the hatch, with nothing to hold him. The void seized him in a breath, a wall of harsh, black air crushing his chest with its cold grip. He tried to cry out. He felt his back and skull explode beneath impact. It was over.

Chapter 1

Chin State, Myanmar, July 2024

Khin Yadanar's machete bit into the banana leaf with dull brutality, releasing milky sap that mingled with mud cascading down the slope. Her body, tense like a bow, wavered under the soil's betrayal, which fleeting clay sucked at her boots with the voraciousness of some beast. The Burmese jungle, gorged on monsoon rains, exhaled a hot breath where dead leaves and hope decayed together. She caught herself on a branch and her nervous laugh dissolved into the roar of the rain. After hours of climbing, the verdict was rendered: at the top she was, at the top she would remain.

Heart hammering, she took a second to catch her breath and sweep her gaze across the succession of rounded peaks drowning in the gray veil of rain. An emerald ocean which waves beat at her feet. The Chin Mountains, the northern reach of the Arakan Range, that reef separating Myanmar and India, stretched their curves like a sluggish Sargasso Sea inviting journey. She knew the duplicity of that somnolent swell that concealed vicious currents that swallowed you whole, body and soul.

She was drenched in sweat. Perspiration burned her lacerated skin, battered by days in this hostile environment which sharp caresses she had endured for days. She lifted her head and felt with delight the tepid water fall in heavy drops across her face, then stream down her ponytail and neck. The impression of coolness lasted only a second, the time it took for the liquid to soak into her rough, soaked uniform, which clung to her body like a second skin.

The student from Yangon had died here, she reflected, in these mountains that transform dreamers into soldiers. Six months of training under the yoke of the Arakan Army, an ally of the CDF-Mindat[2], had metamorphosed her. At only twenty-three, but already one of the oldest in her class, she had been among the first women to complete this program after the 2021 coup. She had suffered under the amused gaze of her Chin comrades, stocky mountain women shaped by the rice paddies. The hunger, the mud, the Kalashnikov shooting sessions, the shivering nights under leaky tarpaulins, the handfuls of rice shared on banana leaves with guerrillas with filthy fingers - all of it had melted away her fat and her illusions. What remained was tough, wiry, respected by her fellow sufferers, and indispensable to the Spring Revolution in this isolated mountain range plagued by clashes with the Tatmadaw[3].

---

[2] Chinland Defense Force-Mindat. Local branch of the Chin people's defense forces, established in 2021 to resist the military coup and protect the civilian population against the junta's attacks in Myanmar.
[3] Myanmar national army under the command of the current junta.

- "*Saya Von*[4]!" An orderly hailed her from below. She scrambled down the ten meters separating her from the rear guard.

- "What's going on, *Ka Behta*[5]?" she asked, stopping two soldiers in camouflage fatigues who were carrying a makeshift stretcher, two strips of cloth lashed to a bamboo pole on which swung the casualty, soaked to the bone, his bare chest wrapped in bandages.

He embodied a people's martyrdom: exsanguine, face drawn by pain yet resolute in silent suffering. He survived by the force of a nation's souls united in one cry: "*doh ayay*[6]!", to bend the knee no more, ready to die standing, three fingers raised to the sky.

- "He's suffocating!"

They were less than a hundred miles from the Indian border. As good as another planet. Myanmar was a parallel universe, isolated by the civil war raging for three years. Everything was scarce. Even bandages and disinfectant were rare commodities. Only a crowdfunding campaign among the Chin diaspora on Facebook had made it possible to receive chest drains. A miracle. They had saved the life of this soldier shot in the lung during the fall of Matupi. Yet the unsanitary environment in which

---

[4] « Doctor » in Chin K'Cho dialect.
[5] « Younger brother » in Chin K'Cho dialect.
[6] Slogan born during the anti-colonial demonstrations of the 1930s meaning "our affair," expressing the Burmese people's will for self-determination, and today their will for democracy.

Khin Yadanar had intervened, followed by transport in deleterious conditions, was worsening his state by the hour. He would not survive without a rapid thoracotomy at the CDF-Mindat clinic near Mount Victoria.

Khin Yadanar crouched. The casualty, a boy of eighteen, perhaps, was gasping, lips gone blue. His thorax heaved in fits and starts. She placed her stethoscope, listening to the deathly silence of a collapsed lung, with that characteristic rubbing sound of abnormal air in the pleural space. Her fingers traced the chest drain, a makeshift tube connected to a plastic bottle, to verify there was no kinking.

- "Pneumothorax." The diagnosis fell, implacable. "I'm raising it from -20 to -40 H2O," she continued, adjusting the device's settings. At once, the boy's chest reinflated and his breathing eased. "Watch him and let me know if it happens again."

The two soldiers resumed their laborious ascent on the narrow trail that snaked through the forest. Behind them, the column moved forward again under the rain, an unwelcome passenger, a torrent of exhaustion that pressed itself forward with pernicious persistence.

Khin Yadanar leaned back against a tree to gather strength, observing with a practiced eye the condition of the shadows passing before her. Wounded soldiers limping alone or leaning on a comrade's arm alternated with families of refugees in tatters, silent children clinging to their mothers' *longyis*, old men with fixed stares, tiny samples of Myanmar's three million internally displaced persons, swinging their meager possessions in soggy bundles, haggard yet alive and victorious. Not a triumphal procession, but hardly a rout either.

They were all returning from Matupi, a town liberated at the end of June by Chin Brotherhood troops. A month of deadly assaults had been waged to defeat the Burmese army infantry battalions entrenched atop the ruined town. The operation was slowed by dissension between the Chin Brotherhood and the Chinland Council, armed groups of the same ethnic group opposed to the junta, but which had degenerated into fratricidal conflict. The former accused the Chinland Council of lacking resolve; the latter, the Chin Brotherhood, of supporting the Arakan Army in its encroachment on southern Chin State. These skirmishes played into the hands of the junta and delayed the liberation of the region.

Nothing surprising for Khin Yadanar, who knew of the mosaic of fifty-three Chin tribes speaking forty-five distinct dialects that the massif harbored. And Chin State itself counted more than twenty CDFs[7], most collaborating with one another, yet all jealously guarding their independence, a sign that unity was not this stubborn mountain people's priority. This dissension, ancient and natural to them, was not destiny. A Tibeto-Burman people from central China, the Chins had wandered until the fifth century to the river that now bore their name, the Chindwin. They had already made it their territory by the time the Burmans arrived in the Irrawaddy valley in later centuries. A biblical legend, born from their recent conversion to Christianity, spoke of a deluge that

---

[7] « Chin Defense Force ».

had fractured them into distinct tribes. Their scattering resulted actually from Shan incursions in the fourteenth century, from the city of Kalemyo built at the foot of their mountains. Khin Yadanar caught herself dreaming that what external pressures had shattered, others might reunite anew. So, she was not surprised but disappointed that political scheming and local parochialism had overshadowed the common cause, leading to the death of several of her compatriots. What a waste!

The Chin Brotherhood, a patchwork of various Chin resistance groups[8], aided by reinforcements from the Arakan Army and the Yaw Army, had nonetheless succeeded in liberating Matupi despite this setback. It was the first significant victory in the region. Its strategic position would allow the linking of Arakan to northern Chin State, and open the field for an offensive eastward, toward Mindat and Pakkokku, to the Irrawaddy and the Burmese Army's munitions factories.

That momentum had found new breath in October 2023, when the Three Brotherhood Alliance launched Operation 1027, seizing several strategic zones. A year later, the junta held barely half the country. With ethnic zones liberated, next offensives would target encirclement of Nay Pyi Taw. The priority was unity, to forge the dozens of independent PDFs into a single regular army, the only force capable of utterly defeating the Tatmadaw,

---

[8] The Chin Brotherhood brings together the Zomi Federal Union, the Chin National Organization, the Mindat Chin National Council, as well as the CDFs from Maraland, Kanpetlet, Matupi and Mindat.

without repeating the errors of the previous uprisings of 1962, 1974, 1988, and 2007.

What made this revolution singular? Ten years of democracy, the internet, better coordination among armed groups, a common cause binding Burmans and ethnic minorities. Keeping under the yoke a population knowing only dictatorship was possible. Returning to bondage a nation that had tasted hope was not. For the first time, breaking the cycle was possible. They only needed to get it right once.

But first, the CDF-Mindat would need to secure its rear, sweep the Chin massif of Tatmadaw stragglers, clear mines from the city and its surroundings, resurrect homes razed by bombardment, and establish an administration capable of breathing new life into this phoenix reduced to ashes. The task was titanic, yet this victory offered hope to all cities destroyed by the junta. More than three years after the coup, after months of armed clashes, atrocities, burned villages, collective rape, bombardment, and pillaging, a victory for the PDF and ethnic armed groups was finally conceivable.

Khin Yadanar finally glimpsed light at the end of the tunnel. The country would be liberated and democracy restored. Before that, Mindat would be freed. The dominoes were aligning. The first, Matupi, had just fallen. It was strange that the fate of a town cut off from the world until the 1920s could determine that of an entire nation. She had volunteered naturally when the CDF-Mindat launched a medical assistance operation to evacuate the most serious cases to their headquarters near Mount Victoria[9]. The roads belonged to them. Yet they had made the difficult but necessary choice to cross the jungle at a forced march, risking landmines, because a column of vehicles would have presented an ideal target for Burmese aviation. It also meant they had to outpace the Tatmadaw stragglers on their heels.

- "Awm Awi, we'll never shake them at this pace."

Kee Mawng's familiar voice cut through her torpor like a blade. He alone still called her by her Chin name since she had no family left. To the others, she existed only as Khin Yadanar, the Burmese surname she'd adopted upon entering the University of Medicine in Yangon. The guerrilla gestured toward the rear guard with a tilt of his chin. Beneath his dripping jungle hat, his emaciated face betrayed that unusual, particular anguish known only to those who have already felt death's breath. She understood without words: the Tatmadaw soldiers shadowing them since Matupi were inexorably closing the distance.

- "The *sit kwe*[10] are less than a mile behind us."

- "How do we shake them? The wounded, the elderly, the children are exhausted by the trek. And the mud isn't helping."

- "We're easy to track," Kee Mawng agreed, observing the trail their column had left in the soil. "We have no chance in armed combat. We'll need to create a diversion."

---

[9] Also known as Nat Ma Taung. Highest peak in Chin State (3,053 meters).
[10] A derogatory nickname used for soldiers of the Burmese army, meaning "dog soldiers.", because they blindly obey their masters, like dogs.

He jogged toward three rear-guard soldiers. Quick words exchanged. One of them moved back up the column while the other two peeled off at a right angle, deliberately pounding the soft ground.

- "They'll create a false trail," Kee Mawng explained upon returning, "and I'll try to cover our tracks, hoping it's enough."

- "I'll help you," Khin Yadanar replied, picking up a branch to rake the ground.

- "Too dangerous! The *sit kwe* will be here any second. Get back with the others!"

Khin Yadanar answered with silence and action. Her companion sighed, defeated, and followed suit, knowing the futility of arguing against such inflexible will forged in the crucible of her grief. Bent backs, eyes fixed on the ground, they labored. Level the mud. Straighten the ferns. Cast branches across the path. The irony imposed itself: man, that destroyer, clumsily attempting to imitate nature's art of erasure, working to erase the traces of his own existence. Minutes slipped away, elusive, marked by beads of sweat mingling with the rain.

- "We're out of time! It'll have to do," Kee Mawng cut short, breathless, assessing the fifty meters of hastily concealed path. His gaze swept the surroundings with the instinct of the hunted. "Come, this will hide us," he ordered, seizing Khin Yadanar by the arm and dragging her toward a mass of vegetation looming upslope.

The young man hacked a passage through the green thickness with his machete. They plunged into the darkness of that vegetable cavern, ignoring the cruel tentacles that scored their skin, as if the jungle itself sought to drive them back. Suddenly, Kee Mawng stopped. A metal wall. His hand struck it and a hollow resonance answered his call. He scaled it and tumbled into the structure, then extended his hand to his companion to hoist her up to him. The structure that welcomed them was a titanic wreck devoured by rust, an artificial colossus asleep at the heart of the mountains.

- "Looks like..." Kee Mawng began.

- "A plane," Khin Yadanar whispered, incredulous.

The incongruous discovery would have to wait. The threat still hung over them, imminent. The young Chin unsheathed his machete, cut an opening onto the path below. They crouched, shouldered their rifles, and waited, prisoners of a silence that only the heavy hammering of the monsoon on the leaves dared disturb. From time to time, the rusty fuselage resonated under the impact of drops, like a drum announcing destiny's approach. The seconds stretched as their gazes remained fixed on that liquid curtain drowning the forest.

Suddenly, Khin Yadanar felt Kee Mawng tense. A movement. A shape detached slowly from behind a trunk. Then another. A row of fifteen grayish specters emerged into their field of vision. Khin Yadanar's breathing suspended of its own accord.

Her heartbeat against her eardrums, a primitive drum marking death's approach.

She recognized the grass-green uniforms of the Tatmadaw. A troop of gaunt wretches, some in flip-flops, others barefoot, miserable yet relentless, bearers of the death they had sown in Mindat three years before. Khin Yadanar felt only hatred and contempt for them, despite their pitiful state. Were these the same men who had tortured her parents and left their bodies to burn in their incinerated home? Anger surged through her, a scalding wave. Mechanically, her Kalashnikov found its place. She drew a bead on the lead soldier, her sight aligned on that faceless mass, without personality, almost abstract. Symbol of that formless enemy that haunted her nightmares.

A hand rested on her shoulder. Kee Mawng shook his head slowly, grave. He understood what she felt, even though his own family had managed to flee to neighboring Mizoram. A tenacious guardian angel, he protected her, even from herself, against those inner demons that longed only to awaken. Between the two of them, they had no chance. It would be suicide. She withdrew her finger and lifted her head slightly. She had never used her weapon against another human being. War had transformed her without corrupting her entirely.

Kee Mawng took his radio with measured gestures. Two brief presses of the PTT button, the signal awaited by the rest of the group. A detonation tore the forest's silence two miles away, followed by a cacophony of birds that fled shrieking. The lead soldier pivoted, his troop followed him toward the gunshot and the false trail. The diversion was working. Kee Mawng pressed the button twice more to alert his men. Natives of these mountains, the two Chins would continue luring the enemy eastward, while their column pressed on toward the south. They would regroup days later at headquarters.

Five minutes elapsed in oppressive silence before they dared breathe fully.

- "We got lucky," Kee Mawng sighed, his eyes taking on that same crease as his smile. Then, sweeping their metal refuge with his gaze: "I wonder what a plane's doing here," he added, delivering a first machete blow to a branch obscuring what had once been the instrument panel.

Khin Yadanar unsheathed her machete in turn. A complicit glance exchanged, and they launched into a tacit competition, attacking the vegetation covering the aircraft with playful rage. The branches collapsed one after another, accumulating at their feet in a disorganized heap, vegetable chaos defeated by human determination. The mysterious aircraft revealed itself gradually through the vegetation tangle that had formed a sarcophagus around it, mummifying its remains. Some trees had grown inside the cockpit, others around fuselage fragments, blurring the boundary between artificial and natural. In places, a piece of fuselage emerged from a trunk like a jackfruit, elsewhere a root burst from the fuselage like a metal excrescence. The aircraft had become part of the forest, just as the forest had become part of the aircraft.

Kee Mawng had never left his native Chin State. This was the first plane he had touched or even seen up close. Despite his ignorance, he guessed that the glazed nose of the wreck had exploded on first contact with the canopy. The wings must have been torn away by trees long before the carcass hit the ground. Advanced oxidation indicated the crash dated back several decades. But when exactly? Perplexed, the two amateur archaeologists stepped back to better embrace their discovery. What remained of the aircraft resembled a metal tube deformed by a giant hand. Rust had eaten at it like cancer, erasing all trace of exterior paint. The *Sleeper in the Valley* rested in its vegetable still life, a relic of another war, another era, yet witness to the same fundamental absurdity.

- "I think it dates from World War Two," Khin Yadanar ventured, climbing the nose to enter the cockpit again.

- "What makes you say that?" Kee Mawng asked, following her.

- "Just a hunch," she replied with a shrug, jumping down onto the interior floor.

A moment of recoil. A skull, resting on what appeared to be the remains of a leather flight jacket, stared at her in silence from the pilot's seat. Empty gaze traversing the decades to meet hers. She took it delicately between her hands, turning this *Yorick* with the professional interest of one intimately acquainted with death. Three years of civil war had made her familiar with such macabre encounters, not to mention the hours spent dissecting cadavers at university.

- "Lethal depressed frontal fracture," she concluded in a professorial tone, noting the visible depression in the frontal bone. "He died on impact, hitting his head on the instrument panel," she explained to her companion, who continued probing the rear of the fuselage with raised eyebrows.

She knew she tended to show off, which certainly contributed to the respectful distance her companions kept. But it was stronger than her, this need to order chaos, to name horror to tame it. Unfazed, she set down the skull and unfolded the jacket covered in mold. Several bones rolled across the floor, accompanied by a metallic tinkle, vulgar refuse abandoned after time had feasted. They were signs of nature's indifference to humanity, reduced to mere vanity in the impressionistic tableau of the jungle. They were nothing. Dust returning to dust. With one hand, she brushed aside some bones and picked up a necklace from which aluminum identification tags hung.

- "J.A. CROMWELL," she began reading. "2945776 RAF," she continued. "RAF? I was right," she called out to Kee Mawng, who was busily working at the rear of the aircraft, "it really is a World War Two plane. A POS? PLT OFF? C OF E?" she asked, reading the last two lines. "No idea," she concluded, tucking the plates into her pants pocket.

- "Look what I found," Kee Mawng called to her, joining her with a vermin-eaten brown leather satchel, brandishing his trophy victoriously.

Seized by irresistible curiosity, she seized the bag, opened it, and plunged her hand to sound its depths. Her fingers encountered the rough surface of what appeared to be several pieces of flat rock with rounded edges. Intrigued, she first extracted the rectangular tin box corroded by rust that was bothering her, and placed it on the instrument panel, promising herself to return to it. Then she spread the satchel's flaps to let light penetrate. What she discovered at the bottom was simply impossible.

- "What the hell is this?" was all she managed to mutter.

Chapter 2

Cambridge, United Kingdom, July 2024

- "Professor, time for your medicine!" Nancy called out from the kitchen, her voice forced with cheer.

Ayaan tore his gaze from his phone. His great-grandfather lay motionless in his medical bed, a grayish fungus amid the remnants of a life of erudition that surrounded him. The old man could say nothing. His oxygen mask sealed in silence the man who had once made Cambridge's amphitheaters vibrate. A brilliant academic, Professor Preston had devoted his life to Indian history and culture. His pulmonary illness had transformed him in mere months. A withered silhouette, drawn deeper into his mattress each day, as if the earth already called to him. Yet a light persisted in his gaze, testament that the mind remained sharp though imprisoned in a centenarian body.

A groan escaped from the bed. Ayaan recognized in it the old man's exasperation at the infantilizing tone the nurses employed. What irony for this lecturer, reduced to embodying the Sphinx's riddle, now taking instruction from a girl in her thirties after decades of teaching with authority before generations of students.

The sound of a gallop accompanied Nancy's intrusion, causing the bookshelves lining the walls to tremble, laden with books, travel mementos, and trinkets brought back from India. Ayaan looked at these dusty relics, yellowed by the chandelier's light. This cemetery of objects, where the stelae of a slowly fading existence lined up, plunged him into an abyss of melancholy. He repositioned himself in the leather *Professor Chair* where he had been sprawled for over an hour. He turned to face the steeple of Little Saint Mary, glimpsed between the gauze curtains, took a selfie with the salon as backdrop, and posted it on Instagram with the caption "A Brief History of Still Time." The curve of King's Parade hid Gonville & Caius College where Stephen Hawking's memorial stood, but the wink would be understood.

With a sharp gesture, he shoved his earbuds in and scrolled through Barcelona posts: beach photos, clubs, cocktails, brunches at *Jamón y Vino*. He liked them all... Seconds later, notifications cascaded in successive pops. "It sucks! Sorry for you, bro." "We're waiting for you! What are you doing?" "The party isn't the same without you." "Come join us! You've earned it!" "If you stay in Cambridge, you'll end up as pale as your ancestor, man!"

This last message drew a smile from him. He lifted his eyes to the window. His reflection outlined itself faintly there, superimposed over the pale, uniform light filtering from the British sky. This clarity scarcely sufficed for the cold-loving plant to cast a timid shadow on the parquet. In the veil of suspended dust, two solitudes coexisted: that of an old man imprisoned in his body, and that of a young man imprisoned in this suspended time.

No, the summer grayness had not altered his naturally tanned complexion, that of a second-generation Anglo-Indian child. But it gnawed at his soul with the same patience the disease devoured the professor's lungs.

He let out a sigh. His friends' comments scrolled past, joyful pixels of a parallel life under the incendiary Spanish sun, contrasting with the vault-light filtering through curtains that resembled shrouds. To stay. That verb sounded like a verdict, pronounced without appeal by the tribunal of family duty. Neither consent nor rebellion: a capitulation before the immutable edifice of obligations. His frozen fingers gripped the telephone, that small window opened onto a distant azure, which returned him inexorably to the absurdity of his cloistered existence.

He had just completed his second year of law at Cambridge, sixteen hours daily, identical relentless days. Dawn jogs through Parker's Piece, breakfasts between legal treatises, lectures in Gothic amphitheaters where professors' voices echoed like incantations. Lightning lunches at the law library, evenings in seminars, collapse into bed haunted by unfinished essays. Weekends? Mere illusory reprieves, stolen from the mountain of accumulated work, punctuated by meetings at the Pro Bono Project, at the Caius College Law Society or at the Inns of Court, where each calculated handshake added another stone to the edifice of his future network, the indispensable key to obtaining an internship at a prestigious firm.

Cambridge, city of murmuring stones. To tourists, it offered lace spires and *Hogwarts*-like decorum. Ayaan saw an absurd theater where *Dead Poets Society* met *Shawshank Redemption*. Century-old walls evoked less alumni's exploits than gilded-cage bars.

He never complained. Or scarcely. Furtive exchanges at the pub, between two pints, with classmates whose eyes bore the same feverish gleam. All accomplices, all rivals. All aware that this consented suffering was the price to be paid for entering the holy of holies: the law firms of London, where you'd be taught on the first day that "the holidays are over." Would follow years of monastic labor, until the title of junior partner transformed their sacrificed youth into hard currency.

He had chosen this path. Followed the footsteps of an absent father, a phantom in three-piece suit at Sullivan & Cromwell. Dreamed of a fortnight's respite in Barcelona before the hell of summer internships. But destiny, that sadistic ironist, had bound the arrival of summer to the prolonged agony of Anthony Preston. Chronic obstructive pulmonary disease. Clinical words for a collapse. Siblings in London, parents and uncles tangled in their schedules, he had been designated by default as keeper of the tomb. Farewell to all hopes, to Barcelona, to holidays.

His mother, Anjali, had played the irresistible card: debt and guilt. "You owe him everything." How contest it? Family first. Honor was at stake. One did not let die alone the great-grandfather who had opened Caius College's doors. Anthony Preston was a living monument to British academia: Emeritus Professor of South Asian History, fellow of Cambridge's major research, contributor to the Cambridge Studies series, and 33rd Degree Master of the

Isaac Newton Lodge. A titan with multiple prizes. Decades of glory reduced to a century-old body withered beneath an oxygen mask, the last of his generation still honored before death rather than posthumously.

Ayaan knew him scarcely. Tattered memories: a rasping voice at a family dinner, a skeletal hand placed on his at Christmas. Nothing more. Not the slightest feeling at the invocation of that ancestor commemorated with the greatest respect at family gatherings. At Cambridge, nevertheless, his name opened doors. "Great-grandson of Professor Preston?" Respectful whispers in the corridors, gazes that suddenly measured him with anxious deference. The giant's shadow followed him, a benevolent and suffocating specter.

Nancy's heavy footsteps shook the floorboards, each step a tremor in the humid silence of the apartment. Her laughter pierced through the R&B melodies leaking from Ayaan's earbuds. Other artificial laughter emanated from the old television replaying old episodes of Mr. Bean. Professor Preston, prostrate in his bed, stared at the ceiling with a glassy eye, his face masked by the oxygen apparatus betraying only mineral resignation. The nurse had annexed even his last refuges: choice of programs, rhythm of care, insipid menus. The old intellectual attempted escape through reading, forced to set down the book minutes later, he who had found in letters a final refuge after his wife's death. His decaying body forced him to mourn that love, his only consolation an occasional dram of Talisker that Ayaan served him surreptitiously, and the wandering of his mind, awaiting a death that took its time.

The student turned up his music, seeking to drown out the din. Tom Bingham's *The Rule of Law* slipped between his fingers, cruel pages reminding him of the vise of his ambitions. He started a chapter, but the words danced, elusive. A shrill call suddenly pierced through, tearing the soundscape. Nancy, waving an arm like a semaphore, pointed at the telephone.

- "You're going to go deaf!" she thundered, hoisting the patient's torso with routine brutality to administer a treatment. "Can't you get that? I'm busy!"

Only then did the young man notice the telephone's shrill ring cutting through the television. Ayaan removed one earbud, his expression dark. He disliked the nurse's tone but resolved to get up with a muttered curse to answer. The faded receiver vibrated on the low table, an anachronistic vestige of a bygone century.

- "Hello?" Ayaan's voice trailed exhaustion like a learned reflex.

- "Latika Williamson, Director of the Centre for South East Asian Studies in London. May I speak with Professor Preston?"

- "He's indisposed at the moment. Can I take a message?"

- "I know he's been retired for quite some time, but we received an email addressed to him. From Myanmar..." The word dropped like a stone into a well. Silence thickened.

Myanmar meant nothing precise to him. Was he meant to grasp the implication? He waited. Nothing came. Somewhere, a clock ticked off the seconds.

- "A woman claims to have found a notebook dating from 1942 belonging to your great-grandfather. In the mountains of Chin State..."

- "I'm sorry?" It was Ayaan's turn to lose his voice.

- "I didn't know he'd lived there."

- "Neither did I," the young man admitted pensively, fixing his gaze on the skeletal hand clenched on the sheets. The Chin mountains rose before him, their shadow concealing a past that neither books nor family confessions had ever touched.

- "This is a personal message that doesn't concern our organization. It would be best if I forwarded it to you. Can you give me your email?"

Ayaan set the receiver back in its dusty cradle with a sharp click. He returned to the leather chair, deaf to Nancy's calls which dissolved into the muffled hum of the television. The Chin State. These syllables resonated within him like mysterious incantations. No story, no confession had ever touched that name.

He opened his mailbox with a mechanical gesture. The message was already there, waiting. Words streamed across the screen, each sentence a pickaxe blow against the wall of silence. A tale of a plane crashed in Burmese jungles, of a notebook with pages yellowed by time, of a stone tablet covered in forgotten characters... Professor Preston, until then a wax statue, was transforming before his eyes and suddenly seemed less pallid. The academic, on the surface as smooth as his polished furniture, had been young too, he recalled. Perhaps even impetuous, an adventurer, impulsive. Interesting? It was possible. Ayaan did the calculation. 1942. His great-grandfather had been nineteen. He knew nothing of his ancestor's youth. He could bear it no longer. He needed answers. He pulled himself from the chair and walked with determined steps toward the bed.

- "Grandfather, I need to talk to you." He sought Nancy's eyes; she nodded. "The Centre for South East Asian Studies called." No reaction. He continued. "They received an email. From Myanmar. Your notebook and a stone tablet were found in the wreckage of a plane in Chin State. Does that ring a bell?"

A convulsion ran through the old man's body as if lightning had struck his atrophied nerves. His eyelids retracted, revealing pupils suddenly incandescent. The hollow chest heaved in spasms, a disjointed mechanism which every grinding piston threatened to dislocate. Fingers raked at the oxygen mask, pallid nails scraping the plastic with desperation. Nancy lunged, alarmed, but an imperious gesture from the professor froze her. The mask finally slipped, revealing a mouth twisted by effort, translucent skin edged with veins prominent as raw roots. Air whistled between his cyanosed lips, a ragged melody where urgency and excitement mingled. In the pallid light of the salon, his profile seemed for a moment to reclaim its lost sharpness.

- "Win Ka." The name fell like a verdict, charged with senile fury. "The box, in the closet. The group photo. In Burma." He was seized by a violent fit of coughing and replaced his mask.

Ayaan pushed open the bedroom door where the acrid smell of medications and old leather reigned. The mahogany wardrobe exhaled a grudging sigh as he extracted the cardboard box and emptied its withered clutter onto the dining table. Yellowed photo albums, folded letters, dog-eared documents, nothing of consequence. He continued searching through the pile, a prospector plunging bare hands into the clay of time. Until an envelope addressed to Alice Preston, Birmingham, a distant aunt, or cousin of his ancestor. The photograph in it revealed four people before a collapsed brick structure framed by dense jungle: two smiling Westerners flanking a young Asian woman with an impudent air, and an Asian man with a sullen expression standing slightly apart. The old, washed-out black and white print showed an unrecognizable Anthony Preston: a young colonial god with athletic body and swagger, face radiating the arrogance of empire builders. On the back: "Our whole gang, Win Ka, 1941".

Back in the salon, the photograph acted like an electric shock. The old man straightened, mask torn away, his voice broken by urgency:

- "That's it, that's it. You must understand. You must finish what I began," he continued with a vitality and emotion Ayaan had never known him to possess. His breathing remained labored and speaking clearly demanded enormous effort. "My notebook, the tablet... I thought them lost forever."

The skeletal hand gripped his wrist, a grip from beyond the grave. Ayaan felt the weight of generations crash down upon his shoulders. Barcelona, the holidays, vain futilities. Here, in the smell of death and furniture polish, the ultimate battle of a man against oblivion was being waged. Nancy understood and retreated toward the kitchen, the image of Ayaan bent over the dying man's bedside disappearing through the gap of the closing door.

Chapter 3

Chin State, Myanmar, July 2024

Khin Yadanar withdrew her hands from the still chest of the child. Time hung suspended. After minutes of resuscitation, nothing. She straightened, arms hanging limp, shoulders defeated, to survey the naked body of the girl lying motionless on her back. A disjointed puppet fallen to the ground, studded with IV lines. With a slow, almost ritual gesture, she brushed aside the bloodied lock of hair masking the face turned to one side. Pallid features. Expressionless. Eyes closed. Mouth slightly open, seeming almost peaceful, as if sleeping, save for that grayish tint already devouring the pink of cheeks still malleable. Death had not yet fully arrived. *Rigor mortis* would come later, transmuting flesh into marble.

She raised her head, signaled to the nurse. The sheet covered the child. Mechanically - how many times had she repeated this gesture? - she stripped off her gloves, her mask. Discarded them. Washed her forearms. Blood flowed into the sink beneath her distant gaze, a burgundy fluid carrying with it one more life. Her gown stained with brownish spots. "You can shut down the generator," she said, hurrying from the operating theater, a metal table set at the center of a room which walls bore an uncertain hue. It was the only solid structure in the camp. She quickly crossed the space that separated her from the main building, a wooden shack crowned with a tin roof, at the edge of that jungle that devoured everything. Inside, the sick and wounded were crammed onto rows of wooden beds. Life and death played out there, in that paltry setting. Hundreds of patients treated daily by a team of ten. Now came the dreaded moment. In her mind looped the prepared phrases, worn threadbare, empty of meaning.

Two hunched silhouettes waited further on, eyes fixed to the ground. She planted herself before them, a stiff and clumsy stake. Their gazes crossed hers, red, imploring. The young couple rose. She did not wait. No words, however carefully chosen, could attenuate the loss of a child. Her rehearsed discourse seemed vain, artificial:

- "I'm sorry," she said, abrupt and awkward, "we did everything we could, but she'd lost too much blood. I'm sorry," she repeated.

The words rang false. Her mind asphyxiated, incapable of producing an explanation that might give sense to what made none. The young mother collapsed in tears against her husband. The man's eyes, swollen, streaming, questioned Khin Yadanar's one last time. Motionless, she remained there. Her arms hung. Her index finger tapped the tip of her thumb, a nervous tic, a derisory bulwark against helplessness. The man managed finally to murmur "thank you" through the sobs that heaved his shoulders. Obscene gratitude. It was too much. She fled outside, circled the building, found an isolated corner, collapsed on a stone. Head in her hands, a stifled cry. Her tears, uncontrollable, released the tension accumulated over these relentless hours.

In the mountains of Chin State, war raged on, relentless. Tatmadaw aviation had struck again. A school, children. Daily tragedy, unbearable routine. The army was losing ground and taking revenge on the weakest out of spite and cowardice. A calculated strategy, the "four cuts": collectively punish civilians to sever them from the resistance. Food, funds, information, recruits, all had to be cut off. But hatred grew. Three years of atrocities had only amplified the insurgency. A Pyrrhic victory that translated into repeated cataclysms for the most vulnerable.

The children, caught by surprise, had no time to run toward the trench dug near their school. Three of them and their teacher had died on impact. Dozens of others had been rushed to the clinic in haste, carried on backs, on improvised stretchers, by every means available. Often too late: roads bogged down by the rainy season immobilized motorcycles. The father had arrived last, exhausted, a *pietà* bearing his bloodied daughter at arm's length. Shrapnel had shredded her chest. Too late. Khin Yadanar and her team had fought with their pitiful means. Without result. It was not her fault. Not the father's either. But that angelic face would continue to haunt their nights.

Her function demanded detachment. Impossible. Each day ended in tears. *Sisyphus* in white coat. She was respected, feared, for her efficiency, her coldness. A mistake. Overwhelmed by emotions she couldn't master, unable to decode others', she analyzed, calculated, forbidding spontaneity, retreating in solitude as a refuge.

An arm enveloped her, drawing her against a chest where she buried her face. She nestled there, wrapped her arms around those strong shoulders, let out another uncontrollable wail, her body shaking with each sob. Kee Mawng remained motionless, a statue of flesh bearing the weight of that pain. He always knew how to appear when she needed him most, no doubt having waited all afternoon at the hospital's edge or returning from a mission. His rough fingers drew a wayward strand behind her ear, surreptitiously caressing her cheek, a fragile balance between affection and warrior's restraint. Khin Yadanar lifted her head, wiped her nose with the back of her hand, and plunged her gaze into his. Behind the van dyke and military cut, she recognized the childhood friend, a memory rescued from times of innocence, before the war, before her parents' death.

Together, they rose slowly, one step, then another, he supported her as if fearing to feel her buckle. They advanced in lopsided symbiosis, their shadows merging in the oblique light of twilight reflected by the clinic's solar panels. Her strength returned, her body responded, she rested her head on his shoulder, walking with trembling steps toward the wooden barracks where she kept her quarters. The sun slipping beneath the clouds toward the ridge line offered a gentle warmth to her face caressed by the late afternoon breeze. The landscape bathed in a golden glow through the tears that still flooded her eyes.

- "Have you eaten?" he asked finally. She'd had nothing since morning. He was no doctor, but he recognized the signs, as did she. She shook her head. "Come on, I'll take you to the kitchen," he said with an attempt at cheer, "they might have some *oi-sa prüp*[11]."

She smiled. He remembered her favorite dish. But he knew, just like she did, that this meal which once graced their daily life was now reserved for festive occasions in these times of scarcity. They would be lucky if they were served corn soup with a hard-boiled egg. They were barely ten meters from promised land when a soldier caught up with them running.

- "We got a message on Signal," he said with urgency. "Helicopters just took off from Toungoo heading our way. They've already passed Pyay. We need to evacuate the hospital!"

The alert transformed the camp into a methodical anthill. Urgency, yes, but no panic. Kee Mawng and Khin Yadanar ran toward the clinic where resistance troops assisted the medical staff in carrying patients to bunkers dug into the hillside. Stretchers slid from one end of the camp to the other in an unceasing back-and-forth, bearers and borne joined in silent choreography. They separated, Kee Mawng moving off with a stretcher, Khin Yadanar supporting an amputee, an IV bag at arm's length, both limping toward the shelter a hundred meters away. Multiple round trips were made in minutes, until at last the building was completely

---

[11] Traditional K'cho dish made with chicken.

emptied of its occupants. Khin Yadanar plunged back into the clinic to inspect every corner.

- "Come on, Awm Awi, we can't stay here!" Kee Mawng admonished her. They were the last exposed.

She didn't answer and continued her rounds, frantically gathering every precious piece of equipment she could carry. Tubes. Needles. Sterile gauze. Each one making the difference between life and death. She'd forgotten her weakness, a machine with precise movements defying her latent tremors, adrenaline compensating for her hypoglycemia.

- Kee Mawng took her by the arm. "We don't have time!" he commanded with authority.

She let it happen. One last glance over her shoulder when suddenly she broke free, rushed to a table, grabbed her backpack, and joined Kee Mawng, who grumbled with impatience. Their hundred-meter sprint through the forest brought them to an opening in the ground, a menacing dark mouth ready to swallow them. They plunged between sandbags into a trench crammed with dozens of comrades, sitting in silence in darkness, on the sodden earth, their outsized shadows swaying like those of boat people beneath the lightbulb that oscillated from the wooden ceiling of their makeshift shelter. Nothing left but to wait. This was what Khin Yadanar dreaded most, those long minutes that stretched like hours, spent listening for the slightest sound, motionless, her back pressed against the cold damp wall, legs folded for lack of space. The smell of wet earth mingled with that of fear. All prayed silently to be spared. All knew that if they survived, others might die.

They were fortunate to receive a Signal warning. Each PDF had encrypted channels where lookouts and *watermelons*[12] shared troop movements and aircraft passages. Minutes. The difference between life and death. In Chin State, where the SAC[13] cut internet for months, information rarely reached civilians. The schoolchildren had paid the price.

Kee Mawng seized a guitar like a weapon, his scraped fingers made the strings wail. Church hymns rose in chorus. Khin Yadanar could take no more. She pulled out her phone, shoved in her earbuds, and let herself drown in an ocean of decibels. The music of punk band Rebel Riot tore through her eardrums, an electric catharsis plunging her deep within herself. Exhausted by social interaction, she needed to recharge her batteries. She closed her eyes, watching the morning's faces parade past: the child with shattered ribs, the father with trembling arms, the nurses with dark-circled eyes. Each note was a scalpel opening abscesses of helplessness. Kee Mawng caught her gaze. A fleeting smile, complicity of survivors. He knew that behind her clinical coldness lay a tempest. Hunched beneath the low ceiling, he continued leading the religious chants, pious incantations against the surrounding madness. Faces relaxed, voices entered communion,

---

[12] Soldier-spies who secretly provide intelligence to pro-democracy forces. They appear "green" on the outside, like the color of their uniform, but are "red" on the inside, like the color of the democratic opposition's flag.
[13] State Administration Council. Official name of the Burmese junta that seized power following the military coup of February 2021.

as if his smile exorcised fear. His mere presence was enough to soothe those around him. He healed souls. She healed bodies.

She seized her phone and plunged into the blue-lit screen, a luminous refuge in the bunker's darkness. Connected to Starlink, a fragment of normalcy torn from chaos, she opened her email. A subject line imposed itself immediately on her tired eyes: "Regarding Professor Anthony Preston."

"Hi Khin Yadanar," she began to read, "I'm the great-grandson of Professor Anthony Preston, whose journal you've recovered. His health doesn't allow him to reply, and he's asked me to thank you for your message. If it's possible, I'd like to exchange with you about your discovery, by email or on WhatsApp. My phone number is in my signature. Thanks. Ayaan Carter."

Curiosity overwhelmed fatigue. WhatsApp wasn't secure, but he'd fortunately set up Signal. The bunker walls seemed to tighten around her, but this message opened a window onto elsewhere.

- "Hi, it's Khin Yadanar. We can talk here, it's safer."

No wait. Her phone vibrated immediately in her hand. Ayaan was online.

- "Hey, thanks for replying. Could you send me the satchel and its contents by DHL? It's really urgent."

The request hit, without preamble. A brief laugh escaped her, an incongruous flash of hilarity in this underground refuge.

He was joking, obviously. Two nurses crouched beside her stared at her with surprise and disapproval. The moment forbade laughter, but she had to admit this Ayaan had a warped sense of humor. Such ignorance and insensitivity necessarily amounted to sarcasm. Unless... Could it be? She needed to know for sure.

- "Sure," she replied, irony inflecting the words. "By mule or helicopter? The helicopter's expensive, but faster. The army's already on the way." A smiley concluded her reply, a shield against possible misunderstanding.

- The response came like lead: "You're joking? I'm serious. I absolutely need to get my great-grandfather's stuff quickly."

- "Sorry, it's impossible," she answered soberly, her smile definitively erased.

- "He's 101 and gravely ill. Seeing the tablet and his notebook before he dies is crucial for him. You understand?"

Irritation rose in Khin Yadanar like dengue. Her empty stomach protested; her day had been a perpetual struggle against death. A dull pulsation hammered her temples, fatigue, hunger, bottled anger. This wasn't the time. Outside the clinic, the bodies of children, lined up under simple shrouds, still awaited return to earth. And this brat, thousands of miles away, was talking to her about urgency because a centenarian *thosaung kala*[14] was about to die peacefully in his bed? "Who the hell does this bastard think he

---

[14] "Foreigner wearing sheep wool," used to refer to the British, and by extension Westerners, and now used with a pejorative connotation.

is!" She imagined Ayaan, clean jeans, coffee in hand, typing these words from an air-conditioned apartment.

The fate of this old colonialist meant little to her. Eighty years that Myanmar had bled. And English invasion was the root of all ills. Buddhist nationalism in reaction to British racist and discriminatory administration. Interethnic conflicts succeeding their "divide and conquer" policy. Aung San's Burma Independence Army, which became the Tatmadaw, assassinating its own people. The savage capitalism that pillaged and exported the country's wealth to enrich a handful of cronies.

He was the ghost of a past determining everything for eighty years, that rebels could finally bury. The opportunity presented itself to start anew. Cleanly. *Tabula rasa.* Turn the page, including Aung San Suu Kyi and the NLD's[15] old guard, too *Bamar* for minorities. Half of the exiled democratic government came from minorities. Their common objective? A federal democracy, diverse, equitable, in which each could decide its own future. Collegiate governance. No more providential leader. The people led the struggle alone, with makeshift means and limited international support.

She inhaled the heavy air deeply, three times. Her gaze crossed Kee Mawng's, guitar in hand, still cradling collective pain. He sensed her tension, questioned her with a raised eyebrow. She lifted an appeasing hand. "Don't feed the troll, don't feed the troll,"

---

[15] National Unity Government. Provisional government in exile formed in April 2021 by democratically elected Burmese parliamentarians to oppose the military junta that seized power in a coup d'état on February 1, 2021.

she intoned inwardly. The Burmese principle of "*ah na de*", that cultural reluctance to cause others discomfort, had never fully inhabited her. For her, it was less tact than hypocrisy. Truth, always, even if it wounded.

She gripped the phone until her knuckles whitened, breathed deeply before striking the virtual keys:

- "The journal belongs to your great-grandfather. But your museums are already overflowing with antiquities looted during colonization. So, there's no way I'll send you the tablet, which belongs to the Burmese people!" Her fingers animated themselves with their own life, borne on long-contained anger: "What you're asking is simply impossible. I'm 600 kilometers from the nearest city in Mizoram where international courier exists. The monsoon turns roads to mud slicks. The slightest medicine must cross the Indian border, 100 kilometers from here, by smuggling trails through jungle and minefields. It's slow, dangerous, horribly expensive. We only use this route for what's essential. We're fighting with makeshift weapons against a junta that massacres our people, without any material support from your country, which is nonetheless responsible for the mess we're in since the independence. So no, we don't have the time or means to send you a DHL package!"

The digital silence stretched as if her words had crossed space to strike him physically. Then the reply appeared, hesitant:

- "Sorry, I had no idea how serious things are. You must think I'm a complete asshole."

- "YES!" her mind howled, while her fingers typed: "No. I know our situation doesn't make headlines. I just had a terrible day, sorry. But you should've informed yourself before writing to me..."

- "You're right, I'll do that. In the meantime, and I don't mean to push ("and yet you're pushing", Khin Yadanar sighed, but something in her resistance had softened), could you send me photos of the tablet and each page of the notebook? It's mainly their content that interests me."

- "That'll take time. We're powered only by solar panels and generator. When Starlink's down, we have no connection because of the junta's blackout. I'll do my best. By the way, the stone is broken into several pieces. It was already like that when I found it."

- "I understand. Do what you can."

The young woman's curiosity finally awakened, splitting the bark of her irritation:

- "Why is this so important? What could be so urgent after all this time? It's just an old notebook and an ancient tablet..."

- "My great-grandfather is dying. Pulmonary disease. He made a major discovery before the war. He's asked me to help him solve this enigma, to finish what he began. It's his final wish."

- "How did they end up in the plane?" asked the doctor, who had no interest in archaeology. She had no time to devote to ancient history when all her efforts consisted of writing a new one.

- "No idea," Ayaan admitted. "The Professor ("funny way to call his ancestor", thought Khin Yadanar) wouldn't tell me anything. I only know he'd just begun his research when he lost them. So, we've a lot left to discover. And time's pressing."

- "There he goes insisting again," she muttered with irritation while typing: "I'll do my best. Tomorrow, if the clinic isn't slammed."

- "You're a nurse?"

- "Doctor," she replied abruptly, before qualifying, "well, not quite. I was in my fourth year of medicine when the coup happened. We treat the wounded as best we can. I'm learning on the job and from online tutorials..."

- "Impressive. How can I help?"

A shudder ran through the bunker like a wave. Khin Yadanar raised her eyes from the screen. Kee Mawng had stopped playing, was now giving instructions to his men, voice low but firm. She removed her earbuds, strained toward the real world. A distant drone was growing, swelling in crescendo over the nervous murmur stirring the group.

- "I must go," she wrote with urgency. "There's an attack," she concluded before powering down her phone.

A man switched off the light. Darkness fell, total, primitive. The smell of humus invaded her nostrils; the helicopter's rotors became audible. Was it truly approaching or did the loss of sight sharpen her other senses? Impossible to confirm. The tension, palpable, vibrated in the confined air. Children cried, soothed by lullabies their parents whispered in their ears to calm them. A first explosion, still distant, tore the silence. Exclamations of terror fused immediately, like sparks in the night.

- "Don't be afraid," encouraged Kee Mawng, "that's still far off. Remember: hold the safety position, protect your heads and ears."

Khin Yadanar folded her legs against her chest, bowed her neck, clasped her head in crossed hands. Another explosion, closer, shook the air. The drone swelled again, like a famished monster seeking its prey. She pressed her forearms more tightly against her ears, derisory shields against the horror rushing toward them. The detonations drew nearer, each shock seeming to shake the very foundations of their refuge, cascades of sand pouring down on their heads from the ceiling. The helicopter was upon them.

Chapter 4

Cambridge, United Kingdom, July 2024

Ayaan hurled the photograph across the table. Preston and colleagues before Win Ka *stûpa*, red brick indistinguishable from thousand other sites. How many hours scrutinizing each detail to find a clue? A complete impasse. Frustration rose in him with the violence of a tide. His muscles tensed as though wrestling an invisible adversary. He was going to explode. He held his breath, stifled the oath burning his lips. Meters away, Professor Preston slept, fragile and diminished, prisoner of a body abandoning him piece by piece. How much longer? The thought cut through him like a blade.

Two days since Khin Yadanar had given no sign of life: "There's an attack." Ayaan had devoured Burmese media - a succession of macabre images - incinerated villages, martyrs in coffins, families in grief. Three years of war had transformed horror into routine. What if she were among them? He might have scrolled past her corpse without noticing. A name on Signal, that was all that bound her to him. Not even a face. Not even certainty the name was hers.

Was he worried about her? Or merely infuriated that his quest should halt precisely as it took shape? He had to admit it: the enigma had seized him. More than curiosity, it had become obsession. His last thought before sleep, first upon waking. Ayaan recognized this fever that had carried him to Cambridge. He'd banished half-measures. Racehorse at full gallop, blinders riveted. Yet fragile too, like stallions that snap an ankle and lie thereafter, wounded by failure.

He wanted to erase Preston's imprint from his ascent, to obliterate paternal influence. To reach the summit alone, without a sherpa, as if merit guaranteed success. How could he accept that a stranger at the other end of the globe would end this fixation that occupied his last days of leave? For the first time, should he admit defeat? The idea was unbearable to him. It violated what he was, all he had built. In Cambridge's silence, with only a dying old man for company, Ayaan felt something crack within him. Something that dangerously resembled defeat.

With a sharp gesture, he seized a sheaf of papers cluttering the table. There had to be clues somewhere. He opened an envelope, reread the letter. Sarah Cromwell: "My only consolation is John wasn't alone when the aircraft crashed." Probably the one Khin Yadanar discovered. "I suffer thinking his resting place will remain unknown, that he had no Christian funeral. But his soul rests beside God." I am sending you a photograph of him and his comrades during training. He was so proud the day he received his wings. I know you will always preserve the memory of his sacrifice, if not of the vibrant man you had no time to know."

He pulled the black-and-white photograph from the envelope. His fingernails pressed into it, leaving pale crescents. Ten men posed before the nose of an aircraft, four crouching in front, the others behind with arms around shoulders. Chests thrust out, gazes proud, smiles frank or shy, sometimes rendered grimacing by cigarettes dangling from lips. They were the embodiment of youth, its insolence, its vanity, its impetuosity. All were dead now, their faces, their immaculately pressed uniforms, insignia gleaming on their caps, forever fixed.

"Of no importance," the old man had dismissed with a wave of his hand, eyes clouded, when Ayaan had questioned him about the photograph. "We must finish what I started." Preston's broken voice echoed in his skull, the refrain of a worn-out litany. Ayaan wanted nothing more, but his ancestor offered no help whatsoever. Still, Ayaan had filed an official request for information on John Cromwell with the national archives. There were probably thousands of them. He would have to be patient. But patience was precisely what he lacked.

He continued sorting through the box's contents: a ring set with a cabochon ruby, and a gold pocket watch. Two further letters, official ones this time, containing the obituaries of a Sergeant Myers and a Soldier Pitt. Finally, his attention settled on the Burma Star, which he gripped until its edges cut into his palm. A decoration for what? For having survived? The details provided by relatives were scant, useless. Anthony had served as Second Lieutenant in the Duke of Wellington's Regiment after enlisting in Kolkata. The defense of Assam, the Arakan campaign with Slim's

14th Army, the battles of Imphal and Kohima. Demobilized Captain, in August 1945. Nothing useful for his quest.

Ayaan had grown up surrounded by other family veterans who had sacrificed their youth so he could have his own. Cradled in stories blending horror with obsolete values like camaraderie, solidarity, honor, he had formed a romantic image of that period. Lincoln's words from Gettysburg returned ceaselessly. The speech burned, bitter as remorse. They were the men he wished to be, forbidden by the times. He invented a thousand excuses. They had believed - country, liberty, ideals. Him? An entomologist of heroism, pinning dead butterflies. "Perhaps one day," he lied to himself, hoping never to discover if he was made of the same metal.

He recalled Khin Yadanar risking her life daily, mirror of his own cowardice. Easier for her: no choice, nothing to lose. He lived his dream of glory vicariously, standard-bearer of his ancestor's exploits, trying to solve an enigma without clues. An impasse. Throw in the towel? The possibility loomed ever larger.

His phone vibrated. A notification. His friends provoking him with another mojito photo from Barcelona? Another *meme* about the Myanmar war? In rage, he sent the phone sliding to the far end of the table. He hadn't finished dissecting the jumble of documents sprawled before him. He would find something useful eventually. Another vibration. The temptation was too strong. He could see the hook behind the bait, but he had to bite. He seized the device and saw the Signal icon appear. A message from Khin Yadanar. Finally!

Ayaan hastened to download the first image she had sent. A broken stone tablet, its fragments assembled like pieces of an ancient puzzle. She had attempted to clean it, but the inscriptions remained illegible. He would need to enlarge it, print it, show it to the Professor, if he could still speak. A second file appeared. Then a third. Ayaan shook his phone, frustrated by the sluggish bandwidth failing in Chin State. Two notebook pages: a schematic plan, sketches of bas-reliefs. Then these lines of unknown characters, secrets laid on paper by his ancestor. Several more images reached him in succession of beeps.

- "Hey," he finally decided to write, "thanks for the photos. You alright? I was worried about you after your last message," he half-lied.

- The response arrived, brutal in its simplicity: "I'm okay. The helicopter flew over without bombing us this time. But the next village got razed. Luckily, the residents had fled because of the warning. No casualties. But they lost everything."

- Ayaan searched for words. This war seemed so distant to him, so abstract. "Sorry to hear that." The words sounded hollow, even to his own ears. "Must be difficult day to day," he added, hoping the phrase would be enough to mask his indifference.

- Khin Yadanar changed the subject: "You got the photos?" Perhaps she had sensed his detachment, that coldness he could never seem to hide.

- "Yes, thanks. I'm not sure what it is, but I'm going to show this to Professor Preston." Why did he persist in calling him that? This distance, this formula, she must surely find him pretentious.

- "I started with those pages because they seemed important for your research. There are others in the same script. The rest contains his excavation notes, a journal. I'll try to send everything, but it depends on the situation here."

- "I understand. That's already fantastic. Now, we can move forward!" His enthusiasm rekindled despite himself. Finally, something concrete.

- "Where are you at?"

- "Nowhere," he admitted straightforwardly. "Nothing useful in Preston's documents so far."

- "Still hasn't explained to you how the tablet and notebook ended up in the plane wreck?"

Ayaan glanced toward the adjacent room where the old man slept, the oxygen mask on his face.

- "No. He refuses to talk about it. A letter suggests he was in the plane, piloted by someone named John Cromwell, who died in the crash. How Preston made it out... A mystery."

- The response shot back. "Cromwell? I found his tags in the cockpit! Here: J.A. CROMWELL, 2945776 RAF, A POS, PLT OFF, C OF E."

- Ayaan felt excitement rise. "Fantastic! With that, I can get his file. Already one enigma solved... But I'm stuck on the rest. Preston insists the tablet and notebook are essential to solving the puzzle."

- "Like a real Indiana Jones movie!" The emoji that followed, a mocking "LOL", stung.

- "Preston told me the tablet and notebook lead to the earliest Buddha hair relics, buried in the lost capital of the Suvannabhumi kingdom..." He leaned back in his chair, satisfied. That should shut her up.

- "That's your mystery? Everyone knows the legend of the merchants Taphussa and Bhallika, and the relics brought from India to the Mon kingdom of Ramanna, the 'Land of Gold.' You can read about it at the Shwedagon Pagoda! That's what's so important? You're wasting my time!"

- Irritation rose in him, but he restrained himself: "I'm not a specialist. Preston says it could be the first *stūpa* built in the country after the Buddha's death. An exceptional discovery, archaeologically and spiritually..."

- "That's nice, but we die by the thousands under the bombs, millions of refugees are living in the mud, and we risk our lives every day defending our freedom! So frankly, searching for a pagoda that's two thousand years old isn't exactly a priority!"

- Anger was building in him, but Ayaan held it back: "I know." He acknowledged it reluctantly, incapable of fully accepting that she was right. "I don't claim this discovery will solve everyone's problems. But maybe it would draw international attention to your situation? I just want to fulfill my great-grandfather's last wish."

- "Basically, you don't give a shit about what's happening here! All you care about is using our history for your hobby and your fifteen minutes of glory!"

- He growled, frustrated by the terrible truth she had managed to read in him. "I expressed myself poorly, I apologize if I seemed insensitive." He recited mechanically what he'd learned in a negotiation course: "I admit I know little about Myanmar and I really want to learn more. I'll do everything I can to help." Even he doubted his sincerity.

A minute passed. The screen remained silent. Had she disconnected?

- A cold message appeared: "I said I would send you those photos and I'll keep my word. But once I've sent all the pages, that's it for me. I'm starting to regret finding that plane."

- Ayaan clenched his teeth: "Noted. Thanks again." He typed with rage before flinging the phone across the table.

The rustle of sheets tore through the silence. It had awakened the patient, who stirred, his livid arm emerging from the covers. Ayaan rose. He must speak, he thought, before night claimed him. The respirator mask engulfed the old man's face, mist escaping in gasps. Only his eyes persisted, two sapphires fixing him with disquieting acuity. They seemed to know that each minute spent at this dying man's bedside was a theft from his own ambitions. Time was running out. Their project risked an abrupt end. What could he gain from it? A vague idea germinated in his mind. He needed an alternative, safer, more dependable. The crystalline eyes continued to interrogate him, but he already paid them no heed. He did not even see the hand reaching to grasp his.

Nancy entered the room. "Time for your medication," she called, a broken record fixated on its groove. Ayaan stepped back and bumped into the side table where the phone lay. His gaze caught the name, Latika Williamson, the Director of the Centre for South East Asian Studies, scrawled on the Post-it pad. He knew what he had to do.

Chapter 5

Chin State, Myanmar, July 2024

Khin Yadanar split the steamed sweet potato in two, then bit with delight and voraciousness into the smoking flesh. Pain shot through her, a stifled cry, mouth ablaze. The spat pieces splattered on her neighbor's feet, who jolted back in disgust. That hunger. Always that hunger devouring her, making her lose all patience. "*Bilu ma*," her comrades murmured, "*the ogress*." They watched her in silence, both amused and disapproving. Her bunkmate and fellow doctor had warned her, handing her the banana leaf wrapping this burning coal. Khin Yadanar had done exactly as she pleased. Bravado? Contrariness? She swallowed with a provocative smile despite the burning that descended her esophagus. Her scorched tastebuds would no longer savor the subtle perfume of her favorite snack. She resented herself, without letting it show.

- "Now that's a dinner-show you're putting on for us," Thang Pam, a young nurse in her unit, called out, flicking a plume of cigarette smoke into the air. Laughter rippled across the group.

The four young women sat on the wooden stairs outside their barracks, savoring the warm breeze of that sunny late afternoon. Flocks of starlings chirped and traced arabesques, waves that plunged and rose from tree to tree. Soon the tide would withdraw and give way to the discreet chirping of nocturnal crickets. Khin Yadanar drank in this moment of serenity. Cotton tracksuit, coolness of the river bath lingering in the jasmine of her wet hair gathered in a bun. The yam warmed between her teeth, diffusing its sweet flavor.

It had not rained since the previous week, the sky had cleared, the humus hardened. They had taken the opportunity to hang their laundry on the facade, breaking with the tradition of feminine undergarments displayed out of sight. Khin Yadanar thought back with pride to the "Longyi Revolution" after the 2021 coup. She and her comrades had hung their skirts above the barricades. Soldiers dared not pass beneath them, fearing the loss of their virility. An effective tactic that had slowed the crackdown and a feminist declaration questioning military authority and Burmese patriarchal norms. Yet the leering gazes and whistles of men of the CDF at this profusion of panties and bustiers fluttering in the wind proved the cause was far from won. Even among those who challenged the established order.

- "Did you hear what happened to Dai Phyu?" Thang Pam broke the silence as two young recruits passed by, sniggering and multiplying winks in their direction. "Sergeant Shing Ling cornered her during night patrol. He said he needed to 'inspect her equipment.' She refused and he threatened her with citing her for insubordination."

- "Shing Ling again?" Shing Tui cursed. She was one of the few women fighting regularly on the front line as a sniper after being trained in the North by AIF[16] volunteers. "That pig! He thinks he's untouchable because of his 'exploits' at Matupi," she added with contempt, downing a large gulp of *khaung*[17].

- "He's not the only one," Mana Yawng continued. Another nurse. Khin Yadanar appreciated her work ethic, her sense of humor. Today, no humor. "Last month, a patient grabbed my waist and said: 'You revolutionaries aren't supposed to serve the people?' I felt so... dirty."

- "*Aw mai ca*[18]! Why didn't you report it to me?" Khin Yadanar asked. "I'd have filed a complaint with the Commander."

- "What difference would it make?" Mana Yawng shot back with bitter laughter, taking the liquor her companion offered. "What did he say about the doctor who was harassing me?"

- "He laughed," Khin Yadanar admitted with helplessness. "Then he said: 'We all make sacrifices. Don't distract our heroes with women's stories.'"

- "Same when I complained about Shing Ling groping recruits," Shing Tui continued. "'Do you want to be responsible for

---

[16] Anti-fascist Internationalist Front. Armed group of international volunteers engaged in the civil war alongside the local resistance, with an anti-fascist, anti-capitalist, and internationalist ideology.
[17] Traditional beer consumed particularly in the southern part of Chin State.
[18] K'cho expression used to express compassion, sorrow, or anger in response to the difficult situation that a loved one is enduring.

the division of our forces?' he asked. 'These men risk their lives every day.'"

- "The complaint squad," Thang Pam added. "That's what they call us behind our backs." She hurled the sweet potato skin she'd just finished in an angry gesture. Khin Yadanar did the same. "It's like we're fighting two wars. One against the junta, and one just to exist safely in our own ranks."

- "*A yäi ca*[19]! Same old refrain!" Khin Yadanar fumed. "'We'll deal with it after we win. Focus on the real enemy.'"

Incomprehension gnawed at her. A movement that claimed it wanted to restore democracy, human rights, dismantle the military regime, patriarchy, corruption... and yet sidelined, postponed the well-being of half the population. Yet, women's liberation in Myanmar was not peripheral. It was the very soul of the Spring Revolution. The cement of its success.

The Tatmadaw reduced women to furniture. Widows redistributed at random among the troops, like spoils of war. Soldiers' wives condemned to serve those of officers. Hostages slowly dying in frontier outposts. Valueless objects to the military. As for civilians... Khin Yadanar recalled the medical reports: torn uteruses, fractured ribs, empty gazes of those who had survived systematic rape. The resistance must be this flawless mirror, reflecting back to the army its own monstrous face. To win over soldiers' wives, to show them their husbands were dying for a

---

[19] K'cho expression similar to "Aw mai ca".

system that would reduce them to slaves, so they would push them to desert.

She observed her companions. Twilight gilded their weary faces. They were not those rifle-toting dolls in propaganda videos. No. Their callous hands held the registers of clandestine schools, adjusted drone sights, cast metal for makeshift shells. Their fingers sutured wounds at the front, diffused mines, encrypted messages to inform the world. Their blood had nourished the soil of the homeland as much as men's. Respect? Protection? Men owed it to them now. Not as reward, but to bring about the annihilation of the junta.

- "Even the river's become their territory," Mana Yawng growled, crushing her cigarette against the worm-eaten wood of the stairs. An ember died out in an angry crackle. "They hide behind the rocks and ogle us. Impossible to maintain decent hygiene under these conditions."

- "What if we gave them a lecture on vaginal yeast infections?" Khin Yadanar quipped. "That should keep them away."

- "With pictures!" Mana Yawng added, miming a camera pointed between her thighs. The cascade of laughter that greeted the suggestion drowned out the voice of Sophia Everest, whose song *Shin Yal* played on Thang Pam's phone.

These were the kinds of exchanges that earned women resistance fighters the contempt of their elders. They were criticized for their crudeness, their bawdy jokes, their refusal to abide by traditions. Their parents despaired of bringing them back to the village to marry them off. They were forgetting these women's tenacity, their determination to use this opportunity to transform society, to claim the place in society that they had been denied until now. They embodied the hope of a Myanmar freed from old demons, ready to take its place in this new century.

- "I'll have to take a lover," Thang Pam said, fixing her gaze on the horizon. "These predators don't bother girls who are in couples."

- "Keep dreaming!" Mana Yawng laughed. "You'll need a shitload of makeup to attract a guy with that face!" She pursed her lips in a mock kiss in response to the bird that Thang Pam flipped at her.

- "You're joking?" Khin Yadanar interjected. "You're not seriously going to throw yourself at the first guy for that reason? That's not the solution and it sends the wrong message."

- "Easy for you to say! You're with Kee Mawng, the local rock star. You're untouchable!" Shing Tui cut in sharply.

- "That and her shitty personality," Thang Pam added mischievously.

- "What are you talking about?" Khin Yadanar rushed to correct. "We're not together. We're just childhood friends."

- "No way! You mean you've never...?" Mana Yawng asked with a wink, inserting a finger through the circle she made with her other hand.

They all burst out laughing at Khin Yadanar's obvious discomfort. She felt a dull heat rise to her cheeks. A doctor, she saw, observed, touched, manipulated, operated, cut, sutured, repaired naked bodies all day long. She wasn't a virgin either. A brief affair with a medical student. So why this embarrassment at the mention of Kee Mawng? Why these images that surfaced: his calloused hands caressing her neck, his sweat-covered chest, his lips when he smiled at her...

- "If you're not together, I'll take my shot," Thang Pam teased with a falsely angelic smile.

- "Wait, isn't he your cousin?" Shing Tui cut in.

- "That wouldn't stop her," Mana Yawng jeered, lighting a fresh cigarette. "She's desperate and only relatives would have her." A quip met with another middle finger.

Their antics irritated Khin Yadanar, forcing her to examine the mirror of her emotions, and rather than confront them, she chose to extract her mobile phone. Digital escape. She hoped this form of passive resistance would invite them to change the subject. She opened Signal and sent the photo of the final notebook page to Ayaan. It was done, she'd kept her word, she could finally cut ties with that pompous jerk. The tablet remained, accursed artifact or national treasure? Should she alert the NUG[20]? The government in exile had no Ministry of Culture.

---

[20] National Unity Government. Government in exile formed by elected parliamentarians who were ousted during the 2021 coup in Myanmar.

- "Speak of the devil," Shing Tui murmured with a tilt of her head toward a soldier approaching their group.

Kee Mawng walked toward them, his uniform caked with dried mud. His assault rifle swung with the rhythm of his stride. Khin Yadanar fixed her gaze on her screen, feigning indifference. A sharp elbow from Thang Pam made her flinch.

- "*Om law*[21] Kee Mawng," they sang out in unison.

He smiled, that smile that never left him, even in exhaustion. He looked shattered. He'd just returned from the field.

- "Hey everyone. Awm Awi, can you come? I need you."

Laughter erupted. Khin Yadanar jumped to her feet. "Stop messing around!" She took Kee Mawng by the arm, felt beneath her fingers the fatigue that stiffened his muscles. "What can I do?"

The trio continued to tease them as they moved away toward the medical building. Around them, the camp hummed with its routine of war.

- "We ran into soldiers who'd fled Matupi last month." His voice was heavy. "Two hours of gunfight. They surrendered finally. About a hundred people. We separated the women, children, and elderly. We need you to check on them."

Khin Yadanar nodded immediately.

---

[21] Informal greeting used in K'cho dialect, reserved for friends and family members. Shortened version of "*Mei Om Law*," which is the formal greeting.

- "They're dehydrated and malnourished. Some dysentery cases and probably malaria, I think."

- "I'll grab my equipment."

Five minutes later, they joined the team in the long wooden shack at the camp's edge. The smell seized them, that smell of human misery that Khin Yadanar knew only too well. About fifty women, children, and elderly lay sprawled on the beaten earth floor, filthy and in rags. The same haggard faces, empty gazes she had tended for months among civilian refugees. They belonged to the other camp this time. A month in the jungle had marked them. Their skeletal bodies testified to this precarious survival, sustained on rodents and bamboo shoots. Khin Yadanar felt that pity reserved for the innocent, not for the Tatmadaw men locked in the camp's prison. She approached a young woman clutching an infant with jutting ribs against her. The scrawny child sucked desperately at a withered breast.

- "I'm going to examine you." Her movements were precise, automatic. The stethoscope revealed an alarming tachycardia symptomatic of dehydration. "How old is he?" She pinched the skin on the baby's arm to confirm her diagnosis.

- "Almost two months."

- "When did your milk dry up?" Khin Yadanar placed the instrument against the skeletal chest of the mother.

- "Two days ago. I tried to give him some herb broth..." Her voice broke.

Khin Yadanar opened the soiled diaper crusted with dry, brownish traces stuck to the infant's skin. She removed it completely and tossed it aside. They would have to burn it.

- "That was irresponsible," she declared flatly, without emotion. "Even boiled, your child can't digest that yet. The diarrhea has worsened his dehydration."

- "I'm sorry."

Khin Yadanar stood up. In her notes, she wrote down the diagnosis.

- "We're going to prepare a rehydration solution. And a meal will be served soon. Priority is getting both of you back in shape. And hygiene is absolutely crucial. A nurse will show you what to do. If the diarrhea doesn't stop, we'll need to put him on an IV. You understand?"

- The young woman seized her hand, in tears. "Thank you, *Saya Ma*[22]. The gratitude was palpable in her voice trembling with emotion. "If we'd known... The *bogyo*[23] kept telling us you, the 'terrorists,' would torture us..."

The word hung in the air. Khin Yadanar smiled sadly. The irony struck her like a punch to the gut. Her parents, both doctors of the CDM[24], had been assassinated by the Tatmadaw during the capture of Mindat three years before. No mercy, not even a decent

---

[22] « Doctor » in Burmese.
[23] « General » in Burmese.
[24] Civil Disobedience Movement. Launched by Burmese civil servants and citizens to oppose the 2021 military coup.

burial. Their bodies had been abandoned in the blaze of the family home. And they, the generals, called them "terrorists". She went to join Kee Mawng, who watched the scene from the doorway.

- "You hear that?" she asked him, intertwining her fingers with in his with unusual tenderness.

- "Yeah." He tucked a strand of her hair behind her ear, a tender gesture that bound them beyond words. His fingers were blackened with earth. "That explains the fifty corpses from last week. They preferred to starve in the forest rather than be captured. There were women, children."

- "Brainwashed by decades of propaganda." Khin Yadanar shook her head in disgust. "If soldiers knew the truth, they'd all switch sides."

She observed the patients still waiting and became aware of her companion's exhaustion.

- "I'll be here for a while. Get some rest. And take a shower," she added, pretending to sniff him with a wrinkled nose and a small mocking laugh.

Without warning, he pressed his lips to hers. Surprise coursed through her, but she did not pull away. Something within her yielded, then answered this embrace with a fervor she did not know she possessed. When their mouths parted, their gazes remained locked in a silence heavy with promises. She smiled at him tenderly as she slipped her flip-flops back on, then took a few steps at his side outside, their fingers intertwined. Behind the barracks, a honeyed sun was setting. Beyond the peaks, Mount

Victoria raised its imposing summit, its head resting on a pillow of clouds like a sleeping divinity. A majestic tableau, a gift from Mother Nature to celebrate the birth of their romance.

- "See you soon," she promised. "I need to get back." Her hand slid along his face to rest against his rough cheek. "You need a shave," she teased, gently scratching his Van Dyke. He laughed and resumed his walk.

She remained in the middle of the clearing, watching his figure shrink, his gait dragging, his shoulders hunched. A silent storm rose within her. How could she tame this intimacy that shattered her order? Did she genuinely love him, or was it the desperate yearning of two lost souls? She wanted neither to wound him with refusal nor to lead him astray with hasty consent. She had stifled these questions beneath the revolutionary urgency. The war forbade love. For three years already the conflict had ravaged the country, for three years she had chosen to serve the cause rather than her own happiness. How much longer would she have to wait before she could allow herself to dream of anything but liberation? Was she punishing herself, and Kee Mawng by extension, for her parents' death?

A roar tore through the air. She barely caught sight of the MiG's silhouette before a deafening explosion set the landscape ablaze in a blinding flash. The blast compressed her entire being and hurled her several meters backward. The impact was merciless; her head struck the ground violently and she lost consciousness.

When she emerged from that void, each particle of air burned her lungs. The silence quickly gave way to a deafening whistle submerging muffled screams that barely pierced the cottony veil of concussion. She tried to breathe and was seized by uncontrollable coughing. Ash dust lacerated her throat, desiccating her tongue, giving her the impression of being buried alive. Her spitting, tasting acrid and metallic, soiled the ground in brownish sprays, each spasm reviving the sharp pain radiating through her chest. She struggled to open her eyes, dripping with dust and tears, to discover a theater of blurred, dancing shadows that collided and thrashed in all directions. She tried to raise herself once, immediately stopped by the pain clamping her skull like an incandescent crown. She thought she heard herself scream, but the incessant whistling swallowed her cry along with all her thoughts. Her fingers groped the back of her head. Her hand came back slick with blood, but the knowledge drowned in the nausea that twisted her skull.

She lay back, motionless, breathed deeply, reopened her eyes to the dark azure sprinkled with leaves and debris floating above her. The cries and commotion grew clearer, the screams detaching themselves from the sound of running feet. She had to rise. She pushed on her arms. Still that unbearable discharge radiating through her body. Two hands came to seize her and help her up. The world lurched, her legs gave way. Only her guardian angel's support kept her standing. The vertigo subsided. The MiG, the bomb. She was wounded, but alive. Her feet dug more firmly into the ground. Her strength was returning. She turned her head toward him. It was not Kee Mawng, just an unknown face marked by fear. In her mind, a single thought, a single image: her lover walking toward the explosion.

Panic seized her, a black veil that smothered all faculty of thought. She broke free from the soldier's grasp and bolted, drunk with anguish, legs trembling, stumbling with each stride, screaming Kee Mawng's name until her throat bled. Frantic, unable to process the whirlwind of information from her surroundings, she continued her erratic run through the smoke. One cry, one name. Nothing else mattered. Suddenly, she saw the gray form lying on the ground. She plunged toward the inert body shrouded in twilight's pall, a shadow puppet cast by flames. His left leg was nearly completely shattered from the knee down. His name, called out hoarsely, was swallowed by sobs. He did not respond.

A switch flipped within her. Her instincts took over, the weeping girl replaced by the war medic. She tilted his head back, observed the movements of his chest, her ear at his mouth. He was unconscious but still breathing! She examined the leg. Shreds of muscle hung beside the crushed bone laid bare, a crater from which blood gurgled, drenching the humus in continuous pulses. The femoral artery was hit. He would die in three minutes. She removed her jacket and tied it near the wound. It was insufficient. She raised her head and called out a soldier.

- "Come here!" He stopped dead in his tracks. "Give me your belt!" She placed it around his thigh above her jacket. "Tighten it hard!" He obeyed.

Kee Mawng regained consciousness with a piercing shriek of agony. Unfortunately, they had no morphine.

- "Stay there! Keep his legs elevated!" she commanded. "And keep him awake at all costs!"

She ran toward the clinic, stuffed supplies into a bag, then ran back, requisitioning two stretcher-bearers. Kneeling in bloody mud, she packed the wound with sterile gauze, then placed a tourniquet above the belt. She twisted it with all her strength, causing another acute wail from her lover. The hemorrhage stopped. A second tourniquet would have been ideal. But this basic material - twenty dollars in any country - was extraordinarily rare in their mountains. Like all elementary medical equipment and treatments. Twilight surrendered to night and she continued to examine the wound by the light of the fire. No other visible injury.

- "Take him to surgery! Absolute priority! The surgeon must operate immediately!" The stretcher-bearers complied.

She wanted to go with him, to ensure he was being treated. He'd need amputation, she knew that, but she preferred to repress that nightmare, to banish its future consequences from her mind for now. If he made it. No. He couldn't die. Should she follow them, watch over him, wait for the surgery to end? The dilemma made her oscillate between the distraught lover and the field medic. The latter finally prevailed. Other lives were at stake. She had to trust her colleagues.

She scanned the scene for survivors. The camp thrashed feverishly behind a curtain of smoke. Burning trees exhaled resin, searing her nostrils and eyes. The wind shifted and revealed it: hell. A mass of black forms passing buckets, desperately dousing the charred skeletons of buildings that shrieked and vomited tongues of flame. Shouts. Orders flung into the chaos. A crack, a shriek tore the air - a roof collapsed with a crash, scattering sparks that the wind scattered like fireflies, igniting the neighboring trees at once. The inferno radiated into the night; she felt its scorching breath on her face, mesmerized by its terrible beauty, drained hollow by the crackling that hollowed her out.

The women's quarters lay at the heart of the furnace. A sickening premonition seized her gut. She ran hard enough to dislocate her ankles toward her barracks, striding across waves of people that blocked her view. She finally caught sight of it. What remained of it. The carbonized structure, flattened by a giant's hand, finished consuming itself under sprays of water buckets from volunteers clustered at its side. Nothing was left. And there, at the foot of the building, lay three women's bodies aligned side by side, petrified, bloodied, disfigured, blackened by soot, resting forever in silence. Khin Yadanar fell to her knees with a cry of despair and dissolved into tears.

Chapter VI

Win Ka, Burma, February 1942

Anthony Preston closed his notebook slowly. The characters carved into the wall had finally yielded their secrets to his patient pen. Or at least their visible form had, for their deeper meaning would remain veiled for many months yet. He thought of the long days that awaited him and Professor Sayer, bent over these ancient signs in the quiet studiousness of Rangoon University. For the old Mon language - that tongue which the expeditions of Forchhammer[25] and Taw Sein Ko[26] had scarcely begun to rescue from centuries of silence - guarded its mysteries jealously. Each new text was a labyrinth of riddles and challenges.

But all that would have to wait. The urgency of their times allowed no delay. They had to gather hastily every fragment, every inscription, before returning to Rangoon where, they still believed, the safety of civilization awaited them, safety that would grant them time to extract its secrets.

---

[25] Emanuel Forchhammer (1851-1890). Swiss Indologist and Orientalist, specialist in Pali and the first professor of Pali at Rangoon College in Burma.
[26] Taw Sein Ko (1864-1930). First recognized archaeologist in Burma, who held the position of Superintendent of the Archaeological Survey of Burma.

Anthony's shadow, shrunken as if to shield itself from the growing ardor of the tropical zenith, told him the morning was already nearing its end. The *pauk*, those lacquer trees with scarlet flowers, raised their tongues of fire toward the relentless azure. Carried by the fragrance of silken cotton trees, they swirled in the scorching waves that escaped the ground. Another day would not be long in evaporating without their work being finished. This race against time that was also a race against History itself.

A thorn pricked his thumb as he closed his leather pouch. By an instinctive gesture, he brought the finger to his lips and tasted that drop of copper-tinged blood that beaded there. It was then he became aware of his position: he stood in the middle of a thornbush, absorbed in contemplation of his archaeological treasure. His gaze was captivated by the figure rising at eye level. It was of striking beauty. Coiling from blocks of black laterite was a *naga*, a mythic serpent with scales still tinged the emerald green that had once covered it entirely. He gently pulled away the clump of grass that masked the left portion. An ogre's head emerged into the light. A *yakkha*, guardian of the celestial realms surrounding Mount Meru, the sacred mountain at the center of the Buddhist universe. The bestial face had been gnawed by time, rendering it nearly unrecognizable. One could barely discern the brow ridges looming above gaping and menacing eye sockets, as well as the broad and flattened nose. Only the lower jaw remained intact, revealing a maw from which four monstrous fangs protruded, ready to devour the reckless who dared violate this sanctuary.

Similar bas-reliefs ranged along this partially visible wall: a capital with three lions, noble emblem of the Ashoka empire, flanked by a bull and a horse; a blooming lotus and a *Dhammacakka*, the eight-spoked wheel of law, first symbol of Buddhism; a white elephant evoking the sacred animal that appeared in a dream to the Buddha's mother. And many other figures adorned these fifty meters of blocks emerging from the ground, crowned with grasses and climbing plants. The rest of the wall lay buried beneath the alluvium of centuries or had been dismantled to be repurposed in secular constructions, the common fate of so many monuments that indifference delivered slowly to oblivion. This section of wall was all their expedition had managed to exhume from the ramparts that had once encircled the *stūpa*. Or rather, the ruins of what it had once been, for only the circular platform remained, surmounted by a mass of collapsed bricks.

Professor Sayer, who directed the excavations with the meticulous passion of a true scholar, had immediately grasped the significance of this discovery. First, the symbols of evident antiquity that preceded human representations of the Buddha. Second, the use of clay bricks mixed with straw and rice chaff, measuring exactly four hundred sixty-one cubic inches. Finally, the employment of a "butter" type mortar, in use before the adoption of dolomitic lime. All these elements corresponded to techniques employed in India during the third century before Christ. To these were added the finger-marked motifs, an artistic innovation distinctive to the Pyus[27] and the early Mon kingdoms. Sayer was convinced of it, and nothing could have shaken his conviction: they had just uncovered one of Burma's most ancient monuments, the remains of Suvannabhumi, that golden kingdom of the Mons which legend traced back to the Buddha's lifetime, founded by King Siharaja according to the chronicles. From the third century before our era, the Ceylonese annals of the *Mahavamsa* and *Dipavamsa* had recorded it as the first *Theravada* Buddhist civilization in Southeast Asia. True, the hypothesis was difficult to substantiate; the inscriptions relating to King Ashoka's missions made no explicit mention of it, but Professor Sayer believed in it with that ardent faith which animates true seekers.

For fifteen years he had devoted his life to this vanished civilization. Through his erudition and intuition, he had led the expedition to the summit of the hill overlooking Win Ka. Laborers had cleared the site during winter. His university budget and personal savings had been swallowed up, much to the dismay of his colleagues. It was he too who had engaged Anthony, then a young man of eighteen fresh from Winchester College, to serve as his assistant. He had charged him with drawing the site plans, sketching the bas-reliefs, and recording their excavation work. The young man had proved an invaluable collaborator. Beyond the

---

[27] Tibeto-Burman speaking people who migrated from the Tibetan plateau to the Irrawaddy Valley in the 2nd century BC and established the first historically documented Buddhist urban civilization in Southeast Asia, creating fortified city-states that flourished for over a thousand years until the mid-11th century.

enthusiasm of youth, he displayed that disdain for comfort so precious in the field. Having spent his childhood between Rangoon and Maymyo until his departure for boarding school at twelve, he spoke Burmese fluently. His resourcefulness in negotiating with the local population for the necessary equipment proved precious in those troubled times when war drew inexorably closer.

Japanese aircraft had struck Rangoon on December 23rd, leaving more than two thousand dead among the curious crowds gathered along Strand Road, oblivious to the danger overhead. The capital, until then an inviolable sanctuary, stood defenseless: the few shelters that existed would have been worse than useless against such bombs.

The British administration, caught entirely off guard, had seen nothing coming. A month earlier, all had still been celebrating Saint Andrew's at the Scots Kirk[28], dancing until three in the morning in that hushed atmosphere peculiar to the colonial clubs, sheltered by the conviction that war would never reach them, nestled in their small Eden built at the Empire's margins, between gilded pagodas and flourishing trading posts. Only the sudden departure of the Japanese community a fortnight before might have awakened their suspicion. The precision of the bombardment confirmed the presence of an invisible fifth column feeding intelligence to the enemy. The strategic sites, the docks among them, but also Watson's establishments, which imported

---

[28] Presbyterian church on Signal Pagoda Road and frequented by the Scottish community, including members of Masonic Lodges affiliated with the Grand Lodge of Scotland.

American trucks through the Lend-Lease Act, had been struck with an accuracy that owed nothing to chance.

The raids had reduced the poor quarters to ashes, transforming Rangoon into an open-air mass grave. Two days later, on Christmas Day, five thousand more civilians perished. Only the heroic intervention of the Brewster Buffalos and Tomahawk P-40s of the Flying Tigers prevented the toll from mounting still higher.

A panic, unprecedented in scale, seized the capital. Shops, stores, and markets closed as if responding to a single command. As for the Indians, they carried vivid memories of the racial riots of 1938 and knew they would become targets should the British abandon the city. The wealthier among them departed for India by ship. Three hundred thousand others, mostly coolies, took to the roads westward on foot, hoping to reach East Bengal[29] through the unforgiving jungle of Arakan. The city emptied of half its population within days, stretching into an endless column along Prome Road[30].

The military authorities were forced to deny travel permits to adult males and restrict movement authorizations to prevent utter paralysis. Officers' wives became secretaries, nurses, and laundresses by necessity, while administrative staff continued their duties as best they could, consoled only by the hope of soon rejoining their families in the north.

---

[29] Present-day Bangladesh.
[30] Present-day Pyay Road.

With no means of escape, the people of Rangoon dug trenches and shelters in their gardens, while Lactogen, essential to the English tea ceremony, transformed into a precious and scarce delicacy, prompting the authorities to impose rationing. Sirens soon punctuated daily life, succeeding one another hour after hour through the nights, once the Japanese abandoned daytime bombing to concentrate their efforts on Mingaladon airfield.

Rangoon had gradually seized up like a wounded animal stiffening before death. The governor's appeal not to abandon the city convinced no one, particularly when government offices began transferring north, creating the impression that the crew was abandoning a ship on the verge of sinking.

Since then, Japanese forces had crossed the Thai border, Moulmein had fallen, and Mandalay was enduring its first bombardments. The flow of contradictory information progressively drained the population's remaining resolve. The university closed its doors when the administration commandeered its premises. Nothing now held Professor Sayer in Rangoon, that capital consumed by a morbid and frenzied fever.

Weary of sleeping only in two-hour intervals before a new siren tore him from bed to force him into the makeshift shelter, damp and cold, dug in the garden like an anticipated grave; weary of remaining huddled in darkness unable to find rest because of the cloud of mosquitoes that harassed him; weary of hoping that Japanese aircraft would hurry and arrive so they could finally return to bed, yet they never came; weary of walking empty markets the next day to hear only talk of war and its mad rumors.

Professor Sayer had chosen this forced sabbatical to devote himself entirely to his field research, before access was denied to them by the inexorable advance of the front. What was more comforting than taking refuge in the past, a territory frozen like inscriptions carved in stone, when the present offered only uncertainty? They had just spent two months clearing the site, two months of patient toil that had brought them to the threshold of discoveries which importance they sensed without yet grasping their full scope.

Thus, despite the manifest reluctance of the Burma Railway Company employee, a man with graying temples who regarded their tickets as if they were passes to the afterlife, their small group had boarded the train for Kyaikto on the Sittang Valley State Railway line. This same line which terminus was Martaban, facing Moulmein across the Salween River, which had just fallen into Japanese hands. They had been virtually the only passengers on this journey that crossed Pegu and then the Sittang Bridge. The line was primarily used to organize the methodical retreat of troops between Martaban and Thaton, in the face of the inexorable advance of the Rising Sun forces.

Cut off from the outside world and its tragedies for more than a month now, their small team had been wandering over the mausoleum of one of Southeast Asia's principal civilizations, one that still awaited revealing its greatest secret.

- "Professor, come see this!"

- "Dr. Win Thu, have you found something?"

Professor Sayer extricated himself from the thorns with great flailing gestures, his cream-colored cotton suit torn and covered in prickles. At last free, he drew out a handkerchief, lifted his bamboo pith helmet, and wiped his brow: no cool breeze reached this clearing where the parched vegetation exhaled yellow tendrils, mirages rolling beneath the impenetrable thickets. The exaltation of a discovery so near made the heat burn all the more fiercely. He made his way toward the assistant professor, a Burmese man in his thirties, barefoot in *longyi* and white shirt, standing proudly beside the collapsed dome of the *stūpa*, from which he had begun removing bricks one by one, as testified by the perfect cube he had stacked beside the monument. Ordinarily expressionless, he now wore a triumphant smile, holding what appeared to be a stone tablet.

- "Show me that," said Professor Sayer with curiosity. "Looks like a votive tablet."

He seized it reverently and examined the carvings. His eyes widened, his lips parted.

- "Anthony!" he called out, his voice hoarse with ecstasy. "Look, my boy! Southern *Brahmi* script!" he exclaimed, pointing to the characters carved in stone. "It will take time to translate. But unless I'm very much mistaken, the name of Emperor Ashoka is mentioned! The tablet and *stūpa* would date to three hundred years before our era! Gordon Luce[31] had better watch himself!"

He flashed him a brilliant smile, then placed his friendly hands on the young man's shoulders, anticipating his savory victory over the preeminent historian of the Burma Research Society[32], who had been quite vocal in his public skepticism of Sayer's revolutionary theses on the chronology of Suvannabhumi. In the academic debates that opposed them, scholars knew how to display the same ferocity as soldiers on a battlefield.

- "You heard that, Nandar Aye?" Anthony called out to the young woman reclining at a distance, in the shade of a stand of flowering Cassia trees.

The young Burmese woman looked up and gave him a knowing smile before burying herself once more in her reading of *Gone Myint Thu*, the latest novel by Dagon Khin Khin Lay[33]. Like the students at Rangoon University, this acerbic portrait of colonial society captivated her. The book never left her side. For long seconds, Anthony contemplated this tableau. Stretched out on a blanket, her silhouette was framed by the chandelier of yellow flowers cascading overhead. She lay on her side, an elbow propped

---

[31] Gordon Hannington Luce (1889-1979). European scholar of Burmese history, a specialist in epigraphy, archaeology and the ancient languages of Burma, author of the magisterial work "Old Burma - Early Pagan".
[32] Learned society founded in 1910 in Rangoon, dedicated to the study and promotion of art, science, and literature related to Burma and neighboring countries.
[33] Dagon Khin Khin Lay (1904–1981). Burmese novelist, screenwriter and filmmaker, founder of the Dagon Publishing Company and one of the few female publishers in Burma.

languorously beneath her head, in an attitude of beguiling languor. Through her white cotton chemise showed the lace of a corset embracing a slender bosom and waist, prolonged by the curve of a hip defined by a becoming *longyi* in mauve and blue patterns. A strand of hair lustrous as lacquer escaped her chignon and caressed delicately her face. With a graceful gesture, she wound it nonchalantly around her finger, while her foot danced mechanically, a sandal hanging from her toe swaying to the rhythm of an imaginary song. Abandoned in this innocent posture, she seemed to taunt with an effrontery not entirely unintentional the three men laboring in the dust at the foot of a pile of old stones.

Sensing she was being watched, the young woman lifted her eyes and met Anthony's gaze, sustaining it briefly but intensely. Their minds exchanged a spark he felt down to the pit of his stomach. From the corner of his eye, he saw Win Thu staring at him with evident ill will behind his large round spectacles, his lips pursed in a disdainful sneer around the eternal cheroot he kept clamped between his teeth.

- "Remains to be seen what other treasures this *stūpa* might hold," Professor Sayer continued, his face illuminated by an almost joyful expectancy.

The slap he landed on Anthony's shoulder pulled him from his reverie.

- "Ashoka?" he murmured, his mind suddenly awakened. "Could this be the *stūpa* built to enshrine Buddha's relics? Could the legend of Sona and Uttara be true?"

- "Who can say? What a discovery that would be! Only one way to know: let's finish excavating the monument."

He had scarcely taken a step toward the pagoda when the first explosion shook the hillside. Soon, the echo of other blasts scattered the forest in a cacophony of branches and panicked birds. A roar rose up, powerful, tearing through the air. Bursting from behind thick foliage, an aircraft cleaved the sky just above their heads, projecting its menacing shadow upon them. It climbed in a chandelle, banked, dove obliquely toward the earth, then turned away toward Thaton. The fighter flew with the sun behind it, concealed in the glare. Anthony raised his hand above his eyes, squinting at its fuselage, which dwindled before his gaze. Sudden dread seized him at the sight of the red circles that shone distinctly on the aircraft's side and beneath its wings.

Chapter VII

Bilin, Burma, February 1942

Sergeant Myers scanned the eastern bank of the Bilin with anxious eyes, seeking some movement of the enemy. This narrow stream of water constituted a fragile frontier between the two armies. It all seemed peaceful, yet this quiet did not soothe him. His company had been tasked with retaking and holding a bridge upstream from Danyingon, which the enemy had destroyed that morning. The latter had likely already positioned itself on their bank, in the jungle that bordered the road.

He marched at the head of his section, knuckles clenched white around his carbine, ready to fire. His uniform, saturated with sweat, irritated his skin, but he perceived only the pain that twisted his entrails. He was not sick, no, he was afraid. A fear that ebbed when the gaping wounds radiating from the soles of his feet cruelly reminded him of their presence. Remnants of their forced march following their rout at Moulmein. A debacle more bitter than physical suffering. He had been fortunate. How many exhausted comrades had to be abandoned during their retreat, armed only with a canteen and their rifle? Likely dead by now. "March or die." The men of the 1st Burma Division had quickly made this motto of the French Foreign Legion their own. This tragic episode had decimated his former unit, which few survivors had been incorporated into the 2nd Battalion of the KOYLI at Bilin.

This catastrophe had dealt a severe blow to the troops' morale. The Salween estuary, hundreds of meters wide and bordered by mangroves, had constituted a far better defensive line than the Bilin now was. Yet it had not prevented the Japanese from gradually encircling the 17th Indian Division, attacking from the east after having crossed a jungle deemed impassable.

And here was the catastrophic scenario about to replay itself, as evidenced by the destruction of the bridge. The Japanese had already crossed the river and were preparing to outflank their lines from the north, employing the same maneuver as at Moulmein. The defensive line was stretched so thin that an entire army could have infiltrated between the companies. And perhaps it already had.

They had harbored no illusions. From their arrival, they knew this position would prove untenable. In the dry season, the Bilin was only a few meters wide and never rose higher than the knee. It was nothing but a stream easily crossed by infantry, along which the British troops, hastily regrouped after the fall of Moulmein, had been scattered.

Muffled detonations sounded at intervals. He had not yet glimpsed the enemy, but he knew it was there, crouched in shadow, awaiting the opportunity to unleash hell upon them. He scanned the vegetation intensely, so much so that it seemed to him the enemy was everywhere, as if the jungle itself had transformed into a forest of soldiers.

They did not even benefit from the protection of armored vehicles, Lieutenant Goldthorpe's vehicles having fallen behind. They would rejoin them at the bridge with forty Indian sappers. He felt naked and vulnerable without the Bren guns mounted on the vehicles, the only ones the company possessed, heavy armament being rare in the Burmese army.

The 2nd Battalion of the KOYLI, though numbered among the Empire's finest troops, was nevertheless ill-prepared to face such a force. From 1939, its best elements had been transferred to North Africa, leaving the battalion based at Maymyo to reconstitute itself with fresh recruits. Its modern equipment had not been renewed, the war effort barely sufficing to maintain troops in Europe. The Burma campaign, viewed from London, was nothing but the wrong war, in the wrong place, at the wrong time.

These men had therefore been sent to southern Burma with only the materiel they could gather on the spot, striving valiantly to repel an enemy hardened by three years of conflict in China, with only three Bren guns, a handful of light armored vehicles, a few grenades, no sniper rifles, no Thompson submachine guns, no spades to dig trenches, insufficient ammunition for their Lee-Enfields, a dozen local machetes of poor quality, some twenty compasses for the entire battalion, and the slouch hat of the Gurkhas in place of the regulation steel helmet, which had the advantage of being able to deflect the 25-caliber rounds used by the Japanese.

To this was added everything the Burmese army had lost in hastily abandoning Moulmein, including most of their rations. The only anti-tank launcher had disappeared with soldier Cryer, who had refused to part with it during the rout and had gradually fallen behind.

Myers and his men could not rely on their training to compensate for the lack of proper equipment either. The British command, judging the jungle impassable, had based its exercises on the European model, emphasizing discipline and orderly marching rather than mobility. They were incapable of responding to the Japanese tactics of infiltration and encirclement, which proved the enemy apparently did not find the jungle so impassable after all.

Myers finally caught sight of the bridge, a hundred meters ahead, beyond a curve in the road. The entire column rushed toward it in silence, discovering the charred structure lying at the bottom of the stream bed like a wreck of blackened wood.

- "Good God, where the devil are those sappers?" thundered Lieutenant Atkinson, watching south where heat mirages shimmered across the horizon. "Let's not hang about in the open, that's certain death. Sergeant Myers!"

- "Yes, sir!"

- "Disperse the men in defensive positions while we wait for Goldthorpe. Sections eight and nine on the far bank! Section seven this side! Make sure the men get cover. The Japs aren't far!"

- "Aye, sir!"

The order had scarcely been relayed when a roar of engines, mingled with the sharp cracks of rifles, poured from the south, down the road they had followed. The KOYLI instinctively pressed themselves behind rubble, stumps, and embankments, bayonets fixed like a handful of poilus from the Great War. Atkinson raised his field glasses to his eyes, scanning the bend.

- "Goldthorpe!" he cried at the sight of two light armored vehicles emerging two hundred meters distant.

The machines bore down, shaking the air with hellish breath. In their wake a cloud of dust and black smoke swirled. Beyond the din, Myers could make out the wild spattering of enemy bullets on their armor. At one hundred meters, the fire ceased, granting the steel monsters the fragile respiration necessary to reach the bridge.

An officer bounded from the lead armored car. His face, a mask of dust, bore the white mark left by goggles drawn round his neck. Violet shadows beneath his eyes, worn features, lips cracked with thirst amid an incipient beard, clothes crusted with grime and oil, everything spoke of the terrible days they had endured and announced those yet to come.

- "The sappers?" barked Atkinson, allowing Goldthorpe no time to catch his breath.

- "Dead!"

- "All of them?" Atkinson's face fell.

- "All of them!" Goldthorpe confirmed, his jaw clenched. "The Japs cut the line south of your position. Hiding in the jungle ten meters from the road. The sappers were dead before they even left the truck. The two other vehicles made for HQ. You can't stay here! Another formation's outflanking you to the north to encircle."

He delivered his report in a single breath, almost without pausing, shouting as if the projectiles that had hammered his vehicle had deafened him.

- "Thank you for the warning! Myers, inform the men. We're pulling out!"

The very instant the order rang out, the first mortar shells exploded, streaking the dust, accompanied by the ricochets of bullets whistling from the forest. In an instant hell descended upon them. It was too late to flee. They would have to hold against an enemy superior in numbers, better equipped, better trained. Hold to the last if necessary. Hold as only the KOYLI knew how. For the KOYLI never abandon, never surrender. *Cede nullis*[34]. Such was their motto.

Huddled in a shell crater, Myers raised his head. Two figures crawled from the jungle, clutching a machine gun. In a sharp reflex, he shouldered his rifle, cocked it, pressed the trigger.

---

[34] "Yield to none."

The first gunner rolled in the dust. Without catching his breath, without taking his eyes from the sights, he cocked and fired again. The second collapsed.

It lasted only three seconds. Three seconds of eternity during which the rest of the world had vanished. Three seconds to kill two men, instinctively, as easily as on the range. By reflex, by habit, but by desire as well. The desire to avenge his fallen comrades, the desire to make the enemy pay for the humiliation of Moulmein. Then time resumed its tumult: flashes of tracer fire, guttural cries, the stench of sulfur mingled with blood. Fear gripped his viscera like an iron hand. He had to act quickly, save those he commanded.

- "Sergeant Myers!"

The voice pierced the din at last. Private Doug Pitt, a small red-haired fellow with a ready wit whose garrulousness usually cheered the bivouacs, crawled toward him at twenty meters. Myers sprang up, bent low, and plunged beside him.

- "What is it, Pitt?"

- "The Lieutenant wants sections eight and nine on this side of the bridge. And you to lead the seven. We're pulling back south, toward HQ."

- "South? By the road? He's mad! We'll be cut to pieces!"

- "I don't write the orders, Sergeant! I just pass 'em on!" replied the soldier, managing a wry smile that shrapnel had failed to rob him of.

Even in such straits, he had to quip, he couldn't help it.

- "Goldthorpe's vehicles will cover you! That's what he said!"

With that, Pitt darted off, streaking along the ground. Myers relayed the order. Bayonets fixed, the men prepared to force the Japanese jaw open. If they did not hurry, sections eight and nine would find themselves encircled.

A dull rumble warned Myers that the armored vehicles were getting underway. He gave them a few meters' head start, then hurried, bent low, behind the tracks churning up the dust. At once the jungle tore open under a storm of shrapnel and shells. The machine guns of the armored vehicles answered, relentless, vomiting their streams of fire. From the corner of his eye, Myers glimpsed two of his men topple with a strangled cry. Whether they were already dead or merely pinned to the ground by agony, his duty commanded him to advance, lest the rest be engulfed.

- "Forward! Forward, for God's sake!" he thundered, his arm sweeping the horizon like a desperate semaphore.

While the infantrymen tried to combine running with firing, the crews of the armored vehicles sprayed the jungle with grenades. Each explosion tore at the landscape: clouds of leaves, coils of smoke, screams of men. This chaos loosened the grip. The section gained a few dozen meters before the enemy could snap the jaws shut again. The volleys became less intense. Myers hoped the same respite would be granted to the two sections behind them.

It was then that Goldthorpe's armored vehicles accelerated, maneuvering to draw the enemy's artillery fire. They had not gone a hundred meters when a new deluge enveloped them. Myers watched them recede, answering shot for shot, barking like two raging metal Cerberuses. Soon they vanished in a cloud of dust and leaves, leaving the road bare, Myers and his men exposed, as the fire resumed.

No alternative remained. Myers rushed toward the jungle. If the enemy had been able to traverse it to infiltrate their positions, so could they. A quick glance over his shoulder. Several of his men followed him. How many? Impossible to say in the chaos. How many would remain inert on the road? He had no choice. They would all be slaughtered if they stayed. A bullet whistled past his ear. He crouched low and plunged headlong into the tropical vegetation, which closed its dark and hostile arms around him, swallowing him whole.

Chapter VIII

Between Kyaikto and Moke Pa Lin, Burma, February 1942

The cartwheel exhaled its complaint with that inexorable regularity which marks the hours of defeat, alternating its mournful cadence with the dull tramping of hooves that raised clouds of dust. The acrid stench of the animal mingled with that of this rout which transformed an army into a cortege of specters. For that was precisely what Anthony beheld: a procession of booted shadows, the same color as the ground they trod with weary steps. He straightened his spine to scan this fiery horizon that the pitiless sky crushed beneath its furnace. The yellowed and charred branches of the rubber plantation offered derisory shade to this human procession that unfolded from Kyaikto toward Moke Pa Lin. An illusory respite that could not temper the heat that warped both landscape and souls. The wheel laboriously surmounted a stump and fell back with a dull thud to continue its hypnotic routine.

His tongue touched his cracked lips, a futile gesture against the thirst that gnawed at him. His throat seemed obstructed by the dense air he breathed with difficulty. He felt the crust of earth crack upon his face, hardened like marble. For hours now he had not perspired. No tears either to wash his eyes of those resinous vapors. His entire body had become parched, each fiber like that of dead wood. Each step demanded conscious will. For a moment, he hesitated to unscrew his canteen stopper, a vain hope to which he had yielded many times. It had been hours since he had offered its last drop to Nandar Aye.

Around him stretched the debris of this British army that the Japanese invader had dogged since Bilin. Among this human tide, his group had found its place by necessity. They did not wear the same uniform, yet all bore the same garb of defeat. They too were forced to abandon the summit of Win Ka, constrained by the invader, unable to complete their excavations. They had carried away the tablet that Anthony guarded carefully in his pouch along with his notebook and Nandar Aye's book, but had been forced to renounce piercing the secrets still hidden within the *stūpa*.

It was with reluctance that Professor Sayer had announced, the day before, their departure for Rangoon, his hand forced by circumstances. After a brief night spent stowing their belongings in the cart, they had departed at dawn, almost backwards, casting a final glance toward that summit where the thousand-year-old monument stood, with the hope of returning to complete their work once the army had repelled the invader.

The spectacle that greeted them upon reaching the Moke Pa Lin road had taught them that this deadline would likely prove impossible. They discovered there a long column of faces carved by sleeplessness, bristling with rifles now useless, borne by hollow legs. Soldiers stumbling in pairs, arm in arm in gestures of a fraternity that resists chaos. Too much suffering, too much despair in eyes that no longer even rose to question their incongruous cart.

The canteens had been empty since dawn. The water of the ponds, heavy with mosquitoes and buffalo carcasses, had become a nauseating potion these wretched shadows dared not renounce. Anthony had felt revulsion at the sight of a soldier lapping at a puddle. But the choice was simple: survive or succumb to thirst. As their journey progressed, the wounded had gradually been crammed into the rear of their vehicle, while their equipment had been left by the wayside. This gathering continued until the passengers themselves had to surrender their places.

Win Thu had protested vehemently when Professor Sayer decided that only Nandar Aye would remain in the carriage. To no avail. Sayer was his elder and his superior. To persist would have caused him to lose face. He now walked, his face sullen, his longyi and feet covered in dust. Anthony would not have failed to find it amusing had he not been so exhausted. Everything about the assistant professor was antipathetic to him: those pinched lips, that strict coiffure, those intellectual spectacles. So much so that he could not refrain from casting a contemptuous look at him across the cart. The Burmese answered with silent hatred. Professor Sayer noticed nothing. He labored at the front, his shoulders sagging, his emaciated frame floating in his ample clothing, guiding the beast by the reins in leaden silence, his mind doubtless entirely absorbed by the discoveries they had had to abandon.

Anthony knew the source of the disdain Win Thu harbored for Nandar Aye. She was not merely a woman, but of humble extraction as well. Win Thu belonged to a noble family of Mandalay. Their genealogical tree had burned in the British invasion of 1885. Yet the properties they owned throughout the country testified to their lineage. His father, a former student of Cambridge, numbered among the most prominent lawyers of the Rangoon court, moving with equal ease in British intellectual circles and Burmese high society, where he took pleasure in promoting, like his son, a drawing-room nationalism, citing Gandhi, condemning the segregation of the Pegu Club[35], while continuing to trade with His Majesty's empire. From their residence on the shores of Royal Lake[36], sheltered from the economic crisis that had raged for a decade, Win Thu and his father condemned the Saya San[37] revolt, yet preached for an emancipation of the Burmese people, not so they could freely decide their own destiny, but so the local elite, of which they considered themselves members, could at last resume governance according to the natural order of things.

Win Thu's contempt for the young woman had transformed into a fierce rancor, which cause Anthony knew well: she had rejected him. He who constituted one of the best matches in the capital, squandering the family fortune on alcohol and

---

[35] A British social club in Rangoon strictly reserved for Europeans, an emblem of a segregationist policy that barred access to any Asian, even those of high rank.
[36] Present-day Kandawgyi Lake.
[37] Buddhist monk, healer, and leader of the 1930-1932 peasant rebellion against the British. Died by hanging along with 125 other rebels.

women. She, nearly orphaned, possessing nothing but her intellect and this bewitching body. She had rejected him. Did she not live in concubinage with Professor Sayer? Did she not make eyes at Anthony? That was what he could not forgive her: this attraction to the *thakins*, this preference for Europeans, which constantly reminded him of the place of Burmans like himself in the racial hierarchy of colonial society. An irreparable loss of face, a wound to his Burman pride continually reopened by the ostentatious reading of *Gone Myint Thu*, that novel recounting the obstacles overcome by a young man of humble station for love of a woman of superior rank. A constant affront he could not forgive.

As if he could have read his thoughts, Anthony saw Win Thu pull out his lighter with a metallic click to light the cheroot clenched between his jaws. He exhaled a plume of smoke with an air of defiance.

- "Tell your servant not to smoke. The smell of tobacco will draw the Japs!"

The voice, hoarse and stripped bare by exhaustion, rose like a growl into the clammy heat. Anthony turned his attention toward it, capturing the source of the command: a man whose threadbare uniform seemed to resist through sheer pride its own dereliction. The non-commissioned officer remained upright, frozen in his own authority, like those ancient statues one believes will stand forever even as the world crumbles around them.

- "He is not my servant," replied Sayer, his voice brief, direct, yet not without weariness. He turned then toward his assistant, his face drawn by sleeplessness and sun. "Dr. Win Thu, would you mind?"

Win Thu, making no effort to conceal a fiery glance directed at the military, resigned himself. With his heel he crushed the tobacco residue in an angry gesture.

- "Thank you," the non-commissioned officer said to Sayer, without a glance for Win Thu. "How did you end up here? Do you own a plantation?" What other explanation could there be for their presence in the midst of conflict, so far from the capital?

- "I am a historian at Rangoon University. These are my assistants. We were conducting archaeological excavations at Win Ka when we were interrupted," he explained with a grim air.

The infantryman surveyed the group with a gaze where curiosity collided with disbelief: not a trace, in those dusty silhouettes, of the cliché of the gentleman-archaeologist in white shirt, mustache impeccably groomed, hair pomaded, conjured by the discovery of Tutankhamun's tomb two decades before.

- "I thank you for offering your cart to our wounded. Otherwise, they'd be left rottin' by the side of the road," admitted the sergeant, casting a look at the bodies heaped within. His voice then became abrupt. "Pitt! What in God's name are you doin' in there, you daft bugger?"

- "Sergeant Myers?" A mass of red hair emerged, revealing the unruffled effrontery of a broad grin. "Blimey! Bloody hell, I'm glad to see your face! I reckon the jungle would've had you for its supper by now!"

- "Get out at once! I know you're not wounded, you malingerin' sod!," the NCO rebuked him. "You're lettin' that idle bastard swing the lead?" Myers asked Sayer with a hint of reproach.

- "I am not a physician," answered the academic curtly without even turning, his features chiseled by lack of rest.

Pitt, seemingly docile, jumped from the cart, his gait full of the weary provocation of survivors. He crossed the incandescent gaze of Win Thu, who had been obliged to demean himself by walking to yield the space to this shameless slouch. The lad from Leeds took on the air of a wise guy and, true to the reputation of Yorkshire folk, answered with a provocative jut of the chin indicating he was ready for a row if one was being offered. The Burman averted his eyes with a mutter, whilst Pitt rejoined Myers and their conversation began, under the attentive ear of Anthony who hoped to learn more of the conflict's progress.

- "Company's been bled white, it 'as. All them lads scarpered: McDonald, Clarke, Abbott...", the soldier enumerated, his ordinarily cheerful face now dark as thunder. "There weren't nowt left but a handful of us. We hung about waitin' for it to get dark, then legged it to join up wi' HQ. Bloody 'ell, we'd hardly got there when they says, 'Right lads, time to shift! We're off to Kyaikto!' Didn't even get time for a cuppa, never mind owt to eat. Had to get crackin' straight away, so we left half our kit back at Bilin. Japs were pourin' in from every direction, thick as flies they were. Had to tab twenty miles through the dark, gettin' plastered from all sides. Same malarkey this mornin' as well. So, when I spotted this cart with a duck pullin' it, I thought, 'That'll do for me.' Grabbed meself a kip, I did. Not that I were shirkin', mind you. I've done me feet in proper, runnin' about in boots that don't fit," he said with a grimace of apology.

At the plantation's edge, the road opened like a wound, its surface scorched by the sun. To the left, dense forest threw up a curtain of humid shadow; to the right, a patchwork of russet paddies, crevassed and silent. The carcasses of trucks, disemboweled by shrapnel, twisted by fire, left to cool along the verge, added to the furnace.

- "What about you then, Sergeant?"

- "I went through the jungle," replied Myers, his jaw tight as a clam, his eyes fixed on that wall of greenery. "Couldn't see more'n ten meters in front of me, and I'd no idea if I were goin' the right way or not. One crack of a twig, one little clink of me pack, and I'd have been done for. Had to steer clear of the tracks too, 'cause there were Japs crawlin' all over the place like ants on a picnic. So, there I was, wanderin' through on me own, in the quiet, listenin' to every bloomin' sound. Tell you what, Pitt, I'd have given anythin' for your forced march with the rest of the company. Anyway, come the next night, I got into Kyaikto, or what were left of it, nowt but smoke and rubble. I fell in with the bluecoats from the 2nd Battalion Duke of Wellington's, then found the KOYLI again. Had some grub, got a decent night's kip, then down comes the order: 'Fall back to Sittang along the railway line.' You know how it's gone since then: off we go at first light, nice little walk through the countryside, then the Japs comes over droppin' bombs so we wouldn't get bored. And 'ere we are now, still got twenty miles to go before we reach that bridge!"

- "You're 'avin' me on, Sergeant? Twenty miles?"

Myers cut him short by raising his hand for silence. Anthony too pricked up his ears at the distant hum gradually filling the air. All lifted their eyes to scan the azure in anxious expectancy. In a flash, an aircraft cleft the space, its snout emblazoned with a shark's grin. Pitt, in a laugh defying all prudence, flailed his arms frantically above his head:

- "A Flying Tiger! Yahoo!"

The Curtis P-40 Tomahawk fighter tore through the column, then vanished as rapidly as it appeared. As it dwindled to a speck, it climbed and began to bank to come back down on them. Myers grasped the threat in an instant.

- "Get down!" he roared with imperious voice.

All the soldiers plunged as one into the ditch. Anthony, moved by ancestral instinct, seized Nandar Aye by the arm, dragging her toward the verge. Sayer, petrified, remained standing until Myers hurled him to the ground, shielding him with his own body. Machine-gun fire erupted across the road, tore through the air and dust, plowed through the cart's wood with a deafening crash, as the fighter passed at treetop height in a thunderous roar. A second later, it vanished into the sun, leaving only gravel cascading down like stinging rain on the nape of necks.

- "Bloody madman!" cursed Pitt with rage. "We're on the same side!"

An obvious truth on the ground. A harder one to discern from the air, when uniforms and faces all wore the same earthen tint.

Then silence. A long moment in which the heartbeat slowed gradually. Around them, forms came back to life: soldiers straightening, brushing dust from their clothing, gathering weapons. Only Anthony remained prostrate for a moment beside Nandar Aye, whose face, drained of fear, had taken on the color of *thanaka*, her chest wracked by shock. In a brief gesture, she squeezed his hand intensely, murmuring more gratitude than any words could have contained.

The young man still did not move, staring at the crimson trickle that escaped from the vehicle. Then he rose and approached, joined in silence by Pitt and Myers. At the rear, the wounded had frozen in death, their bodies torn to pieces. The cart would go no farther. The horse lay on its side, its breathing emitting faint whinnies of pain, its brown coat bathed in a river of red. Myers knelt, stroked its mane, and plunged his bayonet into its neck. Bullets were too precious.

Already, a few soldiers converged, blades gleaming, to carve up the beast and divide the choicest morsels among themselves. Pitt, ordinarily quick to throw himself upon such carrion, remained frozen, his gaze fixed on the rear of the vehicle where he had been lying just minutes before. A mere chance. Luck decided life or death. The absurdity of war. Finally, without a word, he removed his shoes, took the boots from a pair of legs protruding at the rear, verified their size, and pulled them on with a grunt of satisfaction.

Win Thu and Nandar Aye had withdrawn, figures standing on either side of the road, frozen like stone sentinels. Anthony observed them without being able to fathom what they felt. Suddenly, Professor Sayer placed a hand on his shoulder, stammering:

- "Thank you for saving Nandar Aye," he faltered, his eyes bright with genuine gratitude as he gripped his hand.

Sayer, hatless, hair plastered to his scalp, staggering on exhausted legs, now appeared diminished. He wavered a few steps, then made his way toward Sergeant Myers, offering him a discreet sign of acknowledgment. Myers responded with the sangfroid expected of a soldier.

They divided the meager remnants of goods salvaged from the cart, each man adjusting his effects with the grave precision of those for whom every object existed only according to the weight it added to survival. But for Professor Sayer, the essential lay in the satchel that Anthony carried.

With a signal, Myers gave the order to move. The column resumed its march, grinding the burning laterite beneath their feet in mournful silence, each man oscillating between the mechanical effort of walking and the fevered listening to the forest, and the dread of attack at every clearing. There remained, the sergeant affirmed, some twenty miles to cover before reaching Sittang. The enemy, invisible yet so close, seemed to breathe down their necks.

Nandar Aye, now constrained to the same regime without privilege, bore it with detachment and resignation. Anthony walked at her side, almost furtively brushing the back of her hand. She averted her gaze with a reproving gesture, then quickened her pace to rejoin Sayer, leaving between them the fragrance of unspoken frustration. Win Thu observed the scene with a sharp smile, half-cynical, half-vindictive. Anthony swallowed his anger, drifting to the rear of the group.

Two hundred meters farther on, the forest tightened like a green jaw. A detonation cracked, a brutal tear in the torpor. The whistle of a bullet wrenched Anthony from his reverie. A groan followed as a soldier collapsed, hands pressed to his abdomen.

- "Take cover!" roared Myers, throwing himself to the ground at the moment the forest exploded in uninterrupted gunfire.

The wounded screamed, others dragged themselves to aid at the mere gravel, their hands and faces raw with abrasion, heedless. Each knew that to linger thus exposed would quickly mean they would all go down. The men of the 17th Division, spectral silhouettes, attempted to return fire, adjusting their aim as best they could on the fleeting muzzle-flash among the canopy, but what manner of reply was this when the enemy was naught but an invisible shadow?

- "Sergeant, I think I've spotted them."

Clifford, the former boxing champion of Burma, positioned the Bren and fired a furious volley into the dense vegetation. The groans that answered him wrung a grunt of satisfaction. Immediately drowned out by an inhuman clamor. The tree line exploded with a swarm of figures, Japanese pouring forth vociferating, swords and bayonets forward, uttering savage cries. Caught off guard, the KOYLI threw themselves into the fray, borne by that cold panic. The two waves met with unprecedented violence, shoulders against chests, blades against flesh. A chaotic melee of roaring and shrieking beasts.

Myers, swept up in this tide, bellowed without comprehension, fist white-knuckled, eye bloodshot. Reason engulfed, rage lodged in his belly, he ran, a red veil for his field of vision. He saw a face loom before him. Without slowing an instant, he plunged his bayonet into the Japanese officer's stomach, who let out a shrill cry before collapsing. Carried forward, he stumbled, fell heavily. Huddled around his rifle, he saw three phantoms rushing toward him, naked swords, eyes bulging with a madness magnified by the fury of close combat. He was going to die. If he were to go, he would take at least one with him.

Already the steel of the sword descended, ready to slice his flesh. Frozen, he raised his weapon by reflex alone. Then a dark mass swept the three Japanese away and hurled them to the ground. Soldier Barker was already crushing the last one's skull with rifle butts. Several dull blows until the skull gave way. Myers, dazed, sprang to his feet, but already a hand seized him, dragging him from the turmoil.

- "What're you playin' at, Pitt?" he shouted, struggling to break free from the iron grip that were dragging him back.

- "We gotta scram, Sergeant! We'll get our heads blown off if we stop 'ere!" he hollered, pulling hard and not letting go. "Besides, them civvies are gonna cop it if they sit there like lemons!" he finished, jerking his head toward Sayer and his companions, laid out on the road like they were stuck fast.

The thought of resisting flashed through his mind before disappearing. Fear, the survival instinct, those same masters, reasserted themselves. He wanted to live. He let himself be swept along, almost reluctantly at first, then began running doubled over, toward Anthony, whom he pulled roughly upright.

- "Move!" he commanded, going to haul up Sayer.

From the corner of his eye, he saw Pitt do the same with the two Burmans. Without mercy, he pushed them toward the opposite tree line. As he plunged into the verdure, Myers cast a glance behind. Barker still held out, a prodigious colossus holding two enemies by the throat, whose heads he smashed together, while six others hacked him to pieces. His mangled body fell, eyes meeting those of the sergeant one last time in a silent plea. He collapsed, swallowed by the road strewn with corpses. The last image Myers glimpsed between the trees, before continuing his flight, was that of Japanese soldiers launching themselves in pursuit.

Chapter IX

Thaton, Burma, February 1942

Two thousand souls had assembled on the football field of Thaton. No summons had been necessary: nothing could have diverted them from this rendezvous. A murmur ran through this multitude that would have cried out its hatred, yet was held back by the gravity of the moment and the dread that the Japanese army inspired. The anticipation paralyzed them as much as the guilty excitement that possessed them. Before them, because of them, a man was to die.

A section of Burmese soldiers carried the prisoner more than they escorted him. He could no longer walk. Eight days had elapsed since they had confined him without food, after having paraded him in an oxcart from Thebyugone in the company of a pig, under the mockery of those villagers of whom he had previously been in charge. The men of the Burma Independence Army bound him to a goalpost, formed two columns, and presented arms as their officer approached. General Aung San appeared at the entrance of this honor guard, walked its length with solemnity. Thus framed, he appeared smaller than usual.

Captain Kura Kimura despised him. Not for his stature, but because despite all the ceremony, he was no soldier in the eyes of the Kempeitai[38] officer. The training of the Thirty Comrades in Japan was nothing compared to the trial by fire on the Chinese front that he himself had endured. His father, an influential officer and member of the Black Dragon Society, could not tolerate weakness. He had participated in the Mukden Incident of 1931, which had led to the annexation of Manchuria, and had used his connections to ensure his son was placed on the front lines.

Kura had taken his leave of his pregnant wife, to whom he had entrusted a lock of his hair. Thus it was that young Lieutenant Kimura, a graduate of the Nakano Gakko, had participated, as early as 1937, in the first engagements of the Second Sino-Japanese War: at the Marco Polo Bridge and at Lake Khasan, where he was evacuated after a Soviet bullet had pierced his thigh.

His convalescence completed and after instruction at the Tung Wen College, the intelligence school created by the Black Dragon Society within the grounds of Shanghai University, he had joined General Shiro Ishii's Unit 731 at Harbin. There, he had been charged with supplying "patients" to the doctor. He had emptied prisons of their "anti-Japanese agitators" to find men, women, and children of all ages and conditions suitable to serve as material for the scientific experiments conducted in what was officially registered as a sawmill.

---

[38] Military police of the Japanese Imperial Army, also acting as secret police in the occupied territories.

He had been invited to attend several of them. They ranged from vivisection without anesthesia to inoculation with viruses - black plague, bubonic plague, typhus, syphilis, gonorrhea, cholera - to trials of chemical weapons, grenades, flamethrowers, to exposure to X-rays, grafting of animal limbs and organs, to studies of the human body's resistance to acceleration, to falls, to shock, to heat, to cold, to vacuum, to compression, to decompression, to fire, to freezing, to gangrene, to dehydration, to starvation, to hemorrhage, or further to removal of the liver, stomach, kidneys, one lung, the entire or partial intestine, to amputation of all four limbs, or one, or two, or three, and so forth. He had seen the human body, that well-oiled clock, that perfect machine, dislocate, dismember, empty, tear, open, spill, spread, break, liquefy, explode, implode, fracture, swell, rot, wither, turn green, turn black, vomit, piss, shit, stink, cry, scream, shriek; then disappear until nothing remained but a handful of ash carried away by a wind as indifferent as he himself had become.

A young surgeon had confided that his hands had trembled during his first vivisection, but he no longer thought about it by the second time. It was a rite of passage to become a hardened officer and honor his father, his country, and his emperor. Kimura remembered his own. The smell of gunpowder perfumed the aftermath of battle. A dozen prisoners of war, soldiers from Chiang Kai-shek's army, waited, kneeling, and blindfolded. Several corpses — training dummies pierced by the bayonets of the troops — dripped suspended from the charred beam of a house. The others had been reserved for the officers.

Kura unsheathed his saber, sprinkled its blade with water, and positioned himself above the first condemned man, his feet firmly planted on the ground. His heartbeat frantically as tumultuous thoughts flooded his mind: the kendo lessons from his father, stories of samurai ancestors, the humiliation of the Meiji era, his grandfather's revenge achieved through the success of his zaibatsu, his father's initiation into the Black Dragon Society, the promises made before the altar of ancestors.

A long breath. The flood of memories faded before a single determination: not to dishonor his family. His katana fell in a sharp motion against the prisoner's neck. A jet of blood stained his uniform as the grimacing head rolled across the ground. With trembling hand, he cleaned the blade with water and wiped it with the paper his superior handed him, attempting to scrape away the streak of fat clinging to the steel slightly bent by the impact. Another officer, blue like him, took over. His first blow slipped and struck the skull. Two more were needed to finish off the prisoner, who writhed on the ground, screaming.

General Aung San, too, would experience his rite of passage. Watching him approach the emaciated Indian, held upright by ropes that cut into his wrists, Kimura wondered whether he would emerge stronger or lose face like his colleague in China.

The Burmese General raised his voice and recited the sentence: Abdul Rashid, chief of the village of Thebyugone, was found guilty of abuse against the local population and collaboration with the enemy. Officially, this had no connection whatsoever to his Muslim faith. No one was deceived, least of all the helpless Indians witnessing the spectacle in the crowd. The British had maintained their dominance through racial division; the allied populations were now reaping what their masters had sown.

Under the Indian Empire, the minorities who had suffered from the Buddhicization and Burmanization policies of the kings of Mandalay had sided with the European power. The Karens participated in the campaign to suppress resistance following the fall of King Thibaw in 1885. A colonial army composed of Indians and minorities suppressed the revolts of Saya San in the 1930s. The Burmese Army was a force for maintaining order rather than defending against external aggression, the British having always distrusted the Burmans.

It was this distrust that had led the colonial authorities to grant partial autonomy to certain ethnic territories, to prohibit the recruitment of Burmans into the army, to entrust administration to Indian officials, and to guarantee enough seats to minorities so that Burmans would never obtain a majority in their own country. Frustrations and humiliations that had found expression in 1930 through the massacre of Indian dock workers.

The capture of Moulmein and the British retreat had a powerful inhibitory effect, causing history to repeat itself. While the troops of the Burma Independence Army. targeted Karens in their path, Burmese civilians gave free rein to their resentment against Muslims who had not yet fled. Interconfessional violence intensified without the Japanese liberators being able to halt its escalating dynamic. Order must restored, lest the conflict spiral into civil war.

Whether they killed each other, Kimura cared not. He scarcely concerned himself with the fate of these rustics, these degenerates that they all were to him. However, the Japanese army could not waste its energy policing this backwater, nor allow a situation ideal for the Karen fifth column to fester. A public execution was the best solution: a cathartic ritual of the scapegoat expiating the sins of an entire community. General Aung San had accepted reluctantly, knowing he risked alienating the minorities he sought to unite.

Despite the contempt Kimura felt for this young man of barely twenty-seven, he had to acknowledge in him an innate sense of politics. Though he employed Buddhist concepts in his speeches, he invariably advocated for a strictly secular state, which earned him sympathy among peripheral populations. Ethnic cleansing and an execution based on religious targeting could only harm him. Yet he had no choice: injustice rather than disorder.

After reciting the sentence, Aung San slowly drew his sword from its sheath. A deathly silence reigned. With a sharp gesture, he plunged its point into the prisoner's chest, who uttered an inaudible cry. The blade opened a gaping wound from which flowed a crimson stream. Aung San stared at the dying man, the weapon hanging at the end of his arm, as if the fluid wished to return to the earth to sustain the cycle of *Samsara*. The spectacle was over. All departed in silence, save Ma Ahma who rushed to her husband's corpse. In tears, she intoned the name of he who would never answer again. A few Indians came to join her: some attempted to comfort her, others discreetly carried away the body. Aung San departed without a word.

Kimura remained alone at the edge of the field. He had already lost interest in this brief episode to turn his attention to a rain tree burgeoning above the sideline. He could have composed a *haiku* had he been capable. But the only art he mastered was that of war, the *Bushidō*, which contemplative practices he did not disdain. He was already dead, he no longer existed. Like his samurai ancestors before him, it was by meditating each morning on his own emptiness that he drew the courage to face the enemy. If he was already dead, he had nothing to fear. Only family and fatherland mattered and deserved all sacrifices.

- "*Tai-i*[39] Kimura!"

The respite had been brief. He sighed upon recognizing the voice of Colonel Keiji Suzuki, intelligence officer at Imperial General Headquarters, who hailed him from the far end of the stadium, advancing with great strides, a half-smile lighting his round face with an air of joviality.

The *kempei* found it difficult to respect this officer whose weakness toward the Burmans made him a pariah. Yet he had to acknowledge that this small man was responsible for the success of the invasion. It was he who had welcomed the *thakins* Aung San and Hla Myaing to Japan, convinced of the value of supporting the

---

[39] « Captain » in Japanese.

Dobama Asiayone[40]. Only after the British reopened the Burma Road did Suzuki begin to be taken seriously in Tokyo. He was granted resources to train the Thirty Comrades and prepare for the invasion. All of this had led to the creation of the Burma Independence Army in December 1941 in Bangkok, and its participation in the Japanese offensive. The Colonel's strategy had paid off. The problem was not there.

Kimura's animosity toward Suzuki stemmed from the latter's apparent forgetfulness that Aung San and his rabble were merely a means to a single end: the creation of a co-prosperity sphere ensuring Japan secure access to vital resources. Despite the slogan "Asia for the Asians," under which the Black Dragon Society had created independence movements throughout Asia, it was obviously not a question of granting Burma its independence.

Yet Suzuki could not have been so naive, for he had revised Aung San's political program. He had introduced references to Japanese ideology: rejection of parliamentary regime, eugenics and racial unity under the control of a single party, integration of Burma into the Japanese sphere of influence. So many elements opposed Aung San's Marxist principles, which the Colonel had distilled to secure support from military authorities. Aung San had signed the document as if he were its author. Of the two, it was ultimately the young Burman who had best known how to manipulate the other to achieve his ends.

---

[40] "We Burmans Association".Burmese nationalist organization founded in 1930, which members adopted the title of "Thakin" (master) to defy British colonial authority and promote Burma's independence.

Colonel Suzuki had so championed his Burman comrades that he had gone so far as to adopt the occult beliefs upon which the Thirty Comrades founded their political ideology, attempting to present himself to the population as the providential liberator of the Burman people, the *Minlaung*, that messianic king so long awaited, who should restore socio-cosmic order and announce the advent of the next Buddha. This prophecy referred to a quatrain of the *Jagaru Natacron Taik*, a poem composed in the seventeenth century during the restoration of the Taungû Dynasty[41], which proclaimed:

And upon the lake a Tadorne Casarca alighted,

When with a bow a daring hunter slew it;

The parasol's mast struck down the daring hunter,

Yet the mast by lightning was stricken.

There was no doubt, for Burmese people, that the lake described in this prophecy symbolized the Kingdom of Ava, overthrown by the Mons in 1752. Alaungpaya had defeated them that same year and founded the last Konbaung[42] dynasty. The latter had been deposed in 1885 by the British, represented by the umbrella's shaft. The final verse indicated that the Indian Empire would in turn be defeated by thunder. This had prompted Colonel Suzuki to adopt the war name *Bo Mogyo*[43] and to spread the rumor

---

[41] Ruled over the Second Burmese Empire from 1510-1752.

[42] Founded in 1752 by Alaungpaya, it was the last dynasty of Burma until the fall of the Kingdom of Upper Burma in 1885, following the victory of the British army over the troops of King Thibaw.

[43] « Commandant Éclair » en birman.

that he was the son of Prince Myingun, returned to drive out the English and restore a Burmese kingdom. Marching at the head of the young Burmese army, he had been welcomed as a hero in every liberated village.

An effective tactic for manipulating popular beliefs, but a dangerous game that risked turning against him. Aung San, too, had understood the value of addressing the collective imagination to establish his legitimacy. He was a formidable political animal. Kimura had observed him harangue crowds with fervor, distilling in his speeches calls for the establishment of a *lokka-nibbana*[44] and the advent of a radiant *bama khit thit*[45] , comparing his Thirty Comrades to *yeyhiphe*, companies of brave men who accompanied conquering kings during the golden age of Burmese empires, claiming his lineage traced back to Bagan, explaining Marxism through Buddhist concepts, calling for the establishment of an enlightened government, and finally promising the appearance of the *padethabin*, the tree of life guaranteeing abundance and wealth.

Rumors spread that he was the reincarnation of Prince Setkya, saved by the immortal alchemist Bo Bo Aung and destined to become the messianic king. Aung San had named his party the *Htwet Yat Gaing*, "Society of the Path to Escape," a reference to the *zawgyi*, the alchemist who had escaped the cycle of reincarnations. It was also said that his powers, incorporated into

---

[44] « Heaven on Earth ».
[45] "A new Burmese era," in reference to the Buddhist cyclical view of alternating periods of prosperity and periods of chaos.

the talismans and tattoos worn by his soldiers, protected them from bullets, and that the Thirty Comrades had been rendered invulnerable by the *thwe-thauk*[46] ritual.

The risk was great that in the short term, the aura of liberator would shift from Colonel Suzuki to Aung San, making him the messianic sovereign awaited by the population. Kimura, like the Japanese military authorities, had no confidence in Aung San. This mutual distrust had justified the fragmentation of the Burma Independence Army into reduced units dispersed within Japanese forces.

Yet this had not prevented its ranks from swelling with all manner of colonial army deserters, young soldiers, prisoners, brigands, armed peasants, adolescents, students, Buddhist extremists, racists, socialists, Marxists, beggars, and children. This mass was hardly an army, but it could rapidly transform into a fifth column, into a popular movement difficult to control. The excesses, murders, rapes, looting, summary executions, and massacres committed during the chaos following the British withdrawal had delayed the Japanese army, forcing it to transform into a force for maintaining order.

Kimura wondered what would happen if General Aung San's distrust, whose popularity was growing, turned to animosity and he affixed the label of occupation army to his former Japanese allies. The imperial army was certainly achieving rapid victories, but the campaign was not yet won. Singapore had fallen, but

---

[46] A blood-sharing ritual that the men of the "companies of brave warriors" perform by drinking their blood mixed with alcohol.

pressure persisted since the United States had declared war in December. If the warm reception transformed into fierce resistance as in China, their victory would be compromised. It was therefore necessary to ensure that Japanese forces were perceived as liberators and holders of legitimate authority, even if it meant eliminating those among their allies who would eclipse them.

Colonel Suzuki finally presented him with a document, which Kimura seized after saluting his superior:

- "An order of mission from the Imperial General Headquarters."

The captain rapidly scanned the paper, refusing to believe what he was reading. If what he deciphered with perplexity proved accurate, he held in his hands the means to definitively ensure the unshakable support of the Burmans, nay, of all Asia's populations. Winning minds and hearts was the surest way to definitively drive western colonists from the continent by depriving them of all local support.

- "Where does this information come from?" Kimura inquired respectfully.

- "From one of my agents of the Minami Kikan," boasted Suzuki.

In 1940, Colonel Suzuki had gone to Rangoon under the false identity of Minami Masuyo, correspondent for the prestigious Japanese newspaper *Yomiuri Shimbun*, there to establish an intelligence network. A year later, he created the intelligence agency *Minami Kikan* there, with quarters on Judah

Ezekiel Street[47], where he had trained young Burman nationalists to plan clandestine activities. Since the beginning of the invasion, a fifth column had thus conducted guerrilla actions to destabilize the enemy. Agents, often dressed as monks, as well as others operating in all layers of local society.

- "This Sayer has recovered the country's oldest pagoda?"

- "Perhaps the first of Suvannabhumi,'" confirmed Suzuki. "The tablet he found there mentions that the *stūpa* could also contain relics of the Buddha. Imagine the support our army would receive in each city if we entered with them..."

- "Saviors with magical power, liberating the country from its impious invaders to restore Buddhist faith," murmured Kimura to himself.

- "A windfall for the *Shōwa*[48]. We must get this stone at all cost!"

- "Is the tablet important? Why not simply dig the relics from the *stūpa*?"

- "Because we don't know where it is. Our agent knows but hasn't transmitted the site's exact location."

- "And your source is currently with Sayer?"

---

[47] Present-day Thein Byu Street.
[48] Propaganda campaign based on the superiority of the Japanese race and justifying military expansionism under the pretext of liberating Asia from Western imperialism.

- "Yes. They left their excavations near Win Ka and are retreating toward Rangoon with British units."

- "They risk escaping us..."

- "The enemy is already evacuating Rangoon. Take some men under Bo Ne Win's command. They will translate the clues left along the way by our agent. Infiltrate enemy lines and intercept Sayer before he enters Rangoon. After that it will be too late."

Bo Ne Win was the war name of Thakin Shu Maung[49], one of the Thirty Comrades. A sobriquet meaning "Commander Radiant Sun," as ridiculous for Kimura as Suzuki's "Commander Lightning." He commanded the unit tasked with organizing resistance operations behind British lines.

- "You must absolutely retrieve the tablet and catch Sayer," Suzuki insisted.

- "And if we can't bring him back alive?"

- "This discovery must not fall into British hands! Do you understand, Captain?"

- "Aye, Colonel!" confirmed Kimura.

- "According to the latest reports, their group was spotted on the Kyaikto road heading toward Sittang. Good hunting, Captain," concluded the small man, his fine mustache surmounting a predatory smile.

---

[49] Ne Win seized power in a coup in 1962, then established an isolationist authoritarian socialist regime until 1988.

Chapter X

Moke Pa Lin, Burma, February 1942

Myers, Sayer and their companions had journeyed throughout the day through the jungle, fleeing with the obstinacy that proximity to death confers. Their flight orchestrated to the rhythm of detonations, sporadic at first, then tightening like the mesh of a net. Each explosion drove them toward another, leading them progressively toward some invisible trap. Afternoon brought them to Moke Pa Lin, where the clamors of war enveloped them from all sides. Only one exit remained: the narrow Sittang Bridge, a kilometer to the northeast, spanning the tumultuous river.

Anthony had supported Sayer during these final leagues, the scholar faltering at each step like a man whose strength was abandoning him. Forty-four years old only, yet of a constitution unprepared by either occasional days of archaeological excavation or Sunday excursions by boat on Victoria Lake[50] with the Rangoon Sailing Club. This scholar was discovering the bitter reality of exodus.

---

[50] Present-day Inya Lake in Yangon.

Anthony would have preferred to offer his arm to Nandar Aye, a pretext to feel that gracile body against him and converse with her in hushed tones. But the young Burman woman followed the soldiers' pace with an endurance that would have shamed many of those around her, testimony to a childhood marked by privation. A striking contrast with Win Thu who, hampered in his traditional *longyi*, displayed a grimace of exhaustion where veins and taut muscles protruded, a mask painfully removed from his habitual haughtiness.

In this hasty retreat, their small group had joined a composite detachment of the 2nd KOYLI, reinforced by elements of the 16th and 46th Indian Infantry Brigades, testimony to the confusion reigning among British troops scattered and cut off from their headquarters. Heterogeneous units reconstituted themselves under the authority of willing officers. A singular mixture of British Christians, Hindu Jats, Muslims and Punjabi Rajputs, Sikhs, Dogras, Pathans, Gurkhas, Chins, Karens, and Kachins. No trace of Burmans, prohibited from enlistment until 1935 and excluded from the system of "martial races" since the strike of 1920. Nandar Aye and Win Thu were thus the only Burmans in this rabble of wretches that had rushed upon Moke Pa Lin.

All had thrown themselves upon the muddy pond at the village's entrance, drinking avidly, splashing, bathing in these foul waters where the carcass of a decomposing mule lay festering, diffusing a pestilential odor. Pitt's enthusiastic calls to Sayer and Anthony to join him met with polite refusal, accompanied by a grimace of disgust they could not manage to conceal.

- "We've got orders to hold this hill in case the Japs come at us from the southeast," explained Myers in a firm voice, above the vibrations of the Japanese artillery that continued to pound the surroundings.

- "We'll be a burden if we stay. The wisest course would be for us to cross the bridge and be on our way without you," proposed Sayer, in the hope of being able to distance himself as quickly as possible from the front.

- "Can't do it, I'm afraid. The Japs 'got themselves dug in on that pagoda hill over by the river. They're tryin' to grab the bridgehead that the 3rd Burma Rifles have been holdin' all mornin'," he explained, gesturing toward the northeast from which the most intense explosions and bursts of fire came. "You lot have got to stay put here till we've sent 'em packin'."

These tidings rendered Sayer ashen, but he attempted to compose himself when he saw Anthony rush to support him.

- "We'll try to slip across to that bridge quiet-like when it gets dark," attempted Myers to console him, though his voice didn't sound like he believed a word of it himself. "Till then, find yourself a nice quiet spot and get some kip. You're gonna need your strength for what's comin'. And I'm tellin' you now: no smokin'!" he bellowed, fixating on Win Thu, whose metal lighter kept clicking away nervous-like between his fingers. "You want to draw a shell down on top of us?"

They withdrew toward a group of trees not far away, leaving the soldiers to dig holes and trenches with their bayonets and bare hands, for lack of spades. Each leaned against a trunk in the shadow of the scarlet boughs of these prides of Burma, then, exhausted, sank into an agitated sleep troubled by the dull detonations continuing to make the ground tremble.

Darkness reigned when Myers awakened Sayer with a firm pressure to the shoulder.

- "It's time," he murmured simply.

Anthony raised himself with difficulty, his joints stiffened by his slumber on the ground hard as rock. It seemed to him that he had not closed his eyes, so interrupted had his rest been by gunfire and by those obsessing visions of Japanese soldiers crawling through the darkness, blade between their teeth. More than once, he believed he was waking up screaming, but he was not even certain of it. He could not discern the state of his companions, but it seemed to him they displayed the same erosion of the senses. Only a fierce fear, engine of a survival instinct that crumbled yet remained vivid, still allowed them to place one foot before the other.

Myers and Pitt approached their group and explained the situation in low voices:

- "We're one mile away from that bridge. The Japs are gettin' ready to cut the railway line. Our boys are gonna hit 'em hard at first light to push 'em back. I don't want you lot caught up in all that carnage. So, here's what we're doin': we'll take the long way round, slip along the river headin' west, keep behind our own lines, and make for Bungalow Hill."

All acquiesced in silence, breathing more freely at the thought of distancing themselves from danger, even if it meant prolonging their flight.

- "Now listen, you've got to march in dead silence," resumed Myers, his voice turning sharp. "Enemy patrols have been nippin' at our sentries' heels all through the night. There's a good chance some of 'em have slipped in behind our lines without us noticin'."

The brief illusion of security vanished. They gathered their belongings and set out into the night that engulfed them. Myers walked at the head, Pitt brought up the rear. Only bursts of explosions and sporadic flares allowed them to discern obstacles. They advanced thus for what seemed like hours, their laborious gait punctuated by gunfire amid the dried rice paddies, nearly stumbling over every stone or root, catching themselves on the shadow ahead. Their progress was slowed by the frequent halts Myers imposed at each rustling of undergrowth.

Suddenly, Win Thu struck a branch and collapsed, letting out an exclamation of pain followed by a torrent of imprecations in Burmese.

- "Pipe down!" hissed Pitt between his teeth. "They'll hear you bellyachin' like that all the way to Tokyo!"

- "It wasn't on purpose!" retorted Win Thu sharply. "You can't see anything in this darkness, and I'm not equipped like you to scramble through fields!"

- "Maybe don't dress like some tart then!" mocked the soldier, gesturing at his *longyi*. "Looks like you've never done a hard day's graft in your life! You're a proper skiver who starts whingin' the moment there's real work to be done!", sneered the Englishman, spitting on the ground.

- "A beast like you knows nothing of the effort that intellectual work demands," commented the academic with a condescension that cut through the darkness. "You are incapable of thinking, good only for serving as cannon fodder for an empire that exploits you. At least we Burmans have understood and fight for our independence."

- "Idiot! You reckon the Japs 'gonna just hand it to you on a plate? Ha!", mocked Pitt. "We're the ones fightin' off these fascist bastards for you, and this is how you thank us? Before we came here, this place was a complete dump, it was. Now you've got the railway runnin', and suddenly you want us to scarper off? Traitor!"

- "Traitor?" sneered the Burman with sarcastic tone. "I did not choose to be a subject of the Crown. My allegiance is to the Burmese people. Not to an invader who enslaves us and plunders our wealth!"

- "Keep your gob runnin' like that and you'll get yourself strung up proper!" sniggered Pitt.

- "Not if the Japanese kill you first!" retorted Win Thu with provocation.

Myers interposed himself when Pitt was about to hurl himself at him with an animal growl, pushing back with difficulty the soldier who had already seized the Burman's shirt.

- "That's enough, Pitt!" barked the sergeant.

- "You hearin' what that snake in the grass just said, Sergeant? He'll sell us out to the Japs soon as look at us, knife us in our beds while we're sleepin'. Mark my words!" protested Pitt.

- "I said enough! Get yourself to the head of the column!" he ordered in a voice that brooked no argument. "And you," he continued, turning to Win Thu, "I'm tellin' you straight: keep your mouth shut! In the dark, your Jap' 'friends' might just mistake you for one of us. And don't come cryin' to me when they do..."

A red flare illuminated his face just long enough to reveal the clenched jaw and furrowed brows in the mask of hatred he directed at Win Thu. The near bursts of fire that concluded his words confirmed that he was not speaking lightly.

- "I beg your pardon," offered Sayer, joining Myers at the rear of the column. "He's not a bad sort. A brilliant boy, but he lets himself get carried away. Independence is a subject close to his heart."

- "Clever in the books, maybe, but not bright enough to know there's a time and a place for mouthin' off, is he?", objected the soldier with a bitter edge to his voice. "I don't give a toss about his fancy ideas, Professor, not when they're gonna get me and the lads topped!" growled Myers. "We'll be there soon enough. You make sure that lad keeps his gob shut from here to there. After that, you can have all your tea-and-biscuits jaw-wagging back in Rangoon if you're still breathin'."

Sayer took the blow in silence and resumed his prostrate wandering.

The sky turned slightly gray as they emerged onto an abandoned hamlet at the forest's edge. The dawning light cast a few reflections on the seething river, revealing the structure that spanned it two hundred meters away. The bridge, at last! A marvel of colonial engineering, its metal spans leapt boldly across the five hundred meters separating the two banks. Despite the abandoned vehicles forming a string of twisted metal on its deck, it appeared passable.

Their relief was short-lived. Below, the first glimmers revealed a grave situation. The bridgehead was but a lunar landscape, its craters continuously redrawn by explosions. The bursts of shelling animated the summit of Pagoda Hill, which white pagodas stood out against the morning sky, indifferent witnesses to this tragedy.

At the heart of the battle were the men of the 3rd Battalion Burma Rifles, holding their position since the previous day with two hundred men. A hundred Kachins, fifty Chins, twenty Karens, reinforced by a few British and Indians. Reservists who had held despite successive waves of enemies. Japanese troops were now only a few dozen meters away, threatening to take the bridge at any moment.

Behind them, the situation was scarcely more favorable. The enemy had cut the railway line. They were surrounded. And the planned assault to break free from Moke Pa Lin would only bring the clash to them. They could not remain motionless.

- "Take shelter," ordered Myers, indicating a brick building at the wood's edge. "I'm gonna scout ahead and have a look at what's goin' on down by that bridge. Get some rest while you can. You're gonna need it 'cause we'll likely have to leg it when I get back."

A nod of understanding to Pitt and Myers had vanished into the vegetation. They sat with their backs against the barracks, facing the river, in expectation. Nandar Aye asked Anthony for her book.

- "It soothes me," she explained, opening the volume.

Anthony contemplated her with a mixture of amusement and admiration for this miraculous resilience. She had displayed an iron calm from the beginning of their ordeals, as if their torment remained foreign to her. The last few days had nonetheless marked her: disheveled hair, face covered in dust, shadowed eyes, chapped lips, soiled longyi. Everything clashed with the coquettish student Anthony had known. And yet, she retained that same innate grace, to which was now added a quiet determination previously unnoticed. Silent courage, discreet, the antithesis of the soldiers' noisy bravado, but no less remarkable. Captivated, he observed her clear eyes focused on the pages, as if this world at war no longer existed, those lips that moved silently, and he knew. He knew he would never love another as he loved her.

- "I must isolate myself for a few minutes," she excused herself with modesty, rising and returning the volume to Anthony.

She plunged straight through the trees to escape their gaze. Anthony waited a few minutes, then rose in turn, feigning departure at a perpendicular angle. He turned his head as he made a detour and thought he saw Win Thu observing him. He cared not. The call was too imperious. He entered the grove of rubber trees, pivoted, then approached silently a small building overrun by vegetation, dwarfed by the height of the surrounding trees. Through the trunks, he glimpsed the house on the other side of which the rest of the group remained. They were not far. He had to be discreet. He circled the cabin and finally caught sight of Nandar Aye, standing in front of a wall. His sudden appearance made her start.

- "What are you doing here?" she asked with urgency.

He approached her without a word, encircled her waist, drew her against him, and kissed her with fervor.

- "You're mad!" she protested in muffled voice, pushing him away with a gesture lacking conviction. "They're right there!"

She cast an anxious glance toward where their companions lay and drew him by the hand to the other side of the wall's corner.

- "I don't care!" he answered, wounded as much as excited by her objections. "I can't wait any longer. I miss you!"

He took her in his arms again and tried to slip his hand beneath her *longyi*, but she struggled to free herself.

- "This is not the time!" she cut him off, carefully adjusting the fabric about her waist with a mechanical gesture. "What if he finds us..."

- "Let him find us!", roared Anthony, raising his voice. "I'm tired of playacting, of hiding, of sharing you!"

- "And how shall we live when you've lost your position and reputation? Where will we go when he throws us in the street, my mother and me? To your parents?", she threw at him, her lips curled in a hard, sarcastic smile.

He scowled, the fire that desire and youthful romanticism kindled in him suddenly extinguished by these basely material considerations. She softened at the sight of the sorrow her reproaches had awakened in him.

- "I love you too and I want to be with you," she resumed in a sweet voice, caressing his hair with tenderness. "Didn't your father say he would find you a position at Burmah Oil?"

- "It's not for me. I'd rather pursue an academic career." He hesitated at her surprise. "I heard that Professor Luce is looking for an assistant."

- "You will need a letter of recommendation from Arthur." She temporized but was visibly relieved that an alternative presented itself distant from Sayer. "Then, be patient. When you have a stable position, we can be together."

A nearby detonation suddenly brought Anthony back to reality, reminding him that the world around him, his world, was ablaze.

- "None of this matters anymore, does it?" he asked with intense distress.

- "We don't know." She attempted to comfort him, but her own gaze betrayed her fears. "Let's return to Rangoon and see how the situation evolves," she encouraged him with an affectionate smile.

She encircled his neck with her hands, then rose on tiptoe to kiss him. She pressed her breast against his chest, felt Anthony's desire swell against her belly, whilst his large hands descended along her thighs to raise the fabric of her *longyi*. Their breathing accelerated, panting in synchrony. She pressed her back against the wall whilst he grasped her buttocks, their mouths still united.

Suddenly, a crack attracted their attention. They turned their heads and discovered Win Thu, his hand resting against the wall's corner, a predatory smile illuminating his face. His eyes, narrowed with malignity, fixed Nandar Aye from behind his spectacles with assumed concupiscence whilst she hastily dressed to cover her bare legs. With his other hand, he played with his lighter, opening and closing it with a repetitive gesture, taking a morbid pleasure in the regular clicks filling the air like a threat.

- "Quite a spectacle," he finally uttered with cruel satisfaction. "I wonder what the Professor will think of it," he added with a click of his tongue. He was taking an evident pleasure in the situation.

- "I too can tell him of the time when you tried to rape me," she retorted without wavering, her features tense, her gaze hard.

- "Tell him what you like," Win Thu challenged her. "You really think he'll believe a tramp like you after discovering your infidelity?"

Anthony took a step forward, ready to hurl himself at him, but she held him back.

- " As for you, brat, you can say goodbye to your career at the university. I don't think of anyone who'd want to hire a backstabber like you as an assistant," he promised, his smile entirely erased.

- "What do you want?" interrupted Nandar Aye, her chin raised, understanding he had not rushed to denounce them to Sayer because he wanted something.

They both were at his mercy, she knew it. There was no escape. The question was what their transgression would cost them. Everything? Or less?

- "You already give yourself to two men..." he began. She knew where he was going. "What I want? That you offer yourself to me too when I desire it."

She knew his kind. He was not the first whom her beauty had attracted. These men who desired only what they could not have, what their money could not buy. He wanted to possess her like a hunting trophy, to dominate her, to break her. Such an ego fled self-elevation through effort. He knew his limits, his weaknesses, his sloth. Such an ego could rise only by humiliating those surrounding him. He would take her and then, once tired, once assured she had become his plaything, the slave fulfilling his every desire, he would enjoy destroying her by denouncing her to Sayer. Because she had rejected him. She saw it in his eyes.

- "Easy for a street girl like you, who fucks the first comer..."

Pure provocation, but he could not help himself. She was about to respond when Anthony lunged without her being able to stop him, rushing at him to throw him to the ground. Win Thu just managed to shield his face when the blows began to rain down.

- "I'll kill you, you bastard!" screamed the young Englishman.

Nandar Aye was desperately trying to separate them when Pitt and Sayer came running.

- "What in God's name is all this then?", gasped the soldier between his teeth, face dark as thunder. "You'll have every bloomin' Jap for miles around down on our heads," he growled, hauling each of the two adversaries up by the arm.

He was about to continue when something caught his attention. He approached the wall on which Win Thu had leaned. The greyness of the morning light revealed a series of Burmese numerals, written on the lime-washed wall, some still dripping, fresh. He touched the black ink which left a wet trace on his finger. A mixture of soot and water. With a sharp gesture, he cleared away the plants obstructing the wall's base, searching abruptly beneath the questioning gaze of his companions. He plunged his hand into a tuft of grass and rose, holding a vessel filled with dark liquid, beneath the astonished gaze of the three people who watched him in silence.

- "Son of a bitch! Who in blazes wrote this?" he interrogated, his face flushed, his voice trembling with a rage he contained with difficulty.

- "I don't understand," mouthed Sayer, not seeing what had put the soldier in such a state.

- "It was him!" shouted Nandar Aye before Pitt could answer, pointing to Win Thu. "Look at his hand!"

All turned toward the Burman as he, surprised, checked his hand with a bewildered expression, discovering blackened fingertips. In a flash, Pitt put him in his sights, his rifle on his hip.

- "You dirty rotten bastard! I knew you were a bloody traitor through and through!" growled the soldier, his jaws clenched, his index trembling on the trigger.

- "What's possessing you?" objected Sayer with professorial authority. "This is outrageous! Explain yourself, private!"

- " Oh, I'll tell you straight up, yeah. Your clever friend there, he's a fifth columnist, that's what. He scratched some kind of code on the wall. That's why them Japs have been snappin' at our heels since Kyaikto!"

- "Hold now, this is ridiculous! Dr. Win Thu is not a spy! I vouch for him!" protested Sayer vehemently as he felt the situation slipping from his grasp.

- "He also tried to rape me," Nandar Aye suddenly announced. "Fortunately, Anthony intervened."

Anthony was caught off guard by this lie and stared at her with dread. The young woman's features were impassive, hard, cold, displaying a composure that betrayed no doubt. He knew not whether to admire or fear her. He himself dared not speak for fear of betraying himself and turned toward Win Thu, whose face was livid. Anthony could imagine the thoughts racing behind his eyes, bulging with fear. At the sight of the transformation in Sayer's gaze, Win Thu understood she had reversed the situation in a second. It was he, now, who was at her mercy, a cornered animal desperately seeking an escape.

- "You filthy dog!" barked Pitt, blood rushing to his head. "Scum like you makes me want to chuck! I oughta put a bullet in your belly right now!" He pressed the gun's muzzle against Win Thu's sternum.

- "She's lying!" vociferated the Burman, mad with anguish. "You whore!" he screamed in the direction of the young woman, foam flecking his lips.

He grasped the end of the weapon to free himself, his bloodshot eyes fixed on her, his face swollen with uncontrollable rage, driven by the single idea that obsessed his mind: to avenge himself upon her. Pitt resisted, ordered him to step back, tried to push him away, but the other would not hear. The shot rang out.

Everyone froze. Win Thu, dazed, collapsed backward, his back against the wall, looking astonished. He lowered his eyes toward his chest from which flowed a stream of crimson that soaked his shirt. His face contorted. His cry tore through the air, followed by a coughing fit. His mouth opened like that of a fish out of water, his chest heaving erratically. He tried to speak but could only emit moans covered by bubbles of blood. He began to panic, his arms flailing frantically in the air, as if to grasp their hands in a final appeal. No one moved. They were paralyzed, unable to make a gesture. His lips rapidly turned pale, then bluish. Cyanosis spread. His nostrils flared faster as the wheezing increased. His arms fell, his mouth released a gurgle of blood, his eyes continued to fix on them while his lips formed inaudible words. His body became inert, save for the imperceptible twitching of his chest. Then, even that ceased. A veil passed over his wide-open eyes that dropped toward the ground when his head slumped. Motionless. The blood had stopped flowing and his lighter lay near his open hand.

- "What in God's name is all this bloody racket?" thundered Myers, who came running. He pushed them aside to discover at what they all stared at in silence. "Pitt?" interrogated the sergeant, his features distorted by incomprehension.

- ""Not what it looks like, Sergeant!" protested the soldier vehemently. "He went for my rifle and it went off by accident. I caught the bastard red-handed, I did. A proper informer! He was leavin' signals for the Japs!" he defended himself, pointing to the numerals on the wall.

- "He is telling the truth, Sergeant," confirmed Sayer. "The man also tried to have his way with Nandar Aye. Anthony's brave intervention resulted in an altercation. Your man tried to separate them, but Win Thu resisted..."

Myers looked at them in silence in turn, attempting to form his own opinion of the situation. Anthony turned toward Nandar Aye, disposed to comfort her. Vile though Win Thu had been, their lie had cost him his life. He felt guilty. He imagined she would likewise be assailed by internal demons. She fixed the corpse in silence, her hands clenched into two fists. Was she in shock? She turned her head to meet his gaze. He read no remorse there, only a determination and hatred that dissipated when she recovered her senses and recognized him.

- "You'll have some explainin' to do at a court martial," Myers finally said. "When we get the time for it, that is. Right now, there's nowt we can do for him. We've got to shift! The Japs could be over the bridge any minute now!"

He had scarcely finished his sentence when a gigantic detonation made the hill tremble. Followed by another, equally powerful. Gunfire and mortars fire ceased at once, giving way to a leaden silence that enveloped them like an icy blanket. They exchanged glances and understood immediately: the bridge had just blown. They only started to grasp the peril in which they found themselves when the clamors of war resumed in full force.

Chapter 11

Cambridge, United Kingdom, August 2024

The overhead screen played the latest Olympic events. Ayaan cast an indifferent glance at it. This sporting revelry appeared to him as a farce for unconscious masses. No one in the café paid it any attention. The summer tourist clientele remained glued to their phones awaiting a break in the rain to resume their wanderings through the venerable city. Above the counter, Edison bulbs swayed to the rhythm of artificial Latin music, casting their yellowish light on the woodwork. Against the bay windows, the British drizzle traced its slow arabesques, distorting the hurried silhouettes like so many ghosts.

He seized his oversized cup - a hazelnut-caramel macchiato - while his attention returned to the screen. Paris was celebrating. Hysterical crowds danced beneath multinational logos; that modern "communion" where each deluded themselves about their own humanistic values. Bread and circuses. This compartmentalization of consciousness allowed everyone to avoid the cognitive dissonance that would reveal the imposture.

The contrast with Khin Yadanar's existence, that reality to which no channel would dare expose its public, that struck by its obscenity. They lived on the same planet, but not in the same world. Ayaan had confronted this truth during the internship he was beginning at his father's firm, where he had encountered Burmese asylum seekers. Students, doctors, journalists, all survivors of the civil disobedience movement, all prisoners of British administrative limbo. They waited. Their faces bore that anxiety of the condemned on reprieve: hypothetical acceptance on the British side, passport renewal for a bribe at the embassy, or forced return home where police awaited them. They all lived with fear in their bellies, contemplating that sword of Damocles suspended above their heads.

This discovery had provided him the perfect opportunity: to make the Burmese cause his personal banner within the Cambridge Pro Bono Project. A perfect exotic touch for his curriculum vitae, in addition to the family obligations that had brought him back here for the weekend. Professor Preston was slowly fading in his Cambridge residence, and Ayaan endured this constraint with an heir's impatience. Not that he lacked affection, but the old man's agony impeded his research.

The digital hand marked the wait. His appointment was late. The door slammed. Four massive brutes entered, whose Wrangler jeans, Dr. Martens boots and checkered shirts clashed with the cashmere and flannel that ordinarily clothed the city. A redhead, nose flattened like a beast's, sized up Ayaan with his predatory gaze. A nod of the chin, a pinch of the nose, followed by a knowing smirk at his neighbor. The chairs scraped the floor with the grace of a cleaver as they slumped at a table nearby. Slouched on their elbows, they all stared at him while exchanging mocking whispers.

- "Thank you, come again," the red-haired man drawled, mimicking the accent of Apu, the stereotypical Indian from the Simpsons. Pack laughter. Ape-like onomatopoeia.

Ayaan stared at his cup, fingers clenched around the scalding ceramic. The mocking remarks in a Mancunian accent, echoes of his childhood, resonated in his mind. How many generations would it take? Born here, English in soul and accent, he remained hostage to an inherited complexion, a curse his brother Ethan, with his lighter skin, had miraculously avoided. His national belonging was denied to him by a handful of strangers. Identity, a social phenomenon, was not chosen; it was granted to you. Only the label others imposed upon you mattered.

Other patrons, phones on alert, ready to film the altercation, held their breath. The replies he had wished to offer on other occasions, the fantasized beatings he had given to fascists, thrummed in his heart, drowning his brain in adrenaline. Ayaan measured its absurdity. He breathed deeply, rose, puffing out his chest, revealing his tall stature, moved slowly toward the table where silence had become tense, skirted it without a glance, then approached the counter. The adolescent with pink hair gave him a sad smile. He placed his order, paid, then returned to his seat, impassive.

Two minutes later, the barista approached the intruders with awkward little steps, as impatient to complete her task as reluctant to begin it. She set down the four steaming cups one by one beneath their stupefied gazes.

- "From the gentleman," she murmured.

- "Oi, what the fuck is that, yeah?" growled the stocky one of the group.

- "*Chai.*" The answer offered timidly before she retreated without another word.

- "We didn't order that, for fuck's sake!"

Ayaan held the redhead's gaze, his manner defiant. Silent challenge. The café became an arena. Time suspended, that of ancient tragedies where the hero takes his measure. Alone, he had no chance, yet his ego thrummed with the desire to assert his superiority over those he deemed mediocre. The air became unbreathable. Finally, the redhead produced a carnivorous grimace and cast him a cold stare, a promise of revenge.

- "Let's do one, la! There's no ale in this woke fag's gaff anyway, innit!"

He spat at Ayaan's feet, kicked the door open, and disappeared into the street with his companions. Ayaan exhaled. Around him, the clients averted their eyes, ashamed of their passive complicity. Time flowed once more, marked by the commentary of badminton on television.

The door creaked. A man with graying temples, parted hair, slender frame lost in an oversized brown tweed jacket, struggled with a dripping umbrella. His appointment. He invited him to sit across from him. The scholar let himself fall into the chair, leather briefcase placed on the table before him.

- "Christopher Forsythe. Pleased to meet you."

- "Ayaan Carter. Very kind of you to make the journey all the way from London, Professor. What can I get you to drink?"

- "Black coffee, please. How is your great-grandfather?" the academic inquired with solicitude as Ayaan placed the order.

- "His condition is deteriorating. He can barely speak now. That's why I contacted you."

- "I'm terribly sorry to hear it." He thanked the waitress as she set down his cup. "I never attended his lectures, actually. He was already Professor Emeritus by the time I enrolled. But I did sit in on his seminars on ancient India. Read his books, of course. Brilliant scholar! Though I must say, I had absolutely no idea he'd studied Mon culture as well..."

- "No one knew he'd lived in Burma before the war," Ayaan cut in, irritated by the praise for his ancestor. "Without the discovery of his journal, he would have taken his secret to the grave."

- "Thank heavens that's not the case, because this is rather a significant discovery," Forsythe exclaimed, his eyes blazing with excitement. "You were quite right to contact Latika Williamson. There are only a few of us specialists in Mon studies. And naturally, we all liaise with the Centre for South East Asian Studies."

- "The documents I sent you, do they make sense to you?" Ayaan asked with hope, to whom the reference to Mon history meant nothing.

Khin Yadanar had kept her word. She had sent photos of all the pages of the notebook. After which she had broken off all communication. Ayaan had transmitted them to Forsythe along with those of the tablet, refraining from sharing the sections mentioning Arthur Sayer. His grandfather would be the sole author of the discovery.

- "I'm still working through it," the academic admitted ruefully. "Part of the stone's inscription is illegible. Perhaps with a 3D laser scan and AI software..."

- "That's not possible at the moment," Ayaan interjected. Khin Yadanar had given him a flat refusal. She would never send him the tablet.

- "A pity." The researcher was plainly disappointed but dared not push further. "Fortunately, the journal contains a perfect transcription of the wall's script. Remarkable work! And an unpublished text! I visited Win Ka and Thaton before the coup. I studied the catalogued monuments. Some bear bas-reliefs similar to the notebook's sketches. But none shows any inscription. Which means the site fell into obscurity after the war," Forsythe concluded, his eyes glimmering.

- "You don't know where it is, then?" Ayaan sighed, deflated.

- "No. The notebook's drawings lack sufficient precision. Hardly surprising, really. Win Ka has over forty sites, and only four have been excavated. But the good news is I've deciphered what the inscription says," Forsythe whispered with conspiratorial glee, leaning across the table.

- "You've translated it?" Ayaan exclaimed eagerly. At last, something worthwhile. Even if Khin Yadanar had cut ties with him, he could still move forward.

- "It took a while. That's why I didn't get back to you sooner..." He paused, hesitated, then raised his cup and asked: "Are you familiar with the ancient languages of India?"

- "Not in the slightest." Ayaan had never taken much interest in his great-grandfather's work.

- "No matter. I'll keep it brief." The professor repositioned himself and cracked his neck in preparation for the intellectual effort. "At the time of the Buddha, India operated on oral tradition, with Prakrits as vernacular languages and Vedic for sacred texts. For two centuries, the Buddha's teachings were transmitted orally in Prakrits. Even after they were canonized in Pali, which became the liturgical language of *Theravada*[51]. The first scripts emerged only in the third century BC. Like the classical *Brahmi*, for instance, from which southern *Brahmi* would derive a century later. Are you following me?"

- "So far," Ayaan lied to maintain composure.

---

[51] 'Small Vehicle' Buddhism widespread mainly in Southeast Asia.

- "Five hundred years later, in the third century CE, Pallava Grantha script appeared in southern India. Itself a derivation of southern *Brahmi*. This script eventually reached the Mon people in Lower Burma."

- "The Mon. You mentioned them already..."

- "That civilisation is amongst the oldest in Southeast Asia. Influenced by Indian culture, like the Khmer and Pyu peoples. They used Pallava Grantha to transcribe teachings in Pali and Sanskrit. This is how *Theravada* Buddhism was introduced to the region. They also used it for their own language, Old Mon. The oldest surviving texts on votive tablets date to the sixth century CE. Our only archaeological evidence for dating the Mon presence in Burma. Some scholars, like Dr. Than Tun[52], have argued they were established there centuries earlier. But that was unprovable. Until now," he concluded enigmatically.

- "You mean to say..."

- "Your great-grandfather's discovery provides that proof. And considerably more besides. The script in the notebook is Pallava Grantha. But the tablet's inscription is in southern *Brahmi*. Making it the oldest artifact ever found in Burma. What did Professor Preston tell you?" the researcher pressed urgently.

---

[52] Dr. Than Tun (1923-2005). Burmese historian, specialist in the pre-modern history of Burma, known for his extensive research on Buddhism.

- "That the tablet and his journal point to a *stūpa* containing the first relics of the Buddha in Burma. In the capital of Suvannabhumi..."

- "Revolutionary!" Forsythe burst out. "The entire Buddhist world will be shaken!" His fevered eyes, ablaze, fixed on Ayaan like burning coals.

- "I don't see why." His interlocutor was losing his mind. Who cared about an old pagoda except for a handful of dusty scholars?

- "Consider this: imagine proof that the Romans crossed the Atlantic fifteen centuries before Columbus. That they discovered El Dorado and left behind a relic of Christ. And that it became one of the earliest Christian kingdoms in history, before vanishing under the Conquista. Do you grasp it? It's earth-shattering!"

- "For researchers as yourself," Ayaan said coolly. "But for anyone else?" His tone oozed indolence laced with insolence.

- "Tell that to U Wirathu[53] and Buddhist nationalists! Responsible for the ethnic cleansing of a million Rohingya Muslims!" The reply cracked like a whip. "Don't be deceived by the postmodern bubble you inhabit. Religions still govern the daily lives of billions on this planet. Billions prepared to die or kill for their beliefs. Those relics would be a gift for a junta believing in

---

[53] Ultranationalist Burmese Buddhist monk known for his anti-Muslim rhetoric, who leads the radical 969 movement in Myanmar and was imprisoned before being released by the military junta.

yadaya[54]. It would grant them sacred legitimacy against armed groups, many of which are Christian. Especially if it proves Suvannabhumi existed in the Buddha's time. The military would forge a sacred genealogy, a direct line to him. Enough to galvanise the masses."

- "Suvannabhumi?" Ayaan interjected, keen to change the subject. "My great-grandfather mentioned it..."

- "The 'Golden Land' in Pali. The name Indian traders gave to the region encompassing Lower Burma and parts of Thailand. Also called Ramannadesa, the 'Land of Ramans', Raman being the ancient word for the Mon people. Legend claims this kingdom existed already in the Buddha's time. No evidence supports it, as I explained. According to it, it was ruled by a dynasty of fifty-nine kings, with Thaton as capital. It was conquered in 1057 by Anawrahta, the first Burman king of Bagan. He plundered the *Tipitaka*[55] and carried off every monk and craftsman Thaton possessed, shifting the political and religious centre of gravity to Bagan. That's where history takes over from legend."

- "Suppose the legend were true," Ayaan ventured. "How did the relics reach Suvannabhumi?"

---

[54] Superstitious rituals and occult beliefs associated with *Theravada* Buddhism of Myanmar, although contrary to its dogma, mixing astrology, numerology and symbolic acts.
[55] The collection of sacred texts of Buddhism, particularly of the Theravada school, containing respectively monastic rules, the Buddha's discourses and philosophical treatises, written in the Pali language.

- "Three myths exist. The first is that of Taphussa and Bhallika..."

- "Khin Yadanar told me about that!" Ayaan suddenly interjected. The bitter memory of her mockery revived his interest.

- "A well-known tale indeed. Taphussa and Bhallika, two merchant brothers from Ukkala near the Irrawaddy, journey to India. There they encounter the Buddha in deep meditation and offer him rice cakes dipped in honey. As reward, he grants them his teachings and presents them with eight strands of his hair. They become the Buddha's first lay disciples. Upon returning home, they commission the construction of the Shwedagon, Botataung, and Sule pagodas in Yangon, and the Shwemamdaw in Bago, to enshrine the relics."

- "The legend mentions Yangon and Bago but neither Thaton nor Suvannabhumi."

- "If a kingdom existed in Lower Burma during the Buddha's era, it was necessarily near Thaton, where the earliest traces have been found. The legend's place of origin likely shifted over time for political reasons. Each new kingdom wants sacred legitimacy. Hence the different versions of the same story."

- "You said there are three legends?"

- "The second is that of Gavampati, a disciple of the Buddha. Amongst the first to be ordained and to achieve arhatship[56]. According to the *Sasanavamsa*[57], he travelled to the Mon kingdom of Thaton after the Buddha's death to convert King Siharaja and present him with relics. Finally, the third," Forsythe anticipated, "involves Sona and Uttara, two missionary monks sent by Emperor Ashoka after the Third Buddhist Council in the second century before Christ, to convert the kingdom of Suvannabhumi and bring it relics of the Buddha's hair."

- "So, three different myths, but all describe Buddhism's expansion and the transmission of relics from India to a Mon kingdom shortly after Buddha's death," Ayaan summarized.

- "Or three centuries after his death," the academic corrected. "Still a thousand years earlier than current estimates. A theory reinforced by the fact that the tablet is in southern *Brahmi*, the script that emerged around the third century before Christ and was used for Ashoka's edicts. This places the existence of a Mon kingdom converted to Buddhism at that time, corresponding to the legend of Sona and Uttara. The *stūpa* discovered by your great-grandfather at Win Ka would thus be Southeast Asia's oldest."

- "Yet the legends don't mention Win Ka. They all make Thaton the capital of Suvannabhumi."

---

[56] An arhat is, in Buddhism, a person who has freed himself from the cycle of rebirth (samsara) and achieved nirvana during his lifetime.
[57] Ecclesiastical chronicle written in 1861 by the Burmese monk Pannasami, which relates the history of Buddhism from the birth of the Buddha to its expansion in nine different countries, with emphasis on its development in Ceylon and Burma.

- "It's rather common for new dynasties to relocate their capitals and appropriate the old founding myths to legitimise their power. Likely what happened when Win Ka was abandoned for Thaton. Win Ka would be a logical location for an ancient city. Between the mouths of the Sittang and Bilin rivers. Coastal then, before silt pushed the Gulf of Martaban back several kilometers. The ideal position for a trading port with India."

- "I see," Ayaan mused. "We still need to locate the *stūpa* precisely at Win Ka."

He would need to carefully study the pages of the diary he hadn't shared with Professor Forsythe. They might contain topographical clues. He understood the academic world. He wanted priority on this discovery before sharing the spotlight.

- "And to decipher the tablet," the researcher insisted. "If you can't convince your contact to send it, perhaps she might photograph it from different angles under various lighting. With our software, we could identify every character of the inscription." With that, the academic rose. He had a train to catch back to London.

- "I'll keep you informed," Ayaan promised, shaking the professor's hand. "Thank you for coming. Your explanations have clarified matters considerably."

- "Nearly forgot," Forsythe paused. "As I explained, the notebook's script was Pallava Grantha, later than the stone tablet. Likely from the third CE. In my view, it's the oldest version of the Sona and Uttara legend," he continued, drawing a sheaf of papers from his briefcase and handing them to Ayaan. "I've taken some liberties, as you'll see. Do enjoy the read!" he finished with a wink before heading towards the exit.

Intrigued, Ayaan seized the first page of the stack and began reading.

Chapter 12

Chin State, Myanmar, September 2024

Khin Yadanar straightened against the back of the uncomfortable chair on which she had been slumped for an hour, her gaze lost in the void left by Kee Mawng's missing leg, who slept in the adjacent bed. She drew her knees against her chest and buried her face in them hoping to doze off, lulled by the clinic's noise and the crows croaking. Barely had she closed her eyes when a rustle of fabric pulled her from her torpor. The nurse stood at the foot of the bed. It was time to change the dressing.

The nurse donned latex gloves and began gently removing the bandage, revealing the scarred wound resembling pleated leather. Khin Yadanar had personally managed the treatment over the previous month to prevent infection. The scar was clean, despite a pinkish hue and swelling due to the lack of anti-inflammatories and analgesics. Kee Mawng had suffered martyrdom, the phantom limb pains arriving within a week. Despite his efforts to suppress his moans, he could not refrain from screaming during sudden attacks, comparable to knife thrusts that submerged his consciousness, as if the world had vanished behind a burning veil. Surely that was hell, the impossibility of believing in the existence of any other reality than that of suffering.

Khin Yadanar had been forced to witness his ordeal, unable to ease it, merely able to wipe away his cold sweat. She had even contributed to his torment each time she had to disinfect the wound, compelled to minister to him despite his imploring, sometimes hateful gaze. His body twisted in pain before her and she wept silently, chanting "I am sorry, I am sorry" in long litanies addressed to herself more than to her companion. She had wept each evening, alone, without arms to hold her, without shoulders to rest upon, without a confident. For the first time in her life, she truly knew solitude.

Day by day, the suffering had diminished. A month later, the stump began to taper into a conical shape, with a few bony protuberances. Khin Yadanar acknowledged that her colleagues had done an excellent work given the circumstances. She could not have done better; orthopedic surgery had never been her forte.

The nurse inspected the wound carefully. There was neither pus nor abnormal odor. For lack of sterile saline, she cleaned it with mild soap, causing new complaints from the wounded. It had been an eternity since Khin Yadanar had last seen her companion's smile. The grimacing pout he displayed, while the expert hand carefully tamped his wound, was like a mirror for the suffering that had been draining the young woman's heart since the incident. Fresh compresses were applied with practiced skill, then the nurse moved to the adjacent bed.

Without a word, Khin Yadanar rose as Kee Mawng pulled on his combat trousers, seized the crutches resting against the wall, and handed them to him.

- "Come on, you need to walk," she announced in a neutral voice, offering him her hand to help him up.

The convalescent gave her a forced smile, which she returned, and both left the clinic at a slow pace. The sky was leaden, the air humid and oppressively still, the charnel house of calcined trees adding their scarecrow silhouettes to the lunar landscape. Their wandering pushed them unconsciously toward the forest where young CDF recruits trained on monkey bridges. Their joyful exclamations, their energy only added to her gloom. Khin Yadanar watched them sadly, aware that her lover could never accompany them, even after mastering the prosthetic which was under production in the camp workshops.

She knew she must speak to him. She had made her decision days before, but did not know how to announce it, unable to find the right words. Kee Mawng was the first to break the silence.

- "The drone unit commander told me he had a position for me," he announced with genuine enthusiasm. "I'm starting training on 3D printers and mortar manufacturing next week."

She was genuinely happy for him. She knew he felt a constant need to be useful and would regain his good humor by becoming active again. Calls with his family, refugees in India, helped him. Unlike her, he was not alone in the world. Thus, despite the tragedy, he displayed a resilience she envied, she who felt desperately hollow.

She had continued to fulfill her responsibilities at the clinic robotically, working tirelessly yet unable to find sleep. The days resembled one another, each a little darker. She woke up each night in sweat, heart pounding, searching for her belongings, but all had burned in the attack: her lamp, her bag, her clothes, family photos, the satchel, Preston's notebook, even the stethoscope her father had given her upon entering medical school. Her phone and tablet were the only remnants of her former life. Everything around her was new, devoid of meaning, without history or flavor, as if her past, her very existence, had vanished in flames. In the nocturnal gloom, she sought through the mosquito netting the faces of her friends, replaced by those of her new roommates. Strangers to whom she had not confided, despite their compassion. Their attention, their constant discretion, their careful manner, as one reserves for a wounded bird, only increased the sensation of permanent suffocation she felt, provoking in her frequent bouts of unjust anger that had pushed them to keep their distance. So much so that they no longer came to her bedside to attempt comfort when nightmares woke her with anguished cries, the images of her friends' bodies imprinted on her retinas. It was better this way; she did not wish to know them, to grow attached to them. It was preferable for them: those who approached her all died. Her lack of sleep and appetite, added to her work at the clinic, exhausted her to the point that she spent most of her free time dozing in a chair beside Kee Mawng's bed.

She was incapable of providing the psychological support he deserved, he who had always been there for her, sustaining her through each crisis that had upended her life. She felt useless, ungrateful, selfish. Did she deserve to have survived when those she loved had perished? The sacrifice of these martyrs reflected her weakness, her helplessness, her guilt. It should have been she who left, not them. What gratitude did she offer them? What value did she possess? What reason had she to exist still, if she could not help the last person who mattered to her precisely when he needed her most? As she prepared to add to his suffering, she despised herself, abhorred herself to such a degree that she had imagined, on several occasions, walking into the forest with her weapon to end it, a bullet through her skull. No more pain, no more memories, absolute darkness, peace at last. Only the thought of the additional torment she would inflict on Kee Mawng had prevented her from seeing that desperate act through to completion. She had almost come to resent him and the feelings that bound them, which had only added to her self-hatred. She was caught in a vicious circle, dragged toward an abyss without end.

She had made her decision. Her plan gnawed at her like a scream that filled her lungs, consumed her thoughts. She clenched her jaw to block the words that wanted to escape, but the monster was too powerful. She could bear it no longer. He would not understand. No one could.

- "I'm going to Win Ka," she announced suddenly, abruptly. "I'm going to find the *stūpa* and the Buddha's relics." She had already told him in detail what Ayaan had explained to her about the tablet.

Kee Mawng stopped dead in his tracks, released one of his crutches to seize her by the shoulders, and made her face him.

- "You're joking! That's suicide!" he cried out with urgency.

- "It'd be suicide for me to stay here," she answered in a grave, measured, factual voice, with a clarity and honesty of which she had been incapable for weeks. As their gazes met, she felt all the affection he held for her, and tears came into her eyes. "I love you, you know?" she told him for the first time, her voice trembling, slipping beyond her control.

- "I know," he replied, with emotion. "I knew it before you did."

He was right. He knew her better than she knew herself. Kee Mawng had begun courting her in Mindat when Khin Yadanar's father had treated him for a fracture. His parents had insisted on paying, but the doctor had refused. The Mawng family, farmers living outside the city, had nonetheless returned to offer him a pig specially slaughtered for him. A sacrifice in a region where meat was reserved for great occasions. According to tradition, Kee Mawng had taken to visiting to court Khin Yadanar accompanied by friends under the benevolence of her parents. They had treated the boy with respect. The Mawng clan, however, had shown reluctance, aware that the difference in status precluded any marriage, but also because Khin Yadanar's father was Burmese and Buddhist, which made teeth grit within their

Baptist parish. Concentrating on her studies, Khin Yadanar had been unable to return his attention. He had persisted in his advances even after leaving school at fourteen to work on the family farm. Their faltering relationship had ended when Khin Yadanar departed at sixteen to study in Yangon. Chance or fate—but Khin Yadanar did not believe in such superstitions—had brought them together again at CDF headquarters. Khin Yadanar had grown fond of the one who had buried her parents in her absence and who had subsequently supported her during her military training.

- "Regardless of how much I love you, I can't stay here," she resumed awkwardly. Why was she incapable of expressing her thoughts without wounding those close to her? "I'm suffocating here..." she continued, searching for words. How to make him understand what she felt without hurting him? "I know I love you. At the same time, I can no longer feel... anything, even for you. I feel so empty, so tired, so useless. I don't even have the energy to fight anymore. Like a leaf rolled by the wind, pushed toward a dark hole. I need to retake control of my life."

- "What's stopping you from doing that here? You're free." Kee Mawng clearly did not understand.

- "Free?" she asked sarcastically. "You don't know what it's like to be trapped here day after day," she shot at the farmer who had never left his native region. She regretted it immediately, but continued, nonetheless. "Every day I treat victims of mines, combat, disease. The next day I must start all over again as if what I did meant nothing. It's an endless cycle, like emptying the ocean with a teaspoon. What freedom do I have? I have no control!" Her voice rose until she was nearly shouting without realizing it. Her companion drew her to an isolated spot, away from recruits observing the scene. "A plane comes one day, my friends die, and you lose a leg. In a week, a month, another will come, and it will be your turn to die! Like everyone I love! And I can do nothing to stop it!"

Suddenly, a blast filled the air. Khin Yadanar started, muscles tense, breath held, heart pounding. She spun in alarm to discover a pickup truck with a sputtering exhaust moving away from the clinic. The tension drained from her and she nestled in tears against Kee Mawng, who held her in one arm, the other still gripping his crutch.

- "I'm losing it!" the young woman reproached herself after calming slightly, still unable to face her lover. Finally, she slowly drew back from him, wiping her face with the back of her sleeve, sniffling loudly. "I'm a mess, aren't I?" she asked, as though apologizing.

He offered her a smile full of tenderness by way of reply. He knew this was the moment to listen, to let her confide, to allow her to unburden herself, to evacuate what she had accumulated, but the anxiety sparked by her announcement of departure was too strong. He asked the question burning on his lips.

- "If you feel useless and trapped here, how risking your life to cross the country in the middle of civil war to find an old pagoda will change anything? It's ridiculous..." He was terrified for her; it showed in his eyes. But he understood he could not hold her back by force. She was rational, educated; she would realize the madness of her plan.

- "I've thought about it carefully," she began in a measured voice. Her prefrontal cortex reasserting control. "Like you, I thought: 'who cares about an old tablet and relics,' right? I mean, the junta's committed the worst atrocities for three years and the world doesn't care. Perhaps I must accept the situation, continue to treat symptoms without being able to eradicate the source of the disease." She saw a glimmer of hope cross his face until she continued. "But... risking a single life might be worth the cost if it can draw attention to our situation." Kee Mawng's face darkened at once.

- "We can only rely on ourselves, you know that. We receive no military or financial aid from outside. Only our diaspora supports us. And besides, perhaps it's better if Westerners don't get involved. Remember the sanctions?"

Khin Yadanar knew it well: hell was paved with good intentions. At Aung San Suu Kyi's call, Western nations had imposed drastic sanctions after 1988 and in 2003. The harshest in the world, harsher than those striking North Korea. They had led to factory closures, pushing hundreds of thousands of unemployed young women toward prostitution or illegal emigration to Thailand. Far from bending the junta, they had allowed generals to enrich themselves by circumventing embargoes via China, India, and Thailand. The population, meanwhile, had become the poorest in all of Asia.

- "I know," she conceded. Western intervention would bring even stronger Chinese support to the junta. The war would only be prolonged, perhaps lost. "But the world must know what's happening here. Our victory would impact the whole continent."

There, in this corner of jungle, it was not merely the future of the Burmese people at stake. Each free nation was a candle, a beacon illuminating a corner of the world. A democratic Myanmar was a bulwark against Beijing's despotic ambitions, as Ukraine was against Moscow's. Dikes against the dark tide of authoritarianism. Should even one of them disappear, however minuscule, the entire continent would be diminished, tolling the knell of all humanity. The Americans and the French had had their revolutions in the Age of Enlightenment. The people of Myanmar were having theirs now. Its impact would change the face of the world. This was what Khin Yadanar wanted to cry from the rooftops. Even if only briefly.

- "*Tui kä hmu-pha ne a k'chi a suh*[58]! You'd have to find these relics first! And even if you do, even if the media report on it, the news will shift immediately and Myanmar will be forgotten again after two days. None of this will matter," the soldier interjected, desperate.

- "You're probably right," she admitted. "But two days might be all it takes to attract the attention of donors or governments. In any case, it can't get any worse than it is now. I have nothing to lose," she dared, to convince him.

---

[58] K'cho expression meaning "to remove one's clothes to swim before even seeing the water." Synonym for: "putting the cart before the horse."

It was cruel and unjust toward him, especially that last remark. She did have something to lose, but she had made her decision; nothing could make her change her mind, unfortunately.

- "The clinic's already understaffed." He refused to concede defeat. "Lives depend on you. We need you!" he pleaded, eyes glistening, voice trembling, wavering until he slipped and fell to the ground. She had never seen him so fragile, so vulnerable.

- "I know you need me," she answered with emotion, crouching before him to take his head in her hands and kiss him. "And I know I'm being selfish. You've always been there for me. You're my rock. I'm sorry for abandoning you when it's my turn to take care of you. But I need to do this. I have no choice. If I stay, I won't be able to help anyone, and I'll end up hating you," she admitted with a bitter smile. "And that's the last thing I want, because I can't live without you," she added, kissing him again. Never had she been able to express her feelings so clearly. Never had her thoughts been so limpid. "I'm going... not to die, but to live again. And I will need you," she concluded with a deliberately teasing, provocative tone to try to lighten their conversation.

She knew he could not resist the temptation to be useful. Kee Mawng retrieved his crutches and stood up.

- "What can I do? I'd go with you... but I'd be more of a burden and a liability than an asset in my condition," he acknowledged with blunt realism, his voice hollow.

She understood, from the dull anguish she read on his face, that this was likely the first time the soldier had fully grasped the limitations his new condition imposed. The hothead who had spent his life running the mountains, facing the enemy, would now have to remain behind, with the elderly, women, and children. He could not even protect the woman he loved.

- "You were right earlier," she hastened to continue, lest he sink deeper into depression. "Crossing the country will be dangerous. I'll travel through hostile terrain on roads I don't know. I'll need guides and information. You'll be my eyes and my ears, my travel agency!" she added lightly, trying to make him smile, without success. His heart was heavy. He had just learned he would lose something far more precious than his leg. "Come, help me plan my route," she concluded, taking him toward the barracks.

She understood his sadness, but she felt as if a veil was lifting from her mind at the mere thought of departure, as though daylight were filling a room that had remained dark too long after the curtains had been drawn. An energy inhabited her such as she had not known for a month.

Yet a thought came to temper her enthusiasm. She would have to reestablish contact with Ayaan, which hardly delighted her. But the tablet and the notebook pages could contain essential clues to locating the *stūpa* at Win Ka. She needed his networks and Professor Preston's knowledge to translate them and identify the location. She had lost the journal but still possessed the photographs she had taken and sent to Ayaan. As for the tablet, it was the only thing that survived the fire. It was a sign that the universe wanted her to see this quest through to its end.

Chapter 13

Chin State, Myanmar, September 2024

The sun was at its zenith, piercing the mist escaping from the forest-covered mountains. A few sluggish clouds reluctant to depart clung to the peaks, gliding languidly from summit to summit, to fall asleep as cotton balls in the valley's hollow. As warm wind lashed her face at the back of the motorcycle hurtling down the monsoon-battered road, Khin Yadanar inhaled the musky perfume of the sodden humus, which memory finished flowing in crystalline song at the roadside. Now and then, more from necessity than play, the seasoned driver's zigzags sent the vehicle gleefully splashing through a puddle, drenching the passenger, whose face and clothes gradually covered with a fine layer of mud. She did not mind. She was living again, delighted by the sensation of freedom the warm gusts afforded her as they rushed into her fatigues and hair. She was a bird, soaring over summits smooth as emeralds, framed on one side by the precipice of a shadowed ravine returning the silvery reflections of the stream bathing its feet, on the other by the dense vegetation flashing past. All was azure and brilliant green. Each of her baleful thoughts had evaporated under the sun's invigorating heat. It was her first free time since the coup and she savored every second, aware it would be ephemeral.

- "If only Kee Mawng were here," she sighed, her smile giving way to a wistful pout, her gaze fixed beyond the mountains toward the summits she'd just left. She couldn't even call him or send a message, they were in a blackout zone without connection. She'd have to wait until Chauk to give him news.

A veil came to shadow her exaltation as she recalled her lover's sad face at the moment of their separation, looking so fragile and lost. He had just lost another part of himself and had not understood why. She blamed herself for taking pleasure in having left him. Was she selfish? For three years, her freedom had been reduced to reacting to events imposed from outside: the coup d'état, the death of her parents, the war. She questioned the nature of her feelings for Kee Mawng: were they the fruit of her weariness or did she genuinely love him? It was unjust to project her guilt onto him at the moment she had decided to flee. For it was indeed a flight. She had suffocated under this leaden weight.

Obviously Kee Mawng and those around him could not understand. The notion of individual freedom was an abstraction for them, Christians and Buddhists alike invoking God or Kamma to explain the course their existences took; a course bridled by the shackles of family, clan, religious community, duties, which imposed upon each their place in society. Most, like Kee Mawng, accepted this situation, even accommodated themselves to it to follow the path traced for them. What other choice did they have? What opportunities? Poor, uneducated, cut off from the world, responsible for their kin, they were prisoners of their circumstances. She was different, had always been, as far back as she could remember. She had always done as she pleased, stubborn, unsubmissive. She had succeeded in everything she had undertaken, dismissing all docility or obedience to authority to spare no effort and accomplish what she deemed necessary and just. Life was inequitable, unjust even, and she knew she owed her successes to the favorable environment and natural abilities inherited from her parents. After all, she too was the fruit of the soil that had made her germinate: a couple of rebels executed for having joined the Civil Disobedience Movement and treated the resistance fighters during the Battle of Mindat in May 2021. Like them, she now risked her life, naive to hope that her absurd and desperate quest might save thousands, but invigorated by the illusion of regaining control over her existence. Should she, Don Quixote, survive this attack on windmills, she could then return to her beloved. For, though sometimes doubtful, she was convinced she loved him. Their union would then be a choice despite circumstances. This thought replaced her guilt with a new determination. She had promised him: she would survive and return to him. No matter what.

The motorcycle braked abruptly, skidding on lose ground. Khin Yadanar grabbed the handles to avoid being thrown into a wide trench at which edge the vehicle stopped. A landslide had swallowed the trail, a recurring phenomenon during monsoon. Their descent from CDF headquarters had already been slowed by obstacles and rockfalls they had to overcome. Yet this time they seemed truly blocked. Both dismounted and leaned over the crevasse giving directly onto the ravine. One meter more and it was the end. Khin Yadanar felt vertigo, the void calling her, her legs trembling. They would have to find a way to cross the fissure, or her adventure would end before it began. They were still far from Kanpetlet, their first stop, before continuing southeast toward Chauk, situated on the banks of the Irrawaddy. She felt frustration mounting at the thought of having to perhaps turn back.

Thang Bawi, the guide escorting her at Kee Mawng's request, was examining the cavity while scratching his head. Khin Yadanar seized this forced halt to pull out her canteen and drink greedily the few warm mouthfuls it still contained.

- "I'm going to fetch water," she announced. He answered with an indifferent shrug.

With determined steps, she climbed the embankment, made her way through dense vegetation to a trickle of water escaping from the mountainside. She filled her gourd and slipped a purification tablet into it. Threads of light pierced the canopy, to the immense pleasure of birds and crickets that covered the swaying of leaves. Breathing deeply the air mingling the vapor of new growth with the musky perfume of rotting bamboo, she took a moment to embrace with her gaze her cocoon of verdure. Gaia invited her to let herself be absorbed by the telluric womb, to return to the primordial matrix. There, she glimpsed for the first time her death with serenity, almost a rebirth, a cycle.

Suddenly, the chirping ceased, a shadow extinguished the sun, and the forest transformed into a gray, silent cemetery. Khin

Yadanar perceived the roar piercing the firmament in crescendo. Her body was seized with spasms. She curled up on the damp, cold ground, in the bed of the stream, moaning, trembling, her mind locked in a black box. Despite her eyes shut, she continued to see the flash of the explosion, the light of the flames, bodies covered in soot. She covered her ears, but the screams continued to besiege her. Long seconds passed before the roaring subsided. The birds resumed their songs, the warm light of the sun flowed over her once more. She remained a few seconds longer in her vegetable lair to slow her heart. She was drenched in sweat. Finally, she rose slowly, still somewhat unsteady, and returned to the road. She found Thang Bawi where she had left him. He was nonchalantly chewing a root and watching her with a blasé air.

- "A reconnaissance plane," he simply announced, spitting out his quid and pointing with his chin at a black dot disappearing behind a cloud. "You took your time," he remarked, hacking at a young tree he'd just felled with his machete to strip its branches.

- "I needed to pee," she lied. It was already difficult enough for women to earn respect within the resistance, without her panic episodes serving as excuses for men to relegate them to subordinate tasks. She had to be strong, for herself, for her comrades risking their lives, for her friends who'd lost theirs.

- "Did you piss yourself?" the guide asked in a sarcastic, crude tone, not looking up as he gestured toward the young woman's soaking trousers.

- "I slipped," she simply replied, moving quickly away in search of vines to cut short the conversation.

It took them nearly an hour to fell the trees necessary for assembling a rickety footbridge long enough to span the cavity. Khin Yadanar, sweating profusely through the layer of clay covering her skin, stepped back to admire their work, wondering if it would bear the weight of their vehicle. Fear seized her stomach at the thought of crossing the precipice on this makeshift pontoon. One misstep and she would end up crushed dozens of meters below. Nevertheless, there was no question of retreating.

Without a word, Thang Bawi seized the handlebars and slid the motorcycle into the mud. Khin Yadanar rushed to help. She braced herself and pushed the rear of the bike with a grunt. Her first foot touched the footbridge, then her second. She forced herself not to look down, fixing her gaze on her guide's back. One step, then another. Her breathing gasped, her heartbeat against her eardrums. The footbridge creaked, swayed, but held firm, until finally the rear tire touched solid ground. She let out a cry of victory. They were safe. She wiped her brow with a muddy forearm, sweat burning her eyes, which she planted in the creased slit that hid Thang Bawi's. The fifty-something man with a lean frame spat a brown jet onto the ground of the same color, then pulled out his bottle of *yu*[59] which he held out with mischief. She did not hesitate, swallowed a long swig with a complicit smile. She

---

[59] Traditional liqueur from the Chin mountains of Myanmar, handcrafted from fermented rice or corn.

felt invigorated by the burn down her esophagus. It was time to depart.

After an additional thousand meters of descent, they reached the road connecting Mindat to Kanpetlet, a sleepy hamlet that once served as a base camp for excursions to Mount Victoria. Since the coup, the place had emptied of its inhabitants. Only a meager Tatmadaw garrison remained entrenched on the heights. The surroundings were controlled by the resistance, which decimated the rare military convoys still occasionally attempting to resupply the barracks. Nevertheless, caution was necessary. Thang Bawi, of the Daa Yinbu tribe, knew the area well and had decided to follow forest trails to skirt Kanpetlet until reaching Saw, below in the border valley.

Before the village's outskirts, the pilot suddenly swerved right to plunge onto a goat path skirting the slope toward the southeast. Khin Yadanar clung to her guide, her heavy pack threatening to spill her at each jolt. They rode for an hour, passing Kanpetlet, hidden by the trees above them, their shadow lengthening before them, as if eager to distance them, until finally the sky covered itself with the golden veil of twilight. As a shy gray band disappeared behind them, pushed by the starry vault behind the western peaks, the woods became sparse and they arrived by headlight before the remnants of a village surrounded by abandoned fields. Thang Bawi cut the engine and silent darkness enveloped them. Gradually, Khin Yadanar's eyes grew accustomed to the gloom and glimpsed the Milky Way illuminating the firmament. She recalled the nights spent admiring it in Kee

Mawng's company. That evening, however, the darkness enveloping her made her shiver. She was alone, as alone as she had ever been. She would have liked to call Kee Mawng, to hear his voice, but she had to keep her phone off to conserve its battery, in the absence of electricity.

A shiver gripped her body and she redirected her attention to the forms of the hamlet silhouetted before her: carcasses of eviscerated, collapsed buildings, pieces of charred wood and roofing scattered about, abandoned to the elements and decay. She recognized immediately the signs of past bombardments. She stood in the ruins of a martyr village, a monument to forgotten dead, victims of the war the Tatmadaw waged against its own population.

A crackling pierced the crickets' song and she glimpsed a flickering light through gaps in a makeshift shelter a few meters away, within the rubble itself. Without a word, Thang Bawi and she seized their rifles and approached with velvet steps. The smell of burnt wood grew stronger and whispers reached them. The scent of charcoal immediately revived Khin Yadanar's nightmares, bringing back the terrible images of the fire. She paused, breathing heavily, hands clenched on her weapon, her trembling legs escaping her control. This was not the moment to sink into a panic attack when facing a possible army patrol. She breathed deeply, released her jaw, and concentrated her energy on her exhalation. Once more mistress of herself, she covered the remaining distance in silence, pressed herself behind a post, weapon aimed.

- "*Mei om law*[60]," Khin Yadanar called softly.

- "*Mei om law*," answered a voice from inside the hut. A form swept aside the tarp, revealing a woman in rags who gestured them inside with a wave of her hand.

The two resistance fighters lowered their weapons and entered the shelter. A weak fire of green wood burned there, filling the space with thick smoke escaping through holes in the plastic covering. Around the hearth huddled scrawny individuals in rags, bellies bloated and prominent ribs, their hollow eyes fixed on the intruders with apprehension. Khin Yadanar smiled at them and went to sit on the wet earth, joined by a young woman cradling a whimpering infant, thin and withered. All were nothing but shadows, barely more marked than those the fire danced on the canvas. An old man coughed, lying inert on a bamboo mat. No men in the group. No doubt they were fighting or had been killed.

- "When?" Khin Yadanar asked bluntly, harsher than she'd intended, her throat tight, unsure how to begin.

- "Two weeks ago," their host answered, swaying the baby back and forth in nervous rhythm to try to calm its cries.

- "They came at dawn!" spat the oldest of the boys, jerking his head up abruptly. He was perhaps ten, but his childish voice burned with incongruous rage in such a frail frame. "Two planes," he continued with fury, "they dropped bombs on the church during prayers."

---

[60] Formal greeting in K'cho language

- "Calm yourself, Sang Bik," the young woman intervened with maternal gentleness marked by exhaustion.

- "I saw the pastor die!" the boy insisted, fists clenched. "And Pu Thawng! And Nu Tial with her baby! They were... They were in pieces!" he cried out in sobs. Khin Yadanar's vision blurred in the presence of this grief she knew all too well.

- "We buried them over there," the woman explained above the weeping, pointing a finger toward an imaginary spot. "Couldn't even say a service for them... They're in the same hole as the pastor, I hope that's enough..."

- "And you stay?" interjected Thang Bawi, a root between his teeth, grimacing.

- "Where to go?" answered the refugee, pressing the infant against her dry breast for it to nurse. In vain. "The camps are traps. The Kanpetlet base destroyed the nearest one here with shellfire last week." She caressed the infant's skull, its fontanelle beating slowly.

- "There's always India," the Chin guide insisted with a bewildered expression.

- "The roads are mined. The houses too. That's how his father blew his leg off," she said, drawing Sang Bik against her. "Poor kid! He has no one left... At least here we know where the mines are. And how do you expect us to get to India anyway?" she asked with realism, her gaze circling to rest on each subject of her court of miracles. "We barely have the strength to forage for food in the forest."

- "I kill snakes!" Sang Bik blustered, brandishing a rusty knife under Thang Bawi's nose. "And frogs too!"

A gust shook the tarp, letting in a cold breath that sent ash and sparks flying through the shelter. A southwest wind. It would rain tomorrow, or sooner.

- "I'm Khin Yadanar of the CDF-Mindat. That's Thang Bawi. What's your name?" she asked, fixing her attention on the mummified infant with concern.

- "Man Sung," the mother answered. "But everyone here calls me Anu."

- "When was your last meal, Anu?" the CDF resumed, extending her arms. "Give me your baby." The order cracked out, too imperious. Man Sung stared at her, dumbfounded, almost horrified, drawing back.

- "Give her the baby!" Thang Bawi urged impatiently, "She is a *saya von*!"

- "A doctor... Oh Lord!" Anu sobbed, hastening to relinquish her child, her eyes bright with hope. "It's too late for him," she moaned toward the old man fouling himself, "but save the children, I beg you!"

- "When did you last eat?" Khin Yadanar pressed, beginning to examine the bluish infant that reeked of excrement.

- "Two days ago. Millet porridge. There were a few seeds left in the neighboring field. And two frogs..." she stated, provoking a smile of pride from Sang Bik. "But we can't keep anything..." she apologized shamefully with a knowing air.

- "Cholera," the doctor announced simply, observing the brown streaks, remnants of diarrhea fouling the children's trousers. The epidemic had been decimating the region since the beginning of monsoon season.

A moan rose from the shelter's far end. The old invalid stirred, shoulders heaving with hiccups, murmuring incomprehensible litanies. Khin Yadanar approached the dying man, a decrepit form with sunken eyes, skin stretched over jutting cheekbones. The skin slipped beneath her fingers like an empty envelope. The odor caught in her throat. Dysentery. His cracked lips moved in continuous prayer, his skeletal hands gripping a wooden cross. Critical dehydration, probably advanced renal failure. Without an IV, without antibiotics...

- "He won't make it through the night," she whispered to Anu as she stood.

A rumble of thunder tore into the air. The infant resumed crying. A crackle made the tarp above them vibrate, then another, the percussion accelerated on the drum-skin until it became a deafening beat. A new gust lifted one of the plastic walls, a wave of screaming droplets sought to snuff out the fire that bowed, groaned, but held. All hands pulled at the tarps, fumbling for weights to anchor them to the ground, as the deluge rushed in continuous torrents from all sides. New pieces of wet wood were thrown on the embers, which coughed before relaunching their hissing tongues, like a curse hurled at the rainy sky.

- "The water," Khin Yadanar commanded, returning to the hearth, "it must be boiled!" The order was non-negotiable. "Here!" she ordered, handing her chlorine tablets to Anu. "I'll show you how to purify it if needed. Go fill it out!" She handed her canteen to Sang Bik.

While the child obeyed, plunging with trepidation into the storm raging around them, she explained to the refugee how to use the tablets and the essential hygiene rules to observe. He returned drenched, a spectral apparition accompanied by lightning, rushed to the fire, shook himself, trembling, then handed the canteen to his patron with a hostile look. Khin Yadanar felt somewhat guilty and took pity on his famished appearance. She met Thang Bawi's questioning gaze, where emotion appeared for the first time. There was no need to speak; they understood each other, and she approved with a nod. The guide's voice vibrated through the hut. "We have rations."

The word electrified the room. Khin Yadanar pulled out packages of dried meat, biscuits, flatbread. The children rushed forward with grunts, crooked fingers tearing plastic. It was everything meant to sustain them through their crossing into enemy territory until Chauk, but they didn't hesitate for an instant. The atmosphere relaxed and tongues loosened, exclamations of wonder and pleasure succeeding one another with each victual the travelers extracted from their packs. The distribution ended, a funeral rite. The last mouthfuls fell into stone stomachs with a dull thud. Khin Yadanar observed the scene, jaws working too quickly, eyes watching for the next morsel. It was more than they'd hoped for in days, but less than they needed. For them it was Christmas coming early; for some, the last. All washed down this feast with a sip from the canteen, grimaces answering the chlorine's taste, even the dying man whom Khin Yadanar helped swallow a tablet. It was all she could do under these conditions. Then hands joined around the fire, Thang Bawi reciting a benediction to thank God for this additional day He granted them.

- "You're leaving tomorrow?" Anu asked with apprehension as the fire began to fade. After their departure, death would reclaim its rights.

- "We must reach Chauk as soon as possible," Khin Yadanar confirmed.

- "Take him with you." Anu held out the infant. Her eyes were wet, imploring, but her voice was firm. "With you, he could survive."

The tiny body weighed less than a kitten. Khin Yadanar counted the ribs beneath translucent skin. She clenched her teeth, refusing to weep before people who'd forgotten tears. She hesitated, her hands rose almost, before falling heavily. She couldn't. It was impossible. She hadn't left to save one child, but to save them all.

- "I'll come back," she lied, throat tight.

Thang Bawi lit a cigarette, the ruddy glow underscoring his war-worn warrior's cheekbones.

- "I'll send a message to the CDF for them to come get you. It'll take three days at most," he announced with detachment, exhaling a white plume. They were still in a blackout zone controlled by the junta; they'd have to wait until tomorrow to enter Magwe Region.

- "If we're still alive," Anu replied with fatalism.

Lightning illuminated the shelter as the fire finished dying, returning their thoughts to the night. After their union in prayer, darkness began erecting walls between them. In a few hours, they would be strangers again, walking separate paths.

- "We must sleep now," Thang Bawi said gravely. "Tomorrow, we cross the valley of shadows."

Khin Yadanar let out a long yawn. Tomorrow they would continue their journey on foot, discretely, to avoid checkpoints. Tomorrow they would enter territories controlled by the Tatmadaw. Night fell suddenly, swallowing the last murmurs. She stretched out on the damp ground, her muscles aching from the road, listening to the dying man's rasping gasps as he sank progressively into the night. The other occupants followed suit, huddling together to ward off fear and cold. She closed her eyes, haunted by Anu's face and the child she had rejected. She opened her eyes and turned toward Thang Bawi, who had his back to her.

- "They will come for them, right?" she whispered. No answer.

In the gloom, she observed the sleeping silhouettes, anonymous. They were no one and everyone - a faceless legion, statistics. Today refugees, tomorrow victims. A figure shifting from one column to another, forgotten by all. She remembered her mission, the reason she'd decided to risk her life: to give them a voice, to restore their names. Dying is passivity, but risking one's life is action. She had chosen to act. She sank into restless sleep, cradled by the sound of relentless rain and haunted by the faces of those she left behind.

Chapter 14

Between Chauk and Pyay, Myanmar, September 2024

Khin Yadanar startled awake, the images of the explosion still burning in her mind, her heart beating against her temples, cold sweat running down her neck. She had screamed in her nightmare, Kee Mawng's silhouette engulfed in a ball of fire. She looked anxiously around her, but the other bus passengers paid her no attention.

The landscape scrolled past the wheezing pachyderm that raced down the road between Chauk and Pyay. Humid gusts rushed through gaping windows, the monster's breath carrying the heavy scent of fertilizer and buffalo dung. Khin Yadanar's stomach churned with each jolt, acidic waves struck her throat. Empty stomach. She had to think of something else. Around her, a patchwork of greens gleamed in flashes of sunlight. But this concert of light masked nothing. Behind the curtain appeared abandoned fields, overgrown with weeds, given over to vermin on which white cranes gorged themselves with impunity. Abandoned dikes, rot, collapsed huts. The lands once vibrant with busy shadows were empty of all verticality. Nothing linking the humus to the sky. Khin Yadanar's eye remained fixed on a sadly motionless horizon.

Death by a thousand cuts. Coup d'état, civil war, economic crisis, mandatory conscription. Young men and women fled before their numbers even came up in the lottery to escape roundups. Many hid in regions controlled by ethnic groups or joined the PDF. The junta was shooting itself in the foot. The countryside emptied. Only couples too old to till, too indebted for seeds remained.

At Chauk, she had crossed the market. Stalls half empty. A few stunted vegetables sold at exorbitant prices. The people fed themselves on rice husks thrown at them. The grain went to export, filling the generals' coffers. Sadness for the country once nicknamed the "rice bowl of Asia." War and sanctions had made it scorched earth, lost in the limbo of globalization. Yet, no curse. This past title was a promise for the future. Resources abounded. The population was young and the diaspora educated. Free and democratic, Myanmar would become an industrial tiger at the crossroads of China, India, and Asean. At the heart of the engine of global growth.

An old, rusted sign announced Yenangyaung. Where Burma's first mechanized derrick had gone into operation in the 1880s, where Burmah Oil, which became BP, was born. A symbol indeed of colonization and systematic pillaging of the country's resources by the British. Since the end of socialism, the Burmese junta had taken up the model. Generals enriched themselves through the mines of Mogok and Hpakan, teak and rice. Yenangyaung remained a vital center for the army's gas and oil production. The bus slowed then stopped abruptly with a long screech. A checkpoint.

Khin Yadanar glimpsed the menacing shadows cut out from the makeshift bunker's shade. Two uniformed youths, submachine guns in hand, boarded, verified the driver's papers, scrutinized the passengers. One of them fixed his gaze at her. Her blood ran cold. Paralyzed. Unable to breathe. It was over. They knew. Yet she had followed directives. Uninstalled all applications, erased data, keeping only links to official media and photos of pagodas. And yet, they knew. They would arrest her. Find the tablet. Torture her, rape her, kill her. She would disappear. Kee Mawng would never know. The tablet would fall into the junta's hands.

The soldier returned the papers to the driver, then descended with his colleague. The barrier rose. The bus resumed its route. Khin Yadanar finally took a deep breath. Momentary reprieve. Other inspections awaited her on the road to Pyay. She had to calm herself.

She had anticipated continuous surveillance, the omnipresent army, systematic checkpoints. But planning in the shelter of mountains was only theory. Reality bit flesh. Senses alert, hypervigilance, the reptilian brain in command. Fear. She knew it well: a block of ice in her gut, a paralyzing electric shock. She had buried it under the mountains. She had forgotten it. She was rediscovering it now. The Battle of Sanchaung resurfaced. Images which flow she could not stem. The smell first. Tear gas and burning tires. Mingled with the grease of the bus, it twisted her stomach.

March 8, 2021. Yangon. Three hundred protesters, slingshots, stones, makeshift shields in hand, massed behind their barricades, facing hundreds of Goliaths armed to the teeth. The sun was setting over the intersection of Kyun Taw and Bargaryar at the entrance to Sanchaung, the working-class quarter where opposing processions had converged. One more day since the coup. Another rung on the ladder of repression. The martyrs were already counted by the dozens. The latest, Kyal Sin, nineteen years old, killed the week before in Mandalay, haunted every mind and the t-shirts that read "Everything will be OK." A tribute. A provocation. Everyone knew it. Nothing would be OK. The Tatmadaw would show no mercy. Min Aung Hlaing had ordered snipers to aim for the head on the counsel of his monk Vasipake Sayadaw, an expert in yadaya[61]. The shadows of the young pressed against walls, merging into crumbling facades. The standoff lasted two hours.

Eight o'clock. The carillon's sound rose, a rustling that passed tree by tree across the branches, a wind covering the city with its murmur. The clang of pots filled the sky, then the voices united in a single chant, slow, clear, intelligible. One people, one fight, one message hurled at the junta. Kabar Ma Kyay Buu. "We will never forgive you." The barricades joined their voices to those of the city, three fingers raised in defiance. A tremor ran through

---

[61] Occult rituals or superstitious magical practices.

Khin Yadanar's skin. This daily rendezvous always gave her chills. They were not alone.

No turning back was possible. Her generation had grown nearly ten years in freedom, with the Internet. Too young in 2015, she had voted for the first time in 2020. They had been offered hope, the hope of democracy, of a better future. The army was trying now to strip it of them. Unacceptable.

The narrow streets filled with a dull roar when the first shots cracked out. The flashbangs fell first, raining over the barricades, white-light flashes that split the eardrums. Then the bullets. Real bullets. An adolescent collapsed near Khin Yadanar. Pressed to the ground, she rushed forward in a crawl with another medic. Too late. A glutinous, spongy mass seeped across the pavement from the shattered skull. Beside it lay his sign: "We are not insects." The body was hurried away down a side street. Around her, others fell. Cries from all sides, forms jostling in every direction, as if the night were releasing its damned souls. Chaos. The Gavroches starving for freedom rushed toward the buildings. Khin Yadanar guided a group of girls - girls? She realized they were her age, her own youth seeming so distant - a wounded person under one arm, Molotov cocktails under the other, up dark stairwells. Toward the roof! Higher, always higher. The climb seemed endless. A door opened at last onto the platform. The black sky. Nothing else. They would go no higher.

Below, the street vomited soldiers in waves. Cortege of dismantled machines, regurgitated from trucks by the hundreds, helmeted, faceless, followed by armored vehicles grinding *forward, cold steel monsters that crushed the barricades of burning tires. Orders roared through loudspeakers dissolved into the thunder of the stampede. An orange arc traced a curve from a window and exploded in a shower of fire on one of the vehicles. It continued its slow advance, unmoved. The flames licked the metal, a cry overwhelmed the chaos, then gunfire erupted, crackling on concrete, shattering glass, snapping into the night like a curse.*

Khin Yadanar risked a look over the parapet. The protesters were retreating into the tangled alleys where vehicles could not pass. Doors opened, closed, swallowed the fleeing masses. Voices died gradually. The weapons too. Then silence. Terrible. The waiting. The helplessness. The quarter was surrounded.

Twelve-thirty arrived, grim, struck somewhere in the void. The echoes drew nearer. Battering rams burst through doors, rifle butts shattered locks and latches, the sweep continued building to building, floor to floor, apartment to apartment. Trapped. They were trapped, without options, without escape, under open sky, but for how long? Cries and gunfire pierced the silence now and then, accompanying the extraction of individuals in handcuffs, beaten, hurled into the backs of trucks at the end of the street. Already fifty or more. When would their turn come? Khin Yadanar kept her calm despite the imminent fall of the blade. She threw the Molotov cocktails into the water cisterns. The slingshots followed. No other weapons? As if the junta, in its impunity, needed an excuse. "We are not insects." Yet the boots crushed them without discrimination.

Two o'clock. New rumbling at the quarter's entrance. Reinforcements arriving. Random shots into still-intact windows. The searches continued. The same succession of silences broken by the pack's grunts and the cries of their victims. Now and then, a loudspeaker call set the night ablaze, a threat to those harboring protesters. Pointless. Sanchaung, a working-class quarter, sheltered only partisans. Seated against the parapet, the girls waited. Ears strained, hands intertwined, silent prayers, while Khin Yadanar tended the wounded. Suddenly, a dull thud directly below their hideout, followed by a tumult in the stairwell. The enemy was inside the walls. In minutes, the door would explode and the night would carry them away in turn.

A discreet call, barely discernible among the shouts, caught the young woman's attention toward the neighboring building. Arms waved in the darkness, a plank was thrown across the void, a new exit opened to them. One by one, the girls straddled the abyss, the first offering their hands to those following, to the wounded. Khin Yadanar hung back so no one would be forgotten. The uproar drew nearer. They were on the floor below. She was the last. Behind her, footsteps. She leapt onto the plank, ran, slipped, tumbled into the void. The wooden board flew beneath her, struck the walls, bounced one last time with a dull sound in the alley. She hung suspended above the chasm, clinging desperately to the parapet, unable to pull herself up, her fingers sliding on the wet surface. The first blow struck the door.

A swarm of hands seized her and began to pull. A second blow. She managed to rest her elbows on the terrace's edge. A third shattered the door as she rolled onto the neighboring building's roof. All pressed themselves to the ground, breath suspended, listening to the sounds coming from their former shelter. "All clear." They waited a while longer before becoming certain enough to embrace their rescuer, a matron who smiled at them with kind familiarity.

Hours later, Khin Yadanar watched the dawn break over the rooftops. The sun's heat drove away the last army patrols. Survivors emerged from the city's depths, discovering the walls pocked with bullet strikes, asphalt smeared with dried blood, scraps of cloth snagged on barbed wire, eyes lifted toward the sun to burn away the memory of that accursed night. A new day, like so many others. Yet everything had changed that morning. The Battle of Sanchaung had been as brief as it was decisive. A catalyst. After the suppressions of 1974, 1988, 2007, resistance had finally learned from its past errors. It had understood that it could not prevail, without weapons or training, in urban combat against the junta. Barricades continued for a few more months, each crushed in an escalation of violence. But gradually, the opponents had left the cities for ethnic zones, to receive necessary training and join the People Defense Forces.

Khin Yadanar remained in Yangon as long as she could, passing from hideout to hideout, from barricade to barricade. The following week, she attended the funeral of Khant Nyar Hein, a medical student gunned down by the army, the same day as sixty civilians were massacred in Hlaing Tharyar. Twelve hours during which security forces had shot at will into the trapped crowd. The following month, she treated the victims of the Bago siege. A hundred opponents obliterated by machine-gun and rocket fire, then finished by the dozen with bayonets. Finally, she had decided to rejoin her native Chin State in late April, at the outbreak of the Battle of Mindat. Too late. Kee Mawng had told her of her parents' martyrdom before she could reach the besieged town.

The bus lurched, tearing Khin Yadanar from her reminiscences. The sacrifices of the past still permeated her thoughts, rekindling a flame smoldering beneath the embers. Fear, hatred were still there, night lights illuminating the most remote corners of her mind. Yet a blinding light had just reignited and interposed itself before their pale glow. Her determination had changed. It was far more than revolt. Hope. She was no longer the trembling beast, cornered. It was the Tatmadaw that was now in a crisis, its territories shrinking. Already there was talk of what came after, of this federal, democratic, multiethnic republic that would succeed the dictatorship. They could win. No, they would win. The hours were numbered. They would have already won but for the steadfast support of Russia and China to the junta. She would contribute by placing Myanmar in the media spotlight. But caution: the wounded animal, back to the wall, remains the most dangerous.

The Express Shwe Pyi Thar slowed with a screech of tires, raising a cloud of dust, finally coming to a halt before a checkpoint.

The last one before their arrival in Pyay. As always, the driver's assistant rose, face tense, positioned himself before the passengers, and recited the safety instructions in a mechanical voice: "Identity cards in hand. No filming. Keep your hands visible at all time."

Three silhouettes detached themselves from the corrugated-metal shelter, two raw recruits in ill-fitting fatigues and a sergeant with a square jaw who spat a long jet of red betel onto the asphalt. He mounted the vehicle with deliberate slowness, a stride heavy with drama, reeking of ego and malice. He proceeded up the aisle, heels thumping on the floor, narrow eyes sweeping the cabin in synchronized rhythm with his submachine gun, finger caressing the trigger like an organ of pleasure. He planted himself before a trembling man in his thirties, head bowed, who attempted in vain to vanish behind the seat. "NRC[62]," the military barked, waving an impatient hand. An identity card was thrust toward him, accompanied by a thick sheaf of bills. The thug counted them, made a dismissive face, then roared: "Get down! Join the others!" He pointed to three young men lined up under guard at the foot of a truck. The victim was seized brutally, barely time to grab his backpack. All would be forcibly conscripted to stanch the Tatmadaw's hemorrhage. The lucky ones might call their parents one last time. The others would be returned in a plastic bag or vanish without trace.

The Bamars were finally discovering the truth that minorities had lived in their flesh since independence. MRTV, The

---

[62] National Registration Card, citizenship document reserved for nationals.

Global New Light of Myanmar: nationalist propaganda, lies. For decades, the same bullshit hammered, repeated, driven home. They had believed. They had wanted to believe, nurturing racial discrimination against non-Buddhist ethnicities. Now they understood. There was only one enemy within: the Tatmadaw. It was not the guardian of unity but the cause of division. The other ethnicities? Victims. The true culprits had worn uniforms for eighty years. The police state had not been born three years before but at the independence itself. Even under Thein Sein, even during that "democratization" which had been nothing but a mask. While cities at the center had prospered, atrocities had continued at the periphery. Confiscations. Deprivations. Conflicts. Khin Yadanar had witnessed them in Chin State, a poor region, deprived of the fruits of growth, martyred. The ethnic cleansing in Arakan was another stark example. Twenty-five thousand Rohingya massacred by the army and Buddhist militias. More than a million refugees in Bangladesh. At the time, Buddhists, drowned in nationalist propaganda that flooded Facebook, had defended what they believed was an anti-terrorist operation. After all, the ARSA had attacked police posts. Even Aung San Suu Kyi had said nothing, drawing the ire of the international community. Today, all understood it was the army's *modus operandi* whenever faced with any dissent. An army over which the Nobel Peace laureate had never wielded influence. Thus Kachins, Chins, and Arakanese broke the ceasefire before 2021. Taken up arms again. Not from separatist ambitions, no. In hopes of living in peace. Like the Bamars who had joined them after the coup.

The NCO continued his inspection, the *athet amakhan kyay*[63] pocketed with a grunt. Khin Yadanar's turn came. She slipped a ten-thousand-kyat note under her identity card. Double the usual amount. The soldier snatched it from her hands and inspected it with attention.

- "Chin, huh?" he hissed with contempt. His odor - sweat mingled with alcohol - assaulted her senses. She pressed herself against the window. He advanced a step into her row, as if to corner her. "They got Buddhists among the Chins?"

- "My father was Bamar." She answered as respectfully as his sneering tone allowed, silently thanking her parents for registering her as Buddhist in the official records. It was difficult enough being registered as "Bamar-Chin" in the nationalist, racist Burma that General Ne Win had built after his 1962 coup.

The Citizenship Law had created a caste system imposing a hierarchy among ethnicities. With Buddhist Bamars at the summit, of course. A model inherited from British colonization. The junta had simply inverted the pyramid. Rohingya, Chinese, and Indians were excluded from the list of 135 "national races," denied citizenship and issued an "FRC[64]" instead of the "NRC." Access to public services, education, administrative posts, even travel, all was restricted. Beyond ethnicity and religion, the card indicated one's region of origin. A veritable surveillance and control instrument for minorities, allowing the imposition of

---

[63] "Living expenses", slang for bribes extorted by soldiers from civilians.
[64] Foreign Registration Card, status card given to those considered to be non-nationals, equivalent to the US Green Card.

movement restrictions on certain groups. A single glance at Khin Yadanar's card had allowed the sergeant to slot her toward the bottom of the hierarchy. He could do with her as he pleased.

- "They say Chin girls tattoo their faces to make themselves ugly and avoid kidnapping," he mocked. "Must say, you're not bad looking..."

A predatory smile lit his face, revealing two rows of betel-rotten teeth. She was legally old enough to be conscripted, she knew. He could have her dragged down and subjected to the worst obscenities. She was at his mercy. He leaned toward her again, predator's gaze fixed coldly on prey, two rough hands planted on the headrests as he bent closer. His warm, fetid breath clawed at her face. Her back pressed to the window, she was trapped.

- "Traveling alone?"

- "She's with me. She's my niece," came a calm, authoritative voice from the row behind.

Startled, the sergeant straightened to look at the interloper. Khin Yadanar turned as well and discovered the smooth dome of a monk's head rising above the seats.

- "We've just returned from a pilgrimage to Bagan," he continued serenely, "and we're on our way to Akauk Taung to make offerings."

The soldier fell silent, visibly annoyed, weighing his options. He turned his attention back to Khin Yadanar, inspected her with a deliberate gaze. She was grateful she had chosen to wear the brown robes of Buddhist laypeople before arriving in Chauk. Her garb would save her life. He opened his mouth to speak when a commotion erupted outside. A young soldier was struggling with a conscript who thrashed about, refusing to climb into the truck where others were crammed together, unwilling. "Damn it! Incompetents!" the sergeant growled before bellowing at the two soldiers behind him: "What are you waiting for? Go help, you idiots!" His attention diverted, he tossed Khin Yadanar's card onto the seat with a dismissive gesture, not even looking at her. "You're lucky... This time," he spat, haughty, his heavy footstep receding toward the exit.

Outside, the altercation intensified. The prisoner, desperate, screamed in terror: "I can't! I must get home! My son was just born!" No one came to help. The passengers kept their heads forward, gazes fixed ahead, lips compressed with guilt. Khin Yadanar felt anger surge within her, her body tense, legs bent, fingers gripping the armrest, ready to spring. She turned to the monk, questioning with her eyes. He shook his head. He knew. She knew. There was nothing to do. It was not only her life she would risk, but those of the other passengers as well. She sank back into her seat with resignation, unable to tear her eyes from the tragedy. The prisoner suddenly arched his legs against the bumper and pushed with all his strength. The soldier holding him fell backward on his back. The conscript broke free and began to run, as fast as his *longyi* allowed him, barefoot, his flip-flops lost in the scuffle. He rushed toward the bushes bordering the road. Nearly there. If he plunged in, he might have a chance. Khin Yadanar held her breath. A detonation. A gasp rippled through the bus. The boy collapsed at once, face down, motionless, like a toppled scarecrow. A halo of red spread across his back.

- "You're fucking stupid or what?" the sergeant bellowed, striking the soldier who had fired. "The Colonel would've paid two lakhs for him, you moron! That comes out of your bonus!"

He waved the bus onward. Behind, other vehicles waited to furnish their quota of cannon fodder. The driver pulled away at high speed. The gesticulating sergeant, the truck, the inert body, all dissolved into a haze of dust. The report would record an attempted desertion, punishable by death under Article 27 of the military penal code. If there was a report at all. The body would probably be buried hastily. Quicker. Less effort. Another child would grow up with a missing father. A daily banality.

Khin Yadanar turned her gaze back to her rescuer: a Buddhist monk of uncertain age, eyes closed, legs folded on his seat, fingering his rosary while reciting *Anicca Vata Sankhāra*[65].

- "I thank you deeply, *Sayadaw*[66]," she ventured despite her hesitation at interrupting his prayer. "You saved my life."

The fingers stilled on a bead. The eyes opened with a sad smile.

- "The *Karaniya Metta Sutta*[67]," he replied, eyelids half-closed, "teaches that 'as a mother protects her only child with her

---

[65] Opening phrase of Buddhist funeral rites: "Impermanent, alas, are all conditioned things".
[66] Honorific title for a Buddhist monk.
[67] Buddhist teaching on universal compassion for all beings.

own life, so should one cherish all living beings.' You are not truly my niece, but it was my duty to help you."

- "They shot him in the back... Like a dog," she ruminated, teeth clenched, lost in the void.

- "Men lost in the cycle of violence. Like the bandit Angulimala[68] before he met the Awakened One and followed the *Dhamma*. Their *kamma* will catch them. They wear their own chains."

- "And our chains? The ones they force upon us? The massacres, the bombardments, the summary executions? Who will free us from them?" Khin Yadanar was not religious; she did not believe in cosmic justice. The country had to change now. Punishments had to rain down now.

- "Hatred never ends hatred. Only love can end it. This is the eternal law. The *Dhamma* is like water: it wears away stone without struggle."

- "Then we must hope? Wait for their *kamma* to consume them?" she pressed, incredulous.

- "We must act without hatred. As the Buddha did before King Pasenadi's army: he did not curse the king but illuminated his mind. The junta will fall when their hearts recognize their own darkness."

---

[68] Legendary bandit who became a disciple of the Buddha, symbol of redemption through spiritual transformation.

Khin Yadanar recalled the Saffron Revolution of 2007. The processions of monks reciting the *Mettā Sutta*[69] peacefully. Then, monks beaten, executed by soldiers, nighttime raids on monasteries, bodies in crimson robes floating in rivers. Twenty years already. Did he remember? Since then, nothing had changed. The soldiers' hearts had not glimpsed "their own darkness." The genocide of the Rohingya had been followed by the martyrdom of minorities, then Bamars. All with the blessing of nationalist monks, who ignited minds with their racist sermons.

- "How about us, meanwhile?" she pressed.

- "We wage a revolution against ignorance. We prepare the advent of a just society, freed from fear. Even tigers sleep one day," he concluded with a knowing smile.

Khin Yadanar replied with a polite smile and turned away without a word to return him to his prayer. They wanted the same thing. They traveled the same direction, but on separate paths. Time pressed. She had chosen a shortcut that crossed precipices and rivers of fire. Would she arrive faster? Would she arrive at all? Would she lose her way? History would tell. For now, the next phase of her journey loomed ahead. Pyay. This was where she would descend.

---

[69] The Sutta on loving-kindness/compassion.

Chapter 15

Pyay, Myanmar, September 2024

- "I've arrived safely in Pyay. Found the guide. I'll message you when we reach Minhla. Love you."

Khin Yadanar uninstalled the Signal app from her phone before powering it off. The black screen reflected her troubled face. She missed Kee Mawng's voice, but the Chin Mountains lay in a blackout zone. He was her eyes in this war, her link to the underground networks threading through army-held lands, the guardian angel who arranged her escort at each stage. She would try to reach him later, through Voice IP, under a VPN. For now, time pressed. Silence, anonymity, both meant staying alive. Each hesitation could close her fate.

Kyaw Zaw waited by his scooter, a tense shape against the chaos of Pyay's market. Barely eighteen, a soldier of the PDF Battalion 3602, he wore his youth like a burden. Around them, the crowd swarmed in its theater of indifference, vendors, travelers, all actors in the comedy of normality. But Kyaw Zaw knew: a sudden checkpoint, a random search, and the entire resistance cell would vanish into the military prisons. She had changed clothes to a faded pair of jeans and a plain t-shirt like his. No weapon.

Nothing to catch the probing eyes of patrols, except the broken tablet wrapped in cloth at the bottom of her bag, sleeping like a deadly secret. Her ID was hidden in the lining. Two young people, brother and sister, returning home. That was their cover.

Through encrypted exchanges with Kee Mawng, Kyaw Zaw had secured his commander's permission to take the young woman as far as Hpa Yar Gyi, beyond the Bago Range. Days of travel through broken tracks, anything but the highways where the Tatmadaw spread its checkpoints like snares. "A real pleasure cruise," she thought bitterly as she climbed onto the scooter behind him. The engine roared; Pyay vanished in their wake.

- "I know a path that runs along the road to Paungde!" shouted the boy above the engine's fury as the town fell away. "Tomorrow, we cut through on foot. Southeast. Toward the mountains."

The afternoon unfolded beneath an ochre veil. They rode through fields like a green sea, sunflowers, cotton, maize, sesame wavering under the wind. Above, black clouds rolled with an angry tide, striking the bamboo roofs of scattered huts. Fragile pillars bent beneath the coming deluge. Beyond them, the sky churned, a celestial ocean that no sunlight broke. The light was that of an eclipse. The storm neared. The wind lashed their faces but could not dispel the suffocating weight of air. Thunder rolled, heralding the tempest.

- "Almost there!" Kyaw Zaw cried. "We'll make it before the rain!" He sped up along a slope fringed with ficus trees.

Two kilometers later, he stopped abruptly. The engine died. Silence fell for the first time in hours.

- "Something's wrong." His voice was taut.

Khin Yadanar listened. Thunder still muttered, the guttural growl of a beast approaching. Swallows swooped through clouds of insects driven low by pressure, their cries sharp in the thick air. Nothing else. She was about to speak when another sound surfaced through the wind: dry, metallic, faint beneath the storm's murmur but unmistakable. Gunfire. Distant but real. Their eyes met, no words were needed. Unarmed, but compelled by the same instinct older than fear: they had to see.

- "The village is just beyond the ridge," whispered Kyaw Zaw, hiding the scooter behind a massive trunk. "We go through the forest."

She followed, running obliquely, her bag thudding against her spine like a second heart. The detonations grew clearer, layered now with human voices, cries. Through the vegetation appeared the outline of huts. They advanced low, tree to tree, shadows among shadows. Twenty meters from the first dwellings, he signaled her to crawl. They reached the edge and froze in the tall grass. The horror was complete.

On the packed earth lay the dead - old men, women, children - sprawled in crimson pools, limbs twisted, throats slit, skulls crushed, bellies open. Chickens and pigs ran squealing among them, and a gaunt ox, eyes bulging in terror, strained at the rope cutting its neck. Behind the huts came other cries, other gunshots, fusing with the thunder's bass.

Then a teenage girl burst from between two houses, hair tangled, face distorted by pure terror. She ran as one pursued by death itself. Khin Yadanar stirred, driven by reflex, but three soldiers had already appeared, hunting her down. The girl tripped, fell hard. The pack was on her instantly, snarling. Two men pinned her down. Her screams tore upward, lost in the indifferent sky, while her body writhed in helpless defiance. The third, face twisted by lust, yanked up her *longyi*, dropped his trousers, and fell upon her with an animal grunt. He ripped the blouse open; adolescent breasts barely formed crushed under his palm as his hips moved to a primitive rhythm.

Khin Yadanar felt rage flooding her veins, blind, shattering. She was about to rise when Kyaw Zaw threw himself upon her, hand over her mouth. They were two, unarmed. Hopeless. His grip saved her life while condemning her to witness the child's martyrdom. Irritated by her sobbing, the soldier punched her, short, precise, silencing. Blood ran from her nose, forming a red path over the still face. Her inert body shuddered as he finished, before pulling away with a groan of pleasure. The other two took their turns, methodical, using her as if she no longer existed.

- "It's like screwing a corpse," spat one as he fastened his belt. "Next time I go first. You hit too hard."

- "Shut it," the first barked, shouldering his rifle. "You just have what it takes to fuck a starfish. You should thank me, I did the hard part." He grinned, teeth red from betel, and spat beside the girl's body.

- "Enough!" snapped the third, a corporal. "Dump all this filth inside the hut."

- "And her?"

- "With the rest. No witnesses, no traces." His gaze swept the area, passing over their hiding place without stopping. "Five minutes. Move. The PDFs are near."

He vanished behind the houses. The two remaining soldiers lifted bodies, dragging them one by one.

- "The PDF? Fuck'em! Where are your heroes now, huh?!" one jeered, interrogating the corpse of a sickly old man. His throat was slit from side to side, and his head swung at impossible angles.

- "No one to save you! They abandon you like dogs!" shouted the other toward the forest. Same silence from the little boy whom they threw like a bag of sand into the hut.

- "Come and save them, you cowards!" », copied his acolyte with a cheeky laugh, while a woman went to join the other dead.

The coming and going continued, until only the teenage girl remained, lying unconscious. They stood on each side, looked at her mockingly, two artists admiring their work, then seized her by the limbs.

- "We'll rape your sisters like we did that bitch!" », sneered the first.

- "And we'll burn your families like these huts!" », the second hissed.

The soldiers grabbed a jerrycan and doused the inside of the hut, then the bamboo walls. Their movements were methodical, precise in that terrible way of men who have made destruction their trade. The click of lighters followed, sparks leaping into tinder. They set the next dwelling ablaze as well. Flames shot up into the black sky, hissing, ravenous, licking the roofs with animal hunger. The two men vanished, their silhouettes swallowed by thick smoke that wrapped the village like a shroud. The roar of the fire soon drowned the last cries rising behind the incandescent veil, fanned by the wind that heralded the coming storm.

The emaciated ox finally broke free of its tether, fleeing in panic, bellowing at the burning sky. Kyaw Zaw's grip slackened. Khin Yadanar tore free and ran toward the burning hut. Her companion's shouts dissolved behind her. She heard only her heartbeat and that voice inside, a voice that insisted one life could still be saved.

She plunged into the hut. In the middle of the room, the victims lay piled like bundles of wood. Tongues of fire fell from the thatched roof; the blaze crawled up the bamboo walls, the air thick with acrid vapors that made her cough violently. Tears streaming from her eyes, her vision blurred, she still saw the girl amid the smoke that lacerated her lungs. She crawled toward her, each breath torture, her head spinning in the slow spiral of suffocation. Her hands found the girl's arms. She pulled. The body barely moved, dead weight. Again. She summoned everything she had left, useless. Alone, she would never make it. A strong hand pressed her shoulder.

- "Get out! I'll get her," Kyaw Zaw ordered.

She obeyed, crawling out of that inferno on all fours before collapsing outside, breathless, coughing out cinders that scorched her throat. She turned just in time to see Kyaw Zaw emerge from the flames, his burden in his arms, as the roof behind him exploded in a shower of sparks. He laid the girl gently on the ground. Her chest did not rise.

- "Let me," said Khin Yadanar, shrugging off her bag, pushing him aside to kneel beside the girl, palms pressing the still sternum.

- "Stand up!"

A voice barked behind her, just as she was about to start compressions. She was about to protest when a brutal kick to the back sent her rolling into the mud.

- "I said stand up!"

She turned, breath knocked out, pain shooting down her spine. Two soldiers loomed over them, storm-faced, rifles lowered with the carelessness of men who kill for pleasure. The two rebels stood slowly, hands on their heads. One soldier stared down at the girl's body, his eyes cold, detached, as if gazing at an insect. Without emotion, he lowered his weapon, aimed at her chest, and fired. The shot cracked clean, final. Khin Yadanar screamed, a raw, soundless cry, swallowed by the gust that carried away the smoke. Then she glared at the killer, hatred burning through her fear. Pure hatred, born of absolute injustice. But she did not move.

- "No traces. Orders," the man said. Turning to his companion, his bloodshot eyes glimmering with *Yaa Baa*[70]: "watch them while I deal with this."

He grabbed the girl's body by the ankles and dragged it toward the fire, leaving a bloody trail behind. With a kick, he rolled the corpse into the burning structure. The flames devoured it instantly. Task complete, he brushed his hands off, picked up Khin Yadanar's backpack, then motioned with his rifle. They marched. Around them, the burning village towered, an incandescent volcano, a roaring beast breathing fire into their faces like a curse, its claws of flame reaching to seize them. The famished creature seemed eager to feed on the two new captives of the Tatmadaw.

The gun pressed into her back, hard. Metal against bone. She stumbled, her slippers sliding in the muddy soot covering the path. Pain sharpened her anger as her eyes locked on a carbonized figure smoldering in the ruins. The reek of burned flesh rose, sickening. Tears of fury carved pale lines on her darkened cheeks. Her parents at Mindat had suffered the same fate. Then anger turned to sorrow, mourning not only for her kin but for her country, dismembered for decades. So much violence. So much blood. Why? So, a few could cling to power? Small men with

---

[70] Synthetic drug, made of a mixture of methamphetamine and caffeine, nicknamed "medicine that makes you crazy".

swollen egos, ready to ignite the world to quiet their fear and overcompensate their inadequacy. Min Aung Hlaing, Vladimir Putin, Xi Jinping, Donald Trump, Kim Jong Un, all different faces of the same disease corrupting mankind. That hunger for domination was alien to her. Had evolution rewarded the most violent? The struggle for control, like atoms coveting an electron. For centuries, culture and law had tried to counterbalance that fall, in vain. Cooperation, creation, other natural drives, demanded such effort. Taking was easier. The universe moved toward entropy. Was human order doomed to the same unraveling?

No. She was wrong. Despotism required constant energy, immense, exhausting, to sustain itself in its abnormality. A spring wound against nature, held tense through brute force. Freedom, on the other hand, was an instinct. A primal pulse. An idea reborn again and again. A dormant virus beneath the ice of dictatorships, revived with every Spring. One day, the iron hand would tire. The cramp had already begun. The junta's reservoirs dwindled, weapons, repression, endless waves of broken men to keep it alive. But those men? She turned slightly toward the escorting soldiers. Another blow struck her back. Sharp reminder. Poor, uneducated, despised, mistreated by their own officers. Buddhists, too. They were the same people. Yet they'd chosen the executioner's side. Why?

- "The banality of evil," she whispered, lips cracked by smoke and thirst. Hannah Arendt's words returned from an illegal pamphlet she'd read secretly after the coup.

But here, there were no Aryans with blue eyes lifted from a history book, no Nazi clerk in spotless uniform signing deportation orders. The killers had familiar faces. Men who offered flowers at the pagoda one day, slit villagers' throats the next. No cold bureaucracy, only a proximity obscene and incomprehensible. Submission? Indoctrination? Yes. The generals' uniforms and nationalist propaganda replaced Milgram's white coats. Collective frenzy? Yes, that too. Group pressure turned to madness. How many obeyed from fear of falling? How many surrendered to the intoxication of power? The Tatmadaw offered them rifles, and absolution. Immunity. Permission to abandon conscience. But could theory explain cruelty? Some must simply enjoy it. The memory of the rape rose again. Rage followed. Whatever reasons they claimed, there was no excuse. Each had made a choice between deserter, watermelon' or *sit kwe*[71]. They had chosen. And they would pay, in battle, by rope, before judges. Or, if the monk was right, their *kamma* would pursue them beyond the grave.

Thunder rolled, and rain came in furious sheets, as if heaven itself strained to wash the desecration from the earth. Steam replaced smoke. Blood and ash drifted away in the water. The martyred hamlet froze in its gray mourning, a cemetery without names. Oradour-sur-Glane, the name surfaced from somewhere deep within her. Khin Yadanar raised her face to the sky, mouth open to drink this last offering to the condemned. Fear ebbed away with the rain streaming down her body. Only rage remained, alive, electric under the warm drops. Whatever awaited

---

[71] "Dog soldiers" in Burmese.

her, she would give them nothing. No surrender. No satisfaction. She was ready.

At the village entrance, rows of military trucks stood in the pouring rain, dark hulks masked by water and smoke. A company of soldiers moved with mechanical precision, preparing to depart. At their feet, civilians knelt in mud, hands bound behind their backs, awaiting judgment. An officer walked the line, strong men sorted for transport or conscription, women and children for detention. The crippled, the defiant? Already corpses. Orders cracked through the wet air. Families split, lovers torn apart with a gesture, packed into trucks. Sobs stifled by fear, silence heavier than screams.

- "*Bo Gyi*[72], found these two," said one soldier, shoving them forward. "They're not from the village. She had this bag."

The officer took it, overturned it. Clothes, phone, cables, food, a first-aid kit, flashlight. The broken tablet fell last, thudding like a bell for the dead. He bent down, examined one fragment with cold curiosity, the predator's interest in new prey.

- "Who are you? PDF? Smugglers?" His bark pierced the curtain of rain, sharp and used to obedience.

They said nothing. He stepped close to Khin Yadanar, brandishing the shard, his frustration mounting.

- "What is this? Where did you find it?"

---

[72] "Captain" in Burmese.

Their silence hardened. She met his gaze without flinching in pure defiance. This war dog who expected submission at a glance. The slap came before she saw it, back of the hand, iron across her jaw. The pain rang in her skull. She fell into mud, spat blood, wiped it away, and rose, slow, deliberate, the insolence of those who refuse to bend.

- "Still proud?" he sneered. "They'll make you talk in Okpho. Tie them up. Load them with the others."

He ordered the soldier to repack the bag and walked away without a backward glance. Already, they were no longer his concern, but the OCMSA's[73]. At the name, her stomach tightened. That place north of Pyay, the intelligence center of horrors. Sensory deprivation. Endless torture. Mock executions. Sexual assaults carried out with military discipline. Enhanced interrogations were carried by a confidant of Min Aung Hlaing himself. The lesser prisoners were handed to ex-convicts from Insein[74], their sentences traded for cruelty. Brutes who beat until death. None left alive, except through the door leading to the crematorium. Her head spun as they pushed her toward the truck. She had not eaten since morning. Bile rose. A convulsive spasm, and she vomited over a soldier's boots. He swore and struck her with the rifle butt.

- "Move! Now!"

---

[73] Office of the Chief of Military Security Affairs. The Tatmadaw's military intelligence service, responsible for political surveillance, repression of dissidents and interrogations.
[74] Largest and most infamous prison in Yangon.

The truck roared onto the rough road, jolting the ten silent prisoners crammed at their guards' feet. Rain hammered the tarp, drowning out the mockery of the men above. Cruel laughter paced their funeral ride. In the dark, Khin Yadanar silently begged Kyaw Zaw's forgiveness. He turned away, leaving her in solitude. It was her fault. Her haste to leave hiding, her decision to quit the Chin hills, absurd choices leading to torture and death. And before that, perhaps betrayal, words torn out of them that would doom their comrades.

The quest for the *stūpa* seemed vain now beside so much loss. Yet she knew rage was not enough. Hope was needed, a symbol strong enough to gather what had been scattered. That was what she had tried to give her people. But as the burning village receded behind them, she realized she no longer had any. Soon she would die without hearing Kee Mawng's voice again, without telling him she was sorry. Without telling him she loved him.

Chapter XVI

Sittang Bridge, Burma, February 1942

- "Follow me!" hailed Sergeant Myers with urgency, rushing toward the building to retrieve their packs.

Scarcely had they reached the building when the truth appeared to them, cruel and final. From the hilltop, the spectacle left no room for illusion: a column of black smoke rose from the rubble of the bridge's central section, which steel girders lay twisted in the abyss separating the two portions still standing. Was it the work of enemy artillery? None could have determined it. Perhaps some hope remained of crossing the watercourse by means of boats. They had to ascertain this without delay.

Anthony seized his satchel, imitated by his companions who rushed toward the bank south of the bridge, forgetting fatigue, hunger, and thirst. Only the pulsations of blood pounding their temples remained, and that primitive fear drowning their reason. Professor Sayer stumbled several times, his body seeming to want to capitulate, but Anthony helped him up each time, urging him to maintain their frenzied pace. They emerged, breathless, onto the muddy banks of the Sittang bathed in the wan light of dawn. Wisps of mist caressed the legs of hundreds of ragged soldiers who, like them, came to assault the river in hopes of finding salvation there. But it proved empty of all promise. No boat within reach. Skiffs mocked them from the opposite bank, where they had been brought back the day before to prevent the enemy's passage. They were trapped, backs to the river, with a more numerous and better-equipped enemy about to close the trap definitively.

The northern perimeter, at the foot of the pagoda hill above the bridgehead, remained strangely silent, as if the Japanese had suspended their assault. Had they achieved their objective? Improbable. No doubt they had wished to seize the bridge to pursue their lightning offensive toward Rangoon. Its destruction had stripped them of all sense of urgency. British troops would soon be encircled, as attested by the intense crackling of mortars that persisted to the south.

- "Stay put," ordered Myers, "I'm gonna have a look round for a way across."

Anthony watched Myers depart and felt some relief seeing Pitt accompany him. The soldier's presence had unsettled him since the altercation with Win Thu. He had never liked the Burman, but the role he had played in his death turned his stomach. Nandar Aye had lied. So had he, by omission. The man was dead, and it was as if they themselves had pulled the trigger. Was he a spy? What did those numbers mean? They would never know. Doubtless this incident did not even rise to the level of tragedy, compared to the daily carnage since Win Ka. But what did those thousands of strangers represent to him? His proximity to the deceased gave his disappearance a personal dimension. It was not some anonymous person whose eyes had gone out in his own, filled with terror. Eyes that haunted him as soon as he closed his.

He helped Sayer settle against a tree, took his canteen, then went to fill it in the river. The coolness soothed his battered feet. He breathed deeply and fixed on that promised land, five hundred meters away, so close yet so inaccessible. Around him, soldiers feverishly constructed makeshift rafts. Several, seized with panic, plunged into the waters, abandoned rifles and equipment, then began to swim, deaf to warnings. Anthony watched with horror as they drifted rapidly, struggled against the current, exhausted themselves, before sinking beneath the muddy surface. These visions placed him before the mirror of his own terrors. He turned away to return to shore.

He spotted Nandar Aye crouching near Sayer, offering comfort. He approached and held out the canteen filled with water. Each joyfully drank their share of the silt-tasting liquid. He sat down, intentionally placing Sayer between the young woman and himself. He could neither look at her nor speak to her. Too many feelings jostled. Beyond guilt, the fear of being discovered had reawakened. They had been reckless and had nearly lost everything. But the incident might lead Sayer to question. They would need to remain discreet to allay his suspicions. Anthony welcomed this forced separation with relief. Nandar Aye's reaction, her lie, her coldness in the face of Win Thu's death had plunged him into profound unease, revealing so many unknown facets of his lover. Could he attribute this to survival instinct, when she continued to display perfect composure while everything sank into chaos?

He still loved her but no longer felt that intimacy that had united them. He admired her courage, but a certain awkwardness had taken hold as he became aware that the balance of power had reversed. Unless it had always been thus. She met his gaze and read his turmoil there, looking away to hide her own thoughts.

- "I'll see if I can make myself useful at the infirmary," she announced, visibly eager to put distance between them.

- "I'll stay here with the professor," he answered, gesturing toward the historian, benumbed and slumped with eyes fixed on the distance.

Anthony watched her depart in the direction of the aid post, oblivious to the chaos that surrounded her. Nothing seemed capable of rousing Sayer from his lethargy, neither the mortar shells that continued to churn the earth nearby nor the frantic screams of soldiers running in all directions searching for an exit. They thus remained seated in silence, fixed nuclei in space around which all these free electrons seemed to revolve in confusion.

- "I never would've believed he was capable of something like this. Such a bright boy, from such a respectable family." The professor suddenly broke the silence, contemplating the horizon. "A spy, a Jubelo[75] that I brought into the lodge myself," he

---

[75] Jubela, Jubelo and Jubelum are the three wicked companions who murder the architect Hiram Abiff in Masonic legend and symbolize the three voids of ignorance, fanaticism, and ambition.

concluded, his features divided between sorrow and anger, fixing the ring on his right pinky finger that bore the square and compasses.

Anthony knew of Sayer's membership in the University of Rangoon Lodge. Far from hiding it, the historian proudly displayed his affiliation with the Sons of the Widow, an organization that demonstrated exemplary progressivism in the face of colonial segregation. Not only had it opened its columns to Brothers of all origins, but Burmans held the highest positions. The historian saw in it the cenacle that would give birth to the enlightened elite of independent Burma which cause he supported, despite the ostracism he suffered. He, an excessive optimist, contemplated at this moment his blindness: he had introduced the worm into the fruit. A naïveté that Anthony and Nandar Aye also abused, they too betraying the trusting hand that fed them. Anthony dared not look at this generous but pitiable being who reflected his own mediocrity. Certainly, Nandar Aye and he loved each other, but they lacked the courage to do so openly, preferring to profit from their patron's largesse. To try to convince himself that they kept him in ignorance out of consideration for his feelings would be a lie. This contemplation produced in him an irrepressible self-disgust.

- "We shouldn't just sit here doing nothing," encouraged Anthony, rising. "Come on, let's help them out. It'll take our minds off things," he added, gesturing toward Indian soldiers who labored to construct a raft.

Sayer allowed himself to be drawn along to join these castaways of The Medusa. Other similar crews were forming, several taking to the river as soon as their craft permitted. Over the minutes, the surface of the Sittang populated with an armada of dozens of tiny floating mounds heading toward the opposite bank.

Two hours passed without their having seen Myers again. They had continued to lend their assistance to the improvised shipyards, remaining faithful to the noncom's orders. However, as time flew and opportunities to flee dwindled with the decreasing number of available rafts, they began to worry and wonder whether it was not time to fetch Nandar Aye to attempt the crossing.

Most of the craft had not crossed half the distance when a swarm of Japanese Ki-43 Oscar fighters invaded the sky and began strafing the men in the water, helpless and unarmed. The brown surface rapidly stained with long scarlet streaks, while mangled bodies drifted in the current, debris that would soon feed the depths of the Gulf of Martaban. Rage seized the men who remained on dry land. They began to exhaust their last ammunition on the aircraft circling above their heads. Suddenly, Anthony heard a shout of joy: a Yorkshire lad had just riddled an Oscar with bullets, which plunged before crashing into a rice paddy. Derisory triumph amid the general rout.

Scarcely had the cheers died down when the neighboring village burst into flames under the bombs. The straw huts consumed in a breath, releasing thick black smoke that descended upon them, swallowing the sun. Abruptly, a rumbling shook the earth: the last crates of British artillery shells exploded in a geyser of flames, fireworks immediately followed by a volley of chain explosions which burning blast they felt when they were thrown to the ground.

- "Are you all right, Professor?" asked Anthony, offering him his hand as he rose. His lips moved, but Anthony heard no answer through the whistling that pierced his eardrums. "Nandar Aye!" he suddenly cried, abandoning his companion to rush toward the aid post.

All around him, men ran in every direction, some aflame, all blinded by smoke. Upon arriving, he discovered a trench dug beneath a pile of shattered bamboo, where a heap of bloodied, moaning bodies was piled. At the far end, he finally spotted her, standing straight amid makeshift tourniquets and improvised drips. She was assisting a major who struggled to saw through the mangled leg of a wounded man howling in pain, for lack of anesthesia. He could not help but admire this Artemis, her clothes stained red, her disheveled hair that she brushed aside with the back of her arm, passing compresses, phenol, or bandages to the doctor with calm, precise gestures. She was that lotus blooming in the mire, illuminating the mud surrounding it. It was at that moment that Myers appeared, covered in soot, his uniform in tatters.

- "Orders are through!" he cried to be heard above the din. "General retreat! Now or never, lads! The smoke'll cover us, but our lads holdin' the line to the south won't last much longer."

Anthony crossed the makeshift infirmary to reach Nandar Aye.

- "Forgive me, Major," he apologized, seizing her by the arm. "Come, Myers will get us across the river. If we don't do it now, we're done for!"

She gave the surgeon an inquiring look, who nodded with understanding.

- "I thank you for your assistance," he declared, returning his attention to the leg that now hung by a shred of skin. "May God help you!"

She slowly set down the instruments she held, contemplating one final time the rows of wounded around her, as if asking them silently for forgiveness, then followed Anthony and Myers toward the river. In the distance, they glimpsed Sayer in company of Pitt, who was shifting with impatience. Sayer's face decomposed with horror when he saw her covered in blood and he rushed toward her, arms extended, as if to catch her in case of collapse.

- "Are you wounded, my dear?"

- "I'm fine," she reassured him with a forced smile. "It's the blood of the wounded," she added, provoking a grimace of horror on the professor's face who took her in his arms and held her close for a long moment.

The news of the retreat spread through the troops like wildfire. Ragged columns set in motion as the evacuation of the wounded began: Gurkhas hobbling on bare feet, bloodied Indians, KOYLI soldiers covered in bandages limping. Some, too weak, collapsed and did not rise again. Spare grenades were thrown into rice paddies, weapons abandoned or broken. The survivors carried only what would float: empty cans, planks torn from huts. Charred bamboo crackled in the fire, barely covering the roar of aircraft that continued to decimate the survivors. Death struck at random, a shell fragment here, a stray bullet there. At the water's edge, the spectacle defied comprehension. Hundreds of heads emerged and disappeared in the waters where they plunged en masse. Between two crests of foam, Anthony spotted a group of Gurkhas astride a submerged log, paddling with obstinate slowness while machine-gun bursts lacerated the surface.

He picked up a rectangular steel mess tin lying on the ground, then went to fetch his satchel from which he extracted his journal and Nandar Aye's book, carefully placing them in the metal container before sealing it hermetically. He replaced the box in his bag, carefully tightening the cloth protecting the stone tablet, then went to rejoin the rest of the group on the bank. Myers and Pitt, in underwear and shirts, were finishing the construction of a raft with planks and bamboo, testing its buoyancy by pressing on it with their bare feet. They nodded with satisfied expressions.

- "Let's go!" announced the sergeant, calling his charges to join him.

Nandar Aye, her *longyi* pulled over her blouse around her chest as if preparing for bathing, was donning an oversized combat trouser discovered abandoned in the sand. She knotted shoelaces between belt loops and tightened them to secure the garment around her waist. She took a few steps into the water to rejoin her companions, already assembled around the ephemeral craft they were slowly pushing toward the open.

- "I don't know how to swim," she confessed with apprehension as the water already reached her belly. It was the first time Anthony perceived fear in her voice.

- "Nor can I!" seconded Pitt with solidarity. "But if a mangy dog can do it, we bloomin' well can too! You just got to thrash about like you're fightin' the water." He mimed dogpaddling with a ridiculousness that would have made them laugh had they not all been preoccupied with their survival.

- "Stay beside me. I'll look after you," offered Anthony, showing her where to grip whilst positioning himself between her and Sayer, exhausted, who gave him a grateful look.

Anthony placed his satchel in the middle of the raft, gripped it with one hand while firmly holding Nandar Aye's with the other. In a few steps, they lost their footing and felt the current sweep them away with force. Anthony and the two soldiers began kicking to steer their craft diagonally. Nandar Aye attempted to master her panic each time a wave submerged her, her breathing gasping, her arms clenched to maintain herself on their heap of debris. The professor struggled against his fatigue while trying to maintain his grip.

Despite their efforts, it seemed they were not advancing and the opposite bank appeared always as distant. Sprays of water were lifted from the surface all around them. A machine gun took them for target, raking their flotilla. Cries and calls rang out in all directions. Two men slipped from a wooden panel and found themselves swept in their direction, waving their arms in despair. They disappeared beneath the surface ten meters from him, never to reappear. Anthony himself began to feel exhaustion overcome him and had to struggle to continue moving his legs. Several times, Nandar Aye slipped and nearly went under. Each time, he held her and helped her back up.

The sounds grew more muffled as they moved away from the eastern bank. The ricochets of bullets became more sporadic, then ceased. After an hour, they finally reached the middle of the river. In silence, they turned their gaze toward the gaping hole that cut the bridge in two. They understood now. It was Major-General Smyth who had ordered the destruction of the bridge by the sappers to check the Japanese advance. He who had also destroyed the boats to deny them to the enemy. He who had thus abandoned half the 17th Division to their fate on the eastern bank.

- "Right then, five minutes we'll take," proposed Myers. "Then we'll work in shifts so nobody gets completely knackered."

- "No complaints from me!" gasped Pitt, who collapsed on the plank before him.

Yet their respite lasted scarcely long. A growing hum filled the air. A new barrage of detonations pierced the silence, raising spouts just meters away. The Japanese fighters resumed their deadly ballet above the river.

- "Come on, move!" ordered the sergeant. "We'll be done for if we stop muckin' about in the middle of this river!"

Nearly an hour later, they finally approached the western bank. Anthony could no longer feel his legs, only the proximity of dry land offering him the strength to continue. He relaxed as their deliverance drew near and felt Nandar Aye's wrist slip from his hand.

In a second, the young woman disappeared beneath the waters. He plunged without hesitation, driven by terror like an electric shock. He swam frantically in the direction she had taken, his hands searching desperately in the dark waters for his companion. Opening his eyes was useless. He could not even see his hand before him. Yet he continued. Screaming in his head, barely restraining himself from calling her name to preserve his air. It began to fail him, a burning sensation seizing his lungs. But he refused to yield to the primitive instinct pushing him to the surface. He was seized by a first convulsion but fought on. Suddenly, his hand felt the caress of seaweed. No, not seaweed. Hair. She was there! He gave one final kick and closed his arms around the lifeless body of the young woman, bringing her up with him. He broke the surface, gasped avidly, and raised her head to hold it in the open air.

A reflex finally awakened her and convulsed her body with raspy coughs. Anthony laughed with relief mingled with tears, whispering his love in her ear, while her breathing returned to a regular rhythm. He held her close to prevent her from sinking again and brought her back to the bank where the other crew members waited anxiously. He dragged her and laid her on the sand, then collapsed beside her, utterly exhausted. Sayer rushed to the young woman, taking her in his arms weeping, stroking her hair. Anthony raised himself to contemplate the eastern bank from which black columns of smoke still escaped. They had succeeded. They had crossed the Styx and fled hell. Half-naked, without equipment, without water or food, yet safe and sound. Myers handed him his satchel with a pat on the back, while Nandar Aye and Sayer looked at him with gazes charged with gratitude.

- "Don't go droppin' off!" Pitt teased. "We've still got forty miles to Pegu!" he declared, slapping his shoulder like some devilish Charon.

Chapter XVII

Between Sittang and Pegu, Burma, February 1942

The sun was declining when Myers was torn from his sleep. Exhausted by their crossing, they had abandoned themselves to the lulling of distant detonations that continued to tear at the eastern bank, and had sunk into unconsciousness on the warm sand. He opened his eyes in panic at the touch of a hand grazing his arm, sitting bolt upright like a spring, muscles tensed for confrontation. His heart slowed at the sight of a Gurkha's smiling face, only inches from his own.

- "We can't stay here, Sergeant!"

Myers seized the outstretched hand to rise, surprised by the vigor concealed in this squat lad who could hardly measure more than five and a half feet. The Gurkhas formed the most esteemed troops of the Indian Army: cheerful in spirit, faithful, valiant, they never deserted nor fled combat, fear remaining to them a perfectly foreign sentiment. In truth, there existed no better friend nor worse enemy than a Gurkha. Myers made out a second Nepali who stood apart, clad in the tatters of a mismatched uniform. None was armed. They possessed nothing. Human shadows who, like him, had probably ingested nothing for days.

His last meal dated to the day before their arrival at Moke Pa Lin, when he had managed to shoot a monkey, sharing this charred flesh with the company. Pitt had found it had an aftertaste of pork. Myers retained only the memory of its charcoal flavor. Yet, hungry as he was, he had to rise and continue, and he hastened to drag his companions from their stupor.

Their column set in motion again, carefully avoiding the main road that ran alongside the railway. Japanese aviation reigned as absolute master of the skies. Myers in the lead, their serpentine file plunged through a field of elephant grass two meters high that bordered the bank, deliberately striking the ground to drive away cobras and vipers that might lurk there. Their progress was laborious, the vegetation gripping them like arms seeking to engulf them in this Sargasso Sea. A hundred meters further on, they emerged onto desiccated rice paddies that unfurled their monotonous expanse as far as the eye could see. Scarcely had they set foot on the cracked earth than they immediately regretted the meager shade of the grasses. The sunbaked soil burned their feet. The little coolness their swim had brought vanished instantly.

They marched forward in single file, with no protection against the star that lashed them without mercy. They were hot, hungry, and thirsty, and two to three days' march still separated them from their destination. Not a puddle, nothing that suggested the presence of water in this lunar landscape, save the roiling billows that traced mirages on the horizon. Anthony had almost come to regret those hours of calm that Sayer and he had enjoyed that morning, leaning against a tree, despite the shells that had continued to rain around them.

At the end of the plot, they reached the edge of the earthen dikes that gridded the fields. Their relief was heightened when the Gurkhas discovered ribwort plantains at the edge of the path. Under the astonished gaze of the British, one of them broke off the central stem and began to chew it with relish. He tore off other plants and handed them to his companions who imitated him. Anthony crushed his stem with apprehension between his teeth, before feeling a trickle of water with an herbaceous scent flooding his mouth. He swallowed greedily this nectar, the best he had ever tasted it seemed to him, letting out a burst of laughter.

- "Sergeant, I'll have a bottle of this!" jested Sayer, who was recovering some color.

- "This vintage's better than Château Sittang," added Anthony, recalling the muddy taste of the river water.

- "Doesn't compare to Moke Pa Lin!" argued Pitt, referring to the putrid pond from which he had drunk the day before.

The four Englishmen laughed heartily. For the first time, they thought they might manage. Certain now that they would not die of thirst, their priority became finding sustenance. They continued to wind between the fields on the dike's path, encountering no living soul for a good hour. Finally, they glimpsed silhouettes that stood out as shadow puppets against the sun plunging toward the horizon. The huts of a village broke the sad horizontality of the landscape.

- "Come on then, let's have a look round. But keep your wits about you, stay sharp!" cautioned Myers.

At their approach, children tending buffalo scattered with cries of terror toward the interior of the hamlet. They were about to enter when a group of men emerged from the houses and massed to bar their passage, armed with *dahs*, sticks, and forbidding expressions. The crowd encircled them, advancing with threatening intent. The Gurkhas seized sharp bamboo poles lying on the ground, promptly imitated by Pitt and Myers. They formed a defensive position, back to back, with their three charges in the center. The vise was tightening, announcing mortal confrontation. They would not hold long, at one against ten, exhausted as they were, with their makeshift weapons. Suddenly, Nandar Aye pushed past Myers and advanced toward the eldest of the villagers, a lean, graying man, bare-chested, his *longyi* knotted like shorts, his thighs covered with tattoos.

- "Stop!"

The order cracked as he brandished his machete above his head in a threatening manner, causing Myers and Pitt to take a step forward, ready to leap to rescue the girl. Impassive, she made a sign with her hand for them to remain behind.

- "*Mingala bah, Thu-Gyi U*[76]," she began with assurance. "May peace be upon you, venerable father of the village. We wish you no harm. I offer you my most humble respects."

---

[76] A polite greeting intended for a village chief.

The old man appeared to soften somewhat, without lowering his guard. Sayer and Anthony, who understood Burmese, followed the conversation attentively, in expectation of its outcome. The soldiers, meanwhile, grasping nothing of what was being said, continued to watch the crowd facing them with an air of defiance.

- "*Thami*[77], you speak with politeness. But your appearance contradicts your words. If you think you can deceive me..."

He directed his gaze toward the trousers Nandar Aye wore with a moue of contempt, mistrust anchored in his pupils.

- "These men with you, in tatters and without arms... Are you criminals who escaped from prison? The guards freed the convicts before fleeing!"

- "These men are British soldiers. We wish only a little food before continuing our journey."

- "*Tho-saung kala*[78] soldiers? Where are their uniforms? You lie!"

- "*Thu-Gyi U*, we've marched for days, pursued by the Japanese, without drinking nor eating. We crossed the river swimming after the bridge's explosion. We've lost everything."

- "The bridge exploded?" It seemed inconceivable to him that such a metal structure could simply be annihilated.

---

[77] « Daughter » in Burmese.
[78] "Foreigners sheep" in Burmese, in reference to their woolen clothes.

- "*Thu-gyi U*," resumed the young woman, seizing on his confusion. "We're not criminals. Look at them. They're no danger to you. They can scarcely stand. We ask for only a little rice and water, in the name of the hospitality our ancestors taught us."

The village chief appeared to reflect. Already, around him, the men surrounding him began to murmur and lower their weapons.

- "Maung Tin!" shouted a female voice from the rear of the rank.

The men parted before an old woman, thin and bent double, yet who walked with a firm and resolved step.

- "Let them pass!" she ordered with authority. "Do you think criminals would beg alms in broad daylight instead of waiting for night to attack us?" she interrogated with both hands on her hips.

Without awaiting response, she smiled at Nandar Aye and took her by the hand to lead her toward the village with surprising energy for so frail a being.

- "Come, my child! And tell these poor wretches to follow us. We'll put some flesh back on your bones!"

Nandar Aye invited her companions with a wave of her hand. Anthony and Sayer, who had grasped everything, were the first to follow her lead, followed by the soldiers who let their improvised spears fall. The village chief remained standing there, his knife dangling at the end of his arm, watching the procession file past without knowing how to react to his wife's intervention.

- "*Kyeizu tin bah de*[79]," said Anthony in perfect Burmese, which drew a smile from the old man who offered a broad crimson grin, his teeth ravaged by betel.

The procession passed through the crowd, now more curious than threatening, which observed them with interest. Some were seeing Europeans for the first time and pushed their children toward this cohort of wretches with pallid complexions, then laughed when they returned alarmed. All dispersed when the refugees entered the chief's dwelling, while the sun finished stretching the shadows against the night.

At their hostess's invitation, they all collapsed onto woven bamboo flooring, throwing themselves like rustics upon the green tea she served while chatting cheerfully with Nandar Aye. The rest of the evening was devoted to savoring the feast she prepared for them. For indeed it appeared to them as such: a dish of rice garnished with shrimp and dried fish, accompanied by vegetables and *nga pi*[80], served abundantly on banana leaves. Unfortunately, their stomachs, weakened by their forced fast, could not assimilate the quantity they would have wished to consume. Yet they nonetheless had the pleasant sensation of being quite replete when they lit the cheroots their host distributed generously, accompanied by a draught of rice liquor.

---

[79] "Thank you very much" in Burmese.
[80] Fermented fish paste. A traditional condiment in Burmese cuisine.

Nandar Aye came to retrieve her book from Anthony, who extracted it from the mess tin, intact. She went to sit near Sayer to read it by candlelight. Anthony would have liked to speak to her, to take advantage of this unexpected respite. But the incident of the previous day was too present. Not only the guilt due to the lie and Win Thu's death, but also the terror he had felt when the Burman discovered them. He came to his senses realizing he had been staring at Nandar Aye, who was feigning to ignore him. Then his gaze caught Sayer's, who was studying him, lips pressed thin and features frozen with suspicion. Anthony immediately averted his eyes. Did he know? Had he guessed that they were deceiving him? How much longer could they continue this charade? Each passing day made their deception harder to maintain and their betrayal more unforgivable.

From the corner of his eye, he saw Nandar Aye hand the book to Sayer and rise toward the exit. It was out of the question that he followed her as he had the previous night. This would not fail to confirm Sayer's suspicions. Myers and Pitt themselves regularly cast oblique glances at him. Reluctantly, he drew closer to the KOYLIs who were launching at full voice, aided by alcohol, into *Sod 'Em All*. The Gurkhas and the village chief responded with songs in their own languages. He took the bamboo cup offered to him and drank it in one draft, feeling the beverage sear his throat. They promptly refilled it, also filled their own cups, raised them with multiple euphoric "cheers," then drained them in a single draught, the two Gurkhas striking their chests with evident pleasure. The third glass went down even better, seeming to have scarcely any effect at all.

Anthony felt the blood return to his numbed limbs and the pain fade. His muscles relaxed and his mind grew hazy. He felt good for the first time since... he could not remember. Probably when Nandar Aye and he had consummated their union, their bodies in the complete relaxation that followed. He wanted to live, to take advantage of each moment of pleasure. Far from the suffocating boarding school where his parents had exiled him. Far from the discipline of the British community. Far from the continuous self-control in Sayer's presence, that good but terribly sad man. He wanted to be with Nandar Aye. It was decided; he would confess everything to Sayer upon their return to Rangoon. And damn the scandal, the prejudices, the rumors. And so, what if he lost his university position and Sayer put her on the street? He would find other employment. They would live together. Perhaps they would live on less. But what does material comfort matter when you are in love and the future lays before you? He suddenly recalled that the Japanese were invading Burma. He dismissed this ridiculous thought from his mind. They had reached Sittang, but these savages would go no further. Reinforcements had just arrived. Rangoon would never fall.

Thereupon he rose, staggering, to begin *Chit Ya Lat*, the most popular song of May Shin. The assembly was delighted, impressed by his performance in impeccable Burmese. Pitt whistled, Myers launched "huzzas," and the village chief rose to accompany him. Then they reseated themselves to take fresh cups of liqueur. Anthony drained his in a single draft, just as Nandar Aye returned to the hut. He cast her an intense gaze. She replied with a detached, almost haughty air in which he read disappointment. She went to sit by Sayer without a word. Anthony felt anger boil within him. It was decided; he would confess everything this evening, immediately. He could bear it no longer. He was about to speak when an even more pressing instinct possessed him entirely. He rushed outside the hut and vomited loudly at the foot of the wooden steps, doubled over, scarcely able to stand. Everything came up, including the dinner he had not yet digested.

He heard, above him, exclamations of disgust and laughter from his companions, climbed back in staggering steps, offered an embarrassed smile to the soldiers, and went to collapse in a corner, not daring to look at Nandar Aye and Sayer. His head was spinning, he had the impression of being borne again by the waters of the Sittang. Despite the lies he told himself, he knew. He knew he was afraid, not merely of present danger, of the Japanese army, of death. No, he was terrified at the thought of losing everything: Nandar Aye, his status, his future, when Sayer discovered their affair, or when Rangoon fell under the sway of the Empire of the Rising Sun. It was his life, his bearings, his very identity that was melting before his eyes. He had no control over events. All he could do was survive. Nandar Aye was Burmese, her mother lived in Rangoon. Would she agree to follow him if the invasion forced him to flee?

He discreetly opened his eyes. The songs grew quieter, fatigue and intoxication overwhelming the soldiers. No one knew what tomorrow would bring. Sayer had stretched out and appeared to sleep. Anthony noticed that Nandar Aye, for her part, was looking at him. No longer with disdain, but with sadness and affection. No doubt she shared his doubts and his fears. He felt despair submerge him like a slow tide, gentle but inexorable. He closed his eyes and wept silently, then finally fell asleep.

Chapter XVIII

Between Sittang and Pegu, Burma, February 1942

The rooster's song pried them from their early-morning stupor. Already, the village hummed with activity, while they emerged, heavy-limbed and unwilling, from the depths of a leaden sleep. A sleep that, for all its restorative powers, could never hope to mend their battered strength. Everyone managed to reclaim a shred of vigor, save for Anthony, whose skull was seized by an iron vise the moment he tried to sit up.

- "Hell of a hangover, eh, mate?" Pitt teased, looking as if last night's torrents of alcohol had left no trace on him.

Anthony emitted a groan but refrained from responding. Migraine and hunger cruelly reminded him of the previous day's excesses. However, the aroma of sesame rice rekindled some hope. He greeted their hostess with a grateful smile. All rushed upon these provisions, devouring them while washing them down with tea, paying homage to the munificence of the couple who had sheltered them. Had they been at the prestigious Strand in Rangoon, they could not have been happier. Yet Myers came to disturb their peace. The Japanese army might be crossing the river. They had to take the road without delay. Faces closed, their reality recalling itself mercilessly to them. Their situation was nonetheless less desperate: they had eaten and regained some strength. They could count on the assistance of the local populations during the three-day march that still separated them from their destination.

Myers requested Nandar Aye's services to speak with their host. The latter agreed to guide them to the next hamlet. They thus hoped to progress from village to village, finding at each stage the resources necessary to reach Pegu. Myers suggested cutting across the fields to the railway, which they would follow toward Ka Li, to finally reach the road. This route had the advantage of avoiding the axes that Japanese aviation would certainly survey. His proposal was adopted unanimously.

The chief's wife reappeared with her arms laden with gifts. Each received a *longyi* and a conical bamboo hat. Myers and Pitt manifested the liveliest gratitude, they who had traveled since the day before in undergarments. She also recommended that they cover their faces and exposed parts of their bodies with mud, which would protect them not only from mosquitoes and the sun, but would make them pass for natives in the eyes of Japanese pilots.

- "Smart old lass, eh?" Pitt whistled admiringly at the old woman's ingenuity. "I'll tell you, Sergeant, your own mother wouldn't know you now!" he joked as the NCO finished tying on his *longyi*, the headman assisting with a deft knot in front.

They thanked their benefactress with expansive gratitude, words, even skillfully translated by Nandar Aye, proving powerless to express their recognition. She had accomplished far more than saving their lives: she had restored their hope. Then they departed under the curious and amused gazes of villagers taking the path to their fields, escorted by a troop of children, still wary but less terrified, who quickly turned back toward the village that dissolved into the morning mist.

In the days that followed, they continued to advance through the immense mosaic of rice paddies. Nothing broke the monotonous horizontality save the *stūpa* of a pagoda rising here and there in the distance, a tiny finger pointing toward the infinite azure that enveloped them. No shadow to shelter them. Each village chief had conducted them to his counterpart in the next, who had accepted, despite the risk of reprisals, to lead them to the following stage. Thus, they had benefited from a network of relays. It was not a pleasant stroll, but they no longer suffered from that extreme exhaustion, and their destination finally seemed attainable.

On the fourth day, they reached the railway, as Myers had predicted. Their guide left them now that it was impossible for them to go astray. All they had to do was follow the rails, and they could hope to reach Pegu by evening, if they maintained their pace.

Noon surprised them at the edge of a village like those they had crossed so far. Myers proposed making one last halt there. That evening, they would be guests of the British Army, and the four Englishmen began to dream of *corned beef* after the monotonous rice seasoned with *ngapi* that had constituted their diet since their flight.

They were about to enter when a gathering of armed men barred their passage, as before. The soldiers did not bother to gather sticks to defend themselves, remaining back while Nandar Aye advanced to parley. Yet, before she could speak a word, one of the villagers rushed forward, his *dah* raised, to strike it down upon Pitt. The blade deeply cut the forearm he had raised by reflex to parry the blow. His cry of pain tore through the tense silence that had prevailed until then, answered by the growls and vociferations of the mob. The soldiers formed a circle to confront their assailants. Yet this time they had nothing with which to defend themselves. They stood no chance against this crowd armed to the teeth. Myers promptly tore one of the sleeves from his shirt and tied it around the bloodied limb that Pitt clutched while uttering oaths drowned beneath his sharp cries.

- "My brothers!" Nandar Aye called out, voice ringing clear as she raised her arms to calm the villagers. "Lower your weapons! These men are not convicts escaped from prison!"

- "We know that!" snapped a commanding voice. "They're *kala pyu*[81] soldiers!"

A shaven-headed monk, draped in a crimson robe, stepped forward to face the young woman. Silence reigned. Even Pitt choked back his pain.

---

[81] Literally "white Indian" in Burmese, a derogatory term used for Westerners, especially the British.

- "Venerable *Sayadaw*," Nandar Aye addressed him with reverence, "these men are indeed British soldiers, but they mean you no harm. Allow us safe passage to Pegu, and they will leave you in peace."

The monk eyed her with contempt, his voice cracking like a whip:

- "How dare you talk to me like that? You're siding with our enemies! These oppressors have contaminated our sacred land for far too long. The time for liberation is here! Justice has to strike them down now!"

A growl of approval stirred the crowd when he designated the soldiers with an accusatory gesture. Anthony and Sayer trembled at these words. The soldiers needed no understanding to grasp that their end was approaching. Nandar Aye could do nothing to save them this time. They stood braced, muscles taut, ready to rush upon the first adversary who presented himself. They would likely die, but not without taking several to hell with them.

- "Look at them," the monk pressed on. "Even when they dress like us, you can smell their masters' arrogance on them. The Japanese are coming to break the British yoke. It's a sign of *kamma*. These demons must be destroyed, right here, right now!"

Nandar Aye lowered her gaze, weighing her response. When she looked up, her eyes blazed with conviction.

- "Venerable *Sayadaw*, your words touch the heart of every child of our sacred land. I share your fury at oppression, your burning wish to see Burma free and independent. The shackles imposed on us by colonizers have too long bound the spirit of our people!"

She was speaking now chiefly to the crowd, who murmured agreement, swaying them with the same fervor as the monk. She paused, letting her words take root before she resumed:

- "But if I may, let me humbly remind you of what the Buddha taught. Doesn't the first precept forbid us from harming living beings? These men are unarmed and begging for charity. Isn't that humiliation enough for these *thakins*?" she asked, her tone sharpened with irony on the final word. "Wouldn't it be more compassionate to let them live?"

The monk gave a harsh laugh, his features hardening:

- "You just repeat the scriptures without understanding them, you ignorant woman! You forget that the *Dhamma*[82] itself must be protected! When demons like these threaten the Sacred Law, defending ourselves is our duty. These invaders have desecrated our pagodas by refusing to take off their shoes in our holy places!"

His voice soared as he turned his back to Nandar Aye to rouse the villagers:

- "The blood of these oppressors will nourish our soil! Let their corpses be offerings to the *nats*[83] and a warning to all their kind!"

---

[82] The Buddha's teachings (in Pali).
[83] Animist spirits incorporated into Burmese *Theravada* Buddhism.

The villagers moved closer, faces twisted with hate, eyes burning with a hunger for blood. Nandar Aye shifted, still standing firm before her companions. Her voice now urgent, yet retaining the respect demanded by the situation:

- "Venerable *Sayadaw*," she called, sweeping the crowd with her gaze, ""I didn't say that for the sake of these *kala pyus*, but to protect my own people, my brothers."

The crowd wavered; every eye turned to her.

- "Explain yourself!" barked a villager.

- "British reinforcements have arrived from England. Fresh troops, well equipped, and with those terrifying machines of war they call tanks. They are giant vehicles, unstoppable, running on iron tracks instead of wheels..."

A ripple of anxiety ran through the throng. Sensing their hesitation, she pressed on:

- "They are only a few *kawthas*[84] away, between Pegu and Waw, getting ready to launch a counterattack. If they hear you've killed Britons, the reprisals will be brutal. Those tanks could flatten your homes like elephants crushing sugarcane. Is getting rid of a few enemies worth risking the lives of a whole village?"

The monk was thunderstruck, but already voices were rising all around:

---

[84] A traditional Burmese unit of distance, approximately 1.28 km.

- "She speaks the truth, my cousins in Ka Li saw those machines..."

- "My brother, who trades along the Pegu road, told of thousands of *kala pyu* soldiers camped there..."

Doubt spread as fast as wildfire. The monk, sensing his sway erode, bellowed:

- "Lies! This harlot's in league with the enemy and trying to deceive you with her stories. Don't listen to her!"

But the villagers were no longer listening to him, speaking amongst themselves, their *dahs* gradually lowering. The murderous unanimity was fracturing into a hubbub of worried discussion. Nandar Aye cast a discrete glance at her companions. With an imperceptible nod of her head, she indicated they should follow her. With deliberate slowness, they began to retreat, their measured steps assuming an orderly withdrawal, never turning their backs. They were not fleeing; they were simply resuming their journey with the peaceful confidence of those whose conscience was clear. Pitt refrained from emitting the slightest whimper that might awaken the killer instinct in the mob. The monk desperately tried to regain the attention of his flock, but they persevered in their debate. The atmosphere of lynching had turned into anxious deliberation.

Nandar Aye and her charges finally managed to reach the railway, which they resumed following, moving away from the dwellings, the murmur of disputes gradually fading. A few villagers undertook to stalk them at respectable distance, hostile, yet without attempting to approach. Then, weary, their shadows vanished. It was only when the village disappeared behind a grove of palms that they dared breathe freely.

Nandar Aye stopped to lean against a telegraph pole, eyes closed, her legs trembling. Myers took the opportunity to examine Pitt's wound. His life was not in danger, but the cut demanded the care of a doctor as soon as possible. Myers and Pitt met her gaze, expressing silently their gratitude to she who had saved them through intelligence alone. Sayer and Anthony, seeing her vulnerability, rushed toward her.

- "Are you alright, dear?" the professor asked, concern etched into his voice.

- "I'm fine, thank you," she replied, her voice still uncertain as she straightened, visibly irritated at having shown weakness.

Anthony longed to offer her support, to take her in his arms and comfort her, but propriety demanded distance. Yet as their group resumed its march toward Pegu, with Myers and his men leading the way, he positioned himself at her side.

- "Nandar Aye, you're incredible!" He forced himself to maintain the respectful tone he used in Sayer's presence. "The way you turned that scoundrel monk's arguments against him! You're so convincing they never realized you were misleading them!"

- "I wasn't misleading them. I told them exactly what I believed," she shot back with blunt honesty, not slowing her pace, her gaze fixed ahead.

Anthony felt as though the wind had been knocked from his chest.

- "Surely you weren't serious about defending independence? You're better than that!"

She stopped abruptly, turned to face him, and fixed him with a look so full of anger that he sensed she was barely restraining the urge to slap him. She resumed walking with a stride that radiated controlled fury. Deep down, he knew he should have held his tongue, but he pressed on regardless.

- "I can see you're angry, but you can't deny the benefits the Empire has brought to our country! " She seemed taken aback by his appropriation of Burma. For him, it was self-evident: he was born in the colony. "Look at this railway, the hospitals, the schools where you and your generation were educated. Without us, this place would still be a backward kingdom stuck in ignorance and barbarism!"

Her eyes flashed. She straightened and answered him in a voice trembling with rage:

- "Barbarism, Anthony? Barbarism? Our monasteries were teaching writing when your ancestors were still painting their faces blue to wage naked warfare against the Romans. Think of the tablet we found at Win Ka: who were the illiterate barbarians in the age of our first Buddhist kingdoms?" She anticipated his objection and added swiftly: "And our literacy rate was sixty percent before your invasion! We did perfectly well without your schools!"

- "You're romanticizing your past, Nandar Aye," Anthony countered with patronizing certainty. "Your monks taught no science, merely passing down beliefs recited by heart, generation after generation. We brought the light of reason where superstition reigned!"

She quickened her pace, kicking up clouds of red dust beneath her bare feet.

- "John Stuart Mill himself wrote of our moral duty to guide less civilized peoples until they could govern themselves. It's our responsibility."

Nandar Aye gave a bitter laugh.

- "Your responsibility? How noble, dressing systematic pillage in the language of duty. You speak of development, but where does the profit from our rice, our teak, our oil, go?"

She turned her face toward him as she walked, her eyes brilliant with tears of rage:

- "Your so-called 'moral duty' to civilize us is nothing but a pretext for enslavement. We produce, but we do not own! Our farmers have become serfs on their own soil, if they haven't been driven out by the moneylenders you brought from India. Your 'benefits' have impoverished us! So, spare us these gifts. Take them back, I beg you!"

Anthony could not believe it. They had never spoken of politics. Despite their intimacy, she had never broached such subjects. He studied her as he might have an unknown woman, perceiving with horror that he knew nothing of what animated her. Was their passion merely carnal? How could he claim to love a person so different from him, the opposite of the image he had formed of her? The dreamy, romantic student had faded behind the fierce revolutionary. Had she played the comedy before him, full of duplicity, as she did with Sayer? Did she genuinely love him when she visibly abhorred all that he represented? He felt deceived, betrayed, and anger took hold.

- "Demagoguery!" he hissed sarcastically. "Your rice? It wouldn't even exist without the irrigation systems we built that turned Burma into Asia's rice bowl. Your oil? You wouldn't even know about it if we hadn't drilled for it. And our trains connect you to the world. Before, your goods just rotted in the villages because there was no way to move them. We're the ones who created jobs, opportunities, a modern economy!"

- "An extraction economy that made us your coolies! And when we demand our share, our due, you answer with repression!"

She thrust a finger accusingly beneath his nose:

- "*Your* laws protect only *your* interests! Your 'rule of law' is merely the rule of *your* rights! A two-tiered justice that shields the white man! The institutional racism you've imposed is designed to divide and conquer, sowing discord among Burma's peoples. There were no 'ethnic tensions' before your arrival. You created them with your classification of 'races,' placing us Burmans at the very bottom of the hierarchy in our own land!"

Anthony, realizing that their exchanges were degenerating into sterile confrontation, attempted to calm the situation. After all, he himself was shocked by the segregation imposed by the colonial administration. He loved Burma, its people, its culture. And he had to acknowledge that the Empire sometimes made mistakes in the management of its colonies.

- "You're right about that. But things are changing. The new reforms will afford our country greater autonomy" – that possessive "our" again, which invariably set Nandar Aye's teeth on edge - "with all the protections our impartial legal system offers. Isn't that progress compared to the feudal system we ended, which subjected you to the whims of a despotic king?"

- "Tell me, Anthony," she challenged, "you speak of rights. What of the Burmans' right to self-determination? Did you ever ask us if we wanted your 'civilization'? If democracy is a sound principle, shouldn't it apply universally? Would the English accept a foreign power governing them, however benevolently? Then why impose it upon us?"

She had scored a direct hit. Anthony was completely unmoored. Unable to admit defeat, he grasped at the first argument that came to mind:

- "Because you aren't ready yet! You lack the experience, the institutions, the proper education..."

- "Ready? Were the Americans ready when they wrested their independence from you? And what would Britain be today without their support? A German colony! It's for us to decide when we're ready. And how shall we ever be if you persist in treating us as children? It's a vicious circle!"

She saw the confusion written across his face and drove home her point:

- "I tell you: we're ready! Perhaps it's you who aren't ready to grant us the freedom we deserve and demand. So don't blame us if we seek it from those who promise it!"

And with that, she quickened her pace, leaving him behind as she rejoined the soldiers marching ahead, leaving Anthony reeling. It was Sayer's calm, almost paternal voice that drew him back to himself:

- "Don't hold it against her," the scholar began. "Not that she's wrong. I share her sympathies. But you can't understand her sensitivity on these matters without knowing her personal story."

Anthony flinched. For a moment, he was tempted to protest: he knew Nandar Aye intimately, better than anyone, or so he believed. Yet that certainty fractured immediately. Of her origins, he knew almost nothing, only scattered fragments she had let slip.

- "Her personal story?"

Sayer inclined his head, like a man forced to touch upon a wound still raw.

- "What happened to her father, to her family," the academic explained. "You didn't know, but our march to Pegu is a painful pilgrimage for her. Like returning to a grave. She was born there, where her parents, humble farmers, once owned a small plot of land."

- "What happened?"

- "The same to what happened to thousands of others. Ruined by their debts to the *Chettiars*[85] during the Depression of the thirties, they lost everything. They made their way to Rangoon in the depths of recession, begging for work."

- "That's terrible," Anthony whispered. "I didn't know." He immediately regretted the violence with which he had just treated her.

- "That's only the beginning. Her father found work as a coolie on the docks. Her mother sold vegetables at street corners. Her grandmother minded the children. You think you've suffered these past days? It's nothing compared to what she endured then. Her brother and sister didn't reach adolescence."

Silence hung heavily. Sayer's gaze lingered on the silhouette of the young woman walking ahead of them. Anthony, despite himself, felt his eyes begin to blur. He turned away and brushed a tear from his cheek with the back of his hand, trying to hide it. Sayer continued, his voice stripped of all emphasis:

- "Already, Burmans were watching their jobs disappear to Indians, wretched souls themselves, but willing to work for pittance. Can you blame them? They were fleeing famine in

---

[85] Community of moneylenders originating from Tamil Nadu who dominated the Burmese credit market, typically charging relatively moderate rates compared to local usurers.

Madras or Bihar, hoping for something better here. Companies stopped hiring Burmans altogether."

- "The riots," Anthony said, the word half a guess.

- "The riots," Sayer confirmed. "She was only eight when those of 1930 broke out. Her father took part, was arrested, and locked away in Insein for a few months. When he was freed, he couldn't find work. So, he opened a miserable stall - cheroots, betel nuts - just to survive. But with interest rates at twenty percent, you can imagine what that meant. Income shrank while rice prices soared. For thousands, a daily meal became a luxury."

- "I remember little of it," Anthony said slowly, shaking his head. "I was already away at Winchester, only coming back to Rangoon during Summer, spending other holidays in Birmingham with my aunt. But I know what I read: the poverty, the unemployment, waves of migrants fleeing the countryside for Rangoon, the peasant rebellion of Saya San... A terrible time."

- "Precisely," Sayer continued. "Tensions mounted further, building toward the riots of 1938. She lived through them at sixteen, watching her father beaten to death by military police before her eyes. Don't think I'm attempting to absolve anyone: dozens of Indians were massacred by U Saw's *Myochit* nationalists. The army responded to violence with blind violence of its own. But for her," he sighed, "her father was a martyr. Never take that from her. She would never forgive you."

- "What happened to her afterward?" Anthony asked, his voice trembling.

- "As you can imagine, her mother's meager income was no longer sufficient. Her grandmother, fortunately..." He paused. "I say 'fortunately,' though it's absolutely terrible - what else can one say? - Her grandmother succumbed to grief, one mouth fewer to feed. Even then, they found themselves on the street. Then, a miracle: the director of a Methodist school noticed Nandar Aye's gifts, paid for her schooling, and asked for my support. I took her mother into my employ and have housed them both at my home since," he concluded, offering no further details.

Anthony observed that Sayer had omitted to make any allusion to the relationship he maintained with Nandar Aye, avoiding describing how she had become his mistress. This discretion hardly surprised him and he preferred, truth be told, to know nothing of it. What he had just learned had so profoundly upset him that no other consideration could have mattered compared to the suffering in which the young woman had grown.

Through a movement of selfishness he immediately recognized, he felt some bitterness at never having received directly from her the account of this ordeal. But this wound to his pride promptly dissipated beneath a flood of immense tenderness. He finally understood whence came the strength she had manifested since their flight: her endurance, her resolution, the courage she drew from mysterious reserves. He also grasped the deep roots of her pro-independence convictions. He marveled even more at her magnanimity at Sittang, ministering to the British wounded, to these enemies, living symbols of the empire that had caused all her ills. What did he represent himself in her eyes? This question tortured him. Could he ever be anything other than the incarnation of an oppression she abhorred?

He burned to hold her in his arms, to testify to his love, this sudden adoration that overwhelmed him, to declare that he was ready to renounce his prejudices for her. But he constrained himself to continue his march at Sayer's side, condemned to cherish in silence she who walked before him, out of reach.

Chapter XIX

Pegu, Burma, March 1942

- "You confirm that he was a spy?"

Lieutenant Colonel Thomas Bromhead Butt asked the question without lifting his eyes from the report that commanded his attention. The headquarters of the 2nd KOYLI at Pegu consisted of nothing more than a waterproof canvas tent, a three-meter square shelter for the modest remains of command: a folding metal table, the single chair he occupied, a camp bed banished to the shadows, and empty ammunition crates repurposed as makeshift file cabinets, overflowing with crumpled maps and papers which disorder faithfully mirrored the disintegration of the British army.

- "Can't say for certain, sir, but looks that way," Sergeant Myers replied cautiously, standing rigidly at attention. "His fingers were black with soot, what he'd used to scrawl numbers on the wall of the building. Trouble is, we've no idea if it were nowt but scribbles or some kind of code..."

The officer remained silent, allowing a hush to thicken that was disturbed only by the scratching of his pen signing a report with energetic flourishes. He handed it to an orderly, stiff as a magistrate, who snapped a salute and vanished promptly. Only then did Butt deign to cast his tired eyes on the five people crowding his cramped tent.

- "The shot was accidental?"

The fifty-something veteran of the Great War weighed each word as if rationing munitions in these times of dire need.

"Aye, sir! No question!" Pitt exclaimed quickly, his voice pitched by anxiety. "That rotten bugger grabbed hold o' me rifle and wouldn't let go. Fought like wild, he did, and then the gun just went off on its own! Swear down, Colonel!" pleaded the soldier, his fingers drumming nervously on the seam of his khaki trousers.

The Lieutenant Colonel, whose scrutinizing gaze seemed to probe the depths of the soldier's soul, raised a calming hand. An aide interrupted, delivering a new document which Butt skimmed before setting it aside.

- "Mr. Sayer..."

- "Professor," the academic corrected softly.

- "Professor Sayer," Butt continued, unfazed by the interruption.

A professional officer, he recognized the importance of titles and decorum. Yet he studied his interlocutor closely, lips pursed at the sight of the rumpled *longyi* that both Sayer and Anthony still wore, a conspicuous, if not outright ridiculous, outfit for one of his compatriots who claimed such a title. The two soldiers who accompanied them, for their part, were again in uniform. He pressed on:

- "All this is certainly a tragic incident. But this Win Thu…"

- "Doctor Win Thu," Sayer insisted, earning an irritated glance this time.

- "Doctor Win Thu was quite obviously in league with the enemy. Under the present circumstances, I see no reason to spend more resources investigating the accidental death of a spy. This is war, Professor."

- "But Colonel…" Sayer began to protest.

Butt cut him off with an authoritative gesture. He rose wearily, his uniform revealing his Great War decorations. Crossing to the tent's entrance with a martial stride, he stood with his back to his visitors, surveying the feverish agitation of the camp, like an anthill freshly trampled.

- "Professor," he resumed, "these two men have gotten you here safely. A fate most of my troops did not share. Two thirds of them were on the wrong side of the bridge when it blew. Six hundred are still missing. Only one hundred and fifty have rejoined us."

He paused, absorbed by the spectacle of tragedy before him, then turned to meet their gazes.

- "We've managed to feed them, clothe them, dress their wounds," he explained, pointing to the bandage around Pitt's forearm, "but we cannot rearm them. Tomorrow, we'll have to send them back into battle with just five hundred Lee-Enfields, ten Bren guns and twelve Thompsons for the entire division, to face the Japanese who've just crossed the Sittang. We have more urgent matters than a crisis of conscience. As far as I'm concerned, the incident is closed. Besides, we're short of men to guarantee your protection. I can't allow you to proceed to Rangoon."

- "We must get there!" Sayer protested vehemently. "It's imperative!"

- "Order E for general evacuation has been issued and signal W sent," replied Butt coolly. "Martial law is in force. Only essential personnel and those involved in demolition operations are permitted in the city. You won't get past the checkpoints."

- "But Anthony must be reunited with his parents!"

- "Where does your father work?" Butt enquired impassively, turning to Anthony.

- "At the Burmah Oil Company."

- "They've already been evacuated," Butt said with finality. "Their employees were among the first to be moved. Rangoon is a ghost town now. You won't find a living soul there," he explained with clinical detachment.

The Lieutenant Colonel seemed unmoved by the distress that flickered across the young man's face. He had lost hundreds of soldiers younger than Anthony; a temporary separation of an adult from his parents, even under these circumstances, left him unmoved.

- "They've probably left me a note at the house," the teenager murmured.

- "What about Nandar Aye's mother? She's alone..." Sayer pressed.

- "She's Burmese. She doesn't need a pass to go there," the officer cut in, not even bothering to spare the young woman a glance.

- "You can't be serious!" the professor cried indignantly. "It's unthinkable she travel alone in such conditions! We must stay together!"

Butt seemed startled by his interlocutor's reaction. His gaze moved between Sayer and Nandar Aye, probing the nature of their relationship. A raised eyebrow accompanied his revelation.

- "I see," he drawled, lips pressed in disdain.

Anthony wondered. The grimace, was it distaste for mixed relationships, or rather for the age gap between the historian and his mistress? Butt returned to his seat, re-establishing the distance imposed by his rank.

- "I won't waste more time on this matter!" he announced curtly, as a sergeant interrupted to deliver yet another report. The enemy was approaching and he was eager to rid himself of these interlopers. "Since you insist," he continued, scrawling with evident annoyance on a scrap of paper, "here's a pass that will let you through the checkpoints to Rangoon."

He handed the signed document to Sayer, his gesture betraying his impatience.

- "You'll travel in a supply truck. But I strongly advise you to take the first train north to Prome[86]. God only knows how much longer we can hold the city. Sergeant Myers!"

- "Yes, sir?"

- "Escort them to the convoy. Then you and Pitt will return to your unit."

- "Aye, sir!" Myers replied, saluting crisply.

He and Pitt both snapped impeccable salutes.

- "Thank you, Colonel," Sayer managed in a dry voice as he departed the tent. The officer did not even glance up from his reading. They had ceased to exist for him, they were no longer his responsibility.

Myers escorted them to a row of brown trucks, where soldiers were finishing the loading. They would travel in the back among a jumble of crates and bags, and the prospect of motor transport, uncomfortable as it was, already felt like a blessing after days of forced marches. Their farewells were brief, despite the intensity of what they'd endured together. War separated them as naturally as it had brought them together, now that their priorities diverged: the military men braced for the next fight, the civilians wished only to avoid it. The chill between Sayer and Pitt was

---

86 Present-day Pyay.

tangible, the death of Win Thu having dug an unbridgeable gulf between them forever. Pitt, by contrast, was affable with Nandar Aye, helping her up into the truck and thanking her warmly for her help in the village. She replied only with a shy smile.

The trio settled onto the cargo, jostling beneath the engine's vibrations. A backfire and the Bedford lumbered laboriously into motion, the silhouettes of Myers and Pitt disappearing into a cloud of exhaust. The driver had raised the rear canvas to spare them the rigors of the heat. Yet the breeze that brushed their skin was insufficient to attenuate the sensation of suffocation that oppressed them, while the dust raised by the vehicle infiltrated the truck bed to mingle with their perspiration. The impression of asphyxiation, as much as the fear of swallowing sand, imposed silence upon them during the journey. Words would have failed them anyway before the spectacle unfolding in the frame of the rear opening.

The road they painfully covered was bordered on both sides by an incessant stream of refugees ascending it in the opposite direction beneath the implacable sun. Rangoon was emptying of its inhabitants. The most fortunate crowded into an unbroken file of trucks, automobiles, oxcarts and handcarts, bicycles, everything that rolled, laden with suitcases, furniture, trunks, crates, and household effects. An endless centipede crawling with the slowness of a snail. Accompanying the vehicles progressed a compact mass of the impoverished on foot, encumbered with all they could carry. An interminable procession of overburdened families, women carrying children on their hips, elderly leaning upon sticks, faces marked by that peculiar fatigue of those fleeing without knowing toward what. It was a living river, viscous as a mud flow, which their truck penetrated and pushed aside with difficulty, with incessant blasts of the horn and oaths, the driver's Scottish burr drowning in the engine's roar as he attempted to force a passage.

Anthony noted that this human tide was essentially made of Indians, doubtless impatient to put as much distance as possible between themselves and the Burma Independence Army, following rumors of atrocities visited upon Muslims in its wake. No trace of Burmans. The Chinese, for their part, had doubtless taken the initiative thanks to their own evacuation networks. He turned his attention back to Nandar Aye, half expecting to find her indifferent to the fate of those she held responsible for her family's suffering. Instead, he found her rigid, her eyes glistening, her gaze fixed with distress upon a couple struggling twenty meters away. The woman carried bundles upon her head, at arm's length, and in cloth knotted about her torso, exhaustion visible in her faltering gait. The father, burdened himself as much as his strength allowed, held a child against his chest. The little girl, chin resting on her father's shoulder, fixed Nandar Aye with empty eyes, testimony to her incomprehension. Then they too finally vanished, tiny points in the anonymous mass of the exodus.

Anthony felt his own eyes grow misty. Was it compassion for these strangers or crocodile tears consequent to his petty thoughts? He was ashamed to have allowed their recent discord to tarnish the image he held of his mistress. No doubt he had been swept away by jealousy upon discovering that Professor Sayer, his rival, knew more of the young woman's secret wounds. Certainly, he did not know everything about her. But he knew her. Her sensitivity, her intelligence, her integrity, her compassion. She supported independence, yet she would never have wished it obtained at such a price. He contemplated her with renewed tenderness, her contrite face, while the landscape of desiccated rice paddies in which she was born passed around them, the Eden from which her parents had been driven, as these refugees were driven today. Feeling observed, she turned her head toward him and offered him a mournful smile.

- "Would you like your book?" Anthony asked, opening the satchel he kept close, hoping to distract her.

- "No, thank you," she replied abruptly, her gesture sharp, her brow furrowed.

Nandar Aye's expression changed in an instant. Her features hardened and she gave him a chilling look, then turned away and took Sayer's hand, almost in defiance. Anthony was left bewildered by such behavior. Was she still upset by their quarrel? Frustration replaced surprise; he snapped his bag closed and turned his silent gaze back to the road.

The convoy slowed abruptly. Anthony peered out past the canvas: a military police checkpoint. A Master Sergeant in sweat-stained khaki spoke briefly with their driver, then walked up to them.

- "Papers!" he demanded, impatience showing in his shaking hand, with eyes that had seen too much in too little time.

Around them, the flow of exiles continued to stream past, the torrent skirting them like a rock. Sayer extended the safe conduct signed by Butt, which the NCO examined at length, before studying the trio, particularly Nandar Aye, with undisguised suspicion. Around them, other soldiers searched the refugees, overturning bundles, questioning in curt tones those who did not speak English.

- "You headin' to Rangoon?" he asked incredulously, with a hint of sarcasm. "If I were you, I'd keep my nose well away. Wouldn't even bother going," he mocked, gesturing toward the refugees. "But suit yourself," he finished, brusquely handing back the papers.

Sayer retrieved the pass without a word, visibly irritated but aware he couldn't protest.

- "Mov' on!" barked the Master Sergeant, slapping the truck before returning to grill two young coolies, hands on heads at the roadside.

The truck rumbled onward, but the mood had changed. Their anxiety was palpable; now their thoughts focused grimly on what awaited them at journey's end. Anthony finally recognized the peril of returning to a city not yet fully besieged, but which could fall at any moment.

A distant, barely perceptible drone, submerged in the engine's thrum, sealed his fear.

- "Planes," Sayer confirmed.

- "Japanese," Anthony added with dread, craning out the truck to scan the sky.

They braced suddenly; the truck jerked to a halt, slamming them painfully against the crates. Shouts replaced engine noise as the crowd scattered into the fields, shrieking, abandoning everything that slowed their flight. Anthony leapt from the platform first, Sayer close behind, both helping Nandar Aye, tangled in her *longyi*, to escape the vehicle. The moment her feet touched earth, a razor-hum filled the air; three metallic shapes, gleaming like insects, streaked above the palm trees on the road's axis. The Nakajima Ki-43 "Oscars" were upon them.

- "Get down! Down!" someone shrieked amid the chaos.

The first bullets raked the vehicles as they flung themselves into the roadside ditch. Screams rose everywhere; the air thickened with oil and fuel fumes.

- "Stay down!" the same voice ordered, while the reckless dashed back to rescue their last possessions.

A loud, rising whistle heralded the second pass, this time the planes strafing the refugees sheltering in the fields with lethal intent. Anthony heard the staccato fire sweeping the paddy, earth thrown up by bullets just a meter away. Panic screamed at him to run, fast and far, from this threat he was powerless to resist. But he knew he could never outrun a plane. Like a trembling hare in an open field, stalked by hawks, he gambled his immobility would make him invisible, a target among thousands. To calm himself as the third pass exploded the road behind them, he tried to calculate the chance of being randomly hit - about one in twenty, he reckoned - until the engine sounds faded. Black vapors rose swiftly, obscuring the sun behind an opaque curtain; then the planes vanished. No one moved; landscape froze in silence, pierced only by burning vehicles and the cries of the wounded. Little by little, people rose, until Anthony, too, helped his companions up.

- "The road's clear!" shouted the same voice.

Suddenly, clamorous survivors rushed toward the bodies that would join the earth forever. Their tears mingled with black ash falling in shrouds over the silent dead of the impromptu cemetery. While some mourned loved ones, others wandered back, stunned, rediscovering burned-out cars, shattered carts, ruined loads. In seconds, all were poorer, frailer, more vulnerable, as war's work of leveling down humanity continued unceasingly.

Anthony observed that the Bedford awaited them, riddled with impacts, yet still in working order. Two other trucks had not fared so well, black masses consumed by flames. Seized with panic, he rushed toward the truck bed in which he had abandoned his satchel. He scrambled onto the platform and discovered a heap of debris. He cleared it frantically, scraping his hands. Finally, the satchel appeared. He opened it hastily and felt its contents. The tablet and metal box containing his journal and Nandar Aye's book were intact. He heaved a sigh of relief.

- "We're moving out!" called the driver, starting the engine.

The other vehicles in the convoy resumed their rumbling, indifferent to the tragedies unfolding around them. There was nothing they could have done anyway. Their mission led them in the opposite direction from that followed by this tide of the dispossessed. Anthony, Sayer, and Nandar Aye found a place among the overturned crates. The burning vehicles, which swarms of shadows around them desperately tried to extinguish, gradually disappeared behind the crowd of refugees that once again surrounded their column, as if nothing had happened. During the hour that followed, the infernal roar of the engine mingled with the grinding of springs tortured by the ruts in the road, tormenting the passengers as much as what remained of the cargo. Suddenly, through the canvas flapping in the hot wind, Mingaladon aerodrome appeared on their left.

The sight was striking. The metal hangars, disemboweled by Japanese bombs, stood like skeletons of twisted iron. Gaping craters pocked the runways in Marsden Matting, some still smoking. The charred remains of two Hurricanes and a P-40 Tomahawk lay near the control tower, their wings pointing in a gesture of metallic agony towards the azure sky. At intervals, helmeted figures raced between the debris, the last RAF mechanics evacuating whatever equipment could still be saved towards Magwe. A convoy of trucks laden with aircraft parts sped away in the opposite direction, raising whirlwinds of ochre dust. Then the aerodrome too vanished as they continued southward towards the city center.

Thirty minutes later, the truck finally came to a halt at the intersection of Commissioners Road[87] and Godwin Road[88]. Anthony and his companions heaved sighs of relief as they descended from the truck bed, while soldiers were already approaching to unload the vehicle. Yet their relief was short-lived. The city they discovered was unrecognizable.

Before them stood Rangoon General Hospital, its imposing Victorian architecture of red brick contrasting sharply with the chaos surrounding it. But even this symbol of colonial grandeur seemed diminished by the atmosphere of rout hovering over the city. The broad avenues, ordinarily teeming with activity, were strangely deserted. Only a few military vehicles rushed past, laden with supplies and soldiers with taut faces. Administrative papers littered the pavements, carried by the hot wind that bore the acrid smell from the docks. At the hospital itself, activity seemed feverish. Ambulances crossed paths constantly, their sirens tearing through the oppressive silence.

Colonial buildings, the government quarter, the administrative offices - all appeared abandoned, their shutters closed like eyelids drawn over a bygone era. A few looters discreetly and with impunity ransacked the deserted shops. In the distance, columns of black smoke rose everywhere across the city, buildings, and warehouses that the British had begun to destroy since the demolition signal "D" had been given an hour earlier, implementing a scorched earth policy in preparation for the arrival

---

[87] Present-day Bogyoke Aung San Road.
[88] Present-day Lanmadaw Road.

of the Japanese. Rangoon was dying in the tropical torpor, counting its last hours of freedom.

More than ever, they understood that their time was running out. They were prey caught in a mousetrap that was closing. Butt had been right: they had to leave the city as soon as possible, hoping it was not already too late.

- "Anthony, go see if your parents left a message," Sayer said, his tone sharp with urgency. "Nandar Aye and I will fetch her mother and pack. You do the same. Only essentials, money, and anything you can sell: jewelry, gold. We'll meet tonight, six p.m., at the station."

- "Alright!" Anthony agreed, eager to shed the *longyi* he'd been tangled in for days, constantly having to retie it, never quite succeeding.

- "Anthony!" called Nandar Aye as he started off, pointing to his satchel.

Now she wanted her book, at such a moment! He snapped the flap open impatiently, plunged his hand into the tin lunchbox, pulled out the novel, and handed it over.

- "Thank you," she said, taking the book. "And the tablet?" her tone was coolly feigned, yet her eyes shone with an odd, intense light.

- "I'll need my satchel. And the stone's heavy. It'd just slow you down."

She didn't reply, unsure whether to insist, turning to Sayer for a wordless inquiry. Her smile was gone.

- "Anthony's right. Don't worry, darling, we'll see him soon. Come, let's not dawdle, we've little time!"

Anthony watched the pair hurry away, perplexed. He lingered, noticing Nandar Aye cast a tense, inquisitive glare over her shoulder. She'd never cared for their research, yet now seemed preoccupied by the artifact. What was going through her mind?

A distant explosion yanked him back to reality; the mystery would have to wait. He sprinted east toward a thick column of black smoke on the horizon, toward Syriam. Then he understood: British engineers had set fire to the Burmah Oil Company refineries and tanks. It was as if all his history - family, childhood, future - was being annihilated in a single *auto-da-fé*. Soon, he thought, all trace of himself would vanish from Burma.

Chapter 20

Cambridge, United-Kingdom, September 2024

The black and white marble checkerboard faded beneath Ayaan's gaze. Absent. As if the mosaic pavement absorbed the light of the wrought iron chandeliers. The rectangular hall extended in its relentless symmetry, its dark oak walls bearing Newton's frescoes measuring light. Squares and compasses intertwined in frieze. Symbols of an inner circle that claimed to measure the immeasurable. Outside, the Masonic temple on Bateman Street raised its grey façade against Cambridge's leaden sky. Among the centuries-old colleges, it was merely another stone in that secular city which collected the tombs of knowledge. Nothing of this seeped inside. Whether day or night, the same light illuminated identically this cabinet of reflection isolated from the profane world. Ayaan, however, was incapable of leaving his metals at the temple's entrance. His foot beat an impatient rhythm against the floor.

He was surely not alone in remaining deaf to the blend of erudition and mysticism offered by the Isaac Newton University Lodge No. 859. The figures spoke for themselves: the number of initiates had halved in fifty years. Despite the aura of mystery that delighted bestselling detective novels, British Freemasonry struggled to recruit. Most of the Brethren had passed sixty. Across from him, on the South column, they lined up in their regalia: white aprons, immaculate gloves, black sashes. Greying members who would have reassured any conspiracy theorist. Ayaan suppressed a smile. This army of weary academics, of portly notables, masters of the world? The very idea was laughable.

The Caius Lodge No. 3355 of Gonville and Caius College had approached him. He still hesitated. Expanding his network, advancing his career—the argument was not negligible. But the idea of wasting his evenings in obsequious ceremonies and obsolete rituals repelled him. So, he sat on the North column, among the profanes, that assembly of guests and academics come for the open white meeting. They were all there. His family, gathered in full for the first time in over ten years. Death, the ultimate separation, was also the only thing capable of bringing together what was scattered.

Three hammer blows rang out from the Orient and awakened Ayaan. The Worshipful Master sat on his throne, dominated by two globes and the Luminous Delta. The black curtain formed a backdrop, like a permanent reminder of what all things tended toward.

- "Friends and Brethren in your grades and qualities," the voice rose, monotone, each syllable weighed according to the Emulation ritual, that legacy of the eighteenth century that the United Grand Lodge of England perpetuated unchanged. "Our beloved Brother Anthony Preston rests before us, overtaken by the fate that, sooner or later, strikes all the children of God."

Ayaan turned his gaze back to the coffin at the center of the temple. A symbol. Like everything here was. Empty, of course. The body had been buried six feet under this morning, after a service at Great St Mary's. The honors kept coming for his grandfather, dead three days earlier. It was now his Brethren's turn.

The day before, Ayaan had visited the apartment on Trumpington Street one last time. A black and white snapshot, frozen in stillness. Silence had replaced the dying man's steady breathing beneath his mask, rendering the place even more dismal. His family had descended upon whatever held value. Alexander's army pillaging Persepolis. The same chaos, methodical and merciless. The library had been given to the Centre for South Asian Studies. No one read anymore. The rest? To the dump. Ayaan had salvaged the box, the one containing his grandfather's personal mementos - except for the ring and gold watch it held. His sole booty. Not from sentimentality or nostalgia. But because Khin Yadanar had decided to depart for Win Ka, and he had to see it through. He didn't usually let emotion take hold, yet gloominess had seized him before this worn and warped box, the only trace of an existence spanning more than a century. A box, and perhaps the name, linked to an archaeological discovery. Posthumously. He would never know. Was that the full measure of a man? What would remain of himself when the time came? Success only held meaning when lived. The memorial ceremonies had only thickened his melancholy. This Masonic ceremony more than the others, given the tedium that its esotericism inspired in him.

The Three Great Lights lay near the coffin: the Bible open to Ecclesiastes 12:1, the square, and the compass. The column of the First Warden stood at the head, that of the Second lay at the foot. The litanies resumed, monotonous.

- "Neither valor nor virtue, neither wealth nor honor, neither tears of friends nor of family can prevent or delay it. It brings us this lesson often repeated but quickly forgotten: each of us must soon cross the threshold and experience that superior life toward which we advance."

Ayaan's mind wandered. The ritual became background noise, progressing with the heaviness of a Sanskrit manuscript. Latin whispers, codified movements around the coffin. Six brothers with cheeks hollowed by age laid upon the mahogany a master's apron stained with ashes and a sprig of acacia. "Symbol of immortality," whispered the Venerable Master. Ayaan thought of the notebook charred somewhere in the Chinese mountains. Only the tablet had survived. He imagined its pieces clinking together at the bottom of a bag as Khin Yadanar made them cross a country at war. One thing was certain: nothing was immortal. The Worshipful Master continued his musings:

- "Our Brother Anthony crossed the Gate of the East bearing in his hand the torch of Truth..."

Ayaan withdrew with a sigh into his inner temple. The cavernous voice enumerated the Burma campaign, the accomplishments of the deceased. Would this masquerade ever end? A single thought obsessed him: how to pinpoint precisely the *stūpa* of Win Ka? He had combed through every document in the box. Studied each survey, each page of the journal. Nothing precise enough. He was facing a wall. Khin Yadanar would arrive at Win Ka in a few days. A conflict zone where she could not linger. Every minute wasted in this obsolete dance was another step toward failure. Absurdity culminated with the Chain of Union. The Masons formed a circle around the coffin, arms crossed, hands intertwined, chanting in old English. Sterile and endless ravings. Then the reading of Ecclesiastes. "Vanities of vanities…"

Three hammer blows. At last! Time resumed its flow. Ayaan thought he heard the second hand ticking away the seconds as he rose, carried along by the stream that led to the Banquet Hall for the festivities. Brethren and academics, relieved of their ornaments, rushed toward the bar in joyful hubbub. They had accomplished their duty. Life resumed its rights.

Ayaan feigned admiration for the clock presiding over the fireplace mantelpiece, yearning to be left alone with the sole thought consuming him - Win Ka - when he heard a familiar voice:

- "Quite the gathering, isn't it?"

Professor Forsythe handed him an ale and raised his own toward Latika Williamson, director of the Center for South East Asian Studies, who was discussing with the Worshipful Master at the other end of the room. She responded with a discrete nod.

- "Rather dated, don't you think?"

Ayaan tasted the foam, unmoved. Around them, conversations animated beneath Newton's coat of arms. Two crossed tibiae on a black ground. A reference to piracy? To death? It mattered little. Symbolism and heraldry held no interest for him.

Forsythe smiled with a patience tinged with intoxication. "What you see is merely a *façade*. The rituals, the symbols... Tools humans need to give themself a reason to get up in the morning. A quest for meaning. Humanity invents myths to escape the absurd, to believe there is something behind the veil of matter."

- "It seems more like empty, mechanical repetition, doesn't it?" Ayaan, skeptical, turned his glass between his fingers.

Forsythe tilted his head. "Perhaps the form of this ritual doesn't speak to you. But its substance cannot leave you unmoved. It concerns us all. For instance, the relation to the sacred might be symbolised by Olympus, the Sinai, the pyramid, the cathedral spire, the Masonic column, or even a tree. Tell me what gives meaning to your life and I will find your verticality. Freedom? The Statue of Liberty. Money? The Gherkin or Trump Tower. Human society is a forest of symbols that speak to us. They are the secret language of our collective unconscious and memory. They transmit not only beliefs but also a common will: each generation interprets according to its own measure, recycles, deconstructs, reinvents."

The voices around them faded, as if suspended upon this conversation. The academic emptied his ale in a single draught before continuing:

- "This world may seem vain to you. But everything that matters to us - love, honour, fraternity - exists because we decide it does, together, as a society, through signs, words, rituals. So, either you follow Buddha, considering existence as a mere illusion, detaching yourself from what makes us human, withdrawing from the world. Or..."

Forsythe let his sentence trail, savoring the effect, while reaching for another glass from a passing tray.

- "Or?" asked Ayaan, playing along. He smiled. The academic was more likeable with a drink in him.

- "Or... you embrace the theatre of life, give it meaning - the meaning you choose, according to what matters to you. You will then adopt your own symbols and rituals - graduation ceremonies, weddings, medals, gold watches - that your children will in turn find outdated. In any case, you cannot escape the fact that myths, ideas, however immaterial they may be, govern the world..."

A pause. His glassy gaze lost itself on the compass and square on the wall before resuming with enthusiasm, his flushed face drawing closer to Ayaan's as if to confide in him:

- "Ideas! Aren't they extraordinary? So fragile, abstract, non-existent without us, floating from mind to mind like fireflies," he mimed with his hand before Ayaan's face. "And yet capable of vanquishing the greatest armies. Critical mass... It takes only a crowd sharing the same idea and poof!" He spread his hands to simulate an explosion. "Take Myanmar. An entire people behind a common hope: federal democracy. Writing for themselves new founding myths. A will to live together. The ideal solution for this multiethnic country. If the army loses, this concept will transform the region. The power of symbols! Do you see?"

- "Speaking of Myanmar," cut in Ayaan. Forsythe's elaborations amused him less. He had to steer the conversation toward what mattered. "Khin Yadanar arrived in Pyay today. Her contact in Chin State just wrote to me. Tomorrow, she'll cross the Bago Yoma. She'll be at Win Ka in three days. Four at most."

- "What a pity your great-grandfather cannot witness the culmination..." Forsythe paused. "Why did he never resume his research after the war?"

- "No idea." Frustration cut through Ayaan's voice. "He refused to speak of it. Of this, of the tablet on the plane... So many secrets carried to the grave. And his notebook offers no precision regarding the *stūpa*'s location."

- "Regrettable," the academic acknowledged, conciliatory. "But war interrupted him. The urgency. He thought he would return. No doubt why he didn't record the coordinates..."

- "It doesn't matter why!" Ayaan's irritation exploded. Forsythe's excuses exasperated him. "We're facing a wall. Four days! That's all we have, to send the location to Khin Yadanar. I've contacted the Burmese community in London. Associations, social networks, exiled archaeologists. Nothing. They all say the same thing: we need a team on the ground. Impossible! I'm at a dead end!"

- "I understand," Forsythe replied, embarrassed.

After all, his contribution would allow him to attach his name to the discovery, and his expertise to lead the research that would follow. Enough to advance an academic career. This thought sobered him and he resumed his usual professorial tone:

- "I should probably contact Global Xplorer."

- "Global Xplorer?"

- "A crowdsourcing platform that analyses satellite imagery to discover archaeological sites using volunteers on the Internet. If we provide them with the area to search and the sketches from the notebook, they could locate the exact site. If only through vegetation differences, since it was cleared in 1941. That leaves traceable marks. The AI software works miracles."

- "Fantastic!" enthused Ayaan, forgetting where he was. The gazes of his family reminded him to compose himself.

All was not lost. Hope, a thin thread stretched between failure and success. Time tightened around Ayaan, but the puzzle could be solved. His sacrificed vacation, the vigils at the dying man's bedside, the relentless research, the confrontations with Khin Yadanar - all of it would gain meaning. And that quarter hour of glory that would inevitably draw the attention of the university, of prestigious firms. He raised his beer to his lips, savoring the draught this time with a smile of anticipation. There remained Khin Yadanar. The unknown in the equation. The free electron in this perfectly orchestrated chemical reaction. The uncontrollable element upon which, nonetheless, the success of their quest in the field entirely depended. He would have to accommodate her, by necessity rather than choice, despite the unease knotting his stomach.

Forsythe emptied his second glass in a single draught. A sharp gesture. The crystal struck the mantelpiece. He extended his hand toward Ayaan:

- "I must slip away. Return to London. My condolences. I'll contact you as soon as Global Xplorer responds. In the meantime, I'm sending you the final part of the translation..."

The email departed in an instant, invisible electronic vibration. Forsythe was already disappearing, a silhouette cleaving through the crowd clustering in the damp hall. Disappearance. As if the funeral ceremony continued, carrying away the actors of this macabre comedy one by one. Ayaan drew out his phone and began to read the text, leaning against the fireplace, thanking Forsythe for providing him with the excuse to escape his family obligations.

Chapter 21

Pyay region, Myanmar, September 2024

Rain fell like spears, vertical and violent, hammering the tarpaulin of the military truck. Khin Yadanar, hands bound on the front, felt each jolt of the cratered road reverberate through her bruised bones. Around her, in the damp darkness, the silhouettes of other prisoners swayed like silent ghosts. Kicks, insults, and sneers flew from the benches where soldiers sat aligned.

Only an hour since her capture. Light had dissolved with her freedom. She knew the fate reserved for rebels. But knowing and living it in one's flesh, that is what separates idea from reality. How long would she hold? A futile question. No one ever does. Had her recklessness sealed the fate of her comrades, of Kee Mawng? She raised her head, met Kyaw Zaw's gaze. Same fear, same determination. They had chosen this fight. The villagers crammed with them, however, had committed no crime but existing on lands contested by the resistance and the Tatmadaw. Scapegoats. Hostages. Innocence offered no more protection than guilt.

The convoy advanced laboriously along the muddy road winding between the verdant hills of Paungde. Ten military trucks, progressing with the slowness of a wary animal. Khin Yadanar closed her eyes, attempting to ignore the throbbing pain in her back. She calculated the distance to Pyay, to the interrogation center. Refocus. Enter meditation. But always the faces returned - victims she could not save, friends dead in the fire, the village girl. A macabre rogues' gallery followed by Kee Mawng's. His sad expression when she left. A rupture. She summoned all her strength not to weep. These demons fed on suffering. She would not grant them that pleasure.

Suddenly, a deafening explosion tore through the air, so violent that the truck swerved. A blinding flash illuminated the interior of the canvas, revealing for a fraction of a second the terrified faces of the prisoners. Then came the screams, orders shouted, and the crackle of automatic weapons. The truck braked brutally, hurling prisoners against each other.

- "To the ground!" Khin Yadanar screamed. "Stay down!"

Bullets began to perforate the canvas. Streams of rain and light. Several soldiers had no time to rise and remained frozen on their benches like disarticulated puppets. The others leapt from the truck, jumping at orders barked by their NCO, some killed before even touching the ground. Water seeped everywhere, mingling with blood beginning to flow. An old man collapsed near her, struck in the chest, his eyes already veiled, fixed on the void.

The PDF attacked, unleashing hell upon the convoy, ignorant that it transported civilian prisoners. Fire came from all sides, from the hills, the dense jungle bordering the road, where countless flashes crackled. A Tatmadaw soldier abruptly appeared, his face contorted with fear. Rain poured in behind him, glacial and merciless. He levelled his weapon at the prisoners.

- "Out! You'll serve as shields!"

Khin Yadanar rose, unsteady but determined.

- "These are civilians!" she shouted to the soldier, her voice barely audible. "Prisoners!"

Another explosion, closer, shook the ground. The soldier was hurled backward, disappearing into the ditch bordering the road. Khin Yadanar rushed toward the opening, driven by a deep instinct, a rage, a primal cry that took control. To live! Outside there was chaos. Soldiers ran in all directions, desperately seeking shelter against fire raining from the forest. Many already lay in the mud. Motionless. The same color as the earth. Rain swept in scarlet streams the blood of her enemies to irrigate the slime. She felt no pity. "You reap what you sow," she thought. The acrid smell of powder and flames resurrected images of charred bodies in the village.

The first truck was now nothing but a burning husk. Casting dancing shadows on the apocalyptic scene. "IED!" she thought, recognizing the signature. The lead vehicle had been pulverized according to the PDF's customary tactic: block the convoy, establish a killing zone, then attack simultaneously from multiple positions to prevent any retreat or counterattack. A burst cracked near her, sending showers of mud at her feet. She threw herself to the ground, rolling under the truck for shelter. From there, she could see the legs of soldiers running, falling, sometimes rising again. The battle now concentrated on the rear vehicles.

Under the driving rain, she crawled to the front of the truck, emerged from her hiding place, straightened, her back pressed against the door, to cast a sideways glance into the cab. The driver was dead, slumped over his wheel. Beside him, an NCO was dying, hands clenched on his torn abdomen. She recognized the corporal who had participated in the rape in the village. Their eyes met. She hesitated. Before recovering herself. She couldn't – didn't want to? - do anything for him. He would die in the minutes that followed. The reflection of a bayonet in the mud caught her attention. She retrieved it quickly, then plunged back under the truck to cut her bonds. The deluge of fire continued relentlessly around her as she crawled to retrace her path in the opposite direction. A single thought occupied her mind: save the villagers before they became collateral damage.

A group of soldiers attempted a desperate counterattack, regrouping behind a vehicle still intact. They were scythed down by a burst from the hills. Others ran toward the jungle, pursued by furtive shadows. Reaching the rear of the truck, she hauled herself up and found herself nose to nose with a rifle barrel pointed at her head. No shot was fired. The weapon lowered, revealing the tense face of Kyaw Zaw, who gave her a corner-of-the-mouth smile. The kid had nerves of steel, she had to give him that.

- "You can't stay here!" she snapped. "You'll get picked off. The PDF has surrounded the convoy." She held out the knife so he could free himself.

- "It's too dangerous out there," the resistance fighter answered. "They don't know we're civilians. We risk being targeted or catching a stray bullet."

Another explosion set the dusk ablaze. Another truck was burning, crackling under rain and gunfire. She observed the prisoners, whose bonds Kyaw Zaw was cutting, huddled at the bottom, their faces illuminated by the unreal orange glow. Some wounded, all terrified. Trapped between a rock and a hard place.

- "We must get out and identify ourselves!" she shouted to them. "The PDF doesn't know we're here!"

Outside, the battle was receding, the PDF probably pursuing fleeing soldiers into the jungle.

- "At my signal, we'll all go out shouting 'civilian prisoners.' Keep your hands raised, visible above your heads."

Time suspended itself, as if the entire universe held its breath. Rain continued to fall, washing away blood and mud, but not fear. Never fear.

- "Now!"

They emerged into the night, a pathetic group of trembling silhouettes. The battle had moved away, but PDF snipers were still positioned around them.

- "Civilian prisoners!" they screamed in unison, their voices mingling with the roar of bullets whistling past their heads.

The villager just beside her fell with a scream, struck in the thigh. The gunfire became more sporadic, then ceased. Silence. Broken here and there by detonations and cries piercing the curtain of the downpour. A long moment passed, an eternity during which they remained in the middle of the road, arms in the air, their voices united in the same clamor rising from the gut with rage and hope. "Civilian prisoners!" The first silhouettes emerged slowly from the jungle, rifles ready to fire, menacing, soaked helmets and caps hiding anonymous faces. A laugh cleaved the night, then a call, a liberation:

- "Kyaw Zaw? Is that you?"

The young resistance fighter lowered his arms, followed by the hostages. Kyaw Zaw rushed toward the voice he embraced with fervor. It was over. They were saved! Battalion 3602 had found them. Khin Yadanar let out a sigh of relief. Felt her legs give way beneath her. She collapsed in the mud, overwhelmed by an indefinable mixture of emotions: relief, exhaustion, horror at the bodies strewn along the road. And that strange guilt of the survivor. A fighter rushed toward her to offer his canteen. She drank greedily, her throat still tight and incredibly dry despite the torrents of rain pouring down on them. He helped her to her feet as the tremors shaking her subsided. She felt her heart slow, her breathlessness ease, then her thoughts clear. Without a word, she rushed toward the villager writhing in pain at the foot of the truck, his hands clutching his leg where blood flowed in a stream. The image of Kee Mawng after the bombardment flashed back to her. Later. There was urgency.

- "Medic!" she cried. "I need a medic! Now!"

A young man in camouflage fatigues came running.

- "Disinfectant and compresses, quickly!" she ordered in a tone that brooked no question.

She moved aside the wounded man's hands and roughly lowered his *longyi* to assess the severity of the wound. The bullet had torn muscle but seemed not to have touched bone or the femoral artery. The disinfectant was met with a long wail.

- "Hold him while I apply the compresses!"

The medic complied despite the villager's protests as she pressed the cloth against the wound with all her strength. Then, without ceremony, she unfastened the soldier's belt - he had no time even to react to his surprise - and tied it around the compress to staunch the blood flow.

- "He needs to be evacuated immediately!"

The makeshift stretcher was being hurried away when she turned to Kyaw Zaw, who was watching her with fascination.

- "I need to see to the other wounded. Try to find my bag if you can. It's very important."

He understood. He knew why she was there. He left without asking questions, letting her continue her rounds. Priority to the resistance and hostages. Hippocratic Oath or not, the Tatmadaw would wait, if they could hold on that long. She could not forget the massacre they had just committed. She climbed back into the truck filled with motionless bodies. She passed those of the soldiers, slumped in silence - breathless, ashen complexions. Neither sneers nor insults. At the back, she found three prisoners tangled together. Dead. Were their wives waiting for them? Or had they lost them in the attack?

Khin Yadanar knelt beside the bodies. She was accustomed to death. But these were different. These were collateral damage, killed by mistake by those who came to defend them. Immense pity overwhelmed her. She reached toward one of the faces and gently closed his eyelids. A simple gesture. Like an apology, a thank you for his sacrifice. She straightened, drained. How to reconcile the irreconcilable? Her conviction that she fought in a just cause, against these three bodies bearing witness that war makes no distinction between guilty and innocent. Each liberated village brought hope. Each civilian killed, the same question: how much longer? She felt that weight settle into her. A sudden fatigue drained her strength. A profound weariness, a disgust. She was a doctor, she wanted to dedicate herself to saving lives. And here she was, confronted with the price of her daily struggle. The others, the most destitute, the most fragile, always paid. Never her. Was it worth the cost? It would have to be. She finally turned from the bodies. They would have to be buried with dignity. She would have to continue the fight. She would have to live with this guilt. For such was her condition: survivor and witness, doctor and fighter, bearer of hope and remorse. Living, she would become the memory of each anonymous victim, guaranteeing they had not died in vain. Victory or death. It was the only choice.

She stepped out of the truck with heavy legs. Observing her fellow fighters gather the bodies of the Tatmadaw. The ambush had been a military success, but Khin Yadanar could not muster the satisfaction displayed by the men of the People Defense Force. She reviewed the line of corpses. Stopped before one: the soldier who had arrested her. The rapist, the murderer, the torturer. There he was, lying in the mud. Where his dream of power had led him, to its rightful conclusion. She examined his face, banally human. His death brought her only meager consolation as his victims would not return.

She raised her head toward a group of soldiers emerging from the jungle. Hands on their heads, flanked by resistance fighters. These would have the chance to be treated in compliance with the Geneva Convention. A consideration they generally refused to rebels who fell into their hands. She could not help but feel admiration for her comrades who managed to keep their heads cool enough to place their cause above their personal feelings. They thus increased the chances that Tatmadaw soldiers would surrender rather than fight. They won the support of the entire population. They ensured their image as freedom fighters on the international stage. And, in case of final victory, they laid the healthy and solid foundations of a pacified country. A rule of law, where justice would not yield its place to vengeance or chaos. This image gave her hope. It reminded her of why she was fighting. A better future was possible.

Khin Yadanar continued to treat the wounded with the help of the medic. There were few among the PDF troops. She moved on to the enemy soldiers, whose ranks had been decimated. It was her duty. She was in the process of bandaging one of them when she heard her name. She stood and saw a silhouette detach from the group to come toward her with great strides in the backlighting of the flames. It was Kyaw Zaw, carrying a bag at arm's length.

- "I found it!" he called out with pride.

- "Fantastic! My hero!" she exclaimed, seizing it with relief.

As she went to open it, she noticed the brown stains that marred its exterior. She did not have to question Kyaw Zaw. She understood. She was immediately reassured. The captain was dead. The secret of the tablet was safe. For the sake of conscience, she plunged her hand to the bottom of the bag and felt the stone fragments beneath her fingers. Against all expectations, she could continue her mission. She had narrowly escaped. Luck - or fate? - was with her. But would it always be? Her hand met the smooth screen of her phone, which she immediately extracted. She could not wait any longer, especially after coming so close to death. She needed to hear his voice. To tell him she loved him. That he could never doubt the feelings she held for him if luck finally abandoned her. If she disappeared. They were separated only by distance, for never had she felt so close. She reinstalled the VPN, Signal, and placed the call.

Chapter 22

North of Bago, Myanmar, September 2024

- "We'll need a boat!"

Words spilled forth unbidden, Khin Yadanar hearing them resonate in the wind that whipped her face, warm and humid breath carrying the voice of the East. She cast a morose gaze upon the vast brownish ocean stretching beneath her feet. The first she had ever seen in her existence as a mountain dweller. Wilder than she had imagined, for one who could not swim. This muddy sea rolled its dead waves where once bright green fields had spread. The millennia-old dikes had vanished beneath the liquid chaos of the swollen Sittang River that had flooded the plain. Only a few golden pagodas still emerged, pathetic beacons in an archipelago of floating debris, silent witnesses to this sunken Atlantis now lying beneath their feet.

Typhoon Yagi had transformed the Bago region into an apocalyptic landscape. From the aquatic desert rose thatched roofs, phantom islets emerging intermittently when these aquatic monsters drew breath between waves. The sky, tinted the same as the stagnant water, plunged into swirling eddies to drown itself in this mirrorless sea, adding its great sweeps to this tableau of desolation.

It had taken them a week to cross the Bago Yoma massif beneath unleashed elements. A week of relentless downpour, wading through mud, sleeping in caves, feet sodden, clothes continuously clinging to their skin, cold, clammy, and heavy, never managing to dry. Kyaw Zaw had chosen the most treacherous paths out of fear of poachers, mines, and the army. They had encountered no living soul, except a handful of wild elephants, fleeting apparitions through the rain. It was only on their descent toward the Sittang valley that they had collided with the flow of refugees climbing the slope in the opposite direction. A tide of wretches battering the rocky foothills in successive waves. Endless columns of haggard phantoms, fleeing the deluge in search of an ark to shelter with their beasts, the only wealth they had managed to salvage from the disaster. That, and what fit in sodden sacks. Some had tried to convince them to turn back. In vain. Khin Yadanar was not one to stop while a single step remained. The last one had led her to this shore.

The lapping of water licking the tips of her toes brought no solace. No explosion of warm colors, no azure beckoning to travel. Only a brown uniformity, a liquid cemetery from which emerged the vaults of engulfed dwellings. The dismal sun, filtered through the heavy, clammy atmosphere that filled the lungs, cast a dull light upon this inverted landscape where earth and sky merged. They would need a boat to cross, that much was certain. But where to find one? Khin Yadanar cast her gaze as far south as she could reach. It met only emptiness.

- "Let's follow the shore," suggested Kyaw Zaw, as if he had read her thoughts. "We'll eventually find a dinghy."

Their solitary march seemed to last for hours through the frozen landscape that surrounded them. No movement, no sound, save for the plaintive caws of ravens circling overhead. Even the wind appeared to have fallen asleep, exhausted after unleashing its titanic rage upon the small fry of this engulfed plain. Images of Cyclone Nargis surfaced: nearly two hundred thousand dead sacrificed by the paranoid junta that had blocked international aid. Then the pandemic victims, twenty thousand more, hastily buried in mass graves. And now a typhoon in the midst of civil war. It was too much. Had Myanmar not already suffered enough? Khin Yadanar wondered what sins her people had committed to deserve such punishment. Fragments of homily on original sin resurfaced, from the time her mother took her as a child to church. Absurd, and yet difficult not to surrender to the supernatural in the face of catastrophes that pursued Myanmar relentlessly. A nation blessed by the gods for its resources. A nation cursed as far back as memory reached. Could a defeat of the Tatmadaw break this cycle?

Her companion's voice interrupted her thoughts:

- "A village!" He pointed at a cluster of makeshift shelters, built hastily with tarps. Rather a refugee camp, the young woman thought. "Stay here, I'll go look."

- "No, I'm coming with you!" The authority in her voice swept aside her guide's machismo. "Some of them might need my medical attention."

They approached with caution the tangle of multicolored tents, simple canvas flapping in the breeze, planted in the grey mud left by slowly receding water. Meagre protection against the elements. At their sight, a swarm of women and children emerged from the shelters. Hungry shadows that assailed them, pressed against them, hands outstretched, begging with whatever dignity contemplation of death could afford. They were their hope. Derisory hope, she knew. Her bag contained neither rice nor powdered milk. Just a few water purification tablets that might save them from dysentery or cholera. For a day or two. The children fixed her with eyes enlarged by malnutrition, eyes that had seen too much and no longer wept. They pressed against their mothers' legs, bodies wasted by opportunistic diarrhea. Khin Yadanar felt that familiar anger rise within her. That rage against the world's injustice that ensured the poorest always paid the heaviest price.

- "We have no food," she announced. Her voice carried despite herself that hardness given by words one prefers never to have to speak.

She immediately read disappointment and anguish carving the faces, extinguishing the eyes.

- "But I am a doctor. I will examine you, starting with the children." She entered a tent while pointing outside: "form a line here. I'll see each of you in turn."

The villagers obeyed in resigned silence. She methodically withdrew from her pack her medical kit, her stethoscope, all that might bring some semblance of comfort. Kyaw Zaw poked his head through the tent flap:

- "The men have gone to find food and wood. I'm going to meet them and try to get us a boat. See you later."

The rest of the day slipped away unnoticed. Entirely absorbed in her consultations that succeeded one another at a steady pace. She had recovered her reflexes and, above all, her reason for being. As if the depression that had paralyzed her at the CDF clinic had evaporated, sublimated after her passage through fire near Pyay. An alchemy had worked within her. Did tragedy need to wash away trauma? Or simply the proximity of her own death to recover the taste for life? A new light awakened and warmed the previously numb corners of her mind. She mattered. She could make a difference. Each treatment, each pill, each piece of advice might be a life saved. A weight had lifted from her shoulders. She was explaining to a group of women how to purify water when Kyaw Zaw returned, fidgeting in place, impatient to keep her informed.

- "Men saw a truck not far from here. And a group putting a boat into the water. They didn't dare approach. Probably the Tatmadaw. We must go look!"

Khin Yadanar nodded. She had finished anyway, limited in the care and comfort she could offer the refugees. She had done her best. She had to continue her journey. The women experienced her departure as a rupture. She had been a buoy brought by the currents, which the tide carried immediately toward open water. Her presence had reassured them. Now uncertainty, fear, the unknown returned.

The sun, already tilted toward the west, lengthened their silhouettes on the water. The two resistance fighters walked without a word, their hearing dilated, hunting for the slightest rumor of the vehicle, when they finally saw the silhouette detach itself in the distance before them.

- "Follow me," Kyaw Zaw breathed, rushing bent toward a hillock. Both plastered themselves against it, panting, warm grass stuck to their cheeks.

Kyaw Zaw withdrew a pair of binoculars from his pack, which he pointed toward their objective.

- "Damn! The *sit kwe*!" he cursed, handing the instrument to his companion.

Khin Yadanar observed the khaki truck that filled her field of vision. No doubt about it: it was an army vehicle. A dozen soldiers were transferring sacks from a dinghy onto the truck's platform. She let herself fall backward, her gaze captured by the routed clouds. Kyaw Zaw continued to fume quietly beside her. When she straightened up, her decision was already made.

- "Going around would take too long," she began. "And this is just the vanguard. Tomorrow, the area will be swarming with soldiers," she continued, unrolling in her arguments. "And they have a boat...," she concluded.

Kyaw Zaw stared at her slack-jawed, confused. She fixed him without flinching, her lips pursing slightly in a determined moue. A flash crossed his eyes:

- "Steal the boat?" he exclaimed, raising his voice before catching himself. "That's insane! Suicide!" he hissed, attempting to whisper.

- "Not if we wait for *moe thout chain*[89]. The place is quiet. The sentries won't be overzealous. I'll bet you they'll all be asleep. They won't even notice."

He remained mute, confusion and disbelief etched on his face. The shadow of a memory crossed his forehead like a black veil. The episode of the village set ablaze. Was he wondering about her motivations? Was she a thrill-seeker taking incautious risks that would lead him to his doom?

- "I'm not suicidal!" she defended herself. "It's the only solution. We're out of supplies and have no other option for crossing. We watch them tonight and try our chance at first light. At the first doubt, we back down, promised."

---

[89] Burmese expression referring to the hour before dawn, when light begins to appear on the horizon but the sun has not yet risen.

The guerrilla fighter nodded, wariness still clinging to his pupils. She feigned not to notice, stretched out, her head resting on her pack.

- "Take the first watch," she said, letting it fall with false innocence in her voice. "Wake me in three hours."

Night slipped down as a single heavy block, sticky and clammy, wearing at the bodies and drawing sweat from every pore. Though exhausted, Khin Yadanar found no sleep. At her watch, she struggled greatly to stay awake, eyes fixed upon the black mass of the vehicle. Around the pallid campfire, nothing stirred. In the silence punctuated by Kyaw Zaw's breathing, her mind wandered toward Kee Mawng. She pulled out her phone. One bar and a weak 2G connection. She hadn't sent him a word for a week. The lack of network in the massif and the need to save her battery. Or rather because she feared his objections, because part of her doubted her own undertaking.

The expression on Kyaw Zaw's face returned to her memory. Was he right to question her motivations? So much ground covered. Only the final straight stretch remained. Turn back? Impossible. Between them and the Chinese hills stretched a jungle without provisions, zones controlled by the Tatmadaw. No. They had to press forward. Cross to Win Ka, find the *stūpa*, then continue into Thailand. They would have to steal the boat right under the soldiers' noses. A risky wager, but "we have no choice," she intoned to herself. Freedom or death. This alternative imposed itself.

She had to contact Kee Mawng without delay, without risking disappearing again without opening her heart. But she couldn't call him in the dead of night... She was lying. She could if she'd wanted to. He would try to dissuade her, she wouldn't find the words. Their conversation would turn into conflict. It would be his last memory of her. Better to write. A message on Signal he would see upon waking, too late. Cowardice, but she began to type:

My Love,

We've arrived at Daik-U. Kyaw Zaw is a good guide for his age. He reminds me of you. He knows the Bago mountains as you know those of Mindat. I wouldn't have made it without my training at the CDF. I held on to the end because of you. You lifted me when I fell, you made me laugh when I wanted to die. You've become my only family, my reason for living.

And how have I thanked you? I left you when you needed me. Forgive me. But I would have been a burden if I'd stayed. I needed to reclaim control of my life. You must understand: since I left, every danger I face is MY choice. No more anonymous planes deciding my fate. When the Tatmadaw arrested me, when our convoy was ambushed (I didn't tell you so you wouldn't worry), when we crossed the jungle under the typhoon... It was MY decision. Each situation gave me the opportunity to act, to help, or to understand my limits. And tomorrow, we'll attempt to steal a boat from the Tatmadaw to cross the river. We risk death. But it's the only way to continue.

You know now why I'm writing rather than calling: you'd try to stop me. And even if you were right, I'd resent you for it. Because nothing can dissuade me, you know. You know me too well. If I survive, you'll receive another message soon from the other shore. If not... But whatever happens, know that you are everything to me. You've saved me more than once, often from myself. You couldn't this time. You couldn't help it, so don't blame yourself. And whatever the future holds for us, be certain that I can only envision mine in your arms. Take care of yourself. I will return to you, whatever the cost. I love you.

Awm Awi

She read her message once, twice. Corrected a word, softened a phrase. It might be the last she would write to him. Every word had to count. Every silence too. She had to be honest. And he had to understand. She pressed send. In the pallid screen that dimmed, she saw the reflection of her grave face. Night was drawing to a close. Still that leaden immobility around the truck. It was now or never. She shook Kyaw Zaw's shoulder. He opened haggard eyes, groaned, muttered, and wiped a trickle of drool with the back of his hand.

- "It's time."

Adrenaline struck hard and her fatigue vanished. She had barely slept, but what did it matter? "When I am dead," she threw at herself as a challenge. In silence, they performed the oft-repeated motions, packed their rucksacks, crawled to the ridge, observed the objective one last time. Everything was still.

Without a word, they began their approach. Soft footsteps, backs bent, vegetation for cover. To the East, a clear line appeared on the horizon, a demarcation between two infinities that darkness had joined. Dawn was coming. They accelerated. Only twenty meters separated them from the camp. The first birds began their symphony. The soldiers could wake at any second. The long boat had been pulled halfway onto the shore. Between them and this ark of salvation: the truck, a Trojan horse concealing countless unknown dangers. But they were so close to their goal they could almost touch freedom. Kyaw Zaw made a gesture. The moment had come. Khin Yadanar adjusted the straps of her pack. They advanced through the mud, their steps muffled by waterlogged earth. Before them floated the typhoon's wreckage: torn branches, shipwrecked planks, tarps transformed into shrouds. The water took on a metallic sheen, the color of molten tin that gave the landscape a lunar aspect. Mist attempted to rise, laboriously.

Kyaw Zaw reached the boat first. With a precise gesture, he cut the moorings. Carefully, they slid the boat into the water. Khin Yadanar climbed aboard. The faint lapping against the hull sounded to her like a tsunami. But everything remained lifeless around them. They rowed away, with slow, calculated strokes, each time the wood plunged through the surface. Fifty meters already. They were going to make it. Mist rose to the boat's rail, a sea of clouds bearing them toward the sky, which would soon mask their flight. A few dozen meters more and it would be done.

She flashed a triumphant smile at Kyaw Zaw when a shock rocked the boat. A tree trunk had rammed them, torpedo borne by the current, before continuing its course downstream, indifferent. The two rebels turned toward the shore. The back of the truck was stirring. No other choice. Kyaw Zaw pulled the motor cord. It coughed, wouldn't start. The commotion intensified, the first figures jumping from the truck with shouts. He tried again. In vain. A first detonation, followed by a whistle near their heads. He pulled once more. This time, the motor began to purr. Both threw themselves against the floor. Kyaw Zaw seized the helm to steer their blind course. The boat lunged forward, a terrified, trembling prey. Its roar drowned out the barks and gunfire, carrying in its wake a final vision of the gesticulating mob. Several flashes continued to herald the arrival of projectiles that bit the surface around them without ever finding their mark.

Khin Yadanar rose carefully. They were alone in the mist that surrounded them completely, washing away space and time, as if their frantic flight had carried them into another dimension. They floated in an infinite ether, erasing all points of reference. Only the pale light radiating through the frosted glass before them confirmed they were still heading the right way. Assured they were out of range, Kyaw Zaw straightened at the helm, eyes fixed on the uniformity to guide their vessel through the obstacles: thatched roofs, submerged trees, electric poles, forcing him to weave. Gradually, the hands of the nascent sun passed beneath the curtain of mist to lift it, illuminating the traps but transforming the water's surface into a blinding mirror. It was then she heard the noise. A cry more shrill, more powerful, adding to theirs in crescendo. She turned and saw, emerging from the vapors behind them, the silhouette of a boat. The soldiers had called for reinforcements.

- "Kyaw Zaw!" she shouted.

He had seen it. His face hardened. That same expression as during the convoy attack. Behind them, their pursuers drew inexorably closer. He pushed the engine to full throttle. Bullets began to fly again, but with greater precision. Khin Yadanar heard their whistling, felt their deadly breath. One bullet tore a splinter of wood near her hand. Another pierced the hull and water began to seep in. Kyaw Zaw continued to zigzag, using each obstacle as a rampart. He grazed a roofline which scraped the young woman's cheek. Their vessel was not faster, but nimbler. After long minutes, the distance began to increase again. Meanwhile, the sun was finishing its work of chasing away the last wisps of mist. They were exposed.

Before them, the far shore gradually took shape. A row of palms, the ridgeline of the Tenasserim massif, hope. Within a mile, they could disappear into the jungle.

- "We're almost there!" Kyaw Zaw shouted.

It was at that instant that the bullet struck him in the shoulder. Khin Yadanar saw his body arch under the impact. He cried out, his hand released the helm, and he collapsed to the bottom of the boat. His blood was already mingling with the brown water seeping through the holes. The vessel continued on its course, without direction, like a panicked horse in full gallop. Khin Yadanar crawled toward the helm, pack still pressed against her back. Regaining control was an absolute priority. The boat pitched upon the waves, hurling them into the air before catching them hard against its wooden floor. She passed her companion curled up and moaning, finally reached the motor. She seized the helm, straightened to resume course.

It was then she saw it: the corrugated metal roof of a house, emerging flush with the water like a reef, directly in line with the bow.

- "Kyaw Zaw!" she had only time to cry.

Too late. The boat struck the obstacle head-on. The impact hurled the vessel and its occupants into the air before they crashed violently into the muddy water.

Khin Yadanar could not swim. This truth came back like a punch to the stomach. Fortunately, an air pocket in her pack allowed her to float, despite the waves dragging her toward the depths. But water was pouring in and she felt the weight pressing on her back. She beat desperately with arms and legs to keep her head above the surface as the current swept her away. The taste of silt filled her mouth. She wouldn't last long. Around her, debris floated past, nearly striking her.

From the corner of her eye, she spotted a tree coming toward her about ten meters away. Last chance. She redoubled her efforts, at the edge of exhaustion, to accelerate toward its branches. Water poured in nauseating gulps, burning her throat, making her cough. She was running out of air, her lips no longer able to find the surface now that her pack was completely waterlogged. Her legs gave out first, unable to support her torso any longer. Her shoulders followed, carrying her head with them.

She was completely submerged. A bubble of air escaped from her gaping mouth in a silent cry, the last her lungs had managed to preserve.

In one final desperate surge, she thrust her arm out of the water. She felt leaves and bark tear at her skin. Her fingers found a branch and clung to it. She was suddenly jerked but held on. With the energy of desperation, she pulled, managed to grasp with her other arm, finally heaved herself to emerge. She took her first breath, mouth agape and starving for air, coughing, and weeping like a newborn. She managed to rest her elbows, chest, then belly on the branch, dragging the pack that continued to pull her backward. Exhausted, sprawled on her makeshift raft, she was trying to gather her wits when she heard a long, barely audible moan. She lifted her head.

- "Khin Yadanar!"

The call grew clearer, though muffled by the roar of water. She spotted Kyaw Zaw gesticulating dozens of meters away, struggling against the currents with his wounded shoulder. He was swimming awkwardly toward her, trying to grab debris. She was in despair. She could not swim, she was exhausted, she could be of no help to him. Powerless, she cried out to encourage him while trying to direct the trunk with her legs. But nothing worked. The tree was too heavy and continued its momentum toward shore, while the current dragged Kyaw Zaw in the opposite direction.

Gradually, his silhouette shrank, his voice became a murmur, his arm, which she could still see flailing frantically above the waves, finally disappeared. She let out a long bellow of distress, shoulders wracked with sobs, eyes burning with tears. It was as if her entire body had decided to surrender, her energy dissolving into the aquatic landscape. She lost consciousness, hands still clenched upon the tree that carried her into the unknown.

Chapter 23

Cambridge, United-Kingdom, September 2024

My dear Ayaan,

What cruel irony that this illness which has stolen my voice should arrive precisely when I had so much to confide in you. We met too late. Too late, also, my past has reemerged when my body had already abandoned me, preventing me from exorcising the ghosts that came to haunt me. I spent my existence fleeing and burying my demons, instead of confronting them when I still possessed the capacity. It is my fault. Perhaps you will learn from my mistakes.

Doubtless you have wondered at the reason which impelled me to abandon the research I had undertaken in Burma before the war. Independence offered me the opportunity, and the Royal Society would willingly have assumed the formalities. But I preferred to turn the page, as one closes a book which certain chapters have left a bitter taste. You see, this country which was my field of adventure had become my field of ruins. I lost far more there than ancient artefacts. It took everything from me, body and soul. My very ideals rest there still, alongside beings who were so dear to me, somewhere in those humid valleys where silence now reigns. Hatred, violence, death had passed through there.

I contributed to it. I do not seek absolution. My hands are dirty, covered in blood that no tears could wash away. They bear the traces of an epoch when violence reigned and when a grief-stricken young man allowed his anger to guide his acts. I fought, I killed, from rage, without even the noble alibi of patriotism. Thus, I have always hidden my service record, of which my Burma Star was the symbol. I relegated it to the closet, ashamed that one might see a hero in me. Even after the armistice, rancour continued to inhabit me. I was alone, no one remained, including my parents, whose boat sank after their evacuation, without my having the opportunity to say farewell. It nearly happened that I yielded to the temptation of the final voyage, felt my resolutions waver.

Then, I made a choice: that of living, or rather reliving. I methodically rebuilt my existence after my demobilization, with 1945 as my new beginning. Before it, nothing existed. At SOAS, I changed my Burmese studies for India, a scholar's promenade that allowed my mind to breathe air less laden with memories. Then appeared your dear great-grandmother Betty, encountered in the course of my research. A luminous woman who never feared my shadows. We journeyed together from excavations to conferences, settled in Cambridge, saw Michael born, then the entire line that preceded you. Everything moved forward. My past had disappeared behind the screen erected by the military dictatorship to isolate Burma from the rest of the world.

At least, I tried to convince myself of it. But nothing is ever so simple, is it? One can lie to oneself. The problem is there is no one to believe you.

The adage holds that it is better to live with remorse than with regrets. At the time, it was already too late to follow it. Memories, which have the unfortunate habit of resurfacing at the most inopportune moments, broke the surface when night came, assailing me with questions I believed I had buried. What had we discovered? What did the tablet and the inscriptions on the wall say? What remained in the stūpa that we had not had time to excavate? I had lost the tablet and my notebook in the crash. Nevertheless, I could still have found the site again, resumed my research, completed what we had suspended. Instead, I continued trying to repress these questions, each time a bit more deeply. But it was only postponing the day when they would finally erupt into the open.

Then came the message from Khin Yadanar. Destiny's final turn, which seemed to take pleasure in reminding me of my abandonments. The tablet had been found, my old notebook exhumed. But my failing memory would render me incapable of pointing out the exact location of the site on a map. Delicious irony. The hour of academic glory sounds, and your estimable great-grandfather can no longer lay his hands on his own treasure. You inform me it could be a major discovery. But I will die before knowing its contents. Thus goes the human comedy. The sole and ultimate lesson every man must learn facing death:

nothing is ever quite finished. And, to each remorse one nourishes, there comes one or two regrets to accompany it.

Do not believe yourself obliged to repair my failings. I first pushed you to take up the torch, the gentle madness of a centenarian convinced that an unfinished adventure contravenes good manners. A final will by proxy. I sought to make you my instrument, and I beg your pardon. But it seemed to me I saw in your gaze the same flame that animated me. The temptation of challenge, the pleasure of discovery. A game for curious and ambitious minds. So, use this quest only if the allure of research, that frisson which makes the academic's soul vibrate, truly seduces you. Otherwise, let it rest peacefully. Mysteries bear the company of centuries very well.

What a pity my body refused me the vitality and time to conduct this research with you. Through it, I would have liked to learn to know you. Another discovery I would not bring to completion. Another failure. One last regret.

I read, with pleasure mingled with a suspicion of jealousy, the drafts of translation produced by my colleague Forsythe. A brilliant man, though dangerously inclined to lyricism. A fault of our profession when one frequents too many papyri and too little rain. I wish him the opportunity to invest himself more deeply in fieldwork. Nothing allows one better to take the measure of centuries than extracting heaps of earth with a spade. Compliment him on my behalf; simply avoid mentioning my reserve - a phantom must know how to conduct itself discreetly. After all, this work no longer falls to me. We are merely messengers, custodians of knowledge that each generation transmits to the next. My time has passed. Let this become his.

His theory is certainly captivating. It remains to be seen whether what the stūpa contains will confirm it. If Khin Yadanar manages to locate it, naturally. A courageous young woman (Burmese women generally are) who evokes in me the memory of a painful past. Perhaps it is preferable we never met, she and I. The suffering would have been unbearable. I will say no more. There are secrets I will take with me. It is better this way.

As for me, time presses. I feel each beat of my old clock as a reminder of a seminar I can no longer give. There remains for me, however, the ultimate satisfaction of having broken the silence that was imposed upon me and made me a spectator of my own history. Lacking voice, I will have found ink. Lacking presence, these pages. May they reach you with that lightness I envy to autumn leaves, swirling briefly before settling, without sound, where life continues.

I send you my affection. May your paths be marked by discoveries, by fruitful doubts, and above all, by that discreet humour which helps one bear the scars of existence.

Anthony W. Preston

Ayaan set the letter down on the bed. He was in his room at Gonville & Caius College. He lifted his head, his eyes lost in the drizzle that was falling soundlessly against the window in the grey light of morning. This morning, he would not run. He had received the post the day before and decided to wait until the weekend to read it. Classes would resume in two weeks, and his summer digressions had already cost him too much time. He had to pull himself together. He could not allow an old brick monument to jeopardize his future.

Despite his usual composure, the temptation to open the envelope had been unbearable. On the back, Nancy's address with these words: "On behalf of Professor Preston." The hope of a revelation, a message from beyond the grave. It was stronger than him. The mystery continued to obsess him. An addiction. He had become antisocial, distant. His friends returned from Spain seemed trivial to him. When he wasn't studying, he pored over maps of Win Ka, read news from Myanmar, waited for a message from Khin Yadanar. In vain. He felt lost, unable to control his thoughts. This sense of helplessness was an open wound.

Professor Preston's letter brought him no comfort. Instead, a chaos of feelings he couldn't untangle. Disappointment first, in the absence of any new clues. Then pity mixed with contempt for this old man pouring out his regrets. And self-loathing at his own lack of sorrow. His great-grandfather had felt affection for him, even complicity, bound by the mystery that united them. This absence of reciprocity questioned Ayaan's own humanity. The professor apologized for wanting to use him. The truth was the opposite. Ayaan had appropriated the sick man's research, exploited his helplessness to remove him permanently. He had done it without remorse. And even now, he would do it again. All these sensations jostled in a chaos he couldn't order. Above all, frustration surged and churned the ocean of his inner tempest.

Yes, he was frustrated. By the futility of his introspection, the uselessness of the post, his very existence. He received the letter yesterday. The same day, he learned of Khin Yadanar's disappearance. News that brought a brutal end to his quixotic quest.

A message from Kee Mawng on Signal. Despite his approximate English, the meaning was clear: Khin Yadanar had announced, in what amounted to a farewell letter, her intention to steal an army boat. Madness. She had given no sign of life since. "The fool!" he had raged inwardly. What was she thinking? He had replied with the usual courtesies, but his anger would not subside. Khin Yadanar's disappearance marked the death knell of their search. A *stūpa* which location he had never found. The same day. Message and letter, the same day!

His great-grandfather had been right: fate mocked their family, launching them on quests full of promise only to pull the ground from under their feet. Generations of Sisyphus taking turns pushing their rock, never reaching the summit. He took the pages, crumpled them, and hurled them in exasperation. The ball of paper struck the window with a dull thud. His phone rang. Forsythe. Nine o'clock—what could he possibly want? Ayaan picked up in a flat voice:

- "Good morning, Professor."

- "Good morning, Ayaan. I'm not waking you, I hope?" It was not a question. Euphoria transpired from his voice. "The *stūpa*! We found it!" shouted the academic.

Ayaan nearly burst into laughter. Not joy, but spite. Really, fate was playing tricks on him. He was already searching for how to announce it no longer mattered, that they would have to abandon it. For the first time in his life, he would know failure. A bitter, unpleasant taste flooded through him.

- "You heard me?" insisted the professor, surprised by his silence.

- "Yes, sorry. How is that possible?" Ayaan forced himself to ask, more from politeness than genuine interest.

- "Xplorer. I've just sent you their report. It's technical, I'll simplify. They used satellite imagery from Sentinel-2, the European Copernicus programme. But also, from WorldView-2 and TerraSAR-X. No matter. They searched for crop marks, persistent thermal signatures, analysed hydrological anomalies, soil stratigraphy, and detected microtopography. And *voilà*!"

He had enumerated all this in a breath, with palpable excitement. As if obvious. All Greek to Ayaan, but his curiosity was aroused.

- "That sounds interesting. Could you walk me through it?"

- "Of course!" The professor did not need to be asked twice. "Buried structures modify vegetation growth on the surface. The *stūpa*'s excavation before the war left traces. Brick foundations, buried walls, which still affect soil moisture and plant nutrition. Specific signatures like vegetation stressed above buried walls. Conversely, luxuriant above fertile fill left by excavation. Detectable in infrared."

- "That's what you meant by 'crop marks,' then?"

- "Quite right. Infrared analysis also revealed the *stūpa's* distinct thermal signature. A brick structure, even partially buried, has different thermal inertia than soil. And then the hydrological anomalies, that is, differences in soil moisture. Indeed, the 1941 excavation created water-retention zones that persist."

- "You mentioned 'microtopography'?"

- "Indeed, even after eighty years, the microreliefs created by excavation remain visible. Variations in elevation between excavated and intact zones. They revealed the excavation plan corresponding to Preston's sketch notes."

- "You're certain this is the *stūpa* my great-grandfather discovered?"

- "Not a shadow of doubt," confirmed Forsythe. "The 1941 excavations left rectilinear geometric traces, distinct from natural formations. They revealed subsidiary structures, access paths, enclosure walls. This constellation of anomalies forms a unique pattern, identifiable by artificial intelligence. It is the *stūpa*. And its coordinates are: 17.238345°N, 97.085024°E!" he concluded in a triumphant voice.

- "Remarkable," conceded Ayaan. "A shame it's come too late, though," he announced gravely.

- "What do you mean?" asked Forsythe, alarmed.

- "Khin Yadanar went missing in the flooded zone near Bago," offered Ayaan in a hollow voice. "Presumed dead. She had the tablet with her."

- "Good Lord, that's dreadful! Poor woman!" lamented the researcher with genuine empathy. "Did she have family?"

Ayaan did not know how to respond. He had never asked the question. He knew nothing of her beyond what had emerged in their conversations. Nothing personal. She had remained only a means to an end. He did not even have a photograph of her. Almost anonymous. A heavy silence settled. Each searched for words. Finally, Forsythe ventured:

- "I'm terribly sorry to hear it. A woman of remarkable courage, by all accounts. Who risked everything to assist us. Would you be able to pass along the contact of the person who reached you? I'd very much like to know if she had family, and whether there's anything we might do to help."

- "Of course," answered Ayaan. "I'll sort it."

He suspected their conversation was drawing to a close. With it, their collaboration. What more could they tell each other if they abandoned their research?

- "Look, the loss of the tablet is one thing," Forsythe continued, as Ayaan made ready to hang up. "We'll never manage to decipher the text from photographs alone. Possibly the country's oldest artefact, which is genuinely unfortunate from a scholarly standpoint. A real shame. But there's still the *stūpa* itself..."

- "Though without Khin Yadanar on the ground..."

- "Couldn't we simply find someone else?" suggested Forsythe with simplicity.

A flash passed through Ayaan's mind. He had been stuck, focused on the obstacle rather than the solution. He was angry with himself. He must seem like a fool. Wounded in his ego, he hastened to present an alternative.

- "I've built up quite a network within the Burmese community here in London. I can put the word out."

- "Excellent! With any luck..."

- "I'll keep you informed," promised Ayaan, invigorated by this new hope.

- "Even without the tablet, whatever we unearth at the *stūpa* ought to support my hypothesis."

- "What are you hoping to find, exactly?"

- "Well, the Buddha's relics, naturally. The hair that Sona and Uttara brought to Suvannabhumi. Proof that this *stūpa* is the country's first, that a Mon kingdom existed three centuries BC, that Buddhism arrived a thousand years earlier than we'd thought. Rather a major find, archaeologically speaking. Would reshape everything we understand about the region's history. Enough to occupy researchers for decades once this war business is sorted. Absolutely thrilling!" The academic's voice practically crackled with excitement. "It would rather be a coup for the resistance movement as well."

- "How d'you mean?"

- "The junta bangs on about being guardians of Buddhism, right? For years now, their propaganda's painted every general as some warrior king building pagodas, defending the faith against Islam. Imagine the embarrassment of the SAC[90] if the country's first *stūpa* and its relics were excavated by the opposition. Especially by ethnic minorities. Massive loss of face. The resistance could genuinely unite all the Buddhists against the military. As Russell Banks put it rather well: 'More than on battlefields, war is waged these days over symbols like never before.'"

- "Right, I see," approved Ayaan thoughtfully. "So, my inquiry will probably generate considerable interest from Burmese organizations in London."

- "It's certain. We're on the home stretch now. Fingers crossed they can rustle up local support quickly. The situation round Win Ka is unstable and could become a flashpoint any moment. Thaton's been under KNU[91] control for a year. The junta's been beefing up conscription and consolidating positions since June, gearing up for a counter-push. Hard to know what the

---

[90] State Administrative Council. Military junta that has governed Myanmar since the coup of February 1, 2021, led by General Min Aung Hlaing.
[91] Karen National Union. Political organization founded in 1947 that represents the Karen people of Myanmar with its armed wing, the Karen National Liberation Army (KNLA), and has been fighting for Karen self-determination since 1949.

typhoon's done to things. But we've got to locate the *stūpa* before the fighting makes it inaccessible."

- "I'll keep you informed as soon as possible," confirmed Ayaan before bidding his interlocutor farewell.

He knew what he had to do. He opened his email and began sending messages to his Burmese contacts.

Chapter XXIV

Rangoon, Burma, March 1942

Anthony burst into the railway station plaza, breathless, a theatre of desolation evoking apocalypse. Thousands of souls pressed together in a surging mass of flesh and clamor. Indians, Chinese, Burmese - the Europeans having been evacuated first - screamed, pleaded, gestured, jostled, pushed, pulled, ebbed according to the whims of the human torrent churning this desperate multitude. All attempted frantically to force their way through the police cordon regulating access to the building. A heap of baggage cluttered the center of the plaza, abandoned in the hope of securing a place on the last convoys leaving Rangoon. All around, the decay of civil order manifested in every detail. The acrid scent of fear saturated the atmosphere. The air, thick with dark smoke, rose from the burning quarters near the port. Vehicles littered the avenue, neutralized or destroyed to prevent their use by the enemy. Only a few automobiles bearing the "E" - for "Essential" - still circulated, transporting the last British officials toward an uncertain future.

Anthony was late. He had moved cautiously through the deserted streets to avoid armed bands, keeping to the walls and concealing himself at every suspicious sound. Now he wondered how to find Professor Sayer and Nandar Aye in this chaos. He climbed the base of a lamppost and scanned the crowd. He finally spotted Sayer frantically waving his arms at the far end of the plaza, dressed in his habitual uniform: beige cotton trousers and white shirt.

- "Sorry I'm late," Anthony offered as he reached the professor.

Nandar Aye stood beside him with her mother, a small, spare middle-aged woman, wearing a simple brown *longyi* topped with an immaculate blouse. Anthony greeted her respectfully, and she returned a shy smile.

- "Not at all, we've only just arrived," Sayer replied, his gaze falling on Anthony's satchel. "You're travelling light. Sensible choice, that. I've had the devil of a time deciding what to take along," the scholar confessed with a grimace, gesturing to two bulky canvas bags at his feet.

From the angular bulges deforming them, Anthony understood they were books. Each must have weighed thirty pounds at least. How on earth had they managed to carry them here? He himself had brought only a spare shirt, a bar of soap, a toothbrush, besides the stone tablet and the metal box with his notebook, which already filled most of his bag.

- "Any word from your parents?"

- "Butt was spot on," Anthony admitted reluctantly. "They held on as long as they possibly could. In the end, they embarked a week ago with other Burmah Oil and Steel Brothers families, all headed for Madras," he explained, clutching the folded letter in his pocket.

Suu, his former Burmese *ayah*[92], who had remained with his parents after he went to boarding school, had given it to him. The family home had been ransacked completely, but she had somehow hidden the envelope and sealed package that came with it, hoping each day for the prodigal son's return. She had embraced him tenderly, tears streaking the *thanaka* from her cheeks, before letting him go. Both knew the reprisals she'd face if discovered fraternizing with a Briton. He'd left with a broken heart, unable to look back at that figure guarding the ruins of his forever-shattered past. In the package lay Burmese rupees, his father's gold pocket watch, several gold chains, and his mother's ring, set with a magnificent cabochon ruby from Mogok. He silently blessed Suu's loyalty: she had kept, untouched, this treasure that might yet save his life in the days ahead.

- "They're safe. That must be a relief," Sayer stated without emotion. "Now we must find a means to get out of the city..."

- "Impossible to get through to the station entrance with this mob," Anthony protested with a sharp click of his tongue. "Unless..." he concluded cryptically, rushing toward a group of soldiers dismounting from a truck a few meters away.

A minute later, military police were clearing a path through the crowd, beating back Indian refugees with batons and curses, escorting the two Britons and their companions to the station

---

entrance. The journey nearly sparked a riot more than once, but they reached the building unscathed, Sayer and Anthony shouldering the book-laden bags. Two Indian policemen let them pass the barriers, but lowered their weapons to block Nandar Aye and her mother. The two men stopped dead.

- "No Burmans," the soldier stated curtly.

- "They're with us. My wife and daughter," the academic lied, visibly struggling to maintain courtesy despite the anger simmering beneath. "And this is my son-in-law," he continued, gesturing to Anthony.

One of the soldiers grunted, then raised his weapon while aggressively shaking his head to urge the two women to hurry. Without even giving them a glance, he closed the passage and turned his attention back to the mass still writhing on the other side of the barriers.

Passing through the station's gates amounted to entering a Dantean circle where the exodus of an empire was orchestrated. They crossed the main hall packed with a routed humanity: families amid mountains of baggage, children clinging to saris, men feverishly scanning the departure boards. Anthony noted that the next train was scheduled for seven-thirty. They had time.

Their group continued to the platforms, which atmosphere contrasted with the tempest outside, the crowd pressing there with resignation under the watchful eye of a hundred uniformed Indians. They found an unoccupied corner, set down their baggage, and settled in silence. Sayer pulled a book from his sack and began to leaf through it. Nandar Aye did the same with her novel, while her mother fingered her beads in meditation. Anthony had no mind to read. Too many thoughts collided in his mind to allow concentration. He tried to calm himself by focusing on his surroundings.

The great red-brick pylons of the station, built in 1877 in Victorian style, stood like pathetic sentinels against the debacle. The colonial architecture, with its wrought-iron awnings imported from Scotland, suddenly seemed fragile and incongruous amid this desperate human tide. The beauty of the building, which residents once called the "Fairy Station," was sullied by the bitterness of defeat. After the plunder of the family home, the spectacle of the empire's decay brought him no comfort. Nothing remained of his past, his future, his identity.

Depressed, he opened his satchel, extracted the metal box and his notebook. He saw Nandar Aye observing his actions attentively from the corner of her eye before plunging back into her reading as if nothing were amiss. Her behavior bewildered him: she rejected him while continuously spying on him. No doubt she was troubled by the same fears that tormented him. He resolved to speak with her openly as soon as the opportunity arose. But not now, not here. He took a pencil and began to scribble, recording on paper their adventures since Win Ka. Writing would be the outlet that might allow him to exorcise his fears. He plunged into his memories. The station, the refugees, the entire world rapidly disappeared beneath the race of his hand, a metronome that gave new measure to time. He did not even notice the gathering darkness announcing the fall of night.

He had reached their interview with Lieutenant-Colonel Butt at Pegu when three shrill whistles suddenly recalled him to reality. The train was entering the station in reverse. The populace stirred like a flock of starlings jolted awake by gunfire, immediately plunging the platforms into chaos. All rushed upon the convoy like a pack of hyenas upon a carcass, scrambling to climb the carriages which filled within seconds, while the mass remaining on the platform continued to vociferate and press forward demanding its place. The soldiers attempted to contain and control the crowd movement threatening to degenerate into riot. Blows from truncheons rained down. In vain. Sayer and Anthony had gathered their sacks and found themselves at the rear of the throng with their companions, desperately striving to find a space to insert themselves through the mass of compressed bodies. But nothing availed. Despite their efforts to push aside those before them, they proved unable to penetrate further, systematically forced back by new arrivals more virulent and aggressive, heedless of the two women. The train seemed as distant and inaccessible as ever when the engine whistled three times again to signal its imminent departure.

Nandar Aye turned and faced Anthony, gripping his shoulders and raising her eyes to fix him with urgency.

- "Hand me the tablet and leave!" she shouted, her features drawn by a panic he'd never seen in her. "Alone, you still have a chance! The police will help you find a seat because you're white!"

- "Absolutely not!" Anthony shot back, stunned she could think of him capable of abandoning her now.

A metallic grinding sounded as the train composed of hastily requisitioned carriages lurched forward. The engine strained beneath the weight of desperate humanity that bent each compartment into an improvised ark.

- "Go! Please!" she implored. "Hurry! Or it'll be too late!"

Anthony didn't move, paralyzed by his lover's pleas. It was already too late anyway. The train began to glide along the platform as families wrenched apart in agony, not all having found seats. Hands stretched through windows, faces contorted with the effort of holding back tears until distance forced them to let go. Some, in one last spasm of bourgeois dignity, had refused third-class accommodation, their relatives departing with exasperated expressions. On the platform, the left behind watched the taillights recede into dusk with the resignation of those who know they'll face the storm alone. For behind them, Rangoon was already burning, and no one knew if other trains would leave before the Japanese arrived. Anthony and Sayer let their bags of books fall with a dull thud onto the concrete.

- "I'll find out when the next train departs," the professor announced in a tone meant to sound detached and optimistic, moving toward the main hall accompanied by Nandar Aye's mother.

Anthony didn't respond. Nandar Aye looked away to avoid his eyes. He felt accumulated frustration rise uncontrollably.

- "Why did you ask me to leave?" he demanded, struggling to keep calm.

She didn't answer, her gaze fixed on the ground. Her silence and apparent betrayal only fueled his anger and jealousy.

- "Was it so you could send me away and stay alone with him? Is that it?" he exploded with contempt. "You used me," he hissed, his voice glacial and bitter. "You never loved me!"

Nandar Aye suddenly straightened to face him, her eyes brimming with tears fixed upon him with a suffering and fury that made her muscles tremble. Her lips moved, but no words crossed them. Anthony's skull vibrated from a slap he didn't see coming.

- "Sixteen," she whispered suddenly, as if breathless. "I was sixteen when my mother pushed me into his bed!" she continued, fists clenched, as dull rage replaced her distress.

She, who had been silent a second before now, spoke as if no dam could hold back the torrent pouring from her mouth.

- "We lived on the street. It was the only way to survive. He gave us shelter, he saved us. And he gave me opportunities I could never have dreamed of. How many daughters of farmers and coolies make it to university? None! And yet, I get no pride from it, no respect. No one acknowledges my work, my abilities. Burmans and British alike treat me like a whore. They're probably right... Isn't it what I am, in the end? But do you know what it's like to abandon all self-respect? To debase yourself, to enslave yourself entirely because you have no choice? I know he loves me. I'm grateful for his generosity. We owe him everything. And yet, you can't imagine how much I hate him! I'm his slave, forced to give myself to him out of fear of losing everything, out of obligation to my mother. My own body no longer belongs to me. Only my thoughts, my feelings remain mine. But I must constantly hide them. I'm like a lion in a cage, a cage that compresses me, that suffocates me. I'm drowning. I can't take it anymore! How much longer can I hold on before I let myself die or bite the hand that feeds me? Now do you understand why I dream of independence? For myself as much as for my country?"

- "I'm sorry. I had no idea," Anthony offered as he watched her calm down.

He felt filthy, stupid, and contemptible. Consumed by selfish desire, it had never occurred to him to question the nature of Nandar Aye's relationship with Sayer, or the torments and feelings it might stir in her.

- "Then you appeared in my life," she continued, softening. "For the first time, I believed in happiness. A life where love, freedom, and security could coexist, without having to choose. Where I could be myself. I glimpsed a future. Then the war came. What future is left for us now?"

Her gaze darkened suddenly as reality caught up with her. She continued in a somber tone:

- "I'm in no danger if I stay in Rangoon. And I don't care about Arthur's fate. But I couldn't bear it if something happened to you. You must leave!"

- "We'll take another train," Anthony replied with confidence in his voice. "Or find another way. We still have time."

- "Don't lie!" the young Burman shot back, seeing through him. "You know the hours are numbered. We'll never manage to travel as a group, especially with my mother. You saw it just now. Alone, you have a chance. Even if we're separated, I need to know you're safe!"

- "We're not at that point yet," Anthony protested.

- "Promise me that when the time comes, if you have no choice, you'll flee and leave us behind," she pressed urgently. "Promise me!"

She was nearly shouting, hands gripping his forearms, tears filling those eyes fixed on him with intensity. He sighed.

- "I promise," he agreed reluctantly. "Is that why you pushed me away these past days?" he asked, thinking of her recent coldness. "You were trying to make me leave you and save myself?"

- "I'd rather know you alive and hating me far from here, than risk seeing you die beside me out of love," she admitted in a trembling voice.

- "So, you do love me?" Anthony asked, tears of his own finally coming.

- "Of course, you fool!" Nandar Aye confirmed, laughing and crying at once.

He couldn't resist any longer. He drew her into his arms and brought her trembling body against his chest. They gazed at each other in silence with intensity. She rose on tiptoe to reach him. He lowered his face. Their mouths joined in an enthusiastic kiss that made the world disappear. The platform, the crowd, the station, the war. Nothing existed for several seconds. Finally, Nandar Aye buried her face in Anthony's chest, who wrapped his arms around her and placed a kiss upon the crown of her head while inhaling the fragrance of her hair. She ordinarily nourished it with bewitching coconut oil, but it had been days since she had abandoned her coquettish rituals, offering a beauty without artifice that Anthony could not tear his eyes from.

Their bodies separated gently, their joined hands relaxing as well, their faces illuminated by complicit smiles. A movement caught their attention. They turned their heads. Sayer stood ten meters away, rigid, his face scarlet, the muscles of his jaw tensed in an expression of quiet fury. Anthony felt an electric shock run down his spine.

- "Arthur, I..." pleaded Nandar Aye, guilt coloring her voice.

She didn't even finish. The professor turned on his heel and strode rapidly toward the exit without bothering to collect his bags. The two lovers rushed after him.

- "Wait!" Nandar Aye called.

Her appeal had no effect. The scholar didn't even slow. Nandar Aye's mother, who had returned with Sayer, planted herself before them, hands on hips. Nandar Aye had no mind for argument, but the forty-something woman blocked their path.

- "How could you do this?" she cried angrily. "You're nothing but a whore! An ingrate! Have you forgotten everything the professor did for you?"

- "No, I haven't forgotten!" snapped Nandar Aye sarcastically.

The reference to the favors she'd had to grant in exchange was lost on no one. Anthony pretended not to follow the conversation to hide his discomfort. Her mother, by contrast, seemed to feel no guilt or shame.

- "But I don't love him!" the young woman tried to explain, confronted by her mother's "so what?" expression. "I love Anthony."

- "You stupid girl! A penniless boy! How will we live when the professor throws us into the street?" the woman sneered with a contemptuous wave toward the young Englishman.

- "Look around you!" exploded Nandar Aye. "The Japanese will be here in hours! Where will we live if we leave with the professor? And with what money will we live if we stay? It's finished!"

Her mother fell silent, finally seeming to grasp their situation, reproach giving way to terror on her face.

- "In any case, we'll have to manage to survive. You're afraid he'll throw us out? Wake up: we're already out! So why should I continue to sell myself?" she concluded with defiant air.

With that, she pushed past the obstacle without restraint, breaking Burmese custom making filial respect a sacred law, and hurried after Sayer. Anthony followed, abandoning the bags of books behind, his satchel his only luggage. He was immediately followed by the mother, who began trotting as fast as her *longyi* allowed, terrified at the thought of being abandoned by those upon whom her survival now depended.

Anthony glanced at the blackboard as he crossed the main hall of the station. It was empty. Nothing indicated other trains would be arranged. Panic seized him as he realized they'd perhaps missed the last means of evacuating the capital. Terrified, he caught up with Nandar Aye as she passed the barriers to force her way through the shrieking mass still pressing outside the building. All three struggled to swim against the current through the mob. It was already dark when they finally burst into the open air, onto the square they'd had such difficulty leaving hours before. They looked in every direction, scanning desperately empty streets. Sayer had vanished.

Chapter XXV

Rangoon, Burma, March 1942

Anthony stood transfixed by this sudden disappearance. How had his mentor vanished so swiftly into the streets radiating from the plaza? These thoroughfares, deserted to the limits of his sight, stretched into a twilight that the absence of street lighting rendered all the more oppressive. Rangoon lay beneath a shroud of near-absolute darkness, reeking of soot, from which emerged the skeletal silhouettes of abandoned buildings, silent sepulchers in this necropolis. Only the station's façade continued to project its yellowish, flickering light, pulsing in rhythm with the roars of the multitude.

He felt rising within him that same panic radiating from the refugees around him. No one knew if another convoy would depart. And while his survival instinct harassed him—a primitive beast that clawed, bit, tore at every fiber of his consciousness urging him to flee—another part of himself resisted desperately. Shame. That guilt which remained the last beacon capable of guiding a lost soul back to the shores of humanity. How could he have contemplated abandoning Sayer when his own betrayal had precipitated his flight?

Turning, he caught the questioning gazes of Nandar Aye and her mother, who awaited a signal. They remained serene, deaf to the frantic shouts around them, as if the abyss did not exist. The young woman bore that same determination as at Pegu. Despite the animosity she harbored toward the professor, she had not forgotten the debt that bound her to him. They had to find Sayer.

As if to settle their hesitations, a low rumble swelled in the night. First imperceptible, it became a mechanical roar that shook the ground. They turned their heads southward. At the end of the street, shafts of light pierced the darkness. One headlamp, then two, then an entire procession of trucks advancing in convoy, a herd emerging from the depths of night. A dozen in total, moving at measured pace, canvas covers taut, wheels turning in perfect unison. They aligned before the station, their engines idling. An officer leapt from the first vehicle and barked orders. Immediately, the military police abandoned their posts to run toward the vehicles, forcing their way through the crowd that surged like a tsunami into the building, sweeping away barriers, smashing glass, overturning furniture. The first soldiers plunged into the backs of the trucks. Their colleagues from the platforms would not be long in joining them. Anthony moved with quick pace toward the nearest vehicle. A non-commissioned officer had poked his head out to observe the scene.

- "What's all this about, Sergeant?" he hailed.

The MP, an Indian with a thick moustache barring his face, regarded him with mingled surprise and displeasure.

- "What the blazes are you doing here?" the military barked. "All civilians ought to have cleared out!"

- "That's precisely the reason we're here!" Anthony replied, his pride stung by the fellow's impertinence.

These Indians customarily addressed Britons – their *thakins* - with deference. This change in tone proved definitively to him that the Empire was collapsing.

- "We were hoping to catch the next train," he explained.

- "Forget it! There won't be another. We're the last convoy. Forty lorries are combing the city to round up our chaps. After that, we're done for. Rangoon will have to fend for itself..."

Anthony's face fell. The sergeant sighed with frustration.

- "Get aboard! We'll squeeze you in somewhere."

- "Thank you, but that won't do," Anthony apologized, gesturing toward the two Burmese women behind him to make clear he wasn't travelling alone.

- "They're welcome too," the soldier insisted, waving his arm to hurry them along.

- "We must first locate one of our party. We can't abandon him."

- "I can't just leave you here!" the sergeant cried out in frustration, plainly vexed by the young Englishman's stubbornness.

The sergeant made to dismount from the lorry but stopped upon seeing Anthony step back. At that same moment, the officer leading the convoy shouted an order whilst returning to his cab. The engines roared back to life, signaling imminent departure. The sergeant grumbled, clearly vexed at having to abandon Anthony. What trouble would this ungrateful Englishman bring down upon him if word got out? Yet he was no more inclined to risk his life chasing after the lad. He spat onto the ground to tell him to go to hell as the vehicles lurched forward.

- "How about a boat up the river?" Anthony shouted, running after the lorry.

- "Forget the docks!" the sergeant roared over the engine's din. "Force Viper's scuttled all the steamers!"

The distance widened despite Anthony's effort to quicken his pace. The swing of his satchel impeded his running, and the tablet's weight caused a sharp pain in his leg.

- "How can we leave the city, then?" he called out one final time with all his remaining strength, before stopping, exhausted, bent double, hands on his thighs.

- "Steer clear of the road! The Japs have got it cut off at the Bago Yoma!" the soldier hollered, half-hanging from the side, one hand gripping the canopy. "Mingaladon! That's your only shot! The last kites are off tonight!"

These were the last words Anthony managed to catch as the convoy's rear lights vanished at the corner of Sule Pagoda Road, abandoning him to the darkness. He turned about and rejoined

Nandar Aye and her mother, who waited for him, motionless shadows silhouetted against the faint glow emanating from the station. The rest of the square was deserted. Muffled detonations, barely audible, indicated that demolition operations continued near the docks.

- "We must find a car," he declared, his voice carrying a new resolve. "Any that still runs will do."

They set off in search, exploring the streets adjacent to the station. Most abandoned vehicles had been stripped bare - tires slashed, engines dismembered by expert hands, leaving only useless husks. Anthony was beginning to lose hope when he spotted, nestled in a dark alley near Canal Road[93], an Austin Seven bearing the letter "E," apparently intact. No doubt the property of some colonial official who'd abandoned it in his precipitous flight. He forced open the door and slipped behind the wheel. The key was in the ignition. He turned it and engaged the starter switch. The little four-cylinder coughed, sputtered, then began to hum with the reassuring regularity of well-maintained British mechanics.

- "Get in!" he called to the two women standing outside the vehicle.

- "Where are we going?" Nandar Aye asked as she took the seat beside him, her mother settling in the back.

---

[93] Present-day Anawratha Road.

- "To Sayer's, then to Mingaladon," Anthony explained, engaging first gear. "The last aircrafts are taking off tonight!"

They rushed through the streets of Rangoon heading east toward Goodliffe Road[94]. The city was nothing more than the dismal ghost of what it had been. The broad colonial avenues, once teeming with life, were now animated only by tongues of fire spewing from the gaping maws of administrative buildings, casting dancing shadows on the walls. No trace of life, no movement, save for rats emerging panicked from mounds of rubble and collapsed buildings surging suddenly from the darkness, forcing Anthony to swerve without time to brake. He decided to slow upon reaching Fraser Street in the commercial district, spotting figures moving about in the ruins of Rowe & Co., that "Harrods of the Orient" victim to Japanese bombardment. A band of looters, their arms laden with heterogeneous booty, rushed out and fled at their approach with the same swiftness as the rodents encountered earlier, no doubt convinced they were a military police vehicle. Anthony was forced to brake hard and swerve to avoid running one down.

Suddenly, a gang emerged from a side alley and headed toward their car, their intent immediately recognizable from the sticks and machetes they brandished.

- "Drive!" shrieked Nandar Aye as one of them was mere meters from her window.

---

[94] Present-day Saya San Road.

Anthony pressed down with all his weight on the gas pedal and the Austin leapt forward. The man attempted to grab the vehicle, but Anthony jerked the wheel, sending him rolling onto the asphalt. Stones rained down on the bodywork and the rear window shattered amid frightened exclamations from the back passenger. Then silence fell as the gang disappeared in the rearview mirror. Heart pounding, Anthony continued to race northward at breakneck speed, slowing only after a mile. They passed the residential quarters where, until recently, the British community had lived. Without a word, they watched rows of colonial villas flash past, systematically looted. Their wrenched-off doors gaped onto devastated interiors, broken furniture littered the lawns, torn pages of books fluttered in the night wind.

It was then they spotted the first creature. Anthony braked sharply, hardly believing his eyes. In the middle of the road stood a leopard, motionless, its golden eyes reflecting the headlights. The animal observed them for several seconds with that haughty dignity of great beasts, then disappeared with a lithe bound into the bushes of an abandoned garden.

- "They've released the zoo animals," murmured Nandar Aye.

So, the rumors were true. Word had also spread that the authorities had freed prisoners and the mad from the psychiatric hospital. All manner of wild beasts would roam freely in the capital's streets. They resumed their journey with greater caution, scanning the shadows stirring about them. Anthony made out the squat silhouette of a rhinoceros contentedly grazing on the lawn of a colonial villa. Further on, a group of monkeys had taken up residence atop an Anglican church, their cries mingling with the crackling flames consuming a neighboring building.

The air was becoming increasingly unbreathable. In the absence of firefighters, long since evacuated, smoke from the freely spreading braziers rose from all over the city, obscuring the stars. They were Nero, witnessing the gigantic funeral pyre that Rangoon had become. But Anthony was in no mood to compose an epic poem on the agony of this Pearl of the Orient. He had to make several detours to avoid mounds of rubble and overturned vehicles blocking the road, each one lengthening their route and filling him with a dull anxiety. Time was pressing. Every minute lost reduced their chances of finding Sayer and escaping together from the doomed city. They finally reached Goodliffe Road. Most of the houses appeared abandoned, their shutters closed and their gardens already overrun by tropical vegetation demanding to reclaim its rights.

- "We're here!" Nandar Aye suddenly indicated, pointing to a Victorian villa surrounded by a brick wall.

Anthony pulled the Austin up and switched off the engine. All was silent. Nothing emanated from the house, which stood in the gloom. No lights. No sound. Was the professor inside? They descended from the vehicle, slowly pushed the gate, then made their way up the drive. No movement greeted their arrival. Anthony knocked. No answer. Nandar Aye opened the panel, discovering an interior plunged entirely into darkness.

- "Arthur?" she called out as she entered. The echo dissolved into the abyss. "He's not here. What do we do?" she asked with concern, turning to Anthony who was observing the first-floor windows from the garden. He fixed her in silence, seeming to consider.

- "I think I know where he might be!" he answered at last. "Stay here with your mother in case he turns up. I'll pop round and have a look. In any case, meet me back here within the hour so we can make for Mingaladon."

- "Be careful!" Nandar Aye pleaded, pulling him into her arms.

He saw her wave as he raced off westward on King Edward Avenue[95].

A quarter of an hour later, he turned into Simpson Road[96], cut the engine, and looked up at the imposing Masonic Hall, that symbol of the Enlightenment as much as of the cultural uniformity imposed on conquered peoples. *Vae victis*. The British were at home everywhere; the natives nowhere. The two-story building, completed in 1908, revealed its neoclassical lines crowned by the delta of the pediment, embodiment of the mysteries revealed to the Brethren who gathered here in quest of illumination.

He passed the columns of the portico with curiosity mingled with apprehension, troubled by the impression of trespassing. Sayer had sponsored Win Thu to pass under the

---

[95] Present-day Daw Thein Tin Road and Bo Min Kaung Road.
[96] Present-day Pan Tra Street.

hoodwink. The Burmese academic had quickly attained the rank of master of Rangoon University Lodge No. 4603. Anthony was too young to be initiated. He was merely a profane forbidden to cross this threshold laden with secrets. The entrance hall was plunged into darkness. He stood still on the Minton tile floor to let his eyes adjust to the gloom, then made out the door opening to the banquet hall and the adjoining carved arcades. The atmosphere might have been that of a London club transplanted under the tropics.

He began to climb the teak staircase, hand trembling on the wrought-iron banister - a work from Walter Macfarlane & Company's workshops in Glasgow - toward the true sanctuary: the main lodge on the upper floor, from which a faint golden light filtered. He entered and took in the wainscoted walls, the two columns Jachin and Boaz, the mosaic pavement covering the floor behind them, and then the Master's lectern at the Orient, the sole furnishing inhabiting the space, upon which burned a candle casting dancing shadows of the masonic square and compass hung above. Sayer sat upon the floor, back against the pulpit. Anthony could not tell if he'd noticed his arrival, for he showed no reaction. He walked softly and took a seat beside him, not daring to break the silence. The tablet emitted a dull thud as his satchel struck the wooden floor.

- "The secretary left with the furniture..." Sayer declared in a neutral voice that echoed through the lodge. "There's truly nothing left..."

Anthony understood his words extended beyond the empty space they contemplated with somberness. They were witnessing, powerless, the inexorable disappearance of all that had formed the foundation of their lives.

- "I'm sorry," Anthony apologized, conscious of his share of responsibility.

He wanted to say more. He owed it to his companion. But he didn't know where to begin. Silence filled the gloom, deepening the chasm between them.

- "How could I have been so blind?" the professor lamented suddenly. "First Win Thu, and then..." he sighed, unable to finish.

- "It's not your fault," Anthony offered, consumed by guilt.

- "I know!" Sayer replied sharply, turning abruptly toward Anthony. Yet his voice betrayed sadness more than anger. "You're in love. How could I possibly begrudge you that? One can't command feelings. Love won't be forced or forbidden. But the lies, the betrayal..."

- "You're right," Anthony admitted shamefully. "It's inexcusable. We ought to have found the courage to tell you straight. But Nandar Aye was terrified you'd cast them out, her and her mother. Fear does dreadful things to one..."

- "That's what cuts deepest, that she could imagine for even a moment I'd turn them onto the street! I'll grant it may seem queer given the years between us, but I'm devoted to her. Her mind, her spirit... I simply want her to be happy!"

Anthony knew he was sincere, but the road to hell was paved with good intentions, he reminded himself. Yet he preferred to hold his tongue and spare Sayer increased suffering rather than share the revulsion Nandar Aye harbored for her benefactor. The man had genuinely been blinded by his feelings for her. He steered the conversation toward a subject he knew dear to the professor:

- "This temple is magnificent. I've never been inside a lodge before."

A platitude, mere civility, he knew it. But he hoped to draw his companion from the torpor and self-pity into which he'd retreated.

- "The building is imposing," Sayer conceded, "but without the Brethren, it's nothing but an empty shell. It wasn't the stonework, but the discussions conducted here that gave it meaning. We were building Burma's future in this place. Its independence, an end to segregation, leaders for tomorrow. Brick by brick, through reasoned debate, putting discourse before violence. I simply can't comprehend how Win Thu wandered so far off the path."

- "Impatience, perhaps. Opportunity knocking. Or motives rather less than honorable..." Anthony ventured.

He refrained from sharing the animosity he felt for that blackmailer who'd attempted to coerce Nandar Aye in the vilest manner.

- "He seemed to share my aversion to war when I told him about my father," the academic offered sadly.

- "Your father?" Anthony inquired, intrigued.

- "A Boer War veteran came back wounded, a heavy drinker and a violent man. Lost in the bottle most of the time, couldn't hold down a position to save his life. My mother and I were bearing the weight, keeping the family fed, and protecting my brothers from the thrashings he'd give us when he was clear enough to know what he was doing. We could scarcely scrape together the five shillings a week for our miserable East End rooms. Books and my dreams of adventure got me through it all. A scholarship put me through university. My younger brother wasn't so fortunate. He was killed at Verdun, just eighteen. My father couldn't even bring himself to attend the service for him..."

He had recited his account in a colorless voice, features drawn, eyes lost in the void.

- "Where are your parents these days?" Anthony asked.

- "Still in London. I write to my mother regularly, send her money. My father, he can go hang for all I care! I've no wish to lay eyes on him again. That's why, once I'd got my degree, I booked passage on the first ship to Rangoon. I reckoned I could leave the ghosts behind, the war and all... But they've caught me up here and stripped away everything I'd managed to build."

- "Not quite everything!" Anthony interjected, tapping the tablet through his satchel. "You can still decipher what the stone's got to tell us and share it with the world. You said it yourself: it's likely a tremendous find! We'll complete the excavation once the war's done. Mark my words, our chaps will have the Japanese on the run before long. Everything will be as it was. It may take months, or years, but we'll return!" he insisted, feigning cheer.

- "You're young and naive," Sayer said in a hollow voice.

- "Or perhaps just determined to see the best of things," Anthony retorted with a challenging tone. "In any case, I'm not throwing in the towel. And I'm not leaving without you!"

- "Don't be daft," the professor rebuked him wearily, as if addressing a petulant child. "Get yourself clear if you possibly can. Though I suspect it's rather late for all that. No more trains, no more ships. We're done for here."

- "There's still one option," Anthony corrected. "The last aircraft lift off from Mingaladon tonight. And you can't give up, not after what we've already been through. We've got to have a go at it!" he encouraged. "Come along!" he added, rising to his feet.

Seconds passed during which Sayer appeared to reflect.

- "Right then," he finally agreed, grasping the hand Anthony extended to help him up. "What's there to lose, really?"

He turned to face the Orient, straightened, formed a square with his feet, and placed his right hand over his heart to make the sign of Reverence. The Masonic ring gleamed at his little finger.

- "So mote it be[97]!" he declared solemnly, blowing out the flame. "Let us go, now that the shadows of evening close in."

---

[97] Expression, equivalent to "Amen," dating back to the Regius Poem of around 1390, the oldest known Masonic document.

Chapter XXVI

Rangoon, Burma, March 1942

Sayer pulled the Austin up before the gate of the villa, letting the engine idle as he sounded the horn three times. No one appeared. Barely an hour had passed since Anthony's hasty departure, yet the house seemed deserted. Anxiety gripped them as soon as they opened their car doors, until hurried footsteps echoed down the street towards them. The headlights revealed Nandar Aye, breathless, her *longyi* hitched above her knees, hair disheveled, her face shining with feverish energy. Clutching her book to her chest, she stopped abruptly.

- "What happened? Are you alright?" Anthony asked instantly, taking her by the shoulders, his voice trembling with concern.

- "I'm fine," she panted, struggling to catch her breath. "I went searching for Arthur, in case you didn't find him. I lost track of time and ran back when I heard the car. I didn't want you to worry..." she finished, with a forced smile.

An uneasy silence fell as she met the professor's gaze, the memory of the railway station looming over them like a heavy, thunder-laden cloud.

- "I'm sorry, Arthur..." she murmured, her tone cold, only making the discomfort greater.

- "Let's not speak of it," he cut in hastily, his voice feigning detachment.

A rustling on the gravel announced Nandar's mother. This distraction was a welcome relief, providing Anthony with a pretext to change the subject:

- "Let's go, since we're all here," he said, opening the rear door. "We must hurry!"

- "My mother has decided to stay," Nandar Aye announced calmly. "She'll be safe here and can look after the house."

The two Britons exchanged glances, unable to object. They could not afford to squander precious time in fruitless argument. If that was her choice... Sayer took the woman's hands with emotion and pronounced a solemn *kan kaung bah zay*[98], while she softly recited the Mora Sutta[99] to bless their journey. Anthony offered only a polite, distant bow before climbing into the car. Nandar Aye embraced her mother, handed over her book, then joined the others on the back seat.

---

[98] "Good luck" in Burmese.
[99] Buddhist prayer for protection in all directions.

- "Let's go," said Nandar Aye, closing the door as Sayer started up the Austin, which roared off into the night.

- "You're leaving her your novel?" Anthony asked, surprised to see the book abandoned by the one who had guarded it so faithfully.

- "I've finished it at last..." she replied simply, her gaze lost in the darkness, hair whipped by the wind pouring through the window.

Outside, Royal Lake[100] stretched its silvery reflections, but Anthony's mind was elsewhere. Would they reach the airfield in time? What if the planes had already gone? Would they try the road to Prome, risking a breakthrough of enemy lines? He paid no heed to the majestic shadow of Shwedagon Pagoda as they went onto Prome Road[101]. Did he even know this was the last time he would see such beauty? The city melted away swiftly as they rattled northward, until finally a constellation of lights pierced the horizon: Mingaladon.

Sayer stopped the car by a barracks. An almost mineral silence fell as they stepped out, crickets weaving a muffled undercurrent through vegetation at the edge of the airstrip. Anthony raised his head to the Milky Way, unfazed in the ethereal night, inviting contemplation of life's impermanence. Yet the silence only heightened his fear that they were too late: the place looked abandoned.

---

[100] Present-day Inya Lake.
[101] Present-day Pyay Road.

Burners and gooseneck flares cast harsh light on Marsden Matting shot through with bomb craters, tracing out the triangular pattern of runways made of perforated steel plates. Beyond, the ruins of the southern hangar stood skeletal, bearing the scars of a recent bombardment. Tents, huts, and sheds loomed in silent, solitary silhouette in the glow of kerosene lamps. The anti-aircraft positions of the AA Company of the Rangoon Battalion lay deserted, emptied of their Browning machine guns. There was no sign of life.

Faint voices, blown on the swirling wind, rekindled hope. Bypassing the barracks, the group emerged onto a fuel lorry, lit by a kerosene lamp, the tracks behind it still hidden. Sayer picked up the lamp and forged ahead. Soon, they spotted two Bristol Blenheims lurking under mango trees three hundred meters further on, lit brightly by drums of burning petrol. Three figures bustled under the nose of the first, spinning the propeller by hand. A shout - "Clear prop!" - was followed by splutters and explosions as the engine coughed and roared to life. The second engine followed, its own prop spun up. No take-off would happen for at least ten minutes, they were on time.

They were about to race for the aircraft when Anthony caught a movement at the edge of his vision, a fleeting shadow on the periphery.

- "Stop right there!"

The voice, crisp, carried an indeterminate accent. All three turned to see four figures advancing steadily. Sayer's lamp revealed four men dressed in shirts and *longyis*, rifles in hand, their faces set with grim resolve. The fugitives froze as the strangers levelled their guns. Behind, the rotors kept up their infernal roar, so close and yet so unattainable. Nandar Aye stepped forward, perhaps intending to negotiate as she had in the village near Pegu. Anthony tried to stop her. These were not peasant mobs with sticks, easily swayed. These men radiated confidence making them far more dangerous. Seasoned fighters, most likely, ready to open fire without hesitation. Yet the Burmese woman pulled free of his grasp and pressed forward to the tallest man, who lowered his weapon. Then she turned to face the Britons.

- "Give me the satchel," she said to Anthony, hand trembling.

He hesitated, baffled.

- "Nandar Aye, who are these men?" Sayer demanded, a note of accusation in his voice.

- "Men of the BIA[102]," she replied. "And him," pointing to the man beside her, "he's Captain Kimura, an officer of the Kempeitai[103]."

An iron silence descended as they assessed one another.

- "Your book!" cried Anthony, struck by sudden revelation. "It was you, not Win Thu, who wrote those numbers on the wall!

---

[102] Burma Independence Army.
[103] Military police of the Imperial Japanese Army; also functioned as secret police and counter-intelligence service.

The novel held the code reference! You brought them straight to us!"

- "Yes. I was recruited at the university a year ago when the Japanese set up an intelligence network there. They taught me cryptography, but my real job was to win students to our cause."

- "A spy!" Sayer exclaimed, incredulous. "And you let that poor Win Thu be blamed in your place!" he raged.

- "That poor Win Thu?" Nandar Aye's voice dripped with scorn and contempt. "A blackmailer who tried to rape me! You can ask Anthony if you don't believe me," she flared.

Sayer turned to his assistant, who nodded tacitly.

- "You've always blinded yourself with that saviour's complex," the Burmese woman continued, almost tender, "Refusing to see the true nature of those around you. Letting yourself be played..."

Her lantern-lit face showed piercing pity for the academic. The irony of her words, even as she revealed her own betrayal, was clear to all.

- "Why?" Sayer eventually managed, his voice defeated.

- "Anthony knows why," she replied, enigmatic.

- "I know nothing anymore," Anthony objected coldly. "How am I to believe a word you said after so many lies?"

- "I was sincere!" protested Nandar Aye, her trembling voice brimming with emotion she could barely contain. Tears glistened in the lamplight.

- "Anthony... Look at me," she pleaded, as he turned away to hide his own pain. "I never meant any harm. Never. I never sought this, I just fell in love with you against my own will..."

- "But?" Anthony cut in, his confusion obvious.

- "But I love my country as well. I want to be free, and only an independent Burma can give me that."

- "So, you sided with the Japanese..." He gave a laugh, nearly a sob. "You really believe they'll grant you independence?" His bitter gesture toward Kimura finished the thought.

- "I hope so. What other choice do we have? They alone offered to help. We tried the peaceful way, protested, negotiated, pleaded. What did we get? Bullets, prisons, contempt..."

Anthony covered his face with a weary hand. His anger was spent, replaced by a void of sadness.

- "What about us?" he finally asked, voice raw. "Was it ever real, even for a moment?"

- "It was the realest thing in my life. I love you, Anthony, more than anyone before," she said with heartfelt truth, caring nothing for Sayer, who stood motionless, involuntary witness to her confession.

The professor, the soldiers, the roaring planes, all disappeared.

- "But not enough. Not enough to choose me over your cause..."

- "You can't imagine the decision I had to make! Yes, I betrayed you. And I'll live with it until my last breath. I had to choose, Anthony. I chose my country," she whispered through shaking sobs. "But I hope we'll meet again, after the war..."

He said nothing. There was nothing to say. He knew it was wishful thinking. After the war? He'd likely die here, that night. Even if he survived, even if the conflict ended, nothing would be as before. Love would linger, but so would the lies, betrayal, and pain. The Japanese officer at her side grew impatient.

- "Enough!" he shouted in a curt, accented bark. "Give us the tablet!"

Anthony snapped back to reality, fixing his gaze on the officer's square, severe face, who started toward him. The three other soldiers still had them covered, fingers on triggers, ready to shoot. Nandar Aye gestured to calm them.

- "Anthony, your satchel," she urged again.

- "All this for an old stone? What possible difference can it make in your fight for independence?"

- "It's a symbol," the Freemason beside him interjected. "A propaganda tool. They'll use it to rally the people to their cause.

Nothing stirs political feeling more than religion, eh?" he asked, glancing at his former mistress.

- "You're right, Arthur," Nandar Aye agreed. "I'm no historian. But when you explained the tablet came from the first *stūpa* of the legendary kingdom of Suvannabhumi, that it contained the Buddha's first relics, I understood the power of such a discovery."

- "How cynical!" Sayer protested despite himself. "You'll help these fascists turn a symbol of peace and compassion into a means of enslavement! How far you've strayed!"

- "Spare me your sermons, Arthur!" Nandar Aye retorted, her face twisted by rage. "You British were the first to imprison our monks, defile our pagodas, use Christianity to convert our minorities and set us against each other! Besides, you've no say in this. The tablet and relics belong to the Burmese people. Enough! Give me the stone, Anthony!"

She was losing patience, her hand outstretched, trembling. Anthony glanced over his shoulder: the propellers were spinning at full speed, the mechanics climbing aboard. They'd be taking off any minute.

- "What happens to us if we give you the tablet?" Sayer asked.

- "You'll be free to go," Kimura answered curtly.

- "They gave me their word," confirmed Nandar Aye.

- "You were arranging this with them while Anthony was searching for me; weren't you?" the historian asked, finally seeing the last pieces fall into place, painfully, inexorably.

- "Yes, I went to a contact who operates a radio. I informed them we'd be here."

- "I see..." Sayer turned to his companion. "Anthony, my dear boy, I don't think we have a choice," he said, fatalistically.

Anthony surrendered and began to slip the strap off his satchel. Sayer, abruptly, stepped in, swung his arm, and brought his hand down hard. The gunshot rang out as the kerosene lamp crashed to the ground. A violent burst of flame erupted between them and their assailants.

- "Run!" Anthony heard, just as the professor collapsed, both hands at his chest.

Without thinking, he dashed for the fuel tanker, sprinting as gun shadows wheeled toward him.

- "No! Wait!"

Nandar Aye's cry pierced the tumult. He saw her, arms wide, interposing herself between him and the rifles. Another shot rang out, followed by a wail of pain. Then a succession of gunshots reverberated in metallic blasts as he dove behind the lorry.

Flat on the ground, crawling through dust and dry grass, Anthony glimpsed through the lorry's wheels two bodies sprawled, motionless, on either side of the wall of flame. Voices shouted, then faded. The air vibrated. Then came the smell, acrid, suffocating, burning his throat and eyes. Kerosene streamed from the tanker, forming a glistening puddle spreading dangerously toward the flames. Behind him, the rotors swelled, rising to a shrill wail. A Blenheim was already surging forward, engine howling, down the runway. The second waited its turn on the taxiway, ready to leap. Anthony understood: it was now or never.

He bolted, keeping the lorry as cover, his satchel heavy against his hip. His legs barely obeyed, weighed down by fear and exhaustion. He waved his arms, screaming until his throat burned. Useless. The aircraft roared past him and climbed, swallowed by the nocturnal sky. The second Blenheim was turning toward the runway. Suddenly, a yellow flash, then a tremendous blow. The tanker exploded, shaking the earth, drowning even the rotor noise, casting Anthony's shadow dozens of meters ahead.

A hatch opened on the Bristol Blenheim's back, near the rear gun turret. A mechanic hauled himself out, slid down the fuselage, and ran toward him, shouting words lost in the engine roar.

- "Who the devil are you?" he demanded sharply as he bore down on the young Englishman. "And what in God's name do we have here with these chaps?"

Anthony turned and saw four figures silhouetted against the burning debris, closing fast.

- "We must go!" Anthony barked, rushing toward the plane.

The first shots cracked, their high-pitched clamor barely audible, but their flashes unmistakable in the darkness. Rounds perforated the fuselage. The mechanic steadied Anthony onto the wing, then pointed to the hatch the pilot had opened above the cockpit. Anthony felt a bullet's breath graze his ear as he offered his hand to the mechanic. Too late. The man stumbled, his head snapping back. He collapsed, the back of his skull shattered. Anthony scrambled up the fuselage as his pursuers closed in dangerously. He plunged through the narrow opening, nearly losing his satchel, then tumbled hard into the cramped cockpit.

- "What the blazes' happening here?" shouted the pilot as two rounds shattered through the windscreen.

- "Japs!" screamed Anthony.

- "Where's Mike?"

- "Dead! Get us airborne, for God's sake!"

The pilot pushed the throttle. The engines roared furiously, and the aircraft accelerated rapidly down the metal runway, then lifted thirty seconds later. The plane climbed steeply for altitude, then banked sharply north. Through the glazed nose, Anthony gazed upon a sea of darkness from which rose the monstrous glow of fire. Flames were spreading to neighboring barracks. He searched for a movement, any sign of life. Nothing. Did Nandar Aye survive, or was her body burning with Sayer's? He stared into the darkness for an eternity, fists clenched, until the light vanished behind them, offering no answers to the questions tormenting him. His throat constricted as he settled into the navigator's seat, eyes burning, his mind unable to accept the tragedy that had just unfolded.

- "Your name?" the pilot bellowed over the engine.

- "Anthony!"

- "John!" replied the aviator, extending his gloved hand. "Blasted compass!" he cursed, tapping the instrument. "The needle won't hold true! The gyro's completely gone bust!"

Anthony heard no more. In the steady engine's hum, the crash of the night's horror resounded incoherently in his head. He grasped at fragments, fumbling through darkness for the labyrinth's exit. But each memory bounced against his mind's opaque walls like a lost echo. The image of Nandar Aye returned, insistent, tearing. Had she loved him or lied to manipulate him, as she did Sayer? He'd kept his promise: he'd fled to save his life. But had she been sincere when she'd wrung that vow from him? Nandar Aye, a spy... He saw in retrospect their shared moments, the imperceptible trembling of her hands reading by candlelight, the firmness of her gaze when conviction overcame her gentleness. She had been a liar, no doubt, yet burned with sincerity in her lies. She had betrayed to serve a cause greater than their love. Yet in the final instant, she'd offered herself to bullets to save his life. The thought tore at his chest. She had loved him, and what had he done? He'd fled. He felt hollowed out, foul, unworthy. No grave would bear her name. All he'd have would be a memory growing ever more fugitive, destined to fade with time.

The aviator engaged the autopilot and shouted to be heard:

- " The Japs have taken Rangoon already? That was close!" he bawled. " But what the hell were you lot still doing down there?"

Anthony shouted back, his words hacked against the engine roar, telling the aviator in broad strokes what had happened over the past days. The air thick with fuel fumes burned his lungs. When he finished, the pilot sat silent, eyes fixed on the gauges. Like Anthony, he'd also lost a friend tonight. All because of an old tablet. An absurdity upon which both men chose to meditate separately and in silence. Suddenly, the pilot frowned and tapped nervously at one of the two fuel gauges near his left shoulder.

- "The rounds pierced the tank! We've lost too much kerosene! The engines will pack up!," he announced, continuing to check his instruments.

Anthony felt a shiver traverse him, visceral, animal. He understood they would die as well. His breath fractured, a spasm took him. His muscles gave way to terror he couldn't master, his body betraying him as urine ran down his leg. He collapsed, unable to control himself or regain his breath, whilst the pilot beside him took no notice. Air failed him, his mind was slipping, laughter bubbled up, uncontrollable. A nervous, absurd laugh. The irony: to survive bullets, bombs, only to die here, trapped in a steel coffin so near deliverance.

- "Haven't got a clue where we are," the pilot continued, focusing on the darkness enveloping them. "We're over mountains now: the Pegu Yoma or the Chin Hills, Lord knows. Not a sign of a road or clearing. Just jungle."

He felt beneath his seat, drew out a small hatchet with a wrapped handle, and thrust it at Anthony.

- "Cut those rope lines securing the bomb bay hatch!," he shouted, indicating the fuselage aft. "I'll reduce speed at the critical moment. When I give the word, you jump. Keep your body tight. The trees will break your fall. With luck, you'll make it through."

- "What about you?" Anthony cried, suddenly terrified of jumping alone.

John didn't answer. His brief gaze said it all: he'd stay at the controls. He likely wouldn't survive.

Anthony crawled into the metal tunnel, navigating through struts and cables. He finally reached the fuselage's center, at the wing join, where the bomb bay hatch sat. His satchel caught on to the cross-members, blocking him at each movement. In silent fury, he wrenched it from his shoulder and hurled it toward the cockpit. Then he crouched to reach the hatch doors, hammering with rage at the straps holding it shut until they finally gave way under repeated axe blows. The hatch swung open onto the rustling night. Spent, dejected yet resigned, he sat at the edge of the void. He was going to die. Legs dangling, face whipped by the warm wind pouring through, he suddenly tasted the strange quietude of those who no longer hope. This time there was no plan, no providence to hold him back. All he'd thought he commanded - his future, his choices, even his love - had been nothing but mirage. He'd ever been merely a passenger in the tumult, human debris swept along by history's current. He'd been fortunate to survive this long. But it was finished.

- " Stand by! At my signal!" the pilot barked without turning.

The plane pitched abruptly, lurching like a wounded bird. Anthony gripped with all his strength to keep from falling through the hatch. His satchel, sliding side to side, banging on the floor, caught his eye. He wanted to rise, retrieve it. The tablet was all he had left. If he were to vanish, he wanted it with him, close to him. To hold it, like Nandar Aye, his love, one last time in his arms. But at that very moment, one engine cut. The Blenheim lurched violently, his body lifted into the air, legs pedaling in the void, arms opening reflexively. He saw himself with horror tumble through the gaping opening, nothing to hold him. The void seized him in a rush, his chest suddenly compressed by a wall of air. He felt his back and skull explode under the impact. Everything went black.

Chapter 27

Kyauktaga, Myanmar, October 2024

Khin Yadanar opened her eyes with difficulty. Her floating gaze settled on the wooden slats of the ceiling, its white paint peeling in large leprous plaques. Her fingers explored the thin mat separating her from the concrete floor, cold and hard. Every fiber of her body screamed its suffering. She struggled to sit up, each movement sending electrical charges through her muscles.

The room stretched before her in brutal barrenness, offering only a varnished wooden altar where a golden Buddha statue reigned, crowned by an electric garland that flickered obstinately. The pistachio-green walls rolled out their relentless monotony, broken only by the square of sunlight shed by a window behind her. Her brown *longyi* and Hello Kitty t-shirt were not hers. She had been changed. Anguish gripped her throat. She scanned the room with growing agitation. Her backpack rested against her makeshift bed, its contents scattered across the floor. Everything was there. Everything except... She plunged her hand inside. It was empty. The tablet had disappeared. With jerky movements, she gathered her belongings, sprang to her feet, slung the bag over her shoulder, and hurried barefoot from the room.

She emerged onto a gallery flooded with sunlight. It took her long seconds to adjust her vision. She stood on the flank of a hill, at which foot lay the gentle undulations of a patchwork of forests and fields vying in shades of green. Behind her, the terrain continued its ascent, Indian mahogany flowers and hibiscus seeming to soar toward the azure sky. She recognized the style of the white buildings with red roofs at once: a Buddhist monastery, as confirmed by the litanies borne on the wind above the croaks and cries of birds that filled the air.

She made her way up the gallery toward the main building from which voices rose. In the vast hall, a crowd stood aligned beneath a roof supported by columns, all facing a golden Buddha statue several meters high. Seated in the lotus position, monks in crimson robes conducted the ceremony while the laity, kneeling or legs folded to the side, chanted prayers in Pali. The voices blended into an antiphon with a repetitive, mesmerizing rhythm, occasionally punctuated by the tolling of a gong.

Khin Yadanar remained standing outside, not daring to join the congregation. She was not particularly religious, raised in Christianity as much as in Buddhism and in the love of science. Yet this timeless music filled her with a profound serenity, inviting her to close her eyes and revisit memories she believed lost. Excursions to the Mindat pagoda with her father, the rare times he went there for Thatdingyut[104], for Thingyan[105], or for his birthday. Visits with friends to the Shwedagon pagoda to make offerings

---

[104] Festival of Lights, which takes place in October or November.
[105] Buddhist New Year or Water Festival, which takes place in April.

before exams. Outings to the Botataung on Saturday evenings to admire the sunset over the Irrawaddy. Another life. A carefree innocence, a normalcy, perhaps lost forever.

A rustling behind her dispelled these visions. She opened her eyes. An old monk with a placid smile fixed her with benevolence. His frail shoulders, his shrunken silhouette seemed barely able to bear the folds of his long saffron robe. But behind skin withered by age, his eyes sparkled with indomitable vitality.

- "I was just about to check on you," he began, slowly moving away, hands clasped in his curved back.

Surprised, Khin Yadanar fell into step beside him. A thousand questions burned on her lips, but she dared not interrogate her host. He walked in silence beside her, imperturbable, as if unconscious of her presence, an unshakeable smile on his lips. Minutes ticked by. She was famished but said nothing despite her stomach's muted protests. The ecclesiastic continued trotting away from the monastery, nose raised, savoring with delight the perfumes of the monsoon evaporating in the clammy heat. She was barefoot but did not care. Only answers mattered. They finally reached a small kiosk offering an unobstructed view of the valley. An invitation to contemplation. The prayers were now no more than distant rumors mingling with the buzzing of insects. The monk sat in a plastic chair and invited her to do the same. She chose to sit on the floor, following protocol.

- "*Sayadaw*[106]," ventured Khin Yadanar, unable to contain herself, "where am I?"

- "Near Kyauktaga," answered the old man, his gaze fixed on the landscape. "Villagers found you yesterday morning, unconscious by the river. You were clinging to a tree and your backpack. They brought you here, along with other storm victims. They weren't sure you would come to..."

- "Nearly two days," repeated the young woman pensively, not daring to imagine the distress Kee Mawng must be in. Decidedly, she was nothing but a source of suffering for him. "Did they also find a wounded young man?" she asked urgently.

The monk shook his head in silence. His smile had vanished.

- "The river hasn't surrendered all that it took," he resumed gently. "Thousands have vanished. The ceremony you witnessed was intended precisely to appease spirits and generate merit for victims of the catastrophe we had just buried in a mass grave. We couldn't risk cremating them and attracting the army."

Shoulders shaken by sobs, Khin Yadanar wept in silence, her lips pursed and trembling, suppressing cries that sought to escape. The terrified face of Kyaw Zaw, his desperate calls as the currents swept him away, returned to haunt her. She had done nothing. She could do nothing, she knew it. But she had done nothing. And now he was dead. He had jeopardized his existence

---

[106] A term of respect when addressing a Buddhist monk in Myanmar.

to help her. Had saved her more than once. In return, she had foolishly endangered him through recklessness. She saw again his boyish face, features hardened by combat but with a laughing gaze. Another martyr immolated on the altar of revolution. Or rather, of her revolution, of her senseless crusade. No point lying to herself.

- "It's my fault," she exploded with a long wail, covering her face in her hands. "I bring misfortune. No matter how hard I try to help, to save people, to save my country... Everyone who comes near me dies or is touched by tragedy."

- "Do you believe you're so important?" cut the monk.

The provocation struck home. Khin Yadanar raised her head sharply, interrupting her lamentations. Surprised, offended, angry, she wanted to hurl her fury at him, restrained only by embarrassment and respect for his status. She remained paralyzed by this explosion of contradictory emotions battling within her, unable to choose. After a few seconds, she calmed and regained her composure at the sight of the sad smile and empathetic gaze her interlocutor offered. It was unorthodox, no doubt, but effective.

- "You're too hard on yourself, *Thami*[107]," he resumed gently. "You must be more forgiving of yourself."

- "How could I be, *Sayadaw*? My parents are dead. My friends perished in a bombardment. My lover lost his leg in the

---

[107] "My daughter" in Burmese. A traditional way of addressing a much younger girl.

same attack. The Tatmadaw killed the villagers I tried to save. Now Kyaw Zaw... And I'm still here. How can I be forgiving?"

- "Because no one has the power to save everyone... Or to condemn everyone. All we can do is do our best."

He extended his hand, withered and desiccated by time in the direction from which chants still rose.

- "Listen to those prayers. You're still here, you say? They are too. Like you, they've lost loved ones. Children, spouses. Your story is theirs. This is the lot of those who live and survive times like ours."

- "I'm not special," Khin Yadanar concluded in an icy tone. "Does that mean my suffering doesn't matter?"

- "You're not special, no. That's true," the monk acquiesced without being shaken. "The universe doesn't revolve around you; it has no concern for you. Nor for anyone else, for that matter. You're not responsible for what occurs. Each is master of their decisions and actions. This doesn't mean you must deny your suffering. It's the symbol of the love you bear for those you have lost. So long as it remains an expression of compassion without becoming self-pity. It's they who are dead. You can't honour them by weeping over yourself."

His tone was calm, without judgment, tinged with an affection a grandfather would have for his granddaughter. She dried her tears with the back of her hand and offered him a sad smile as a token of gratitude. His candor comforted her. At the CDF-Mindat headquarters, she had been treated like a wounded bird. Embarrassment more than empathy, which had only increased her distress and rage. Here was someone who respected her enough to speak the truth, without cruelty, but without sparing her either. He did not lie. Others had suffered as much or more than she. Such was the world. It would not change for her.

- "What you say isn't truly comforting, *Sayadaw*," she said, emitting a sad laugh.

- "It's both comforting and frightening to be reminded that we are nothing. No absolute responsibility, but also the awareness that whatever we do, it may change nothing. Generations succeed one another, errors repeat themselves, the cycle continues. Man remains man."

- "Yet it's possible for individuals to make a difference, to change the world," the young woman respectfully contended. "After all, Aung San and Aung San Suu Kyi shaped Myanmar's destiny."

- "Of course. But at what cost to them and their loved ones?" the monk acknowledged, nodding slowly. "You see, *Thami*, life's a marathon. There are those who race through it like arrows. And those who watch from the sidelines with their loved ones." He ceased contemplating the landscape, turned toward her and fixed her with a grave expression. "The former will receive medals, but they'll run the race in a flash, alone, leaving everyone behind. For the others, it will seem to last an eternity, in tranquility or tedium, without accomplishing anything great." His eyes settled on the horizon again, as if speaking to himself. "In the end, all eventually cross the finish line sooner or later."

- "Are you saying that nothing we do matters?"

- "I didn't make myself clear," he smiled. "The finish line is the same for all. What counts is how you choose to run your race. Ambition can be solitary, destructive. And inaction unproductive. But there remains the middle path."

- "The middle path?"

- "Running the race not at your own pace, but at that of others. Supporting those who limp, lifting those who stumble, crossing the finish line together, without medal, but with a finer reward. That's for you to choose..."

- "Can a single person make a difference, then?"

- "It's true, but not as you mean it. Attempting to reform society without changing humanity is but vanity doomed to failure. Those who have tried, even with the best intentions, have failed. They ended up creating dictatorial regimes. One can't transform society from the outside, by force. It doesn't work."

- "But then, Buddha?" Khin Yadanar was perplexed.

- "There! Now you understand. He differed from political leaders because he didn't attempt to change others. He sought to purify himself. Only thus was he able to transform society by showing the way. That's the secret."

- "*Sayadaw*, I don't know what to do. How can I find the strength to change myself when everything is collapsing around me?" The young woman's voice trembled with sincere distress.

- "Stop trying to control everything," advised the sage with profound tenderness. "You can't. And you will only be able to help others once you have healed your inner wounds. Only then will you improve the lives of all those around you."

- "But Kyaw Zaw, my friends, all dead... So many sacrificed themselves. Must I not save those I can? How could they otherwise forgive me?"

- "*Thami*, you must learn to forgive yourself. Your duty is to do what you can, nothing more. Once you have understood this, all will be well."

He let his final words linger, savoring with a peaceful air the warm breeze caressing his parchment skin. Khin Yadanar leaned her back against the parapet, mulling over the old monk's advice in silence. The internal struggle that agitated her was not finished. But the tempest seemed to be subsiding. She felt her muscles relaxed, her palms open. She had not even noticed her hands had been clenched in two tight fists.

- "I thank you, *Sayadaw*, your words helped me. But I won't lie to you: it will take time before I manage to put them into practice."

- "Detachment is the work of a lifetime. Several lifetimes, even," the monk conceded with an indulgent laugh. No doubt he was recalling his own past existence in quest of Nibbana. An objective that still eluded him in the twilight of his life, as the finish line drew nearer.

- "I have one more thing to accomplish before I can dedicate myself to that."

- "Ah, there we are!" he declared cheerfully, fixing his sharp, curious eyes on hers. "I was waiting for you to come to that," he indicated with an understanding smile.

- "The tablet?" ventured Khin Yadanar uncertainly.

- "The tablet," he confirmed. "Don't worry, it's safe."

Khin Yadanar was relieved. All was not lost. She could still complete her mission. She gave him a detailed account of the events. The discovery of the plane. The tablet. The notebook. Professor Preston and Ayaan. All the way to crossing the river and Kyaw Zaw's disappearance. The monk listened in silence without interrupting, a raised eyebrow indicating occasionally his surprise or disbelief, undeniably captivated by her improbable tale. A long silence followed, during which he remained thoughtful, eyes closed. Khin Yadanar dared not press him.

- "This is extraordinary," he resumed slowly in his quavering voice. "The first relics in the country's oldest *stūpa*. The very source of the Dhamma's arrival in the kingdom of Suvannabhumi. As you so well put it, this discovery belongs to all Myanmar's people. It must be kept beyond the reach of those impious of the Tatmadaw!"

Buddhist monk though he was, he had lost his restraint, his face freezing into an expression of disdain at the mention of the military. No doubt he was recalling the atrocities committed against monks during the Saffron Revolution of 2007.

- "You'll understand, naturally, that the excavations must be conducted by members of the *Sangha*," he probed her, satisfied to see her nod in agreement. "You said the *stūpa* is in Win Ka?"

- "Yes, but I don't know exactly where," she admitted with a start.

She quickly took the pack she had placed on the ground and began searching inside with impatience. She finally found her mobile. It was dead. Destroyed by its prolonged submersion in the river's waters. She stuffed it back inside in frustration.

- "*Sayadaw*, would you have a phone with Internet access?" Like a conjurer, he extracted a device from the folds of his robe with a smile. "May I borrow it?" she dared ask, embarrassed.

He unlocked it and handed it to her. She took it without deference, quickly installed a VPN and Signal, entered Kee Mawng's contact, then sent a brief message. "It's me, Awm Awi. I'm fine. My phone's broken. You can write or call me on this number. I love you." She was about to return the device when it began to vibrate.

- "Awm Awi, is it really you? I... I thought that..." Kee Mawng's trembling voice sounded so fragile.

- "I'm alive. I'm alive," she reassured him.

- "Two days... Two days without word. After your last message, I thought you were... That the waters had..." His voice shook with sobs.

She felt him lost. Surrounded no doubt, but terribly alone. She dared not imagine what he had endured. The terror, the suffering, the grief. She was its cause. She blamed herself. She closed her eyes to conjure his face. She missed him. She wanted, no, she needed to return to him as soon as possible. It was there, or anywhere else, but near him, that she wished to be.

- "The boat capsized. Kyaw Zaw... Kyaw Zaw drowned." He did not know him personally, but it was he who had convinced him to guide her through her journey.

- "Oh Awm Awi, I'm so sorry. And you, how did you...?"

- "I'm not entirely sure. I woke up in a monastery. They found me unconscious on the riverbank. My phone is destroyed. I'm using a monk's phone to call you."

- "Are you hurt? Where exactly are you?"

- "Just scratches, nothing serious. I'm near Kyauktaga, at the foot of the mountains of Kyaiktiyo[108]."

- "I thought I'd lost you forever. I imagined the worst... It was madness!" His distress was transforming into anger. It was natural. She understood his reaction. She would have had the same. The fear was surfacing.

---

[108] Golden Rock, a sacred Buddhist pilgrimage site in Myanmar.

- "You know why I had to do this. The hardest part is over now. I'm safe here." She was lying and he knew it. No one was safe in Myanmar. Especially not a few miles from Karen State.

- "What are you planning to do?" She sensed the tension in his voice.

- "I still have the tablet. And the monk who took me in wants to help me find the *stūpa*. The problem is I still don't know where it is."

- "You're in luck. I wrote to Ayaan to tell him I hadn't heard from you. He informed me he'd discovered the site's exact coordinates. I don't know how, but that's what he told me. I'm sending them to you."

- "Thank you, my love!" exclaimed Khin Yadanar, before blushing as she remembered the monk's presence. He did not seem to take offence at so little. "I'll finally be able to complete my mission!"

- "And then?" Kee Mawng had asked this question with apprehension.

- "Then? The only way is through. Heading for Thailand!" She paused, realizing her lack of sensitivity. "Then," she resumed gently, "I'll come back. And I won't leave you again."

She was about to add a witticism. Say he would regret having her permanently underfoot, that their separation would be missed, or something similar. But she refrained. The wound, the fear, the loss were still raw. The suffering had been real. She would speak lightly no more, would play with his feelings no longer. She wanted him to know she was serious. She would not leave him again.

- "Be very careful," his voice sounded appeased. He had recovered his customary tenderness. "The situation is unstable at Win Ka and could deteriorate. And you'll need a guide to get you through to Thailand across the minefields while avoiding the army. I'll see what I can do. Above all, I hope you can conduct your excavations peacefully..."

- "Why do you say that?" she asked with apprehension.

- "Ayaan thought you were dead. The idiot's been shouting from the rooftops that he's looking for someone else to excavate the *stūpa* at Win Ka. The whole country will soon know..."

- "What an asshole!" she cursed before bidding Kee Mawng goodbye and hanging up. "Good news," she announced, returning the phone to the monk. "Someone's sending me the *stūpa*'s exact location."

- "And the bad news?" asked the old man.

- "We'll have very little time to find the relics."

Khin Yadanar's stomach chose that moment to emit a dull grumble that broke the silence. Both looked at each other and could not help but laugh.

- "Indeed, you must be hungry, *Thami*," smiled the monk. "Come, we'll find you something to eat. While you recover your strength, it will be my turn to make some calls."

Chapter 28

Win Ka, Myanmar, October 2024

- "We found it!"

Khin Yadanar darted toward the cry. The branches tearing at her arms did not exist. Only urgency remained. She plunged into one of the narrow gaps hacked through the jungle with machetes. Back-breaking work that had taken hours. Hours of battle against every vine, every stubborn branch. Each one an obstacle in this monsoon furnace. The trees, with their twisted hands, had pushed them back with primitive violence. Hours to clear the half-kilometer of labyrinth that separated them from the nearby pagoda.

They overlooked Win Ka. At times, through openings, the chequerboard of rice fields unfolded all the way to the Gulf of Martaban. Meagre windows of light in this vegetal cathedral. The rest lay in motionless shadow, exhaling a musky scent of rot. Time itself had stopped for nearly a century, petrified since man's departure. When they arrived, the second hand had started up again. Hammering blades. The call of the great coucal. The rasp of crickets. Each sound counted off the seconds, reminding them that time was running out.

Khin Yadanar emerged into the clearing. A group of young monks labored under the wary gaze of a family of macaques. Beneath her bare feet, she sensed the lines of a platform. These fledgling archaeologists had exhumed the first bricks. The foundations of the *stūpa* emerged like a colossus awakening after a century-long sleep. More than a legend. It was there. She had finally found it.

The old abbot of Kyauktaga joined her immediately. He had orchestrated everything: recruited some thirty young monks, requisitioned a fleet of pickups, secured the support of the KNLA[109] for their protection. The journey had taken three hours on rutted forest tracks, eyes fixed on the sky in anxious anticipation of an aerial attack. Upon arrival, Battalion One of the KNLA Brigade had stationed one hundred men at several strategic points along the road encircling the Win Ka hills. The command post lay near the Kyauk Htaung monastery, from which their expedition had set out on foot. Khin Yadanar and the abbot exchanged a silent smile. They were within reach. All that remained was to clear the monument before excavation. Time was pressing. The junta's informers could report their presence at any moment.

---

[109] Karen National Liberation Army. Military wing of the Karen National Union (KNU), which has been waging an armed struggle for the self-determination of the Karen people in Myanmar since 1949.

The abbot knew it. Immediately, he issued his instructions. Orders came rapid-fire. Brief, precise. Tools were distributed. Tasks assigned. Robes suspended to work bare-chested in the heat that made bodies sweat. At once the percussion of tools filled the forest with metronomic precision, under the inquisitive gaze of intrigued monkeys. Khin Yadanar had no wish to remain idle. Yet she understood she had no place—lay, woman, caught between two faiths—in the exhumation of the *stūpa*. Especially one that held the first relics of the Buddha in the country. Her participation would only taint the discovery and serve the nationalist propaganda of the *MaBaTha*[110], allied with the junta.

An idea came to her as she recalled Preston's notebook sketches. She took her bearings north, then headed east. She began cutting down a path through the undergrowth. Each step, each swing of the blade cost her water and air. She would stop, breathe, then continue. Step by step, meter by meter. Her arms struck mechanically. Her mind wandered toward the Chin hills. Kee Mawng and their discovery of the plane. Images cascaded back: his laughing eyes fixed on hers, his inspired face, his lips on hers. She had withdrawn to find herself. To finally understand that her life at the clinic was no longer imposed. It was her choice. It was there she wanted to be, with him. Saint-Exupéry. "To love is not to gaze at each other, but to gaze together in the same direction." That direction was Mindat.

---

[110] Ultranationalist Buddhist organization in Myanmar founded in 2014 that advocates the "protection of race and religion" and conducts anti-Muslim campaigns. It is led by extremist monks such as U Wirathu.

A dull thud. The machete struck stone. She ran her fingers across the surface. She felt beneath them the rough patterns carved into the red laterite. She had not been mistaken. The wall was there, untouched since Professor Preston had copied the text that covered it. She recalled the entire pages of characters traced a century before by an expert hand. He had been younger than she was then. Despite their differences, she felt a kinship. Even sympathy. A man of his era—colonial Burma, which she abhorred. Had he participated in its subjugation? She did not know. It mattered little. He had been human too. He had loved, suffered, known war as well. They were now connected by this wall. These stones they had both admired. Stones that had changed their lives. They were the thread linking two eras separated by everything, uniting them beyond time and space.

She had read his notebook. Sketches and excavation notes. A few anecdotes about their retreat to Rangoon during the Japanese invasion. Strangely, she felt she knew him. It was too late. He was dead. The last remnant of an age he carried into the grave with him. He had passed the torch to her. These stones. Khin Yadanar saw in them the symbol of the second struggle for Burmese independence. The one that would realize the unfulfilled dream of 1948, to definitively turn the page on colonization. The one that would completely remake the Burmese state. With him would be buried the remnants of the Tatmadaw, the army created by Aung San. Those of socialism and the military regimes. Those of the NLD, the party of Aung San Suu Kyi, too Burmese, too old, too fixed on the past. These stones traced a continuous line traversing all these epochs. They would be the point of departure for renewal. It was here that Sona and Uttara brought the Illumination. It was here that a new Age of Enlightenment would be born. One of resurrected federalism, making diversity a strength, a beauty, an asset.

Reinvigorated, Khin Yadanar attacked the vegetation. The vines clung fiercely. Her determination cut even more sharply. The bas-reliefs were revealed: lions, ogres with gaping fangs, awakened from a centuries-old slumber. When she cleared the top of the wall, light burst forth, flooding the clearing, revealing the golden pagoda perched on the neighboring hill. She blinked to recover from the dazzling light, pulled out her phone, and captured every angle of the wall. The photographs would be useful to historians. It was regrettable that the journal had burned, but she had photographed every page. Its value, therefore, lay not in the information it contained, but rather in the fact that it had become an artifact in which history was intertwined with that of the wall and the stupa. They still stood, defying the ages and reminding humanity of its futility.

She looked at the wall one last time, as if reluctant to leave it. These millennial stones had witnessed civilizations long vanished. They whispered of impermanence, that all things pass. Civil war would pass, dictatorship would fade. She might yet know peace. Then she too would vanish, a grain of sand on the beach of history. And always, these stones would remain, unmoved witnesses, observing the same horrors until this species too passed away.

Thirst returned her to the present. Her time was not measured in millennia. A life was nothing on the scale of the universe, yet it was all she had. One who drowns cares nothing for the cycle of tides. The hungry remains deaf to seasons. It was now that she must act. Each day snatched from death would be a victory. And anything that hastened the fall of the junta was absolute priority. She turned her gaze from the eternal stones. It was time to return to the realm of men. Not merely to refill her canteen, but to see how the monks fared.

They had worked well. The mound lay bare, stripped of its vegetative crown. Earth and moss had been cleared from the foundations. Only the pile of bricks remained forming a dome above the monument. The real excavation work would begin. She exchanged a satisfied look with the abbot. A cube of stacked bricks caught her attention near the structure. The remnants of Preston's clearances before the war, those that had allowed the tablet to be exhumed. Before History interrupted their history. The bulk of the work still lay ahead.

A dry crackle from the walkie-talkie split the air. It was Saw Kaw Htoo, lieutenant of the 1st Battalion, ensuring their security.

- "Speak," replied the abbot.

- "*Sayadaw*, we've received messages on Signal. The LID44[111] just left Bilin. They'll be here in half an hour. They've been informed of your presence and what you're searching for..."

---

[111] 8th Battalion of the 44th Tatmadaw Light Infantry Division, stationed in the Doo Tha Htoo district, near Bilin, Mon State.

- "Copy that. We're speeding up," concluded the monk. Orders came in rapid fire. The monks redoubled their efforts.

- "That stupid Ayaan!" spat Khin Yadanar.

Eager to find her a replacement after her disappearance, he had spoken too much in London. Without concern for informants. His ambition was now delivering them to three hundred soldiers. She stamped the ground in rage, then suppressed her anger. This was not the hour for wasting her strength. Time was running short. Whether they wished it or not, she would help the monks. Pragmatism imposed itself and she would disregard protocol and patriarchal tradition. She removed her shoes and climbed the platform to begin clearing one corner. She received a few sidelong glances. No remarks. The chain work continued in silence at sustained rhythm. A crackle interrupted the panting breaths.

- "The Tatmadaw's is coming! Two convoys, armored vehicles in front. Coming from North and South. To cut off our retreat. We must evacuate!"

The abbot fixed Khin Yadanar, face grave, eyebrows raised in questioning. She gave him an imploring look. He nodded slowly.

- "Give us a few more minutes," she heard behind her after throwing herself back into her task, doubled over, hurling bricks behind her with the energy of desperation.

- "A few minutes, no more! Otherwise, we're lost!" conceded Lieutenant Saw Kaw Htoo. " We're setting a double block. Rearguard sections will delay as long as possible. Hurry!"

The first explosion shook the forest, then a second. Monkeys abandoned their roosts with shrieks of terror. The rebels had used their Claymore mines to immobilize the lead vehicles. The prelude of fanning fire followed immediately. The whoosh of RPG-7s, the dull percussion of M79s, their bass drum rolls against the armored vehicles. Immediate antiphony of the army's SPG-9 rocket launchers. The baritone of PKM machine guns, the staccato soprano of AK-47s, the saccade of the Karens' M-16s. The *aria di furore* filled the theater of operations. The KNLA conducted a well-honed tactic of elastic defense. Their units would establish successive strongpoints to pin down the convoys, followed by calculated retreats stretching the column into the open. Other Karen sections would wait on the hillsides to take them in the flank. And so on, to delay, exhaust, reduce the enemy forces.

Yet without hope of outright victory. The 8th Battalion of the 44th Light Infantry Division were experienced troops. An enemy well known to the KNLA. Impossible to decimate them completely. To delay them without sustaining losses would already be a miracle.

Beneath the symphony of dull explosions drawing inexorably closer, Khin Yadanar and the monks dug like possessed beings. The dome shrank, far too slowly. Nothing. No relics. Was this site cursed? Was fate toying with them? A Tantalus torment, placing the object of desire within reach only to refuse it at once. Preston had been its victim. Now she would be too, because of war. *Bis repetita.* A cycle. She did not dare meet the abbot's gaze. They were so close to their goal. So many trials, so many dead. It was impossible that she had done all this for nothing. She needed more time.

- "*Sayadaw*, we must evacuate!" crackled the radio. "We're still holding the Kalay Thar intersection to the south. But not much longer. If they break through our positions, our retreat will be cut off. It's now or never!"

- "Received. We're coming," the abbot answered. "You heard. We must go!"

The monks ceased work, their faces closed, twisted in grimaces of disappointment. But the abbot had spoken. And memories of the Saffron Revolution reminded them their robes offered no protection from the whip. Robes, packs, tools. They prepared. Khin Yadanar remained alone, rejecting defeat. One brick, then another. To the last she would wrest each second.

- "*Thami*!" the monk's voice thundered. "We must leave!"

- "One more minute," she implored without lifting her head. "Just one minute, *Sayadaw*. I beg you!"

- "It's finished, *Thami*, I am sorry." His voice was gentle but firm. "We'll return. When the region is liberated," he promised without conviction.

Both knew it was false hope. The army knew of their mission. Upon their departure, the generals would come with their stipendied monks to unearth the relics in grand ceremony. These symbols of peace would serve nationalist propaganda, would validate the worst atrocities. She straightened, face turned toward him, eyes blurred. The monk answered with a sad gaze. He understood. But losing her life here would serve nothing. The abbot would not leave without her. Even ready for sacrifice, she could not condemn the Karens risking their lives protecting them. It would serve nothing to find the relics if the Tatmadaw took them prisoner. She was in a dead end with a single exit. Which was closing with each second she wasted in vain. She acquiesced. Stomach knotted, she began withdrawing. One last look toward the *stūpa*'s remains. One last farewell. This time, nature would not reclaim its own. This time, it would fall to enemy hands. The jumble of disordered bricks reflected her back: her life too was a field of ruins. Nothing upright. A collapse that had buried her hopes. She cursed the day she had found the plane, contacted Preston, abandoned Kee Mawng.

A reflection stopped her. She retraced steps. Sunlight struck the mound. Between bricks, a rounded form reflected golden flashes. She rushed, pushed bricks frantically, scratching herself. What did it matter! She extracted the object, dusted it. The miniature replica of a bell-shaped *stūpa* revealed itself. Reflections emanated from its polished faces, as if illumination shined from its very heart. She cried out in joy.

- "I found it!" she screamed, ecstatic, brandishing the golden *patho* above her head. "I found it!"

The monks prostrated themselves and began reciting the Ratana Sutta. Khin Yadanar realized with horror: she, lay, woman, held the relics in bare hands. Her face flushed with embarrassment, she rushed toward the abbot hurrying over with an immaculate white cloth. He took the object with reverence, his lips murmuring with the rest of the *Sangha*, and gently enveloped the reliquary. The sound of running attracted their attention. Lieutenant Saw Kaw Htoo burst into the clearing, features drawn by urgency, astounded by the spectacle he discovered.

- "You're still here!" he shouted with irritation, whilst attempting to maintain a respectful tone. But frustration seeped from his entire being. "Our last position is about to fall. We must leave or we're all dead!"

This time no order was necessary. The monks rose, gathered their things, departed at a run in the lieutenant's wake. Khin Yadanar seized her pack containing the stone tablet, pressed close to the abbot who moved as quickly as his age permitted, the precious cloth against his chest.

Five minutes later, they emerged onto the pagoda overlooking Kyauk Htaung monastery. Before their eyes stretched the plain to the sea. The detonations continued, close, threatening. Black smoke billowed above the tree line masking the road below. Intense fighting was occurring just at the end of the path leading to the monastery. The enemy was at their door. They possessed the relics but could still lose everything. Another five minutes of grueling running on the muddy track connecting the pagoda to the monastery. Khin Yadanar steadied the abbot several times before he slipped. A woman was not supposed to touch a monk. But after her previous breach and given present circumstances, it was the least of their worries. The pickups waited before the buildings, engines roaring. She hoisted the old monk onto the rear platform.

Door slams. Orders hurled on the fly. The vehicles shot off, devouring the track in a cloud of mud and smoke.

Seated with the abbot, four young monks and two KNLA soldiers, M-16s at ready, Khin Yadanar watched the forest blur past. The vehicles tore down like a spooked herd at gallop. Skids, bounds, wild neighing. At each pothole, passengers lifted, then crashed down hard on metal with cries. No one complained. Comfort mattered little. Only time counted. The vehicle took a sharp left turn onto the main road. Two wheels rose, dropped with a piercing screech. Khin Yadanar risked a glance over the cab. Before them, five hundred meters distant, rose the golden *stūpa* of Shwe Sar Yan. Two hundred meters beyond, wrecks of armored vehicles and trucks aflame. The Tatmadaw. Their escape: a narrow road northward, between the two. Only the thin KNLA contingent holding the intersection protected them, sheltered behind burning buildings.

A bullet whistled past her head. Another struck the body of the car. She dove for cover as a mortar round fell ten meters from the road. They were in the lead vehicle. Behind followed the other monastery pickups and KNLA units retreating from the Northwest. The LID-44 contingent must be on their heels. If they did not pass the intersection, they would be caught between a rock and a hard place. Lost, for certain.

Shells, bullets, fell and whistled ever closer, ever more numerous. The two soldiers rose, their rifles pointed straight ahead and began firing in bursts. Khin Yadanar crouched, hands crossed behind her head, pack between her legs, eyes fixed on the rain of cartridges bouncing at her feet in a brazen tinkling. The Shwe Sar Yan pagoda passed in a flash. The moment of truth. The pickup braked hard, skidded left with a screech, accelerated again. A volley of bullets struck where they had been less than a second before. The road rose. More bullets tearing through air above their heads, piercing metal in staccato, striking houses along the road. Then nothing. The soldiers stopped firing, attention shifted behind them. She risked a look over the edge. Below, she saw the intersection they had just passed, from which thick white smoke rose. The KNLA men had used smoke grenades to mask their approach and cover them. They had made it!

All vehicles had passed, racing toward Kaylar Thapha Ridge. The intersection unit would booby-trap the road, beat a retreat in turn. The Tatmadaw convoy would take hours clearing its destroyed vehicles. Impossible to cut them off when they descended on Pauktaw. Only an air strike could stop them if the planes found them on time. In fifteen minutes, they would turn toward Taung Sun, avoid Bilin and Thaton reinforcements. Then they would follow forest tracks to Kyaikto. Heading north through mountains held by the KNLA. In an hour, they would be beyond reach. After that, Khin Yadanar would continue on foot. A grueling trek across the Tenasserim range toward Thailand. Mae Sariang. Then Chiang Mai, where she would meet a NUG[112] representative.

---

[112] National Unity Government. National unity government in exile formed in April 2021 by democratically elected members of parliament who were overthrown in the military coup of February 1, 2021.

She wedged her back against the body of the car, eyes plunged into the canopy brushing the azure with cloud patterns. Wind lifted her unbound hair. Free. Faces relaxed around her. She checked. No one was wounded. A miracle. The soldiers sat, rifles vertical, cigarettes at smiling lips. The monks in lotus position had resumed the Ratana Sutta interrupted at Win Ka. Her eyes met the abbot's. He fixed her with intensity. Complicit smile. She joined him, sat beside him, breaking all protocol. He hesitated. Finally, he handed her the white cloth without a word. She carefully stored it in her pack, with the tablet similarly wrapped. They had discussed this at length. She had explained her intentions. He accepted, trusted her. These objects would never be safe in Myanmar while the SAC[113] held power. He began reciting the Maha Mangala Sutta to protect her in her journey. She closed her eyes. She was finally going home.

---

[113] State Administration Council. Military junta that has been governing Myanmar since the 2021 coup.

Chapter XXIX

Chin State, Burma, May 1942

- "Are you ready?"

The pastor's footsteps echoed across the floor. Anthony turned from the narrow window through which he'd been gazing at the handful of huts clinging to the hillside, surrounded by parched fields, that comprised the Chin hamlet.

- "Let's go," the young Englishman confirmed, addressing his host.

Anthony picked up the woven cotton *zay chin* bag lying at his feet and cast one last look around the room that had been his universe for two months. It was the only habitable space in the traditional Chin house: a vast rectangle with woven bamboo walls. The steep, overhanging roof was covered with dried thatch that was renewed after each monsoon.

The interior lay bathed in shadow, barely illuminated by small unglazed openings closed with bamboo shutters, allowing light and air to penetrate sparingly. A narrow table, a few stools, and a wooden chest comprised the entire furnishings. At the center, the hearth dug into a clay slab, topped with an iron pot, burned day and night, slowly blackening the roof thatch with greasy smoke. On the eastern wall, a simple wooden cross marked the new allegiance of this house. Yet in the corners, traces of another cosmogony lingered: those spirits of mountains and ancient trees that ancestors had venerated, which immanent presence continued to haunt converted consciences.

His gaze remained fixed on the woven bamboo mats and woven blankets that served as bedding and had been folded away in a corner. It was on one of these pallets that he had remained immobilized, tortured by pain, for more than a month. Anthony did not know how long he had lain unconscious after his fall from the plane. But he had counted two days after regaining consciousness, unable to move a limb, before a hunter discovered him. Several more hours passed before the man returned with villagers equipped with a makeshift stretcher.

Anthony's body had been shattered, but he had been fortunate. The pilot had anticipated it: the dense canopy had broken his fall. He had escaped with severe dehydration, a concussion, and multiple fractures. But he was alive. It was more than he had dared hope for. Certainly, a better fate than that of the pilot, of whom no trace had been found. The plane and he had been swallowed by the jungle.

The days passed slowly. His morose contemplation of the thatch ceiling periodically interrupted by conversations with the pastor, eager to perfect his English and correct his halting Bible reading, as well as by the frugal meals and care provided by his wife. To the physical suffering had been added that of endless hours devoted to remembering the tragedies of recent months. A litany of images of destruction he had turned over and over: each destroyed building in Rangoon, each face of a fallen soldier, each refugee cast onto the roads. A dull hatred had matured in him toward the Japanese and their allies in the Burma Independence Army who had stolen everything from him, beginning with Nandar Aye's love. In his denial, he saw her too as a victim, manipulated by despicable opportunists, ideologues willing to do anything to achieve their ends, who had used her suffering to rally her to their cause and push her to do their dirty work. His delusion had led him to convince himself that she had merely repeated scraps of propaganda learned by heart, that she had never betrayed through duplicity or conviction, but through naïveté and credulity. From agent she had become tool, simply because he could not bring himself to despise her.

Each hour spent on his bed, he'd cursed them, tending in the soil of his hatred the seeds of relentless determination now germinated. He'd reached his decision a month ago: he would make for India and enlist to fight the Japanese and drive them from Burma. Where stood the invasion now? Had his countrymen stemmed it? He had no idea, lost in these isolated mountains where only vague rumors of the conflict had reached. No fresh news since the crash. It didn't matter. He'd know more once in India.

The anger that drove him had compelled him to leave his bed as soon as pain became bearable. Then to subject himself to a regime of rigorous exercise to retrain his battered body. Another month had elapsed before he'd felt strong enough to undertake the long march to Manipur. The route through deep valleys and sharp ridges of the Chin mountains to the Tamu pass was grueling. Several weeks of jungle trekking awaited, traversing passes reaching two thousand meters altitude. It was now or never. The first sporadic rains had just fallen, harbingers of the monsoon that would come in two or three weeks and turn the tracks into impassable swamps.

- "Your guide is waiting outside," the pastor indicated, motioning him to follow.

Anthony slung the cloth bag over his shoulder and made his way toward the exit, descending the wooden steps briskly. The structure rested on bamboo stilts, raising the floor nearly six feet above the ground. The space below housed a few scrawny chickens and served to store agricultural tools. Woven baskets of bamboo strips, filled with dried paddy, hung from the beams with the regularity of a rosary.

Further on, the village stretched along a narrow ridge, nearly a thousand meters in altitude, clinging to the mountainside. A handful of identical houses - structures of bamboo and wood, thatched roofs - connected by beaten dusty paths and dispersed according to ancestral logic that separated the wealthy families from common folk. Children with rosy cheeks ran barefoot, while women, some with faces covered in traditional tattoos, dressed in long robes of vivid colors, toiled in fields bearing the marks of *taungya*, this ancestral practice of slash-and-burn cultivation. The blackened fields, pocked with charred stumps, had been set ablaze in March, shortly after his arrival. Bent double in a millennia-old choreography, they deposited rice seeds into holes opened by men after the first rains. Harsh conditions where a poor harvest could bring famine.

Anthony and the pastor made their way toward the hunter who would serve as their guide. In the slanting morning light, the man, dressed in a short-striped tunic and canvas trousers pulled up to the knees, stood motionless, barefoot, leaning on his long flintlock rifle. He chewed nonchalantly on a root while studying Anthony with curiosity. Slung across his back hung the *nam*, that conical bamboo basket held by a wide frontal band, already laden with provisions of dried rice and compressed tobacco with which he would trade along the route. Anthony had also promised pecuniary reward upon their arrival in Manipur. The pastor and he exchanged a few words, followed by a blessing. Then the clergyman turned toward Anthony:

- "This is Thang Lian," he explained, gesturing toward the hunter. "He'll see you through to Manipur. You can trust him."

- "I don't know how to thank you," Anthony replied, his voice trembling. "You've saved my life."

- The pastor raised his hand gently. "The Lord guided you to me," he said with humility. "Your body and your spirit were both broken when you arrived," he continued, referencing the long nights rent by nightmares that Anthony had spent weeping. "I trust both are at peace today."

Anthony remained silent, seeking to hide the wounds still bruising his heart from his host's searching gaze. No doubt the man would disapprove of the unchristian thirst for vengeance that now animated him. He absorbed the landscape surrounding him, lulled by the call of roosters and migratory birds. The pine forests clothing the rounded summits as if to shield them from spring's chill. The high meadows and rhododendron thickets exploding in scarlet bloom. The centenarian oaks offering their benevolent shade to timber houses. No paradise, this. Life was harsh and austere. Yet a haven of peace that the fire consuming the rest of the world had not yet profaned. With all his heart, he wished these mountains, these villages, these peoples would never know war.

- "What will you do if the Japanese reach here?" he asked with concern, thinking of the muskets alone with which the locals were armed.

- "We shall endure, as we have so many times before. The Shans, the Burmese kings, British soldiers... Waves after waves have broken upon our mountains' shores. Yet always the Chins have fought and prevailed. We are a scattered people, divided even, but we are stubborn folk," he declared with a knowing smile. "One day this land shall be ours again, as it once was. If we can unite our strength. And if God wills it..." he hastened to add, almost reflexively.

- "I wish that for you with all my heart," Anthony agreed swiftly, taking his rescuer's hands in his own with emotion.

- "Go now, it's time to depart," the pastor invited with a benevolent smile. "May God keep you and grant me one day the joy of seeing you again."

Anthony went to join Thang Lian and they set off with purposeful stride. The young man turned one last time to gaze upon the house and bid farewell to the pastor, and to his wife who stood in the doorway waving. He left behind him the boy he'd been - his certainties, his dreams, his loves - engulfed in the green mausoleum where the tablet would sleep eternally. The new man quickened his pace, feet striking the ground with determination, his gaze fixed ahead upon the horizon of uncertainties he was about to confront.

Chapter 30

Mindat, Myanmar, December 2024

The representative of the Myanmar National Unity Government's Ministry of Foreign Affairs to the United Kingdom, a lanky silhouette beneath the glare of spotlights, was concluding his address at the podium. He thanked, one after another, the high dignitaries and officials present. In the front rows of the British Museum's amphitheater, a stiff assembly of dark jackets and austere gazes held its breath. At the stage's edge, rigid as statues, stood Latika Williamson, director of the Centre for South-East Asian Studies, Professor Forsythe, and Ayaan. The latter clutched the portrait of Professor Preston. Khin Yadanar was seeing him for the first time and could not help but feel an intense desire to slap him at the sight of the smile he wore savoring his fifteen minutes of glory.

She recalled the message she had sent him, through the NUG emissary, when she had delivered the relics to him in Chiang Mai: "Ayaan, your ignorance nearly cost lives. You're nothing but a selfish kid. I don't ever want to hear from you again." Certain that *ah na de*, Burmese restraint, would prevent him from repeating those words, she had also sent it via Signal before blocking his contact. He was merely an ambitious careerist, a cold monster, hiding behind the mask of the model great-grandson. Let him count himself fortunate. Had she been present in the room, she might have yielded to the temptation to strangle him.

The panoramic camera revealed the packed hall. One hundred fifty journalists, diaspora members, students, scholars, seated in shadow. To the right of the podium, two glass cases bathed in light. Behind the glass, two objects Khin Yadanar knew better than anyone: the *patho* and the votive tablet. Once pressed against her, carried through ravines and jungles as a she-wolf protects her young, they now lay beyond reach. A pang crossed her heart. Perhaps she would never see them again. These artefacts were not hers. They belonged to the Myanmar people, as she had reminded Ayaan in their first conversation. The British minister had just underscored it in his address: the tablet would be loaned for study, whilst the reliquary, sacred, would remain displayed in a safe place to allow the *Sangha* and the Burmese community to pay respects. No excavations, no learned dissections of the *patho*. Only the silence of devotion, awaiting a possible day when peace would allow their return to Myanmar.

Already, nationalist monks and the junta were raging. In The Global New Light of Myanmar, Myanmar Alin, The Mirror, caricatures succeeded one another. The NUG stood accused of being sold to Western colonialists, of plundering the land and faith of the country. Their rage stemmed chiefly from the agreement signed with an exile government, an act that strengthened the NUG's international legitimacy. Thailand, Sri Lanka, Cambodia were already approaching the organization requesting the loan of the relics. The junta's isolation was intensifying within ASEAN. Meanwhile, several journalists had sought out Khin Yadanar for interviews, thanks to Latika Williamson's good offices. Finally, an opportunity to shine light on the Burmese tragedy. Yet she possessed Kee Mawng's lucidity. Her country's martyrdom would soon be consigned to oblivion. Since Donald Trump's election, Western attention was turning elsewhere. Bad omen for democracy's defenders worldwide.

The NUG representative stepped aside. A video appeared on the stage's backdrop screen. Images flowed, illustrating Myanmar's situation since the 2021 coup. Bruised faces, villages ablaze, blood-soaked bodies. Then the statistics. Cold. Merciless. More than three million internally displaced. Nearly two million refugees in neighboring countries. More than six thousand civilian victims. Nearly one hundred thousand homes destroyed by the army. Twenty-eight thousand political prisoners, two thousand dead in detention. One thousand landmine victims, a world record. Thousands of rapes by soldiers. Half the population below the poverty line, twenty million requiring humanitarian assistance. The world's third most intense conflict. One of the least covered as well.

The film halted. Lights erupted, abrupt, returning each to their conscience, to the icy silk of their neckties. Uncomfortable silence. Throat-clearing, rustling of clothing, bodies shifting in seats. Latika Williamson advanced, master of ceremonies in charge of the event. How to continue after such an abyss?

Impossible. Yet it must be done. The audience would probably welcome the distraction her intervention created with relief. She took the microphone, cleared her throat. She sought no transition. That would have been artificial, indecent. Her clear voice unrolled the story of the discovery: the Preston-Sayer expedition of 1941-42, the war's interruption, the plane uncovered in Chin State...

Soon it would be Khin Yadanar's turn. She checked her connection, smoothed her hair with one hand, mentally rehearsed her address's opening. Days of work condensed into seconds. Each word weighed, sharpened. She took a deep breath. She had never liked speaking in public but today was no mere speech. It was the culmination of her baptism by fire. She was ready.

- "In a few moments, Ayaan Carter, will relate how his great-grandfather, Professor Preston, recently deceased, exhumed the votive tablet in Burma, before the Japanese invasion interrupted his work," announced Williamson in a solemn voice. "Then, Professor Forsythe, expert in Mon history at the Centre for South Asian Studies, will transport us more than two thousand years into the past, to share the history of these relics and this tablet. A fabulous story, that of a legendary civilization, of the golden kingdom of Suvannabhumi."

She captivated her audience almost effortlessly, natural orator, weaving into the air that fragile suspense which secret she possessed. To hear her, one would have thought they had recovered Atlantis from oblivion. Why not, after all? She had received an email from Professor Forsythe. A man on the margins, cordial, yet whose passion seemed reserved for the dead. His entire existence appeared dependent on what might have occurred thousands of years past. The message overflowed with gratitude: thanks to her, the tablet had crossed the sea to London. Cleaned, restored, it had yielded its secrets. Engravings of lions, Bodhi-tree and wheels of law, primordial images of Buddha before he was depicted in human form. Then the text's characters. Finally legible. They confirmed his theories. He had hurried to send her the translation, thinking she would be interested. She was not.

"In the twenty-first year of the reign of King Devanampiya Piyadasi, by order of the great king, the venerable Sona Thera and Uttara Thera, dharma messengers from Jambudipa, established this shrine containing relics of the hair of the Buddha. Dedicated by King Sirimasoka, ruler of Suvannabhumi, for the benefit and welfare of all beings. May the Dhamma endure. May all beings find peace and liberation."

These few lines completed the translation of the inscription traced on the laterite wall. The relics had arrived at Win Ka with Sona and Uttara, two centuries before our era. Their presence fissured the accepted chronology of Mon kingdoms, from Gordon H. Luce to Michael Aung-Thwin. Conversely, they offered new legitimacy to Emanuel Forchhammer, to Bimala Churn Law, those forgotten voices of the nineteenth century. Enough to occupy Forsythe and the next generation of historians for years. She was relieved to speak before him. She anticipated that his passion and the weight of the discovery would drive him to pronounce an interminable discourse. A master lecture was the last thing she wished to occupy her day.

- "Now, allow me to present a remarkable young woman, without whom the discovery of the relics would not have been possible," announced Latika Williamson, her voice laden with sincere emotion. "A medical student in Yangon, she returned to her native Chin State after the coup. Since then, she has been working at the clinic of the People's Defense Forces there. In the jungle of those mountains, in the midst of conflict, she brought back to life the votive tablet and Professor Preston's notebook, which lay dormant in an aircraft wreck for eighty years. Then, she crossed a country at war, braving a thousand dangers, risking her life, to reach the *stūpa* of Win Ka. With the aid of Buddhist monks and democratic forces, she found these precious relics, then brought them to Thailand, to deliver them to the NUG. Ladies and Gentlemen, Khin Yadanar," she concluded with a dramatic gesture toward the screen, unleashing a burst of applause.

Khin Yadanar was seized with unease hearing this portrait drawn of her: restrained praise, irreproachably accurate, yet each word returning her to her disturbance. She had never seen herself thus, designated, celebrated, object of a gaze that transfigures the slightest act into merit. She doubted. Her motivations held nothing heroic. A series of chances, of instincts mingled with remorse, of victims who had followed in her wake. Would they still applaud if they knew? And then there were the absent, the anonymous faces of daily struggle. Kee Mawng and the PDF, standing despite fear. They had remained, had not abandoned their posts, whilst she herself had departed. For them, no trophy, no stage where courage is acclaimed. What determines justice: the voice that recounts, or the hand that acts in shadow? It was precisely for them she wished to speak. Her objective since the first day she found the tablet. This was the moment. She launched:

- "Ladies and Gentlemen."

Her voice trembled. She took a long breath before resuming:

- "Today, as I have the honor to speak from wounded Myanmar, I bring you a message echoed by the relics recovered at Win Ka. A message of peace, hope and freedom."

She was set. Words poured forth in floods, naturally:

- "The discovery of these sacred relics, among the oldest traces of Buddhism in my country, is not merely a historical or religious event. It symbolises the humanistic values that have opposed obscurantism for millennia, to enlighten our societies."

Her voice, borne by emotion, gained force:

- "It is a living reminder that freedom, that first breath of human consciousness, cannot be stifled, neither by centuries nor by weapons. Freedom, in each of us, is as natural, as indispensable as breathing itself. It is not taught: it is experienced, it is lived from birth, in every soul, regardless of our past or origin."

She marked a pause to catch her breath. Her heart pounded fiercely.

- "This idea, universal, spontaneous, indomitable, has traversed time and unites our nation today. In the torment of war, many believed our country condemned to division. Cliché of a nation prey to internal tearing and ethnic conflict. Threat brandished since British colonization, instrumentalized by the military dictatorship to justify its oppression. Yet, these relics prove otherwise. Chins, Burmans, Karens, Buddhists, Christians, Animists, have struggled and risked their lives together, side by side, to save them, to bring them before you. As they've been doing since 2021, in the name of a shared hope, a shared future. A Myanmar, democratic, federal, and united in its diversity."

She let her audience absorb her words before continuing:

- "One hears far too often so-called specialists, or those who wish to sow division, claim that Myanmar would be condemned by this diversity. Do not listen to them. It is not our weakness, but our strength. The foundation, the very soil of our future democracy. For without diversity, there is no debate, no pluralism, no need for elections or parliament. After all, what is democracy but a pacified conflict, where ideas have replaced weapons?"

Her mouth was dry. She took a sip from the glass of water beside her.

- "Thus, the Spring Revolution, this alliance of all Myanmar's peoples against dictatorship, is far more than an uprising. It is an inexorable march toward a future where weapons will have been laid down, will have fallen silent, to let ideas speak. A will to live together. A second struggle for independence. To realize the unfinished dream of 1948. The dream of a nation in which each ethnicity, each culture, would have its place and its rights. A dream confiscated by military dictatorship. Our generation, united in pain and hope, rises today to close forever the wounds of colonization and despotism. To turn together the pages of a painful past. To write those of a shared and better future."

She fixed her gaze on the camera as if to pierce their eyes, moved by intense fervor:

- "Perhaps you wonder why you should support our struggle. After all, Ukraine, Gaza, Sudan are also in full turmoil. Is there a hierarchy of suffering? And besides, Myanmar has been at war for decades. How does our isolated people's current struggle differ and concern you? Because our cause is just. Because, against all odds, without international support, we are defeating an army the world believed invincible. Because what is at stake in Myanmar, a country forgotten by all, is a lesson for all humanity, at a time when democracy and humanistic values are retreating, even in nations that proclaimed themselves their champions. Our resistance, our sacrifices, our solidarities become an example that one day will find its place alongside the great pages of universal history. Alongside the American Revolution, the French Revolution, which offered the world the light of freedom and dignity. Our victory will not be ours alone. It will illuminate all nations still enslaved, it will shine as a beacon for all those who suffer beneath the heel of despots, dictatorships, the powerful who claim violence can crush the will of peoples."

She had stated all this in one breath, respiration ragged with emotion. Conscious she was speaking too quickly, wanting to ensure she was heard, she forced herself to slow.

- "So, I hope that, like me, contemplation of these relics, symbols of peace and compassion, will lead you to see more than the ancient remains of a past relegated to the depths of ages. That their brightness will constitute for you the promise, brilliant and vivid, of a free Myanmar. A universal project. A warning to dictators. And a breath of hope for those who dream of freedom throughout the world. The history of these relics reminds us that, no matter the obstacles, freedom and truth will always find their way. As long as there is a heart impatient to breathe the pure air of justice, they will be reborn, invincible."

The end approached. She emphasized each word.

- "Today, doctors, workers, students, former officials, merchants, farmers, journalists are united in this same cause. All struggle, each with their own weapons, their resources, their means. Fighters or civilians, they risk or lose their lives daily, not merely for themselves, not merely for Myanmar. They are the anonymous heroes of a universal ideal. And like these relics, their courage, their suffering, their sacrifice must be placed in the spotlight, before the world's eyes, to be shared, admired, praised. This struggle and this people deserve all your support. We count on you. I thank you."

She did not hear the applause. She had spoken for only a handful of seconds, perhaps. Yet her breath emptied like an opened cistern, tension escaping drop by drop to her ankles. Latika Williamson returned to the podium, mechanical resumption of the conference, resurgence of the ordinary. Ayaan's voice was preparing to take the relay. Khin Yadanar, for her part, had settled her accounts with the world: nothing depended on her now, as if the thread holding her to these months of vigil had just been cut. The rest escaped her now. With an almost liturgical gesture, she closed the laptop. The muffled click of the lid sounded like the closure of a part of her existence. In that slender noise swept a sensation of space, fresh air, roads without sentries. She felt free. More than ever before.

- "You're done?"

Kee Mawng appeared in the doorway, firm silhouette, supported on both legs. The prosthetic, received a month earlier, betrayed only a discreet limp. She offered him her smile. He answered, certain now the trial was passed.

Outside, the sun made the camp's corrugated metal sheets vibrate. They made their way to the scooter, spontaneous fusion of metal and promise. For several days now, Kee Mawng had walked without crutches: only the inflection of his gait recalled his wound, which Khin Yadanar found herself frequently forgetting. As if life, by a stubborn impulse of the heart, refused the memory of blood. A new normality had slipped between them. He had measured the extent of his limits, then digested them with the same brazen lightness that governed his existence. The front line would now remain forbidden to him. He had thrown himself, body and soul, into the drone workshop, fashioning propellers and detonators with a jeweler's precision. She envied him this cranky acceptance.

She, returned only a week prior, had already resumed her post at the clinic. Thai bureaucracy had wrung her more thoroughly than her crossing through war zones. Supported by the NUG, she had accumulated credentials: refugee status with the UNHCR, Red Cross safe-passage, Indian transit visa for fifteen days. The flights between Bangkok and Kolkata, then Aizawl, had been arranged by the NUG. The capital of Mizoram hosted approximately ten thousand Chin refugees from Myanmar. Khin Yadanar had felt at ease there, recovering the languages, flavors, faces of her childhood. Followed a two-day drive to CDF-Mindat headquarters. A miraculous return, less than three months after exile.

The reunion with Kee Mawng was an effusion of tears, laughter, and exhaustion of existing together. Gradually, they wove the gestures of an unmarried couple: shared tea watches, silent vigils, promises murmured. More complicit, more in love than ever.

Kee Mawng mounted the machine. Khin Yadanar slipped behind him, embracing his flanks. She loved this adhesion: her cheek against his shoulder blade, the warm pulsation of the engine like a second heart. The track launched. Dust, switchbacks, horizon cleft. It was the dry season, with its chaos of stones but its limpid sky. No haste. The afternoon light bathed the valley like tepid water. On the ridge, they regained the Kanpetlet-Matupi road. Three months earlier, she had travelled it southward, guided by a stranger. Today, heading north, two bodies fused in a single breath. Warm wind slapped her hair. The landscape, vast green cloth, unrolled before their eyes. She buried her face in Kee Mawng's neck, closed her eyes for an instant. She was alive. She saw one face, then another: Thang Bawi, Kyaw Zaw, the PDF from Pyay, the abbot of Kyauktaga, the KNLA, the NUG... So many faces etched into memory's clay. She owed them so much. Her gratitude for them formed a gentle litany, almost a prayer.

The motorcycle plunged toward the Chi Chaung bridge. Water rolled, exultant, between the pillars. Sharp curves on the far slope. They devoured the ascension, negotiated the hairpins, regained the ridge, which welcomed them with a sign. Mindat.

The city had been retaken by the Chin Brotherhood four days prior. Kee Mawng slowed, turned onto the central avenue. Not a wheel, not a dog. The road stretched beneath a carpet of twisted corrugated metal, blackened beams, wound barbed wire, shattered brick, bicycle handlebars without wheels. On each side of the deserted streets passed the remains of destroyed dwellings, gutted, incinerated, collapsed, bombarded, exploded, smashed. Everywhere the Tatmadaw had left its imprint, its signature. And silence, nothing but silence to accompany their procession through the martyred, but liberated city.

It was Christmas Day, but no celebration. Fear of mines and air strikes. Yet, as at Matupi six months prior, promise had been made that the town would be cleared and secured with utmost speed. Soon refugees would return from India, carrying life into fissures, to rebuild their houses and their existences. It was a new stage in the region's emancipation. Mindat, first rebel city, was finally delivered. Soon, the entire Chin State, then the Irrawaddy valley, then Nay Pyi Daw. The prophecy rolled in Khin Yadanar's skull like the motorcycle on gravel. She had not returned since the coup. Yet every mango tree, every intersection sprang intact from her memory. She was home. The scooter stopped. The engine died. They dismounted.

They stood, side by side, hand in hand, without saying a word. Before them, a burned house, or what remained of it. A few wooden pillars and charred wall fragments, sprouting in sterile ground covered in soot. Identical to the other destroyed dwellings throughout the city. And yet different. One could see the devastation dated. Rain and time had passed, without managing entirely to clean the ruins. Some tragedies struggle desperately against oblivion. Khin Yadanar felt tears flow along her cheeks, her lower lip tremble, but she restrained her cries. It was not the explosive suffering due to sudden tragedy, but a dull sorrow polished by time. It was her house, her parents'. The one in which their tortured bodies had been burned. Then collected by Kee Mawng to be buried in the cemetery. More than three years already. This mausoleum was all that remained of them. Photos and other memories had also gone up in flames during the bombing of the camp.

Slowly, she withdrew two white roses and placed them. Then she returned to position herself against Kee Mawng, her head inclined on his shoulder. He encircled her. Moment of intimacy, of gathering. Sunlight fell at their backs. Their shadow lengthened in the carcass, mute invitation to enter, to be reborn. One day, soon, they would rebuild. One day, soon, it would be their home. In the distance, in the penumbra of falling night, voices rose. Hymns. A mass was improvising in the remains of a church. Kee Mawng joined his soft voice, taking up the chants in a murmur at Khin Yadanar's ear. It was Christmas. Message of hope. Already new dissensions were appearing among the Chins, promises of fratricidal clashes to come. Already accusations of atrocities against the Rohingyas were multiplying against the Arakan Army. Already China was meddling in the conflict to support the junta and pressure armed groups. But she wanted to believe. Today was a day of hope. Mindat was free. Soon, the rest of Myanmar would follow.

Ready to dive deeper into the story?

Do you want to finally discover what the text engraved on the wall in Win Ka said, the one Anthony Preston copied into his notebook?

Scan the QR code below to receive for free, by email, three bonus chapters unveiling the legend of the relics of the Buddha brought by Sona and Uttara to Win Ka.

Don't miss this hidden part of the narrative.

Acknowledgments

This novel owes its existence to a remarkable discovery in the jungles of Burma. My deepest gratitude goes to Clayton Kuhles, Founder of MIA Recovery, whose recovery of lost WWII aircraft sparked the creative vision that became this book. Clayton's generosity in sharing insights and answering my countless questions proved invaluable in bringing authenticity to these pages.

I am equally indebted to Chrys and Shane, whose intimate knowledge of Chin State's rich cultural tapestry and diverse communities fundamentally shaped my understanding of the region. Their perspectives transformed the world of this novel from imagined to lived.

This book would not have reached its final form without the extraordinary commitment of my early readers, Maryannick, Michel, Gilles, Jean, and Tim, who invested considerable time and thought into providing meticulous feedback and insightful suggestions for its improvement. Their careful attention to detail strengthened every aspect of this work.

Finally, to all those who generously engaged with my solicitations about this project and offered their support: thank you for reminding that the people of Myanmar remain cherished across the globe, and that their courageous struggles continue to inspire solidarity and hope worldwide.

About Jak Bazino

Jak Bazino is a French writer with degrees in political science and public relations. He lived in Myanmar (Burma) for over ten years, first under the military regime and then during the transition period, traveling throughout the country and gaining an in-depth understanding of its people, beliefs, and history.

He left Myanmar shortly after the military coup of February 2021, during which he witnessed firsthand the repression orchestrated by the junta against its population.

In 2012, he published his debut novel in French *Zawgyi, l'alchimiste de Birmanie*.

How to help Myanmar?

Situation in Myanmar 5 years after the 2021 coup:

- 20 million people require urgent humanitarian assistance
- 15 million people face acute food insecurity
- 50% of the population below the national poverty line
- 3.6 million people are displaced within Myanmar
- 1.6 million refugees are recorded in neighboring countries
- 8,000 civilians killed by the military junta and its allies
- 28,000 people, including 5,800 women, arrested
- Highest number of landmine victims in the world

Recommended non-profit organizations needing your support:

- https://www.betterburma.org/
- https://backpackteam.org/
- https://mam.org.mm/
- https://www.freeburmarangers.org/
- https://newmyanmarfoundation.org/
- https://cpintl.org/
- https://maetaoclinic.org/
- https://skillsforhumanity.wordpress.com/

www.ingramcontent.com/pod-product-compliance
Lightning Source LLC
Chambersburg PA
CBHW061044310726
48969CB00004B/1082

9 798902 430568